DATE DUE			
JUL 1 6	MAR 2 9 '97	JUL 21	CT 11 00
JUL 20 96	APR 24 '96	SEP 12 98	
AUG 2 '96	MAY 08 '97	OCT 1 3 '9	MR 12
AUG 2 3 '96	JUL 09 '97	OCT 1 2 '9	APR 27 05
OCT 01 '9	OCT 16 '9	DE 17 '98	
OCT 28 96	DEC 03 97	MR 9 '99	
	DEC 18 97	MR 3 1 '99	
JAN 0 4 199	JAN 10 '98	MY 4 '99	
JAN 2 49 7	5-S	AP 6 '00	
FEB 0 3 '9	MAY 09 '98	AUG 0 3 200	
FEB 2 8 '97	MAY 1 4 '98	DEC 1 9 '0	
3-19-97	JUN 04 '98	MAR 28 01	

TRIAL BY FIRE

Also by Nancy Taylor Rosenberg

Interest of Justice
First Offense
California Angel

Nancy Taylor Rosenberg

TRIAL BY FIRE

WHEELER
PUBLISHING, INC.
ROCKLAND, MA

★ AN AMERICAN COMPANY ★

Copyright © Literacy Inventions, Inc., 1996

Published in Large Print by arrangement with
Dutton, a division of Penguin Books USA Inc.,
in the United States and Canada.

Wheeler Large Print Book Series.

Set in 16 pt. Plantin.

Library of Congress Cataloging-in-Publication Data

Rosenberg, Nancy Taylor.
    Trial by fire / Nancy Taylor Rosenberg.
    p. (large print) cm.—(Wheeler large print book series)
    ISBN 1-56895-305-4 (hardcover)
    1. Public prosecutors—Texas—Dallas—Fiction. 2. Women
lawyers—Texas—Dallas—Fiction. 3. Dallas (Tex.)—
Fiction. 4. Large type books. I. Title. II. Series.
    [PS3568.O7876T7 1996b]
    813'.54—dc20
                                        96-2290
                                        CIP

To my husband, Jerry Rosenberg, on his special birthday: You're the light of my life, the most dynamic man I have ever known, and my very best friend.

ACKNOWLEDGMENTS

Many people contributed to the development of this book, but none played a more important role than my editor and dear friend, Michaela Hamilton. Mike, I know I've said it before, but I must say it again. No one can get me to go that extra mile the way you can. I may kick and scream along the way, but in the end, I'm always smiling.

To my agent, Peter Miller, of PMA Literary and Film Management, I owe a debt of gratitude. The following individuals have also assisted me in various ways: Judge Leonard Goldstein, Alexis Campbell, Dudley Campbell, Carol Beatty, Irene McKeown, Rodney Hillerts, Nick Santangelo, and John and Carol Cataloni, for the generous use of their family name. Also to the entire crew at NAL/Dutton and Penguin USA: Elaine Koster, Peter Mayer, Arnold Dolin, Marvin Brown, Peter Schneider, Lisa Johnson, Jane Leet, Mary Ann Palumbo, Alex Holt, and Neil Stuart, my sincere appreciation.

To my fabulous husband, who makes continual sacrifices and supports me every step of the way, I know I couldn't do this without you. To my wonderful family: Forrest and Jeannie, Chessly and Jimmy, Amy, Hoyt, Nancy Beth, and our newest addition, little Rachel, I love you all dearly.

chapter

ONE

The corridor outside the courtroom resembled the inside of a TV station. Lights, tripods, steel equipment cases, twisted cords, and heavy cables were strewn around in the narrow corridor while technicians sprawled out along the walls, sipping coffee and talking among themselves. A reporter for the *Dallas Morning News* spotted the prosecutor, Stella Cataloni, and the Dallas County District Attorney, Benjamin Growman, huddled in a corner in the corridor. Thinking he might be able to get a statement during the recess, he rushed over. "Do you think Gregory Pelham will be convicted this time?" he said, holding his portable tape recorder up close to the district attorney's face.

"Absolutely." Tall and lean, Growman was dressed in a dark Armani suit and a white starched shirt bearing his initials. His nose was pronounced, his eyes closely set, and his lips thin. At fifty-seven, his hair was sprinkled with gray, but he was still a handsome man, accomplished and confident.

"Why did he get off the first time?"

"The trial resulted in a hung jury," Growman answered. "You know all of this, Abernathy. Give us some space here." He turned back to his

1

conversation, but Abernathy continued thrusting the tape recorder at him.

"Pelham was recently arrested for attempting to molest a child," the reporter said. "Is this why you decided to retry him on the old homicide charges? Why didn't you just prosecute him on the new crime? Aren't you afraid the jury will acquit him this time? Once he's acquitted, he can't be retried again. Isn't that true?"

"Once he's convicted on the murder charges, we'll prosecute him on the new charges," Stella Cataloni interjected. "Turn off the tape recorder, Charley. Ben and I have some things to discuss right now."

At thirty-four, Stella was an intelligent and determined woman whom the press had dubbed the "Italian Wildcat." She was also a Texas beauty. Dressed in a yellow linen suit, she had ebony hair that fell to her shoulders in natural, soft waves. Her luminous brown eyes were flecked with gold, and her skin appeared flawless. She wore the left side of her hair pushed back behind one ear, allowing the other side to spill forward and obscure her face. Her walk was purposeful and her footsteps heavy, belying the lightness of her slender yet curvaceous body.

"How long is the recess?" Growman asked once the reporter had walked off. It was the second week in August and the temperature was a scorching hundred and five degrees. The air-conditioning in the Frank Crowley courts building in downtown Dallas was operating, but when it got this hot, it seldom brought the temperature down below eighty degrees. Taking out his handkerchief, Growman wiped his face and neck.

Stella glanced at her watch. "Only five minutes left," she said, "and I didn't even have time to stop by the office. I wanted to see if the coroner's report on the Walden case has come in yet."

Growman frowned. "Worry about your closing argument right now," he said. "Everything else can wait."

"I'm about to conclude," she said, connecting with his eyes. "Depending on how long the jury deliberates, we could have a verdict by this evening."

"How do you feel?" he said. "Do you think it's in the bag?"

"I feel good," she said, smiling nervously. "Of course if the jury stays out longer than three or four hours, I'll be ready to slit my wrists." The smile disappeared. Outspoken and feisty, Stella had shot to the number-two position in the Dallas County District Attorney's office in only seven years. Riding a wave of good fortune and backing it with talent and skill, she had achieved a remarkable one hundred percent conviction record. She wasn't about to lose a case now.

Ben Growman ran his hands through his hair. "Kominsky said you bullied some of the witnesses," he said. "I've warned you about that. The last thing you want in a case like this is to alienate the jurors."

"It's a six-year-old homicide," Stella fired back, her voice echoing in the tiled corridor. "Even the best memories dull after so long, Ben, and our witnesses were all over the place in there. I was trying to force them to go the distance."

When the defendant, Gregory James Pelham, a drifter and dangerous psychopath, had originally been tried six years before for the murder of a young retarded boy named Ricky McKinley, the jury had been hung and Pelham had been set free. Although the new crime he had been charged with was minor compared to the McKinley homicide, it had brought the defendant back into the limelight and the public was now screaming for vengeance. The media blamed the district attorney's office for letting a dangerous criminal slip through its fingers, the mayor and city council members were crawling up Growman's ass demanding he get the man behind bars, and the whole country was watching the drama unfold on national television.

Growman leaned into Stella's face. "You have to bring in this conviction," he said, his breath as hot as a blowtorch. "We can't let this man go free again. We're lucky he didn't kill this other kid or throw battery acid in his face like he did with the McKinley boy."

"Look," Stella said, her temper flaring, "don't you think I want this as bad as you? I've spent so much time on this case my husband frigging left me. What do you want from me?" she spat. "Blood?"

"Control yourself." Growman jerked his head in the direction of the reporters. "Save your energy for the courtroom."

Stella slapped back against the wall, her dark eyes blazing. Taking several deep breaths, she

4

tried to compose herself. She watched as the doors to the courtroom swung open and people started streaming in and scrambling for seats. Growman had taught her that emotional outbursts were unnecessary expulsions of energy. With careful coaching, he had channeled Stella's raw and somewhat uncontrollable talent into qualities that had made her a consistent winner.

In many ways, though, Stella felt like Growman's invention. His career had been on the skids several years back, and in Stella, he had created the exact vehicle he needed to propel him back to the top. She was his rocket launcher, his henchman, his gunslinger. In her present position Stella acted more as an administrator and counselor to the scores of attorneys who worked beneath her, advising them on finer points of law, helping them devise case strategies, analyze jurors. Dozens of other prosecutors could have tried the Pelham case, able attorneys who had less to lose because they weren't sitting on top of a perfect conviction record. Growman had insisted that she take on the case, though, claiming she was the only one who could bring in the conviction.

"Ricky McKinley is dead," he said, his voice low. "Are you going to let the person who put him in his grave go free? You, of all people, should know the agony he suffered. A poor, pathetic kid, Stella. How many more kids are we going to let this bastard mutilate and kill?"

Stella blinked back tears. Then an idea appeared in her mind. She could dispel her image as a bully in the eyes of the jurors, and at the same time bring the case back to life. Blood rushed to her face. Could she do it? Everyone was counting on her. How could she let this monster walk out of the courtroom again when his fate rested in her hands?

This time, Stella thought with steely determination, Gregory James Pelham was not going to escape punishment. As far as she was concerned, Mr. Pelham had reached the end of the line. "Quick," she said. "I need a rubber band."

Five minutes later, a different prosecutor strode down the aisle to the counsel table. Now Stella's hair was secured in a tight ponytail at the base of her neck, and an ugly, abraded scar was fully visible on the right side of her face. Her walk was more tentative, her eyes downcast, and she sucked a corner of her lip into her mouth to keep it from trembling.

Every seat was taken. Reporters and spectators were standing along the back walls. As Stella continued down the aisle, she heard people gasp and whisper, their combined voices becoming an annoying buzz inside her head. They were like a hive of killer bees, she thought, ready to swarm all over her and sting her to death. When she reached the counsel table and dropped down in her seat, a reporter crept over and started snapping pictures from a kneeling position. "What happened to your face?" he said. "Is that scar real?"

Stella became enraged over the man's stupidity. "You'll get your chance later," she said, lashing out with her hand and knocking the camera aside. Seeing the jurors being led in by the bailiff, she quickly organized her notes on the table and tuned out the cacophony around her. The judge was on the stand, the jury in the box, and Stella was ready to get down to the business at hand.

Stella's co-counsel on the Pelham case was Larry Kominsky, a bright young attorney with red hair and freckles dotting his nose and cheeks. Seated between them at the counsel table was a woman with large expressive eyes and a regal face. Brenda Anderson was the D.A.'s investigator assigned to the case. An African-American, Anderson held an undergraduate degree in computer science and a master's in criminology. She had worked her way up through the ranks of the Dallas Police Department before obtaining her present position, and was now recognized throughout the state as the technical wizard of the Dallas District Attorney's Office. Seeing the scar, she exclaimed, "My God, Stella, what did you do to yourself?"

"I'll tell you later," Stella whispered. "Right now we're going to kick some ass."

"Ms. Cataloni," Judge Malcolm Chambers said into the microphone, pausing until Stella looked up. Chambers's face was tired and lined, his white hair unruly, and his glasses perched far down on his nose. If he noticed the scar, he didn't react. "You may resume where you left off prior to recess."

"Thank you, Your Honor," Stella said. Standing and glancing over at the jurors, she saw the shock register on their faces when they spotted the scar. Look all you want, she told them in her mind, just listen close because I'm about to connect the dots.

"Ladies and gentlemen," she said, turning slightly so she was facing the jurors, but keeping the right side of her face clearly within their sight. "Before we recessed, I reiterated the facts the state has presented in this case. Before you begin your deliberations, I want you to remember the victim in this case. Remember the autopsy photos you viewed during the course of this trial." Stella lowered her voice almost to a whisper. "Imagine, if you can, what Ricky McKinley would have looked like had he managed to survive the defendant's savage attack." She stopped and waited, standing as still as a statue, her face completely expressionless.

"Why am I asking you to do this?" she finally continued. "I'm asking you to do it because Ricky McKinley didn't survive. He isn't here to confront his attacker, to tell you firsthand of the agony and horror he was made to endure at the hands of the defendant. Even if this child had escaped death somehow, he would have led a life of anguish and despair. He would have never looked normal, never been accepted by his peers, never been free of fear. You can't hear his pleas for justice, as they are only ghostly cries from the grave," she said, dropping her eyes. "I can hear his cries, though, just as I can imagine the unbearable pain he must have suffered when the defendant tossed battery acid in his face."

Stella walked over to the jury box. One finger trailing along the railing, she continued, "For six years, Ricky McKinley has been dead. And for six years, the man who brutalized and murdered him has walked the streets as a free man."

The courtroom was silent. No one whispered, no one moved, no clothes rustled. Every eye was glued on Stella, the jurors tracking her as she paced, never for one second looking away. Stella's brow and upper lip were moist with perspiration, and she could feel sweat trickling between her breasts and soaking her armpits. "This despicable person, this predator," she said, throwing her arm out in the direction of the defendant, "lured Ricky McKinley into his car, drove him to a cheap motel, and viciously sodomized him. He then beat him to within an inch of his life, sprayed shaving cream in his mouth and nose, and made him cower in the corner under a table. Was that enough?" she said, arching an eyebrow. "The defendant's perverted cravings were satisfied. What more could he want?" She paused and shrugged, as if she were waiting for someone to give her the answer.

"No," she suddenly shouted, her body trembling with emotion, "it was not enough." Her speech became faster as she gathered momentum. "He proceeded to carry Ricky's bloody and battered body to the trunk of his car. He then drove to an isolated field and threw battery acid in his face, eating the skin off the bone. He didn't care that Ricky was mutilated beyond recognition, that his body would later be identified only through dental records, his face unrecognizable even to the woman who gave birth to him. All the defendant cared about was avoiding arrest, making certain that this pathetic child never identified him and caused him to suffer the consequences of his actions. In order to feel safe," she said, "Gregory Pelham had to blind an eight-year-old child."

Striding back to the counsel table, Stella looked over at Judy McKinley, the victim's mother, seated in the second row behind the counsel table. The woman's shoulders were shaking and tears were streaming down her face. Reaching over and touching her arm, Stella then spun back to the jury box. "Ladies and gentlemen," she said, "the fate of this man now rests in your hands, along with the fate of his future victims." She searched the jurors' faces, as if she were committing them to memory and holding each of them accountable. "Once you have considered the overwhelming evidence the state has presented," she said slowly and distinctly, "you will know that there is only one verdict that can be returned in this case. As Ricky's avenging angels, you must put this man behind bars where he belongs and allow this poor child's soul to finally find peace."

The jury deliberated two hours.

Having been notified by the bailiff that the verdict was in, Stella hurried back to the courtroom with Ben Growman, Larry Kominsky, and Brenda Anderson, all of them anxious. Kominsky appeared younger than his thirty-one years. A West Point graduate, he had abandoned his military career to become an attorney. Next to Stella, he was one of Dallas's finest prosecutors, his diminutive size and fresh-faced appearance making him appear deceptively innocent and naive.

Brenda Anderson was dressed in a conservative knit dress, the hemline several inches below her knees. Her neck was long and elegant, her hair worn in a tight knot at the base of her head. Reserved when she was in a group, but outspoken when she related on an individual basis, she was walking next to Stella with her head down.

"We've got it," Kominsky said, looking up at the ceiling as if the word had just come down from God himself. "The jury was only out two hours. Your decision to expose your scar was brilliant, Stella. There's no way they'll acquit the bastard now."

"Shut the fuck up," Growman said, yanking on his shirt cuffs. He stopped and faced Kominsky, hissing his words through his teeth. "Don't you have an ounce of sense? Don't you realize what it took for this woman to expose herself in front of the cameras?"

The attorney looked at Stella and blanched. Her hair was still tied back and she had placed her hand over her cheek to cover the scar. "I'm sorry, okay," he said. "I didn't think. Please, forgive me, Stella, but . . . it was great, you know. The part I liked best was, 'Imagine, if you can.' Man, was that a piece of work. You should have seen the jurors' faces."

"Thanks, Larry," Stella said, flinging open the door to the courtroom. "Let's just hope it worked."

The three attorneys took their seats. It was

after six and most of the spectators had gone home, not expecting a verdict until the following day. Only the press and members of the immediate family were assembled in the courtroom. Since Growman was present, Brenda Anderson slipped into the front row next to Judy McKinley and a few other members of the victim's family. Once the jury had filed in and been seated, the judge called the court to order and asked the jurors if they had reached a verdict.

"Yes, we have," said the foreman, an older man with wire-framed glasses and red suspenders.

"Will the defendant please rise," the judge said.

Gregory Pelham was a short, dark-skinned man with heavy-lidded eyes and rust-colored hair. He was dressed in an inexpensive brown suit, a paisley print tie, and a pink shirt. When his attorney nudged him, he pushed to his feet and scowled at Stella before turning to face the front of the courtroom.

"You may read the verdict," the judge told the foreman.

"We, the jury," the foreman read, "find the defendant guilty of the offense of murder in the death of Richard W. McKinley, as charged in Count One of the indictment."

Stella bolted straight up in her seat. Growman pulled her back down. He was pleased, but there were additional charges, and he wanted to hear the jurors' decisions on these as well. Due to the age of the case and the lack of substantial evidence that the defendant had premeditated his attack, the state had not filed charges of capital murder, an offense which carried the death penalty. They had, however, filed several other charges, the most significant of them being kidnapping.

"We, the jury," the foreman continued, "find the defendant guilty as charged in the crime of kidnapping, as set forth in Count Two of the indictment."

Kominsky leaned forward and whispered to Stella and Growman, "I'll buy the champagne." No longer concerned about the remainder of the charges, he slipped out the back.

Stella listened as the rest of the verdicts were read, most of the charges classified as lesser or included crimes. Many times the prosecution would file numerous counts, all reflective of the same period of criminal behavior. If the jury convicted on one count, it could not convict on the others; therefore, Pelham was found not guilty on the remaining counts.

Once the foreman had finished reading the verdicts, the judge set a date for sentencing and promptly adjourned. Reporters leaped to their feet and rushed the counsel table, thrusting microphones in Stella's face. "How long do you think Pelham will be in prison?" one male reporter said, shoving several other reporters aside.

"We hope to get the maximum sentence," Stella said, ripping the rubber band out of her hair and pulling the right side forward so it covered her scar. "If the judge sentences consecutively on both the murder and the kidnapping charges, Mr. Pelham may never step outside the prison walls."

"What happened to your face? Was it a recent accident or is it an old injury? Did you decide to expose it at the last minute to influence the jury?"

Questions flew at her from all directions. "No comment," Stella said. She turned to say something to Ben Growman, and then walked over and embraced Judy McKinley. "It's over, Judy," she said. "Maybe you can get on with your life now."

"Thank you," the woman said, sobbing. "I don't know how I'll ever repay you. You were wonderful today. I don't know what happened to you but—"

Stella released her when Growman stepped up beside her. The television cameras were rolling again and the photographers were snapping shots of the two of them together. "You've said you might retire next year," a woman reporter said to Growman. "Are the rumors true that you're grooming Ms. Cataloni as your successor?"

Growman beamed, draping an arm over Stella's shoulder. "That's a clear possibility, young lady," he said, using the relaxed, folksy tone of a seasoned politician. "To tell y'all the truth, I can't think of anyone I'd rather endorse than Stella Cataloni. She's the finest prosecutor we've ever had in this agency." He glanced over at Stella and chuckled. "Maybe I'll even organize her campaign. Heck, I've got to do something after I retire. Of course, that's if she'll have me."

Stella smiled. When a man with twenty years in on a job, one as respected and revered as Ben

14

Growman, issued a glowing recommendation on national TV, it was tantamount to handing over the keys to his office. Feeling his hand brush against her side, she reached down and squeezed it. Stella was on a high, and she loved it. Nothing could stop her now.

Stella, Growman, Kominsky, Anderson, and several other senior D.A.'s were gathered in the conference room, better known as the war room. Once a week Growman assembled the senior staff and department heads, and they all faced one another around the long oak table as he made work assignments and commented about various aspects of ongoing cases. The table was now covered with paper napkins, pizza boxes, plastic cups, and open bottles of champagne, and a festive atmosphere prevailed.

Also present was Samuel Weinstein, Stella's planned dinner companion for the evening. They had made arrangements to get together before she realized the verdict would come in on the Pelham case. Technically, Weinstein was Stella's divorce attorney, but even before she had hired him to represent her in the dissolution of her marriage, they had moved in the same small world. Weinstein was a close acquaintance of Ben Growman's and had met everyone in the room on occasion. Dallas, like many towns, had well-defined social circles. People in the law game generally belonged to the same private clubs, worked out at the same gyms, had drinks at the same bars.

Lately Stella had been spending a great deal

of time with Weinstein, not all of it related to her divorce. Sam was a good-looking man and a dynamite divorce attorney, but in some ways he was old-fashioned. Only forty- three, he had been a widower for over ten years, having lost his young wife to breast cancer. Stella found him appealing, even if he was a tad too conservative. With his curly hair and penetrating eyes, his prominent nose and a strong jaw, the attorney had been a steadying influence as she navigated the emotional waters of her divorce. From time to time, he took her out to dinner, but Stella was still undecided where she wanted the relationship to go.

"You shouldn't drink so much champagne," he told her, scowling. "You'll make yourself sick. You haven't even touched the pizza."

"After today," Stella said, tipping a plastic cup of champagne into her mouth, "I think I deserve to get sloshed. If it all comes back up, so be it."

The rest of the table responded with laughter. Growman stood. "To Stella," he said, holding his champagne glass in the air. "We should all be so dedicated. Take a good look at her, people, because in a few years Stella Cataloni is going to be the new D.A. of Dallas County. Yours truly will be just another old fool puttering around on the golf course."

Stella grabbed her glass and tapped it against every glass at the table, leaning over to reach some of them on the far end.

"Speech," Kominsky called out. He had started drinking the champagne long before the others had arrived.

"I'm too drunk to give a speech," Stella mumbled under her breath. Then she lifted her glass again. "To Ben Growman," she offered. "May he retire posthaste. Then I can sit at the head of the table and make your lives hell." When she tapped Sam's glass, it tipped and champagne spilled down the front of his suit. He reached for a napkin and tried to soak up some of the wine.

"I'm sorry, Sam," Stella said, frowning.

"Coffee," Kominsky yelled. "Get the woman some coffee. We've got a sauced prosecutor on our hands. Two, actually."

Brenda Anderson left to see if there was any coffee left in the kitchen down the hall. Seated next to Stella, Growman leaned over and whispered in her ear. "I had my secretary tape your interview off the television today. Come by my office and I'll give you the tape as a souvenir. If you study it, you'll learn how to present yourself to the media. That's part of the game, you know. Once you start campaigning, you'll want to become more polished."

"Thanks, but no thanks." Stella's lighthearted mood evaporated. She had exposed herself and won the case, but now it was over, and she certainly didn't want a souvenir of herself looking like a freak. "I'm ready to go," she told Sam, patting down the hair on the right side of her face. "It's been a long day, and you're right, if I keep drinking, I'm going to pass out or get sick."

"It's fine with me," he said, helping her to her feet.

Taking his arm, she told herself that Sam was special. She had learned to respect him, even lean on him during the past months. Raising his twelve-year-old son alone while managing a busy law practice had to be a difficult task. Stella was so obsessed with her job that she couldn't even appease her husband, let alone handle the demands associated with raising a child.

A junior attorney, looking haggard, stuck her head in the door. "I have a call for you, Stella," she said. "Do you want to take it or should I have them call back in the morning? It's Holly Oppenheimer from the Houston D.A.'s office."

"What line is she on?" Stella asked. Even though Oppenheimer was a prosecutor in Houston now, she had once been a D.A. in Dallas and the two women had been on friendly terms. Although they rarely socialized outside the office, they had frequently shared a table at lunch and were often seen huddled over coffee in the cafeteria during morning and afternoon recesses. Holly had also been the prosecutor when Pelham was first tried, and Stella had conferred with her on a regular basis before and during the present trial.

"Line three," the woman said. "It's the only line that rings through when the switchboard is closed, and it only rings in my office. Every time I work late, I get stuck with all these calls."

Telling Sam she would be only a few minutes, Stella walked over to the console behind the conference table and picked up the phone. "Holly," she said, "did you hear the news about Pelham?"

"Of course I did, Stella," the woman said. "How could I miss it? You've been on almost

18

every TV channel. The CBS affiliate here in Houston carried it live. I couldn't wait to congratulate you."

"Thanks," Stella said, "but you know what? A lot of what I used was your doing. We filed the same charges, used the same evidence. We tried our best, but we couldn't come up with anything new. I just dug into your old notes and put a slightly different spin on them."

"You'll never know how badly I wanted that case, Stella. I got very close to Ricky's mother. When we lost it and they kicked Pelham free, I felt as if I had failed her."

"She's a nice lady," Stella answered. Seeing Ben Growman glaring at her, she turned to face the wall and lowered her voice. "She asked about you the other day, told me to send her regards."

"How is she?" Holly asked. "This was so hard for her. Ricky was her only child. Since I have a daughter of my own now, I know how a mother feels."

"She's better," Stella said. "I think now that it's over, she can finally get on with her life." Turning introspective, she thought about her own situation. "By the way," she said, "have you had a chance to look over the old reports on the fire? You've got a great eye, Holly, and you might be able to see something the earlier investigators missed. I know your time is limited but I was hoping—"

"Oh," Holly said. "I'm sorry, Stella. I was so excited over the Pelham case that I almost forgot to tell you. Your old boyfriend is back in town. The cops stopped him just last night. He's

19

coming in tomorrow morning to give us a statement."

"Randall?" Stella said, a hand flying to her cheek. She tapped Growman on the shoulder. "They found Tom Randall, Ben. He's back in Houston."

Growman fidgeted in his seat and scowled.

"What time is he coming in?" she asked.

"He's supposed to be here at nine," Holly said. "Listen, Stella," she continued, her voice harsher, "people thought I left the agency because I lost the Pelham case, but I left because Growman sexually harassed me and forced me to resign. Just because the review board didn't take my allegations seriously doesn't mean they weren't valid." She paused and heavy breathing came out over the line. "I know you and he are tight and he's probably sitting right next to you, but to tell you the truth, I really don't care." Before Stella could respond, Holly slammed the phone down in her ear. Stella hung up with a shrug.

"Your biggest fan," she said to Growman.

"Oh, yeah?" he said, tipping his chair back. "Tell me something I don't know." A few moments later, he straightened up, seeing the tense look on Stella's face. "Randall's the man you think set the fire that killed your parents. That means he's the person responsible for your scar, right?"

"Right," Stella said, her eyes flashing with hatred. "You know how much I want this man? You have no idea, Ben."

"What are you going to do?"

"I've waited sixteen years to find this asshole," she snarled, "to make him pay for what he did to me. You want to know what I'm going to do? I'm going to nail his fucking ass to the wall." Her hands locked into fists at her side. "Not only that, I'm going to enjoy every minute of it."

Whereas the people gathered at the table had been chatting and laughing among themselves, they now all fell silent. Before today no one outside of Growman had been aware of Stella's scar, as she had always concealed it beneath her hair.

Brenda stepped back into the room and looked around. "Did I miss something?" she asked. "Did someone just die in here? I thought this was a party, people."

Stella's eyes were glazed over and her mouth set. Her heart was beating like a drum inside her chest. Realizing the other attorneys were waiting for her to say something, she flushed with embarrassment.

Sam quickly stood and pushed his chair back to the table. "Come on, Stella," he said, putting his arm around her, and leading her toward the door. He could feel her trembling. "I'll drive you home. Let's get out of here."

chapter

TWO

The district attorney's office was located on Fannin Street in the downtown section of Houston. A ten-story brown brick building, it housed the more than two hundred prosecutors on staff, plus an enormous contingent of clerical workers and other support personnel. An older man wearing a gray polyester suit, scuffed black shoes, and a large gray Stetson approached the row of glass doors in front and stepped aside, letting a woman, a man, and two small children pass. He then herded them across the lobby like a quarter horse herding cattle, and steered them into an open elevator. Once the doors opened on the ninth floor, they started walking down a long corridor. The little girl began crying and the woman swept her up in her arms, tossed her on her hip, and continued without breaking stride.

"I'm sorry," Detective Carl Winters said to the woman when they reached the door to the interview room, "but you'll have to wait out here, ma'am. There's some vending machines down the hall if you want a drink or a candy bar for the kids."

The woman tugged on the older child's hand and dropped down on a bench with the toddler in her lap. She hugged the little girl close. "We're fine," she said. "How long will he be?"

"Shouldn't be too long," the detective said, tipping his hat back on his head. At sixty, Carl Winters was overdue for retirement, but he was an old-time cop, and the job was his life. His wife had passed away years before, and there were no new females on the horizon. His face was heavily lined, his eyes small and cunning, and his weight had soared in recent years, causing a large blubbery mass to spill over the waistband of his low-slung pants. Why should he retire? He had nothing else to do. When one of his closest friends swallowed his revolver only three months after he turned in his shield, Winters decided to keep plugging away until he fell over in his tracks or some asshole pumped him full of lead. He thrived on the excitement of police work, the never-ending challenges and surprises, the inherent danger. He also liked walking around with a badge in his pocket and a gun strapped to his chest. It gave a man a sense of power and respect. He knew people laughed at him because of the cowboy hat, but he really didn't give a rat's ass what they said. His hair was thinning and he liked the way it felt when he put on his Stetson every morning. It was like a bell to a prizefighter, signifying that it was time to step into the ring.

"In here," he said to Tom Randall, opening the door to the interview room and motioning for him to go inside.

Randall was a pleasant-looking man in his mid-thirties, with light brown hair and a friendly, open face. Wearing a short-sleeve Hawaiian shirt,

Levi's, and loafers, he smiled nervously when he saw the people assembled in the room. He wasn't tall, but he was extremely stocky. His arms were solid muscle, his legs as thick as tree trunks, and his shirt strained over the front of his chest. Winters had no doubt that Randall could do some serious damage if a person pushed the right button.

"Have a seat," Winters said, taking a chair at the table. "This here lady is Holly Oppenheimer," he said, tilting his head toward a woman standing against the wall in the back of the room. "She's one of our hardworking D.A.'s." Holly was dressed in a short black skirt and a long red jacket. Her shapely legs were one of her finest attributes, and she never failed to display them. Her eyes were a brilliant shade of blue, her forehead prominent, and her blond hair was styled in soft curls that spilled forward onto her brow and grazed the back of her neck.

"This fine gentleman over here is Frank Minor," he continued, "the supervisor over the homicide division." Minor was the new breed of cat at the Houston D.A.'s office. Harvard grad, family money, young, ambitious. He dressed in Brooks Brothers suits and power ties, seldom smiled, and would jump through a plate-glass window if it would advance his career. Winters had to admit he was shrewd, though. The man had listened when Winters had come to him, asking that they reopen a sixteen-year-old case when everyone else had laughed in his face. Minor was known around the agency as "the Harvard Prick" or "the Uppie Yuppie," and everyone knew Holly Oppenheimer despised him. Winters, however, was beginning to see him as a stand-up guy.

"Okay, Randall," the detective said in his gravelly voice, "why don't you begin by telling us where you've been for the past sixteen years." After all these years, Tom Randall, the man Winters had always thought of as the state's primary witness, had finally reappeared. The day after the fire, Winters had spoken to Randall and he had indicated that Stella was responsible for setting the fire. The D.A.'s office had accepted the case for prosecution and Stella had been arrested. When Randall fled town a week later, however, the state withdrew the charges against Stella. Without Randall's testimony, the district attorney's office decided, there was not enough evidence to go forward.

Patrol had stopped Tom Randall two days before on a routine traffic violation, and then discovered the old bench warrant for failing to appear on a subpoena as a material witness in the Cataloni homicides. Winters had become so excited when he heard the news, he'd almost peed in his pants. The Cataloni murders had haunted him for sixteen years, more than half of his twenty-seven-year career. He'd almost been ready to give it up when he had seen Stella Cataloni on television during the Pelham proceedings, and then when Randall had surfaced, he had decided there was still a chance to put this one away.

Randall was staring at him, a blank expression on his face. "And you know," Winters said,

25

"while you're at it, maybe you can explain for these good people how come you didn't respond to that subpoena."

"Look," Randall said tensely, "I didn't know you guys had a warrant out for me. I moved away, that's all. I didn't do anything wrong. I didn't even know you were looking for me."

Winters smacked his lips. He hated liars. Sometimes he thought he could even smell them, and right now the room was getting pretty stinky. "That really isn't true now, is it?" he said slowly. "I spoke to your parents five, six years ago, and they said you knew all about the warrant. You just didn't want to deal with it, so you made yourself scarce."

Randall was blinking repeatedly. Beads of perspiration had popped out on his forehead and upper lip. "After the fire and all, I decided to move to Nebraska. That's not exactly a crime."

"I see," Winters said, "and you never came back to Houston, not even to visit your parents and kin?"

"All right," Randall said, capitulating. "You got it right the first time. I didn't want to deal with it, so I split."

"So you did know we were looking for you?" Winters said. "I mean, correct me if I'm wrong here, but even though you moved away, you did speak to your parents on a regular basis, right?"

"Yeah," Randall said, staring down at the table, "I knew you were looking for me, but I didn't think it was such a big deal. I mean, I certainly didn't think you'd still be interested after all these years."

26

"Well," Winters said, removing his Stetson and fanning the air with it before placing it back on his head, "murder is a pretty big deal, son. Two people died in that fire and we'd like to know what happened."

Randall's head jerked to the side, checking out Oppenheimer and Minor before he turned back to Winters. "Isn't there a statute of limitations or something?"

"Not on homicide," Winters said, arching a bushy eyebrow. "Let's start with the day of the fire."

"I have to get back to the school," Randall said, leaping to his feet. "I just moved back to town. I'm the new football coach at St. Elizabeth's. We're supposed to be having practice right now."

Winters just glared at him.

"Fine," Randall said, slumping back down in his seat, his face now flushed with anger. "If I lose my damn job, you can support my fucking wife and kids."

"Why don't you just tell us what happened?" Winters said calmly. "Then you can leave and conduct your football practice."

Randall pulled his collar away from his neck. "Hey," he said, "it was a long time ago, and I don't have such a terrific memory." His mouth tightened and he leaned over the table. "Stella Cataloni put you up to this, didn't she? You know how many years that bitch has been telling lies about me? Shit," he went on, relaxing, "I saw her on TV the other day, though, and she looked pretty good. I mean, right after the fire, I said

damn, this gal ain't never going to look normal."
He issued a good-old-boy laugh, slapping his
thighs. "I never thought someone I once fucked
would become so famous, though. Guess that
makes me famous too, huh?"

Both Winters and Minor chuckled at his
vulgarity. Holly gave all three men a scolding look
and they quickly fell serious. Even though he was
not very bright, Randall had an easy, affable way
about him that the men found hard not to like.

"Let's get back to the night in question,"
Winters said. "Were you inside the Cataloni resi-
dence the night the fire broke out?"

"Yeah," Randall said, dropping his head and
then peering up at them like a chastised child.
"You know I was there . . . I'm being a man here,
guys. I'm ready to get this stuff off my chest."

Winters snapped to attention. Holly pulled up
a chair and took a seat at the table. "Start with
the night of the fire and tell us everything that
happened. Do you mind if we record your statement?" she said, seeing Winters's tape recorder
in position on the table.

"I thought you were already doing that,"
Randall said. "Sure, record whatever you want.
I don't have nothing to hide. If you want, you
can even give me a lie detector test."

"Were you the father of Stella's child?" Holly
asked. With her full breasts and long legs, the
Houston prosecutor had no trouble turning
heads, but her lips were slightly too narrow and
her nose too sharp, making her face sometimes
appear pinched as it did at that moment.

"I already said I fucked her," Randall said.

28

"Isn't that the same thing as admitting I fathered her kid? I mean, when you fuck someone, that's generally what happens."

Winters snickered under his breath.

They made their way through the preliminaries and finally focused on the night of the fire. "Stella insisted I go with her to tell her parents she was knocked up, see. Man, things were good back then," Randall said, his eyes glazing over with fond memories. "I was the star quarterback at St. Michael's, and had a shitload of friends. The day before the fire, they told me my football scholarship to Notre Dame had come through. I had no idea what I was going to do. You know, Stel was pregnant."

"Life's a bitch," Holly said, not nearly as impressed with Randall as the men seemed to be.

"So we go to her house and tell her mother," Randall continued. "She took it pretty well, but the old man wasn't home from work yet. He was a building inspector and straight as an arrow. I once told him I swiped a weather vane off the top of the school, and he reported me to the principal. Can you believe it?"

"Go on," Winters said. "Try not to take so many side trips, Randall. Remember, your wife and kids are out there waiting,"

"Well, if I remember right," he said, "Stel was in the kitchen with her mother. I heard the old man's car out front and went to the window to make sure it was him." He looked around the room. "I was plenty nervous, let me tell you. I was able to defend myself, but Stella's father was

29

one of those wiry little wops that could beat the shit out of you if he wanted to. He was out there with some guy, screaming and yelling about something. When he got excited, he generally started rattling off all this stuff in Italian and throwing his hands around."

Holly cut in, sensing a lead. "Did you know the person her father was arguing with? Had you ever seen him before?"

"Nah," Randall said, shaking his head. "He might have been a neighbor or something and they were fighting over the dog. The Catalonis' dog always crapped on the neighbor's yard."

"You didn't understand anything the men were saying?" Holly asked.

"I think I heard him call the guy a no-good crook or something," he said, "but Stella's father called everybody a crook." Randall cleared his throat and then continued, more focused now. "When he came in and I saw how riled up he was, I thought we should tell him another day, but Stella's mother ran out of the kitchen and told him practically the second he walked in the door. Man," he said, making a little whistling sound, "was he pissed. He just blew. Bang, you know, and he was screaming at me like a maniac. He demanded that I marry Stel, but hey, I wasn't ready to get married and raise a kid. Then he said no daughter of his would ever have an abortion. He managed to slug me a few times, and I started slugging him back. Before you know it, we were rolling around on the floor and Stella got in the middle of it, catching a few punches from her father that I think were meant for me."

His voice softened and he eyed Holly across the table. "That really hurt Stel, you know. I don't think her father had ever hit her before. They were close, see, and she'd gone to him thinking he'd understand and help her."

"What happened then," Holly said, "after you told him?"

"I left," Randall said, "but then I got to worry that her father might rag on her some more, so I walked around the house, trying to find a way to get back in. Finally, I saw a window open that went into the basement and got in that way. The stairway leading from the basement opened up right next to Stella's bedroom, so I just snuck into her room and locked the door behind me."

"Was Stella in the room at the time?" Holly asked.

"Yeah," Randall said, "and she was hot. Boy, was she hot. Stel had some temper." He paused and swiped at his mouth with the back of his hand. "We were just sitting there talking, and all of a sudden she leaps out of the bed and starts going off about her father and what a bastard he was to hit her. She was holding her stomach and crying. Maybe he really hurt her, you know. Hitting a pregnant woman in the stomach isn't too healthy. I was a kid back then, so I didn't know about those kind of things."

"Was she having a miscarriage?" Holly asked. "You know she lost the baby, don't you?"

"I heard," Randall said, stretching his arms over his head and yawning. Then he just sat there staring out over the room.

"When did the fire break out?" Winters asked.

"I'm going to tell you," Randall said. "Can't you give a man time to think? This is serious shit we're into now. I'm trying to get it all straight in my mind." He leaned back in the chair and closed his eyes. Then a few moments later, he put his hands over his face, finally dropping them and straightening up in his seat. "Okay," he said, "you want to know the truth, right? What really happened that night. Well, you want it, you're going to get it." He took a deep breath and then spat it out, his speech rapid-fire now. "Before I knew it, Stella grabbed something off the dresser and ran down the hall. If I'd known she was going to set her old man on fire, I would have stopped her. The next thing I knew, the whole house was burning and everyone was screaming. You know, things were out of control."

Holly looked over at Minor, then quickly turned back to Randall, trying to keep her astonishment off her face. "Stella set her own father on fire? You're certain, absolutely certain? These are serious allegations, Randall. For all we know, you're the one who set the fire."

"That's a crock of shit," Randall shouted. "See," he said, "that's why I had to come clean. I knew Stella was trying to pin this on me. For years she's been trying to track me down. Why do you think I split and never came back to Houston? Damn, woman, this is my hometown. You think I wanted to live in fucking Nebraska, all the time looking over my shoulder, terrified Stella would haul my ass into court one day and try to frame me for killing her parents?"

"Did you see her actually set her father on

fire?" Holly asked. "Maybe the fire was an accident."

"I heard him screaming," he said, his eyes flashing. "I didn't see it firsthand, but I heard it. He was yelling, 'No, no, no,' and saying Stella's name. Sure sounded like she set him on fire. When a person runs out with lighter fluid and matches in their hand, and the next thing you know, you smell flesh burning and hear the guy screaming, I think you can assume that person did what they set out to do."

Holly's jaw dropped. "You saw lighter fluid and matches in her hand?"

"That's what I just said," he tossed out, slouching lower in his chair.

"When did you see the lighter fluid and matches?" Holly said. "Where did she get them? Is that what she picked up off the dresser?"

"Stella was a majorette, see," Randall said. "She twirled those batons that are set up like torches. She always had lighter fluid or gasoline or something around, and everyone has matches. Stel used to collect them from restaurants and keep them in a big bowl on her dresser."

"How did you get out of the house?"

Randall thought for some time before he resumed speaking. "I could have just dived out the bedroom window," he said, "but I had to do something to try to save them. I found Stella's brother in bed where he'd been sleeping and carried him out on my back. I couldn't find Stella or the others. The smoke was too thick and the flames were really blazing. I knew if I went back in the house, I'd be burned to a crisp."

"So," Carl Winters said, "you're the one who called the fire department?"

"Hey," Randall said, "who the hell knows after this many years? I did whatever I was supposed to do. When there's a fire, you call the fire department."

"I see," Winters said, knowing Randall had actually fled like a coward. When the fire department had finally been notified by a neighbor, they arrived to find Stella and her brother unconscious on the lawn, Randall nowhere in sight. Whereas her brother had miraculously escaped injury, Stella had been severely burned, and her life had hung in the balance for days following the fire. But Winters had always believed she was responsible. He knew it took a personal connection to set a human being on fire.

He also suspected that there were things going on between Stella and her father that no one knew about. An incestuous relationship would certainly have given a desperate young girl a motive for murder, particularly if she had gotten herself knocked up by her boyfriend and incited her father's wrath. She could have been afraid her father would retaliate against her once Randall left. And then again, Winters told himself, she could have gotten pregnant specifically to get back at her father. So she kills him, thinking it will look like an accident, foolishly thinking she'd have time to get her brother and mother out of the house.

"Let's back up a little bit," Holly said, a questioning look on her face. "If Stella's father was arguing with someone earlier in the evening, possibly he was the one who set the fire."

"There was no one else in the house," Randall explained. "I came in through the basement, see. The lights were all out, and to the best of my knowledge, Stella's parents were upstairs in their bedroom sleeping."

"Where was Stella's room?" Holly asked. "Did she share a room with Mario?"

"No," he said. "Both of their rooms were downstairs, on opposite ends of the hall. This wasn't a mansion, you know. It was a small place. If a person so much as hiccuped, you could hear it all over the house."

"When you went outside the first time," Holly said, wanting to be perfectly clear on this, "was there a car in the driveway other than her father's car?"

"No," he said. "You can ask me all the questions you want, but I'm telling you no one else was in that house."

Holly turned to Winters. "Could the fire have started outside the house?"

"Nope," he said. "The arson squad listed the origin of the fire as Stella's bed."

"How does that fit Randall's story then?" Holly said, a baffled look on her face. "He was in the bedroom when the fire broke out. He just told us it started down the hall, that Stella ran out of the room to get her father."

"Look," Randall said, "things happened pretty fast and furious that night. Maybe I made a mistake."

"Are you recanting your statement now?"

Holly said, her voice spiked with anger. "You made us sit here and listen to all this crap and now you're going to take it all back?"

"No," he said. "I just might be mistaken about the exact sequence of events. I told you I don't have a perfect memory." He paused, thinking. "Stella's father might have come in the bedroom, and she jumped up and grabbed the lighter fluid. You know," he said, tilting his head toward Winters, "she could have done it right there by the bed like he said. I remember we were talking on the bed. It was late, after twelve o'clock by then, and I might have fallen asleep for a while, then woke up when her old man started screaming."

"But you didn't see it?" Holly said, crossing her arms over her chest. "If you were in the same room, Randall, how could you not see what was happening?"

"There was a lot of smoke and it was hard to see," he said. Then his eyes lit up. "Hey, if I smelled the guy burning, maybe he really was in the same room with me. Stel could have gotten the matches and all and then we both fell asleep. Her father could have decided to come into her room and start up with her again, and she set him on fire then."

"Let me ask you something," Holly said. "If you knew Stella was guilty of this crime, why did you pick up and move away from Houston? Why did you run if you were innocent of any wrongdoing? Didn't you realize that by fleeing you were leaving yourself wide open, that you might be sought as a suspect?"

36

"I loved her," Randall said. "And the poor thing was ruined, you know. All that beauty wasted like that. How could I come forward and tell the truth, knowing she would go to prison? How, huh? How can a man do a thing like that to someone he cares about?"

Winters leaned over and whispered in Holly's ear. "He was ready to implicate her sixteen years ago," he said. "I've got his statement in the file."

A period of silence ensued. Then Holly slapped the table with the palm of her hand, determined to shake Randall's composure. "You're feeding us a line of shit, Randall. You might not have testified, but when the police first contacted you right after the fire, you had no trouble at all pointing the finger at Stella. If it hadn't been for your statements, Detective Winters would never have arrested her. Our office then had to dump the case when you skipped town because we had no other witnesses."

Randall's shoulder started jumping. Now he remembered the old fart. So many years had passed, he had forgotten what Winters looked like, and back in those days, the detective hadn't worn a cowboy hat. "You guys could have found me," he argued. "No one ever came looking for me."

Winters said, "Weren't you using another name?"

"Well, yeah," he said, "but for a hotshot cop like you, Carl, that shouldn't have been such a big problem."

"The warrant was only local," Holly explained. "The judge didn't feel the case was strong enough to extradite a witness from another state. We could charge you with obstruction of justice, though," she said, "now that we know that you willfully withheld information in a homicide."

Leaping to his feet, Randall shouted, "I don't have to take this shit from you people. I'm not under arrest. I came down here to give you guys some information and help you out, and here you are, treating me like I'm a fucking murderer or something. Damn you people. How could you trick me into incriminating myself? Isn't that entrapment?"

"Sit down," Winters barked. Randall put on a good show of being a regular guy, but he was a lot sharper than the detective had originally suspected.

"No, I'm not going to sit down," Randall said, hot and agitated. "I sacrificed my scholarship to Notre Dame for this chick, ran off and hid like some draft dodger or something, just so I didn't have to testify against her. You know how much that meant to me? My father played ball at Notre Dame." He started pacing in front of the table. "All my life, I dreamed of going to that school and playing on that team. If it hadn't been for Stella, I might have turned pro and I'd be sitting on a fucking fortune. Instead, I'm coaching puny high school kids for peanuts and wondering how I'm going to pay the rent." He stopped and faced them. "Can I go now? If you're gonna keep me here against my will, don't you have to arrest me and read me my rights or something?"

During the entire interview Frank Minor had been standing in the back of the room, watching and listening. For a man who had turned thirty only a few weeks back, he had moved up quickly through the ranks. He merely nodded when Holly looked over with a questioning expression. He was analyzing the ramifications of Randall's statements, trying to determine if what he had heard constituted a viable case.

"You can go," Holly said. "If we need anything additional from you, we'll be in touch."

Winters hit the stop button on the tape recorder and stood to leave. Holly walked over next to Minor and whispered, "It doesn't look good for Stella, does it? Do you think everything he said is a lie, or could some of it be truthful?"

"What makes you think he's lying?" Minor said flatly, stepping past her to the door.

Randall was walking out of the room when he suddenly stood stock-still, an astonished look on his face. Stella was standing in the corridor right outside the door, only a few feet away from his wife and kids.

As soon as she saw Randall, she exploded, lashing out and slapping him hard across the face. "You bastard," she screamed, raking her nails down the right side of his face and drawing beads of blood. Whipping her hair back, she shouted, "Look what you did to me, you prick! If I could get away with it, I'd kill you with my bare hands."

Holly grabbed her and tried to pull her away, but Stella broke free and balled up her fist, ready to slug Randall. The man's wife was screaming and the children were crying and clawing at her legs. Several D.A.'s heard the commotion and started running down the hall, but Winters

39

shoved everyone aside and seized Stella around the waist, lifting her off her feet and then setting her down a few feet away. "Whoever you are," he said, his chest heaving from exertion, "make one more move and I'm going to cuff you."

While Frank Minor and the other attorneys escorted Randall and his family down the hall to the outer offices, Holly rushed over and told Winters who Stella was. In the confusion he hadn't recognized her. Even though he had seen her on TV, she looked different today. Her hair was draped over one side of her face, and she was wearing heavy makeup. Since Winters had seen her, he knew she must have undergone extensive reconstructive surgery. Not only had the scar improved in appearance, but many of her other features appeared to have been cosmetically altered as well.

"What did you do to yourself?" Winters asked. "Didn't your nose used to be different? What'd you do? Have a nose job or something?"

"Yeah," Stella said, glaring at him as if she was only seconds away from slapping him as she had Randall. "I tried to make the best of a bad situation, Winters. You don't look the same either, since you mentioned it. You're older and a hell of a lot fatter."

Placing an arm around Stella, Holly led her down the corridor to her office.

Standing in the lobby of the D.A.'s office, Randall was using Minor's handkerchief to dab at the scratch on his face, having dispatched his family to wait outside in the car. "Fuck," he said,

"I never thought I'd get assaulted in a damn D.A.'s office. Can't I swear out a complaint? When a man hits a woman, there's all hell to pay, so why should she be able to get away with this, huh?"

Frank Minor was intrigued. He had been inclined to believe Randall's story from the onset, based on Winters' insistence that Stella had been the one to set the fire, and after seeing her behavior just now, he was even more convinced that there might be something worth investigating. Prosecuting an acting district attorney, however, particularly one as recognized and accomplished as Stella Cataloni, would be a difficult and risky proposition. Minor was far from a risk-taker. People who took risks had to be prepared to suffer the consequences, and he valued his career too much to make a mistake. Apart from Stella's position and influence, it was not just an old case, but an ancient case. After sixteen years many witnesses had probably disappeared, along with a good deal of the evidence. "Would you be willing to testify in court to what you told us back there?" he asked. "I'm not saying we're going to pursue this, but knowing where you stand will help us to arrive at the right decision."

For a long time Randall was quiet, his eyes roaming around the lobby. "Yeah," he finally said, "I'll testify. Stella Cataloni's been fucking with my life for years. She called my parents and told them I was responsible for setting the fire. Hell, she told all my friends. I've got a new job now, and I'm finally getting my shit together. If

41

this is the only way to get the bitch off my back once and for all," he said, smiling as he stuck out his hand and pumped Minor's, "then I guess you've got yourself a deal."

Even though Stella had calmed down, her outburst had left her emotionally drained. Shaky and hollow, she was slouched in a chair in Holly's office feeling as though someone had reached inside and yanked out her internal organs. "How could he have the gall to say such things?" she said. "He really said he carried my brother to safety, that he's been on the lam all these years simply to protect me?" Stella shook her head in disgust. "How could I have fallen for such a creep? Thinking I actually slept with him makes me want to throw up."

Holly sat quietly, her face expressionless and her head braced in one hand. For almost an hour, she had listened to Stella rant and rave. When Holly had told Stella what Randall had said, it had set off another explosive tantrum, and Stella was only now beginning to settle down.

"You know what?" Stella said, staring at a spot on the wall over Holly's head. "I used to wonder about people who killed. How did they get to that point? What pushed them over the edge? You always think it's something big, something monumental, but maybe it's not. Maybe it's something small and hateful, insignificant to the overall situation, but important enough to drive them to commit murder."

"What do you mean?" Holly asked, Randall's statement playing over in her mind.

"I had a case once," Stella told her. "It only involved receiving stolen property, but the guy had a lengthy record, all of it relating to theft. I argued he should serve some time in the slammer. His attorney tried to win the court's sympathy by claiming if he went to jail, his wife and three kids would go hungry." She sneered. "I countered by saying his wife could get off her ass and get a job. I mean, most women with kids work today. All she had to do was put the kids in a day school. It wasn't like I was telling her to put them in an orphanage. Why should this guy's wife be any different than any other woman?"

Feeling like a shrink with a patient on the couch, Holly said, "What does this have to do with Randall? Aren't we getting a little off track, Stella?"

"This guy," she said, "when he got out of jail after serving only thirty lousy days, he tracked me down and took a shot at me. He missed, of course, but you know what he said?"

"What?"

"He wasn't mad at me because I sent him to jail. He wasn't even angry that I called him a compulsive thief in front of the judge. He was outraged that I forced his wife to get a job." Stella laughed. "I guess his wife must not have liked working, but by now she's probably used to it. Taking a shot at me cost him ten years in Huntsville. Only problem is he won't serve ten years. I think the bastard's about to be kicked out any day now."

"Aren't you concerned he may come after you again?" Holly said, doodling on a yellow notepad.

"Not really," Stella said. "The way I feel right now, maybe I should just send him my address."

"I still don't see your point," Holly said, her patience growing thin. Every line on her phone was lit up. She had instructed her secretary to take messages, but she was already ten minutes late for her last court appearance, and from the looks of it, she would have to spend the bulk of the following morning returning phone calls.

"Well," Stella said, her body crunched into a tight ball as she leaned forward in her chair, "I don't know for a fact that Randall set the fire, even though I've always suspected he did. But even if he did set the fire, you know what pisses me off, what makes me want to strangle him until his beady eyes pop out of his head?"

"What?" Holly said. Stella's tone of voice was finally fierce enough to capture her complete attention.

"That he claims he was the one who saved my brother," Stella said. "This guy thinks only of himself twenty-four hours a day. He wouldn't save his own kid if it meant risking his thick neck."

Holly shook her head, causing a few blond curls to tumble onto her forehead. "Then who saved your brother from the fire, Stella?"

"I did," Stella said emphatically. "If I hadn't gone down that hall to get Mario, I would never have been burned, never had to suffer through the agony of all those awful operations."

"I saw Mario, you know," Holly said, having met Stella's brother on several occasions during the time she worked with Stella at the Dallas

44

D.A.'s office. "I ran into him at the gym where I work out a few weeks ago. We had lunch and he told me all about his work. He had an exhibition going of some of his photographs at the time at the Graham Gallery on West Alabama. He asked me to drop by, so I did. He's pretty good, Stella. I was impressed."

This was news to Stella. She thought Mario mainly did fashion layouts and commercial spreads. Her brother had never told her he was trying to become a more serious photographer, but then she hadn't spoken to him in quite some time. "I'm going to try to find him now and take him to lunch," she said, standing to leave. "I tried to call him earlier, but he didn't answer. Sometimes he locks himself in the darkroom and doesn't hear the phone."

When Stella stepped into the outer office, Holly's secretary, a dark-haired woman with intelligent eyes and a warm, open face, came out from behind her desk and extended her hand to Stella. "I'm Janet Hernandez," she said, smiling shyly. "I followed the Pelham case on TV. You were fabulous."

"Thanks," Stella said, wondering where the woman had been when she'd attacked Tom Randall. Her behavior today had been a long way from fabulous. Probably at lunch, she decided, turning to leave.

"I hope you don't consider this an imposition," Janet continued, holding out a piece of paper and a pen, "but would you mind giving me your autograph before you leave?"

45

Holly was watching from the doorway. "Leave her alone," she said, her tone rude and offensive.

Stella glanced back over her shoulder. "It's okay," she said, quickly signing her name and handing the paper back to Janet.

"You don't know how much this means to me," Janet said, clutching the paper to her chest. "If my husband's new job works out, I'm going to enroll in law school this fall. Meeting you will serve as my inspiration."

Holly gave Janet a black look.

"I think you have all the inspiration you need, Janet," Stella said, sizing up the situation and trying her best to diffuse it. "You're working for one of the finest prosecutors in the state."

Janet flushed, but she remained silent, slowly lowering herself back to her seat. She had worked for Holly over a year. The other secretaries in the agency were placing bets as to the exact number of days left before she turned in her resignation. The district attorney went through secretaries the way some people went through paper towels. When they resigned, they were always in tears.

Holly stood in the doorway a few more moments, then slammed the door so hard that both women flinched. Beads of perspiration appeared on Janet's forehead. No matter how difficult Holly was, Janet needed to keep her job until she was accepted into law school or she wouldn't have the necessary funds for her tuition. "I made a mistake, didn't I?"

Stella reached over and touched her hand. "I

wouldn't worry about it if I were you," she said. "We all make mistakes now and then."

Once Stella had left, Frank Minor called and had Janet advise Holly to report to his office. "Tell him I'm on my way to court," Holly said, rushing past the woman's desk, her file and briefcase in hand. "I'm already late, and Judge Rolling is a stickler for punctuality."

"Minor already had me call and advise the clerk to put your case at the end of the afternoon calendar," Janet explained. "He wants to see you now, Holly. I don't think he wants to wait."

"Great," Holly said, hurling her file at Janet's face. "Now I've got you telling me what to do."

Janet ducked and the file struck the wall behind her. She bent down to pick up the scattered papers as Holly continued out of the office. The incident with Stella would cost her dearly. Holly had been on a rampage ever since Stella had won the Pelham case, a case everyone knew Holly had lost. Janet should have known not to express her admiration for Stella in front of Holly. She knew she was a jealous, competitive woman. Holly had to feel superior, not just to underlings like Janet, but to everyone she met. This was particularly true with women. Holly could turn on the charm with the men, but she had few, if any, loyalties when it came to women.

When Holly stepped into Minor's office a few moments later, she looked around at the nicely upholstered furniture, the floor to ceiling windows behind the desk, the mahogany bookcases lining the walls. By rights, this should have been her office. Her eyes then fell on the framed Harvard degree on the wall and her back instantly stiffened. When she and Minor had competed for the supervisory position over the homicide unit several months back, Holly had been certain she would walk away the victor. She had far more trial experience than Minor, and because she had once been a cop, she possessed more insight into arrest procedures, forensic evidence, and the overall intricacies involved in building a criminal case. She had been devastated when Minor had snatched the position right out of her hands.

Unlike Minor, Holly didn't have the advantage of wealthy and influential parents. Her father had died when she was only twelve, plunging the family into poverty. Holly had struggled to become an attorney, working as a cop while she went to an inexpensive Dallas law school, studying all night after putting in a full day. Her education was now catching up to her, though, and she was fearful that she would end up mired in a low-level position for the remainder of her career, stuck in a cramped and miserable office like the one she was working in now. She wasn't deluding herself any longer like so many others with similar backgrounds, people who thought foolishly that if they passed the bar and became accredited attorneys, the future would fall into place and the name on their law degrees would be insignificant.

Holly's father had found himself in a similar situation. After twenty-five years with Mobil Oil, he had competed for an executive position and lost. She remembered the shattered look on his face the day he had come home from work and told her mother. "I didn't look good enough on paper, honey," he'd said. "They don't care that I can do the job, that I have more experience than all the other candidates put together. Graduating from a city college instead of a first-rate university is all they care about. They bypassed me over a lousy piece of paper."

The following morning had been the worst day of Holly's life. She had been a spunky twelve-year-old and the light of her father's life. They weren't wealthy, but they were a happy family and lived a rich life. When she went to the garage that morning to get her bicycle out to go to school, Holly's childhood abruptly ended. Dangling from a rope attached to the rafters was her father's lifeless body, the feet brushing back and forth against the seat of Holly's shiny red bike.

Once Minor noted her presence in the room, Holly took a seat in a highbacked leather chair facing his desk. "Janet said you wanted to see me," she said. "What's going on?"

"I think we have something," Minor said excitedly. "With Randall's statement we might be able to reopen the case and successfully prosecute it."

"What are you saying?" she said. "You think we have enough to prosecute Randall? I don't agree, Frank. I mean, Stella's been after me for ages to reopen the case, but I—"

"Why would we prosecute Randall?" he said. "He just handed us the guilty party. I spoke to him outside, and he assured me he's willing to testify."

"Stella?" Holly exclaimed. "You can't be serious, Frank."

"Why not?" he said. "If you ask me, your friend from Dallas might just turn out to be a murderer."

Holly crossed her legs, then uncrossed them, then a few moments later crossed them again. "I guess you're right," she finally said. "In good conscience, I agree that we can't simply overlook Randall's statements, but if we attempt to prosecute someone as high-placed as Stella Cataloni, the media will eat it up like cotton candy. Both of us could go down the drain on a case like this. If we do move forward, we better make certain we know what we're doing, that we have the goods to make the charges stick." She stopped and studied his face, trying to figure out what he was thinking. "And don't forget the Pelham case. People will see the scars on Stella's face and instantly classify her as a victim."

Instead of responding to her reasoning and backing off, Frank Minor found her comments enormously titillating. He was beginning to see the wealth of opportunity in a case as sensational as this one, particularly now that Stella's success in the Pelham case had given her a certain celebrity status with the media. "On the other hand, both our careers could be made on this case," he told her. "Would you be willing to try it? Because you worked with Stella in Dallas, the dynamics would be perfect. Who wouldn't want to cover this story? Two women prosecutors going at it in the courtroom, one time co-workers, one of them on trial for murder and arson." The more he thought about it, the more animated he became. "More than careers are at stake here, Oppenheimer. We could both haul in a shitload of cash. Book rights, movie rights, you name it."

"Hummm," Holly said, curling a strand of her hair around her finger. "I don't know, Frank. Stella is my friend. I mean, we haven't been that close since I moved away, but from what I know of her, she's a decent woman who's already been through a terrible ordeal." She shrugged. "The way you're presenting it sounds cruel and opportunistic. I don't know if I want to be a part of something like that."

"What if Stella Cataloni did kill her parents?" he said, eager to persuade her. "Did you tell her what Randall said? How did she react?"

"You saw her with Randall," she said, grimacing. "How do you think she reacted? She went ballistic. I almost had to call someone in to help me restrain her."

"See," Minor said, pointing a finger at her, "the woman's violent. I think she did it, and if she did, she should damn well pay."

"Look," Holly said, "Stella has always been high strung and impulsive. Everyone knows she can explode if you push the right buttons. This isn't the first time I've seen her lose it. I once saw her go ballistic right in the courtroom." Her eyes glazed over. "Growman controls her, you know. He's taught her to use her temperament to good advantage." She began picking the lint

51

off her skirt. "No one can crack a witness like Stella Cataloni."

Once Holly looked up, Minor drove his point home. "Are you going to let someone get away with murder just because of a casual relationship?" Then his voice elevated even more and he shouted, "Two people died here, remember, not just one. We're talking double homicide, Oppenheimer." He reached behind him to his credenza, pulled out a file, and removed a stack of photos. "Take a look at these," he said, sliding the photos to the edge of his desk. "Then tell me this is something we should file away and forget."

Holly shuddered as she looked at the gruesome crime scene photos. The bodies of Stella's parents had been so badly burned that they looked like blackened logs out of a fireplace. Holly had to turn the pictures around to see any semblance of humanity. "Where was her father's body found?"

"In the hall somewhere," Minor said. "That's not the important issue. Didn't you hear Winters? The fire originated right around Cataloni's bed. Just because her father's body wasn't found in the same location doesn't mean anything. The man could have staggered down the hall after she set him on fire, then collapsed and died."

Holly tossed the pictures back on his desk and sighed. "Well, you're right about it being an ugly crime. It's funny, you know," she said. "People think one murder is the same as another." She sucked in a deep breath and then slowly let it out. "But these poor people were cremated alive, Frank. They must have died in agony."

"So, your little friend doesn't look so sweet and innocent anymore, huh?" he said with a smirk.

Holly was stoic, unreadable. "She's still one of us," she said. "Randall might be a self-serving asshole who just spoon-fed us a fistful of lies."

"You need this case," Minor said, his lip curling in a sadistic smile. "If you want to get ahead, Oppenheimer, you have to develop the killer instinct. You've lost three cases in a row now. Don't you think it's time you bring in a big one?"

Holly's eyes narrowed, but she quickly checked her resentment. "You're the boss," she said, standing and turning to leave. "Whatever you decide, I guess I'll have to find a way to live with it."

Once she was outside Minor's office, Holly's demeanor shifted, and she hummed to herself as she made her way down the corridor. When she reached her office, she saw Janet Hernandez typing on her word processor. "So you admire Stella, huh?" she said. Janet didn't answer. Sometimes she tried to get the upper hand by giving Holly the silent treatment. "Interesting," Holly said, feeling a rush of pure pleasure.

chapter

THREE

Stella paid the cabdriver and then hiked up the stairs to her brother's apartment, located in a densely populated area near the Houston Astrodome. She rang the bell and waited until he came and opened it, pleased that she had found him at home. "Stella," Mario Cataloni said, his handsome face spread in a broad grin, "what are you doing in Houston? Were you waiting long? I was in the darkroom developing some prints."

Stella stepped into his arms and hugged him, burying her head against his chest. He was tall, his hair dark like Stella's, and above his lip was a neatly trimmed mustache. He wore a pair of snug-fitting Levi's and no shirt, his feet encased in his customary cowboy boots, his upper body glistening with perspiration. Around his neck was the gold crucifix that Stella had given him on his sixteenth birthday.

When she pulled back, she punched him playfully in the stomach, connecting with a solid ridge of muscle. "It's good to see you, you handsome devil," she said. "Do I have to get on a plane and fly here just to see what's going on with my baby brother? I called this morning, but you must not have heard the phone."

Mario laughed, rubbing his stomach. "Hey,

Stel, that hurt. You've got to quit beating up on me now. I'm not a kid anymore, in case you haven't noticed."

"Let me see," Stella said, grinning as she circled him. "Nope, I guess not. What are you going to be next month? The big three-oh? Scary, huh?"

"Yeah," he said, "getting old sucks, but then you should know all about it."

While Mario laughed, Stella sneered, displaying the tough demeanor she always put on for him. "You little shit," she said, kicking the toe of his boot. "Are we going to stand here all day in the heat, or are you going to invite me in? I thought we'd go for lunch."

Once she stepped inside, Stella shook her head in dismay. When Mario had lived with her and her husband, she had tasted his sloppiness first-hand, but now that he was a man, she had expected him to take better care of himself. The apartment was large, with two good-sized bedrooms and a third Mario had converted into a dark- room. He had nice furnishings, so that wasn't the problem. Favoring contemporary decor, her brother had decorated his apartment with black marble tables and white overstuffed sofas, strange lamps made out of stainless steel that looked as if they belonged in an office instead of a home. The walls were covered with poster-size photos that Mario had taken over the years. Most of them were head shots of pretty young women advertising some type of product, but some of them were landscapes and nature shots.

"I hear you're doing some serious work," Stella

said, walking over to study one of the images. "Didn't you have an exhibition recently? This is really good stuff, guy. I'm proud of you."

"I just finished a shoot for a dog food company," Mario said, with a grimace. "I'd like to concentrate on more serious stuff, but it doesn't pay the rent."

As a professional photographer, Mario traveled a great deal, but for Stella there was still no excuse for living in a garbage dump. Newspapers were scattered all over the floor, fast-food wrappers and empty, leaking cups covered almost every solid surface, ashtrays were spilling over with butts, and the white sofas were stained and dirty. "This is disgusting," she said. "They have a new invention. It's called a trash can. One of these days you should try it."

"Quit being a mother, Stel," Mario said, firing up a cigarette and exhaling a stream of smoke in her face. "I like living like this. What's the big deal?"

"Put on a shirt and we'll go," she said. "You haven't had lunch already, have you?"

"To tell you the truth," he answered, "I just had breakfast about thirty minutes ago."

"Great," Stella said. "Is there anything to eat in this place?"

"There's some lunch meat in the refrigerator. Help yourself. I have to check on my prints."

Stella busied herself as she always did, picking up the living room and then moving to the kitchen and a sink full of dirty dishes. Opening the door to the refrigerator, she glanced inside and then closed it, deciding to pass on lunch. Seeing a solitary apple in a bowl on the counter, Stella nibbled on it while she worked.

Mario emerged from the darkroom and they almost had a head-on collision as Stella came down the hall, her finger depressed on a can of air freshener.

Finally, when she saw some improvement, she took a seat on one of the white sofas in the living room and proceeded to tell Mario what had transpired at the police station.

"That fucking bastard," he snarled, jumping to his feet. "After what he did to us, how could he possibly make an accusation like that?"

Stella watched as Mario circled the room, flexing his muscles and slamming his right fist into his opposite palm. "Calm down," she said, sorry now that she had told him. "There's nothing we can do. Besides, no one will take Randall's accusations seriously. You should see him. He's a joke, a buffoon."

"Don't kid yourself, Stella," her brother said. "There are people in this town who'd pay good money to see you fall on your face."

Stella tilted her head and gave him a curious look. "You don't mean—"

"You know Uncle Clem has always believed you were behind Dad's death," he said. "And that old goat . . . what's his name? You know, Stella, the cop that busted you the first time."

"Carl Winters," Stella said.

"Well, he's always been after you," he said. "It's like he thinks you're some big criminal that got away, like something out of that stupid show,

'The Fugitive.' He's going to keep after you until the day he dies."

Stella laughed, thinking his analysis of Winters was fairly accurate.

Mario, though, didn't think it was funny. "Look, I live here, Stella," he said. "I know all the rumors that have flown around this town. For the first six months after I moved back, I got stopped by the Houston P.D. every other day. Don't tell me Uncle Clem wasn't behind it, because I know damn well that he was."

Stella looked down at her hands. Instead of helping her and Mario after the fire, their family had turned against them. "Is he still a captain at the police department?"

"Retired about six months ago," Mario said, "but believe me, he can still pull his weight with the rank and file. When he hears about this new development, well, I just don't know what he'll do." Disappearing into the kitchen, he returned with an open bottle of red wine. "Want some?" he said, swinging the bottle toward Stella.

Stella waved it away. "Why would Uncle Clem harass you?"

"How do I know?" Mario said, flicking the hairs on his mustache. "He's a maniac, if you ask me. Maybe he thinks we were in it together. A friend of mine was in a bar watching your TV interview after the Pelham trial. The guy sitting next to him knew our name from the fire and said he'd heard we were sleeping together. That's why we had to get rid of our parents."

"God," Stella said, picking up a throw pillow

and hugging it to her chest, "you really think Uncle Clem would say something that sick?"

"I bet Randall's stupid family started that rumor. I guess they thought if they told everyone we were lovers, then people would think I was the one who got you pregnant."

"Wonderful," she said, her brows knitted in outrage. "Randall probably made that story up himself, Mario. It sounds like something he'd do."

"I should go over there and break both of his fucking legs," Mario said, taking another slug of wine and then wiping his mouth with the back of his hand. "Shit, I've been wanting to get my hands on this guy for years. Do you know where he's staying? I'll get a couple of my friends and we'll teach him a lesson he'll never forget."

"No," Stella shouted. "Don't even talk that way. That's all we need right now." She started sniffing as if she were about to break down. "I didn't mean to blow up like that and slap him. I only wanted to confront him face to face. When I saw him, though, I just went crazy. I couldn't stop myself."

Her brother placed the bottle of wine on a coffee table and sat down next to Stella on the sofa. For some time they just stared out over the room in silence.

"I love you, Stel," Mario said. "I can't let anyone hurt you. You've been hurt enough. If it hadn't been for you, I wouldn't even be alive today." He looked away, his voice low and strained. "How do you think I feel? I don't have a mark on me. Every time I think of your scars, I wonder why it wasn't me."

"Don't start on this, Mario," Stella said, patting her eyes with a tissue. "Please, you know how it upsets me when you talk this way."

Mario persisted. "Having a few scars wouldn't be the end of the world for a guy," he told her. "I remember how Mom used to always say you would be Miss Texas one day, even make it to the Miss America pageant."

Stella stroked his hand. "All mothers have silly dreams like that," she said. "That doesn't mean they're realistic. Besides, I never wanted to be a beauty queen. That was Momma's dream, not mine."

"You were just so beautiful, Stella," Mario continued. "Why did it have to be you?"

Stella knew she was about to break down, but she suppressed her tears. She was the one who had to be strong. It was her strength that had always carried them. She had often thought that if Mario had died in the fire along with their parents, she would have committed suicide. Instead, she had undergone the agony of repeated operations and skin grafts, knowing she had to look normal enough to go out in public and hold down a job if she was going to find a way to support her fourteen-year-old brother.

Brad Emerson had come along at exactly the right time. He had worked with Stella's father in the construction trade, and she had met him on several occasions when he had stopped by the house. After the tragedy Brad had been attentive and supportive, offering to take Stella's brother under his wing in order to keep the authorities from placing him in foster care. Even though Brad was almost twenty years older and Stella was only eighteen at the time, she had found it easy to love someone who extended such generosity and kindness.

In the beginning she had been Brad's little girl, scarred and wounded. She had willingly let him tell her how to dress, where to go, what to say. He had always been the one to organize their social life and pick their friends. How could she have been anything else back then? He had swept into her life like a guardian angel.

Now that she thought about it, she understood why Brad had finally soured and divorced her. Her devotion to Mario had always been a trouble spot between them, even before she began her career as an attorney. The bond between Stella and her brother was impenetrable. What they had shared was so intense, so tragic, that a person who had not been through it could never understand what they meant to each other. She had always promised Brad that as soon as she got Mario off to college, she would devote more time and energy to him. He was the type of man who liked to be coddled, who wanted to come home every night to a home-cooked meal and a wife waiting to please him. Stella's career had taken off under Growman's careful tutoring, though, and over the years she had blossomed into a confident and successful woman.

Grabbing Mario's hand, Stella sealed it inside her grasp. "There's nothing to worry about," she said. "I'm going back to Dallas tonight and talk it over with Growman, see what he thinks we should do. Now that Randall is back in town to stay, we don't have to rush into anything. We can pick through the case as long as we want. With Holly's help, maybe we'll find something to prove he was responsible for the fire."

"Was Holly there today?" Mario asked, a guarded look on his face.

"Yes," Stella said. "Why do you ask?"

"Will she be the one handling the case?"

"I don't know," she answered. "Right now it's too soon to tell. I'm not certain we even have a case, Mario. The evidence is weak, and Randall's trying to shift all the blame on me. The only way we can prosecute him is to come up with additional evidence and after this much time it's doubtful if that's going to happen. The house burned almost to the ground, so there's not much to work with. That's been the problem with the case all along."

"You mean they're going to let Randall get away with it?" Mario said, his face set in anger.

"Probably," Stella said. "He's gotten away with it all these years."

"That's not right," he said.

"Yeah, well," she shrugged, "life isn't always fair."

Stella stood and asked Mario to drive her to the airport.

"Stay the night, Stel," he urged. "We'll go out to a nice restaurant, try to forget about all this stuff."

"I can't," Stella said. "I have a meeting tonight

with Brad and my attorney to see if we can work out the property settlement."

Mario's face softened at the mention of Brad. Even though Stella's husband had been a stern disciplinarian, Mario had always respected him and was grateful for the things he had done for him. "Tell him I said hello," he said. "You know, if he comes to Houston on business, make certain he gives me a call."

"Sure," Stella said.

"Can't you guys work it out?"

"I'm afraid not," Stella said. "He's seeing someone else, Mario. He was seeing her months before he left me." Her shoulders rose and then quickly fell. "She's twenty-four and beautiful, not a mark on her body. Now that he has her, what does he need me for?"

Stella used her brother's phone to call Sam and ask if he could pick her up in Dallas. Once he agreed, they left, discussing Mario's love life and his latest photography assignments on the drive to the Hobby airport. Before she boarded the plane, Stella reached up and tousled his hair. "So you're dating a stewardess," she said, smiling. "Don't you think it's time to settle down?"

"Ah, shucks, Stel," he said, smiling rakishly, "I'm so ornery, I might never settle down. There's just too many good-looking women in this town. I intend to work my way through every one of them before I put the skids on it and let some broad rope me into marrying her."

Stella frowned. How had he become such a

playboy? Mario walked off, turning around to wave as Stella headed up the ramp to the plane.

Samuel Weinstein's offices were located in a complex near the Central Expressway and Mockingbird Lane, not far from the SMU campus and the Park Cities section of Dallas. The rooms were well appointed and spacious, the walls were covered with valuable art, and four neatly groomed women were clicking away at word processors and fielding phone calls. Sam, Stella, and Brad Emerson were in the conference room, where Sam had prepared identical folders listing the couple's assets and liabilities, placing them on the table in front of each of their chairs.

Brad's manner of dress made him look younger than his fifty-four years. Wearing a black silk T-shirt under a purple Claude Montana jacket, slim-legged pants, and a gold chain around his neck, he appeared to be in his early forties. Stella almost broke out laughing when she spotted the latest addition—a small diamond stud in his right earlobe. But regardless of his new mode of dress, Brad Emerson was one of those men who never seemed to age. Even though his hair was more silver now than blond, his face was tan and unlined, his body fit and lean. When he flashed a smile, women of all ages smiled back. He wasn't a large man, but he was extremely strong, his body developed from years of working in the building trade.

"Mario asked about you," Stella said while Sam left the room to take an important phone call. "I saw him earlier today. He said you should call him if you ever come to Houston."

"Oh, really?" Brad said. "What were you doing in Houston?"

Stella told him about Randall surfacing, and Brad snorted and then looked away. "Now that he's back in town, Brad," she told him, "there's a chance we can reopen the case. That means I might finally find out what happened that night and whether or not Randall was the person who set the fire."

"Why can't you let sleeping dogs lie?" he said. "Chasing after this Randall guy isn't going to bring your parents back to life. Your biggest problem, Stella, is you invest too much in the past. It's the future that should concern you. No matter what you do, you can't change the past."

Stella tensed. She'd heard this speech dozens of times. Brad had never understood her compulsion to find the person responsible for her parents' death, her need to seek revenge. Did he expect her to just forget all the pain and suffering she'd been forced to endure, forget that her parents had died an agonizing death? "If your face was scarred," she snapped, "I bet you wouldn't be so willing to forgive and forget."

"What's Randall doing back in Houston?" Brad said.

Sam stepped through the doorway. "Sorry for the interruption."

"He got a job as the football coach at St. Elizabeth's," Stella continued as Sam made his way to the conference table. "But let me tell you something," she added, "I'm going to go all the way this time, and not you or anyone else is going to stop me. I have connections now, not just in Dallas, but in Houston as well. I'm not an eighteen-year-old girl anymore that no one will take seriously." She pounded the table, wanting to convince herself as much as Brad. "Forensic technology is more advanced now, and our agency has an investigator who can work wonders. We're going to dig through the evidence and put this case together if it's the last thing I ever do."

"Happy hunting," Brad said with a smirk. "Now that you've killed our marriage, you can become a regular Sherlock Holmes for all I care."

"You're the one who killed our marriage," Stella shouted. "You and your cheap little girlfriend. What is she anyway, a tittie dancer at one of those strip bars? Can't you do better than that, Brad?"

"Maybe we should get down to business," Sam said, seeing the sparks flying between Stella and Brad. He didn't want the situation to turn into a screaming match. They were here to settle Stella's affairs.

"I'm ready," Brad said, glancing at his watch. "I didn't intend for this to take the whole night, Weinstein. I have a dinner engagement."

The attorney stated a sum that he felt would be a fair settlement and then leaned back in his chair and waited for Brad to respond.

Brad glared at Stella. "I don't have that kind of money," he spat at her. "That's why my attorney isn't here today. I can't afford to pay some guy a grand to sit here and hold my damn hand. I've told you ten times that money is tight right now." He shifted in his seat, trying to calm himself. "Business is off, see," he said in a more reasonable tone. "I had to dip into our savings for operating expenses. I was going to put the money back as soon as I finished some of my new projects."

"Isn't it true," Sam said crisply, "that you've been burying assets, and that in addition you removed the money in your joint bank accounts not to use in the business but to support your extravagant lifestyle?"

"You're a damn liar," Brad said, red-faced and furious. "What kind of fancy lifestyle do I have? I'm a builder. So, I want to dress up now and then after spending my life in sweaty work clothes." He jerked his head to Stella. "Are you going to deny an old guy a few new threads? Shit, what else are you going to try to take away from me, my fucking business?"

"It's more than that, isn't it?" Sam said, assuming Brad had exhausted their savings buying costly gifts for his young girlfriend, maybe so he could take her on trips. "Not all the money went into the business, did it? If it did, there doesn't appear to be any record to substantiate such a claim."

"What's your problem?" Brad said, directing his venom now at Weinstein. "You're fucking my wife, aren't you? You smug little piece of shit. You're fucking my damn wife. I can see it in your face."

The air was thick with tension. Stella looked

down at her hands, while Weinstein tapped his pen on the table.

"You damn lawyers are all the same," Brad said. "All you want is to get your hands on our money, bleed us until there's nothing left." He stopped and took a breath, and then said, "What kind of a name is Weinstein? You're Jewish, aren't you? Everyone knows you people don't give a shit about anything but money." Then he turned to Stella. "As soon as you quit paying this blood-sucker, babe, he'll drop you like a hot potato."

Stella scowled. "Let's not get carried away, Brad."

"Carried away?" he said, springing to his feet. "This asshole served me with a restraining order today like a common criminal while I was having lunch with my friend. Said I can't get within a hundred feet of my own house or my own wife. Embarrassed the fuck out of me and made her think I'm a wife-beater."

Her? Stella thought, knowing Brad had slipped. So, they had embarrassed him in front of his young girlfriend, made her think twice about what kind of man she was getting involved with. Feeling a sense of satisfaction, Stella then saw the vicious look in her husband's eyes. "I'm the one who signed the restraining order," she said, wanting to take the heat off Sam. "It's customary in a divorce. Everyone does it, Brad. And you did knock me down and cause me to bruise my elbow that day. How do I know you won't come over and shoot me or something?"

"Customary, huh?" he barked, his designer jacket now stained under the armpits with perspiration. "Well, I'm getting a restraining order on you, Miss Hotshot. How do you like those apples?"

"Fine," Stella said. "If you feel that's necessary, then go ahead. It's just a piece of paper."

Sam tried to regain control of the situation, wanting them to settle the financial agreement so they could move forward with the divorce. "Why don't you both relax and look over the paperwork I've prepared for you? It's a lot better to agree on a division of property rather than force the court to do it for you."

"Fuck you," Brad snarled, advancing on Sam. "I'm not giving anybody anything. If you want to take away a man's last dime, then you'll have to come and get it."

Sam collected himself and stood, his face muscles twitching. "Is that a challenge, Emerson?"

"Yeah," Brad said, throwing up his fists and flexing his biceps. "Come and get it, you slimy ambulance chaser."

"I think you better leave now," Sam said. "If you don't, I'll call the police and have you forcibly removed."

"Stop it, Brad," Stella interjected. "You're acting like a fool. Sam's just an attorney. This isn't personal. If you want to slug someone, slug me. I'm the one you're angry at, not Sam."

Her husband's fists fell and he stared first at Stella and then at Weinstein, his chest heaving. Then he pointed an accusing finger at Sam. "You're fucking my wife," he proclaimed, turning around and storming out of the conference room.

Sam took his seat and glanced down at the folder in front of him. "I guess we're not going to settle this amicably," he said, his voice trailing off in disappointment.

Stella broke out laughing. "Obviously," she said, stifling another nervous giggle. For some reason, she found the meeting almost comical. She could see the earnestness on Sam's face, and wondered how he had ever thought two people as volatile and high strung as she and her husband would sit down across from each other and calmly settle their affairs. He might be a good attorney, she thought, walking over and draping her arms around him from behind, but he had a lot to learn about human nature.

"He thinks we're lovers," Stella said, bending down and touching her lips to the top of his head. The attorney had been a godsend the night before. He had driven her home and tried to console her. He'd gone on to suggest that she fly to Houston and confront Randall, hoping this would put things in perspective. He'd been so kind, so concerned for her well-being. If she hadn't been distraught at the time and self-conscious about her body, she would have been tempted to invite him into her bed. Sam had been somewhat aloof, however. Stella had impulsively kissed him, but he had made no attempt to take it any further. Instead of going inside the house, they had sat outside in his car and talked.

Sam reached up behind him and touched her hand. "Isn't Brad referring to Growman, Stella?"

"What are you talking about?" Stella said, surprised. She circled around and took the chair next to him.

"You know," Sam said, his voice strained. "Don't you and Ben Growman have a thing going?"

"Absolutely not," Stella said, realizing now why he had been so standoffish the night before. "Why would you say that?"

"Well," he said, "everyone knows Growman's a ladies' man. I haven't seen him with a woman in quite some time, but years ago I used to see him with a young blonde. I've met his wife, Stel, so I know it wasn't legit."

"You probably saw him with Holly Oppenheimer," Stella answered. "Something went on between them, but that was years ago. Growman and I are close, Sam, but I promise you I'm not sleeping with him. He's more like a father figure to me than anything."

"Why did Brad get so upset, then?" Sam asked, tilting his head. "I thought he knew you were having an affair and he just wasn't certain who the person was. Therefore, he assumed it was me."

"He's just acting like an ass," Stella said, swinging her leg back and forth. "People have probably seen us out together. I don't know where he gets off screaming at me, though. He was squiring this girl around town for months before he approached me about the divorce. It's humiliating to think that my marriage was over, and everyone knew it but me."

"Hey," Sam said, leaning over and placing a

finger under her chin. "I'm hungry. How about you? Since we're supposedly having a torrid affair, I guess I should at least buy you a decent meal now and then."

Stella laughed, feeling a wonderful release from the tension of the day. She was dead on her feet, but the thought of enjoying a nice meal with a man as pleasant and attentive as Sam made her feel revitalized. "What about Adam?" she said, referring to his son. "Don't you have to get home?"

"That's why God made housekeepers, Stella," Sam said, smiling at her. "Lois has been with us for seven years."

"I want to meet him one day," she said. "I bet he's a great kid."

"Oh, you'll meet him," Sam said, issuing another smile. "But right now, let's go eat. I worked straight through today without lunch and I'm starving."

"Sounds like a plan," she said, standing. "I skipped lunch myself. For the kind of money I'm paying you," she joked, "don't think you can get away with taking me to McDonald's."

"McDonald's?" Sam said with a look of disgust. "I don't even take Adam to McDonald's. That stuff will kill you."

"Just checking," Stella said, giving him a playful shove as they passed through the doorway.

After leaving the restaurant at the prestigious Mansion Hotel on Turtle Creek Boulevard, stuffed from too much rich food and slightly tipsy from the wine they had consumed, Sam and

Stella drove to her house in his black Mercedes. She leaned back against the headrest and inhaled the rich scent of new leather. "I was going to buy a new car next year," she said, sighing as she thought of her ten-year-old BMW with eighty thousand miles on the speedometer. "Now I guess I won't have enough money." Seeing him come alive, Stella knew she had just hit the magic button. Sam might be an attorney, but he was also a money man, someone who considered financial security to be the most important asset a person could possess.

"If you'll let me go forward and fight for what's rightfully yours," he said, cutting his eyes to her, "and not let your husband pressure you into an unfair settlement, you can buy whatever you want."

"Nah," she said, shaking her head, "all this fighting over money is wearing me out. It just isn't worth it, Sam. Besides, I earn a decent income. I can manage on my own without taking anything from Brad. The house isn't much, but it's almost paid for, and if my car breaks down, I'll just get it repaired."

"I'm not talking about alimony," Sam said, pulling the car onto Stella's cobblestone driveway and killing the engine. "You're not eligible for alimony due to your income, but some of those savings accounts that have disappeared represent money you earned and saved. Do you want to let him cheat you like that?"

"Yeah," she said, smiling at him and then quickly falling serious. "Let him have it. Who knows? Maybe he's earned it. From the way he tells it, I've made his life a living hell for the past six or seven years, so—"

"That's ridiculous," Sam said. "Not only that, it's foolish. If you don't fight for it, the court may not even award you the house, Stella. And what happens if you get sick? What if you can't work? What about retirement? Can you live comfortably on your county pension?"

"Hey," Stella told him, reaching over and clasping his hand, "it isn't that I don't appreciate what you're trying to do, it's just that money doesn't matter to me. If I live in a house, fine. If I have to live in an apartment, that's fine too. Besides, I probably won't even live to reach retirement, so why worry about it now?"

They both fell silent. Outside the night air was heavy with moisture. Crickets were chirping around White Rock Lake, only a short distance from where Stella lived. Her house was hidden in a thick batch of elm trees, making it totally private, if not somewhat isolated. An older ramshackle structure that she and her husband had never taken the time to repair, the house had been built in the early 1900s, and then remodeled about thirty years ago. At one time the structure had been a twelve-stall horse stable, belonging to the sprawling mansion that looked down on them from the hill above. Now it contained a living room, two small bedrooms, a study, and a fairly well-appointed kitchen that Stella never found the time to use.

Seeing a light flash through the windshield, she sat forward. "Look, it's lightning. Guess it's going to rain. No wonder it's so sticky and humid. It reminds me of Houston when it gets like this."

"I think you should slow down," Sam said, turning to look at her. "You drive yourself too hard. Stress can cause the body to malfunction. Believe me, I know what I'm talking about. You're a young woman, but that doesn't preclude you from developing heart disease, cancer, even a stroke."

Stella had dozens of unanswered questions about his wife, their marriage, her untimely death, but she was reluctant to ask. Their religious backgrounds were very different as well, as Sam was Jewish and Stella had been raised a Catholic.

Watching as another bolt of lightning zipped across the sky, Stella wondered if Sam knew how vulnerable she was right now. Her career had never been more promising but the pending divorce had left her feeling lonely and dejected. Her husband's leaving her for another woman had affected her more than anyone would ever know. During the frenetic pace of the Pelham trial, she had been unable to give the problem much thought, but now that the case was over, she knew she had to come to terms with it.

Was this why so many women slept with their divorce attorneys? she asked herself—to convince themselves they could do it, go back out in the world and find another man, re-create a new life?

"Let's go inside," Stella said. "It's going to start pouring any minute."

"Oh," he said, "it's late and I'm sure you're

exhausted. Maybe another night would be better."

Stella felt her spirits plummet. Sam was a handsome, successful man and probably had his pick of beautiful women. Dallas was full of them, she reminded herself. Dallas women knew how to dress, how to fix their hair and makeup, how to giggle and beam at just the right moment, making the man they were with feel as if he was the most important person in the world. Stella, though, was not a Dallas girl either by birth or disposition. In the area of feminine wiles she was clearly outclassed.

Why would Sam want someone like her? For all she knew, seeing her scar on television had repulsed him, and she was putting him in an awkward position by coming on to him. "Okay," she said, her hand on the door handle, "then I guess I'll talk to you sometime next week. Thanks for dinner. I really appreciate you taking me out tonight."

"Wait, Stella," he said, scooting across the seat and quickly embracing her. He pulled back and captured her face in his hands, staring down into her eyes before he pressed his lips to hers.

Stella responded immediately, kissing him back and lacing her fingers in his hair. Before she knew it, Sam's hands were everywhere—flitting over her breasts, her buttocks, working their way between her legs. Stella found herself lodged next to the passenger door, partially reclining in an uncomfortable position. "Let's go inside," she whispered.

"I can't wait," he said, bending down to kiss

her neck. "I want you, Stella. God, you don't know how much. I thought you were involved with Growman—"

Rain was splashing against the windshield and as soon as a bolt of lightning appeared, a loud clap of thunder immediately followed. Stella looked up at the roof of the car as Sam pulled her blouse out of the waistband of her skirt, and then fumbled with the snap on her bra. He was too eager, too aggressive. She had expected a shy and tentative lover. Since the fire, she had never let a man other than Brad see her body, let alone make love to her. For Sam, jumping into bed was probably a routine event, she told herself, but for her it was fraught with danger.

She felt his hand inside her panty hose, his fingers stroking her in the most erotic and sensual way. The contact was electrifying and she jumped, never expecting it to feel this way. Sam's fingers were surprisingly soft and padded, and despite her apprehension Stella found her body responding. She leaned back in the seat and sighed with pleasure, embarrassed at the wetness she felt between her legs.

"Wait," she said, pushing Sam away. "We can't do this here. I'm going to break my neck." Seeing the small storage shack she had christened the carriage house, after the actual carriage houses that so many of the older homes around the lake had once possessed, Stella had a brainstorm. "Come on," she said. "I know a great place for us to go. It's a lot better than the house. It'll be an adventure."

Before Sam could protest, Stella had darted

out of the passenger door and was standing outside the car, motioning for Sam to get out and follow her. As soon as he opened the car door, she took off in the direction of the carriage house about a hundred yards away, laughing as she ran through the rain.

Once they were inside the shack, both of them completely drenched, Stella stepped back in a corner and started peeling off her clothes. She had selected the carriage house for a specific reason— there was no electricity and thus no way for Sam to see the scars on her inner thigh or the white patches on her back and buttocks where the surgeons had removed the skin grafts.

"Where are you?" Sam said, fumbling around in the dark.

"Over here," Stella said, trying to make it like a game. "You have to find me, but first you have to get rid of those wet clothes. I can't afford to have my attorney catch a cold."

Sam started unbuttoning his shirt. The room was illuminated by a flash of lightning, and she saw him bypassing the rest of the buttons and yanking the shirt over his head. She heard the zing of his zipper, the rustle of his pants as he stepped out of them and then kicked them aside. His shadow moved toward her, and when he passed through a beam of light from one of the windows, Stella saw he was still wearing his jockey shorts. "Everything," she said, giggling. "Take it all off, Sam. Those are the rules of the game."

"Oh," he said, shoving his jockey shorts down around his ankles and kicking them aside.

Finally he was there, his naked body pressed

against her. Stella felt the same jolt of exhilaration' she had felt in the car. She inhaled his aftershave, then buried her nose in his chest hair. "I don't know what it is," she said, "but when you touch me, my body goes wild. Is that what they call chemistry?"

"You go wild," he said, thrusting his pelvis forward so Stella could feel his erection. "You're driving me crazy. If I don't make love to you, Stella, I'm going to have to go home and stand in a cold shower until the sun comes up." He suddenly became still, dropping his hands to his side. "Don't let me rush you, though," he said. "If you're uncertain about this, just say the word and we'll stop right now."

"Yes," Stella whispered against his chest, her breath coming faster. "Yes, yes, yes." She could feel the heat emerging from his body, the tautness of his thighs. Rubbing her hands over his back, she felt the solid ridge of muscle stretched between his shoulders. Her hands drifted down to his buttocks. "Good ass," she said, kneading the solid flesh with her hands. She had never realized that this portion of a man's anatomy could be so sexually stimulating. Sam's buttocks were perfectly formed, not flat like Brad's, but full and shapely.

"Quit stealing my lines," he said, seizing Stella with both hands cupped under her buttocks and lifting her off her feet. Then he walked around with Stella hanging on his neck, her legs wrapped around his waist, searching for a place for them to make love. When he didn't find anything but the concrete floor and a bunch of cardboard boxes, he backed her up against the wall and held her in place with his body.

Sam kissed her passionately, his hands gently caressing her breasts. Stella moaned in pleasure. She felt so strange, so removed from reality. In the dark carriage house, the wind rattling the rafters and rain pelting the windows, she felt as if she were living out an erotic fantasy.

"Now," she panted. "Please, Sam, I want you."

Sam plunged inside her and Stella's head went back and her body bowed. The feeling was so exquisite that she was certain she was going to sink to the floor in a heap. She felt boneless, unstructured, somehow liquid and weightless. How long they made love, she wasn't certain, but it seemed so quick, so intense, so natural and spontaneous. Stella felt the muscles inside her contracting, and she cried out in pleasure. Only a few moments later, Sam stiffened and moaned, then his body trembled and shook.

Once it was over, he kissed her tenderly on the lips and then promptly swept her up in his arms. "This was just a practice session," he told her, carrying her through the rain to the house. "Wait until I get you in a bed."

Stella was digging into her purse for her keys. They were standing on opposite sides of Sam's car, both of them naked, their clothes left on the floor of the carriage house. "Forget it," Sam said, his arms wrapped around his chest. "You can stay with me tonight. We have a guest room. You need a ride to the office in the morning, anyway.

Your car's still there from the other day. We can't stand out here in the rain like this, Stella."

She opened the passenger car door to use the light as she searched her purse for her keys. "I'm certain I put them in here before I went to the airport today," she said, feeling frustrated and foolish. Turning her purse upside down on the seat, she finally found her keys, then raced back to the porch to unlock the door.

"Did you listen to the radio today?" Sam said, looking up at the sky. "I hope there isn't a tornado brewing out there. I saw a bunch of black clouds just now that look awful menacing."

Once she had unlocked the door, Stella stepped inside the dark entryway. Sam hit the light switch, and she instantly froze. "Turn it off, Sam," she said. "Please, I don't like the light. It's more romantic in the dark."

"Aren't you afraid you'll trip and fall?"

Stella clamped her legs shut, hiding the scar on her inner thigh, her arms crisscrossed over her chest. Then she braced herself against the wall, not wanting him to see the white patches on her back. "Will you check the circuit breaker?" she asked him, thinking she could run upstairs and get her robe while he was gone. "I'm afraid the lights will go out after you leave from the storm."

"Sure," Sam said. Then he gave her a curious look. "If the lights are on now, Stella, checking the circuit breaker will accomplish nothing." He started walking toward her when she darted around the corner into the living room. Sam thought she was playing with him again and immediately went after her, flipping on all the

81

light switches along the walls. He finally found Stella sitting in a chair in a corner, an afghan tossed over her. "I want to see you in the light," he said. "You're beautiful, Stella. Don't deny me this pleasure."

Stella just stared at him without speaking. Sam dropped down on his knees in front of her chair and tugged on the edge of the afghan. "If you don't take this away," he said, smiling at her, "I'm going to stick my head under there."

"Don't," Stella barked, holding tight to the afghan. A moment later, her face softened. "Tonight was great, Sam. I mean it, but—"

"But what?" he said. "I don't take things like this lightly, Stella, if that's what you're thinking. You have to remember where I'm coming from, that I lost my wife. I haven't been with a woman in at least a year now. I care about you. This wasn't some quickie roll in the hay."

"I know that," she said, tears trickling down her face. "I just don't feel well right now."

"Don't cry," he said, reaching out to stroke the tears away. "Why are you crying? Is it something I said?"

"It's nothing," she said. "It was a difficult day. I'm overtired, I guess. I sometimes get emotional when I don't get enough rest."

Sam pushed himself to his feet and leaned back down to kiss her on the forehead. "I understand, Stella," he told her. "You don't have to explain yourself to me."

Stella gazed at his naked body with longing, wishing things didn't have to be this way, that she could take him to her bedroom and make love to him again. Instead, she had to concoct lies and cower in shame. She didn't have the courage to let him see her body. If he saw the scars on her back and thigh, he might never be able to make love to her again, and she couldn't face that kind of rejection. "You don't have to give me a ride tomorrow," she told him. "Larry Kominsky's picking me up. I've already arranged it. He drives right by here on his way to work."

"Will you call me tomorrow, then?" he asked.

"Of course," Stella said, smiling at him. "If you want, I'll call you every ten minutes. You're a fabulous lover, Sam, better than I ever dreamed you would be."

Her remark brought a smile to his face. He turned and walked out of the room. A few moments later, she heard the door close behind him.

chapter

FOUR

Early the next morning, Holly stopped at Janet Hernandez's desk. "Get Ben Growman in Dallas on the line," she said. "If he's in a meeting, tell them to interrupt him."

"What's going on?" Janet asked, seeing the excited look on Holly's face.

Holly ignored her and entered her office. Once she was situated behind her desk, she took several deep breaths and waited until she saw the light illuminated on the phone.

"Mr. Growman's on line two," Janet said from the doorway.

"Shut the door," Holly barked. For a long time she just stared at the flashing light, imagining Growman's impatience. She wanted him to wait, to know that she was a busy, important person. Finally, she picked up the phone and said, "It's been a long time, Ben. How are you doing these days?"

"I've been better," he said, bristling at the sound of her voice. "What can I do for you, Holly?"

"We have a problem," she said, keeping her voice so low he had to strain to hear her. "It's not a small problem, Ben. It's a major problem, one that could cause you and the agency a great deal of embarrassment. One of your employees is in serious trouble. I didn't have to call you, you know. I'm doing this out of professional courtesy. I hope you appreciate it."

"Spit it out, Holly," he said, sighing. "I don't have time to play games. Who are you referring to and what have they done? Did one of my people come down to Houston and get arrested for drunk driving?"

"You wish," she said. "Try Stella Cataloni, the woman you just endorsed on national television. She's about to be charged with murder."

Stella was in her office conferring with Melinda Richardson. The attorney had just been assigned a new robbery and homicide case and autopsy photos were spread all over Stella's desk. She held one of them under her reading lamp in order to see it better. "Is this the only wound?" she asked, indicating a small round entrance hole surrounded by scorched flesh in the center of the man's forehead.

"Yes," said Richardson, a thirty-year-old blonde with green eyes and a round, friendly face. "According to the M.E.'s report, that's the only bullet wound. The victim died instantly."

"I think you have more than a robbery here," Stella said, setting the photo back down on her desk. "The victim is Asian, right? This was an assassination, probably related to drug trafficking. They could be using the market as a front to deal drugs."

"No way," the woman said. "They took all the money in the cash drawer, even some of the store's inventory, and the store owner was an older man, Stella. It had to be a robbery."

"That may just be a cover," Stella said. "First, it's a contact wound. You can tell because of the scorch marks around the wound. Second, have you ever seen a robber in action? One of these days you should set aside some time and look at the film footage the FBI has on file of various bank robberies. These people get enormously excited when they pull off a heist. Many of them are strung out on drugs, of course, so that explains a portion of it, but others simply get turned on by the danger, the thought that they might get caught."

"I don't understand what you're trying to say," Richardson said, a puzzled look on her face.

"When a robbery goes bad," Stella continued, "it turns into complete pandemonium. Innocent bystanders are shot. The offenders panic and keep shooting until they empty their guns completely and then flee. We never see a wound like this, so carefully placed. The shooter in this case held the gun flush against the victim's forehead and fired only one shot." She paused, trying to put it together in her mind. "Do you have the crime scene report with you?" she asked. "Look and see if any other spent shells were found on the floor or embedded in the walls."

The woman brought the file into her lap and started flipping through the pages. "No other shells were found," she said, closing the file and facing Stella again.

"Okay," Stella said, "he fired only once because he knew he only needed one shot—the kill shot." She looked the woman in the eye and said, "The robbery was staged. This was a professional hit, Melinda. It's probably related to China white, the new heroin that's coming in from Asia."

Ben Growman appeared in the door. "I need to see you privately," he snapped, his loud voice echoing out over the room.

"We're just finishing up," Stella said, motioning to Richardson with her hand. Once the woman had collected her paperwork and left, Growman strode over and stood in front of Stella's desk. "What's going on?" she asked, somewhat miffed. "You barked at me like a damn dog in front of Richardson."

"Why didn't you tell me you attacked this

Randall person?" he shouted, his face flushed in anger. "You threatened to kill him. With your bare hands, no less." He threw his hands out to the side and then let them slap back against his thighs. "I told you not to go to Houston, to let the Houston authorities deal with this Randall person, but no, you had to run off like a nut and threaten to kill someone in front of dozens of witnesses."

Stella flushed under his hot stare. "All I did was scratch his face. I wouldn't characterize that as a vicious attack, Ben, and I didn't do it on the steps of the courthouse or anything. A few people were present, but they certainly wouldn't constitute dozens of witnesses."

"They're reopening the old case," he shot out, leaning forward with his palms on her desk.

"Great," she exclaimed, never expecting to hear such good news. "They must have found new evidence linking Randall to the crime. That's fantastic. How did you hear?"

"They're not filing against Randall," he said, linking eyes with her. "They're filing against you. They believe you set the fire that killed your parents."

Stella was flabbergasted. Her breath started coming so fast that Growman had to run to the outer office and get her a drink of water. While Stella drank it and tried to assimilate what he had told her, Growman stood behind her and massaged her shoulders. "Here's what we're going to do," he said. "We're going to fly to Houston this afternoon. I've already arranged a meeting with Jack Fitzgerald and checked on available flights." Fitzgerald was the number-one man, Growman's counterpart in Houston. "If we catch the three o'clock shuttle, we should be able to see him by five o'clock. Get in touch with your brother and have him meet us at Fitzgerald's office. His statement should carry a great deal of weight."

Stella's thoughts were racing. How could they have believed Randall's statement over hers? It just didn't make sense. "Look," she said, sliding her chair back from the desk and glancing up at Growman, "maybe this is a slick maneuver on Holly's part. Someone higher up pushed her to file against me because of the scene I made and Randall's ridiculous statements. Holly decided that once the case is officially reopened and she has a full investigative staff working on it, she can dig up what we need to nail Randall."

"I don't think so, Stella."

"But why?" she cried. "Why would they do this to me? This has to be a mistake. Prosecuting me is preposterous."

Growman circled to the front of her desk and began pacing. "Once Fitzgerald hears your side of the story as well as your brother's, I'm certain he'll put a stop to this foolishness." He spun around and faced her. "But you must take this seriously, Stella," he cautioned. "Holly Oppenheimer is not one to underestimate."

Stella had never confronted Growman about the sexual harassment charges. She tried to avoid gossip, and generally made it a rule to keep her nose out of people's personal affairs. Right now, however, she decided she had to know the details.

88

"Ben," she said, "what really happened between you and Holly?"

"It wasn't what you're thinking," he said, lowering himself into a chair. "I was in love with her. I didn't sexually harass her as she claimed. We had a brief affair, completely consensual."

As Stella had told Sam the night before, she had always speculated that Growman had been seeing Holly on the side. During her conversations with Holly over lunch, however, Holly had held fast to her claim that Growman had used his position to force her to grant him sexual favors. Stella had tried to stay out of it, knowing nothing could be gained by taking sides and endangering her own relationship with Growman. "Why did she do it, then? You know, make such a big stink?"

"Bitterness," Growman said, grimacing. "She was young and naive. I guess she thought our affair would lead somewhere, that I would eventually divorce my wife and marry her."

"Did you promise to marry her?"

"Absolutely not," Growman said, shaking his head. "She knew where I stood from the start, how much my kids meant to me. When we ended it, she constantly wrote me letters and mailed them to my house. She showed up in restaurants where I was having dinner with my wife and kids." He looked over at Stella, his face haggard now and filled with anguish. "I had to let her go, Stella. Not only was she destroying my marriage, she was out to destroy my career."

"I thought she resigned," Stella said, giving him a curious look.

"Oh," he said, "officially, she did resign. After the Pelham case went down, I used it as an excuse to transfer her from homicide back to the fraud division. I knew she would quit at that point. Holly's an ambitious woman."

Stella looked away. She didn't know what to say. She couldn't tell him that he had just dropped several notches in her eyes, that what he had described was dangerously close to the exact allegations Holly Oppenheimer had made. In the area of sexual harassment, women sometimes had a different slant, and Stella's sympathies fell on Holly's side of the fence. Even though she could be difficult on occasion, Holly was a good attorney and from what Stella remembered, she had always done her job and done it well. Regardless of their personal relationship, Growman had had no right to demote her and force her into resigning her position.

"There's only one thing I can tell you about Holly Oppenheimer," he said, standing to leave. "The woman is a mind-fucker, Stella. She'll use anything and anyone to get what she wants. I might have been in love with her, but she wasn't in love with me. She used me to further her career. I gave her the best cases, the most prestigious office, helped her become recognized and respected." He paused and then added, "You must not trust her."

Stella tossed back, "I don't agree, Ben. Just because you had an affair with her and it turned out bad doesn't mean she's a mind-fucking viper. You'll see when we get to Houston. This is some

90

kind of misunderstanding. Either that, or someone higher up forced her hand as I said."

He exploded, shaking his fist at her. "Don't think for a second that this woman is your friend. For all we know, she could be going after you just to get back at me. Do you hear me?"

"I hear you," she said. "We just don't agree on this one."

"Who do you think called and informed me they were reopening the case?" he shouted. "Who do you think gloated when she told me my star prosecutor was about to be arrested and charged with murder?"

"Who?" Stella said, her eyes expanding.

"Your friend," he said, letting the words hang in the air before he strode to the door.

Jackson Boyd Fitzgerald had a large corner office on the tenth floor of the Fannin Street complex that housed the Houston D.A.'s office, but it reeked with a musky odor and what Stella recognized immediately as cigar smoke. As soon as she stepped in the door, her sinuses clogged up and her eyes started watering. She exchanged glances with Mario and then waited for Growman to make the introductions.

Once the formalities were over, Fitzgerald motioned for them to take a seat in a grouping of chairs that faced his desk.

The office was decorated with heavy oak furniture and Western bronzes, and Stella noticed that none of it had apparently been dusted in quite some time. Fitzgerald was almost as old and dusty as one of his bronzes. At sixty-nine he was past

91

his prime, yet such a fixture in Houston politics that any contender for his job didn't stand a chance. His hair was a yellowish gray, his eyes small, watery orbs in his heavily lined face, and his bushy mustache drifted too far below his lip. Dressed in a white summer jacket and a bow tie, he reminded Stella of a character out of the Old South. All he needed was a white straw hat.

Growman began, then quickly handed off to Stella, encouraging her to tell the Houston D.A. her suspicions that Tom Randall had been the one who set the fire. "He was there," she said, "and he was the only person who had a motive."

"How's that?" Fitzgerald said.

"I was pregnant and my father wouldn't allow me to have an abortion. Tom had just been awarded a football scholarship to Notre Dame. If my father had forced him into marrying me, he wouldn't have been able to accept it."

Stella went on to recount what she remembered from the night of the fire. When she had finished, Mario told his side of the story. Unlike Stella, he was plainly angry. "The man's a damn liar," he said. "He even told the police he carried me to safety, when it was my sister who rescued me. He didn't even call the fire department and report the fire. He just left us there to die."

Fitzgerald leaned back in his chair and bit down on his black cigar. "Well," he said slowly in a thick Texas drawl, moving the cigar around in his mouth as he spoke, "I don't know, my friends, but it seems I might have an overzealous prosecutor on my hands."

"Great," Growman said, glancing over at

Stella and then back to the district attorney. "So, you'll call off the dogs and let this poor woman get a decent night's sleep?"

"Now wait just a minute, Growman," Fitzgerald said, fidgeting in his seat. "That's not what I said, is it? I said it *seems* that Ms. Cataloni's story is truthful, but I'm not prepared to make any promises until I confer with my people."

Growman's voice escalated. "Do you know how agonizing this has been for this woman? Put yourself in her shoes, Jack. Would you want to sit around and wait while your future was on the line? Hell, give us a break. At least let the woman know your intentions. Her responsibilities at my office are considerable and I have to know what she's up against."

The older district attorney rubbed the side of his nose with a gnarly finger, his large gold ring reflecting the light from the window. "This is what I'm prepared to do," he said, puffing out a cloud of cigar smoke. "Give me a phone number and I'll confer with my people, sleep on it, and get you an answer first thing in the morning."

Growman had hoped the trip would have accomplished more. "You're making a serious mistake if you pursue this," he said. "If you do, you'll be prosecuting an innocent woman." Wanting to add even more fuel, he said, "For the record, my office will stand behind Stella one hundred percent. That means full use of our investigators and anything else she might need."

The ramifications of this statement registered in Fitzgerald's rheumy eyes. If Growman backed up his belief in Stella with the full force of his agency and position, prosecuting her for any crime would be a formidable task, let alone a crime as serious as the one she had been charged with. "I think that's mighty nice of you," he said, not wanting Growman to know he was intimidated. "It's always good to see a man stand by his employees." He peered over at Stella. "You've got yourself some high- placed friends, little lady."

"Looks like I need them," Stella said, sighing.

They all stood to leave. Stella wrote down her brother's number and placed it on Fitzgerald's cluttered desk. She had decided to spend the night and see what happened in the morning. If they didn't decide to drop the charges, she would have to begin interviewing defense attorneys in Houston right away. Although she had many contacts in Dallas in private practice, it would be far too costly to have a Dallas attorney represent her in another jurisdiction.

"Tell you what," Mario said once they were outside in the lobby, "I'll treat you both to dinner at Lone Star Steaks. It's on NASA Road, so it's a little bit of a drive from here, but they've got the best beef in town."

"Tonight's my daughter's birthday," Growman said, "but I'll be happy to take you up on your offer another time."

Stella informed Growman of her decision to stay in town, and he agreed it was wise. "I rented a car," she told him. "You didn't have to call a cab, Ben. I would have driven you to the airport if you'd only asked."

Mario excused himself to go to the bathroom,

reappearing just as Growman's cab pulled up in front of the building. Before he left, the district attorney pulled Stella aside. "It's going to work out," he said. "Trust me, Stella. By this time next week, your problems should all be behind you."

Mario was leaning against a column in front of the building, moving a toothpick from one side of his mouth to the other. "Why give her false hopes?" he said, spitting the toothpick out on the ground. "That old goat didn't look convinced to me. No, man, not at all," he continued, shaking his head. "If you ask me, he's like a rattlesnake, just waiting until your back is turned to strike."

Growman frowned, unhappy that Stella had to be exposed to this kind of negativity. "It's best to remain optimistic, son, don't you think?"

"Optimistic, huh?" Mario said, his dark eyes flashing. "Maybe you can be optimistic, Ben, but then you're not about to be charged with murder now, are you?" He ran his fingers through his hair. "Stella and I don't work that way, see," he continued, agitated and nervous. "When you've lived the life we have, it's better to expect the worst. That way you're prepared."

For a few moments they just stood there staring at each other. Then Mario grabbed his sister's arm and together they walked away, leaving Growman standing on the curb next to the cab.

The men were assembled in folding chairs in a large room inside the Immaculate Conception church for the monthly meeting of the Houston

95

chapter of the Knights of Columbus, a fraternal organization similar to the Masons or Shriners.

Clementine Cataloni was on the podium about to conclude his talk. He wasn't a tall man, more wiry and compact, but even at fifty-seven the retired police captain was still a formidable presence. His strength was carried in his eyes, dark and penetrating, his stubbornness revealed by the set of his mouth and his squared-off jaw. Although a few strands of gray were visible, most of his hair was dark and thick, slicked back and controlled with some type of hair product that sparkled in the overhead lights.

"We've now raised over ten thousand dollars for the Westchester Children's Home," Cataloni said, his voice booming out over the microphone. "We've surpassed our target goal this year. Next year, we'll do even better."

A round of applause followed and Cataloni stepped down. He headed to the back of the room and in no time found himself surrounded by men. "Hey, Captain," a large red-faced man said, "you got any news for me?"

Cataloni was laughing at a joke one of the other men had told. He instantly fell serious, grabbing the man's arm and yanking him aside. "When I know something, Elders, I'll be in touch. Right?" he said, the word hissing between his teeth.

"Right, sure," the man said, dropping his eyes. "I just thought—"

"Don't think," Cataloni barked, the muscles in his face twitching. A few moments later, he smiled, slapping the man on the back. "That's my job, Charlie. Just relax and let me handle things. How are the wife and kids, by the way? You keeping that redhead you're married to in line?"

"Things aren't that good at home right now," Charlie Elders responded, his voice strained with emotion. Cataloni turned to speak to someone else, though, and Elders just stood there with a dejected look on his face.

Carl Winters elbowed his way into the grouping of men, tugging on Cataloni's sleeve to get his attention. "I tried to call you back this afternoon, Captain," he said. "Guess you were out. Did your wife give you my message?"

"Not now, Winters." Cataloni glanced at the other men gathered around him. "Why don't you guys get some coffee. I'll join you in a few minutes."

Winters tipped his Stetson back on his head, waiting until the men had dispersed to continue speaking. "Stella Cataloni," he said. "The rumors you heard are true. Looks as if your favorite niece is going down."

Cataloni's dark eyes blazed. He swept his tongue over his lips. "I'll believe it when I see it. You've been making promises for sixteen years, Carl. When I make a promise, I deliver. So far, you've been batting zero."

"Well, get out your binoculars," Winters said, chuckling, "'cause this time, we're going all the way. Randall's back. He's agreed to testify."

The captain said, "Is he credible?"

"He's not the best witness I've ever seen," Winters shrugged, "but I don't think he's the worst, either. It's the first break we've had in the case. I thought you'd be pleased."

Cataloni moved closer, his breath hot on Winters's face. "I'll tell you when I'll be pleased," he snarled. "When that murderous bitch is behind bars, and not a moment sooner."

"Hey," Winters said, "we can only do what we can do. If the jury buys Randall's story, they'll convict. If they don't, I guess we'll have to dig up more evidence and try again."

"If they acquit, it's over," Cataloni said. "Randall's not enough. We need more. His statements have to be backed up, or they'll never stand up in court. Where is the bastard? You said he's in Houston, right?"

Winters glanced over his shoulder and then removed a piece of paper from his jacket pocket, handing it to the captain. "Ask and you shall receive," he told him. A few moments later, Clementine Cataloni slipped out the back door.

After a quick dinner at Mario's favorite barbecue house, Stella watched television with him and then headed off to bed in his guest room around ten o'clock. She tossed and turned, unable to sleep, anxious about what Fitzgerald's decision would be. Once when she was about to nod off, she was jarred back awake by the shrill sound of the phone. She started to go into the other room to ask Mario who had called when she realized that was foolish. He was single and had dozens of friends, and besides, it was still early, not yet midnight. Hearing his hushed voice from the other room, she shut her eyes again and tried to drift off.

Sleep simply would not come, and around three o'clock, Stella finally got out of bed and went into the kitchen to fix herself something to eat. Food always settled her nerves and helped her to fall asleep. After choking down a ham and cheese sandwich on stale wheat bread, she headed back down the hall to the guest room, stopping at Mario's door and peeking in. When he had been younger, Stella had checked on him several times a night. After the tragedy, she had suffered from chronic insomnia and was seldom able to sleep through the night. She'd bolt upright in the bed, her body drenched in perspiration, certain the house was on fire and immediately racing to Mario's room to make sure he was safe.

The room was dark and the covers were rumpled, but as Stella tiptoed closer to the bed, she saw that it was empty. Thinking he had fallen asleep on the sofa, she checked the living room, but Mario wasn't there. Her heart started racing, but she quickly reassured herself. Mario had said he was dating a stewardess with a screwy schedule. Stella had to assume that the woman had gotten in from a late flight and called, probably asking her brother to come over. Returning to the guest room, she collapsed in the bed and fell asleep at last.

When Stella opened her eyes, she had no idea what time it was. The drapes were drawn and the room was pitch black. Rising from the bed, she checked the house, and discovered that her brother had not returned. Seeing the light on the answering machine blinking in the living room, she glanced at the wall clock and saw it was past nine o'clock. With trembling fingers she hit the replay button and held her breath until the tape rewound and a man's voice began speaking. "This is Jack Fitzgerald," said a deep, scratchy voice. "I've decided to put this matter on hold for now. If you have any additional concerns, please feel free to call me."

Stella was standing there in her bathrobe, her hand over her chest. She let her breath out in one long whoosh and sank down in a chair. "Thank you, God," she said, tears of relief welling in her eyes.

Eager to leave now, Stella started packing away her cosmetics and the few items of clothing she had brought on the trip, hoping Mario would come home by the time she was finished.

At Frank Minor's direction, Holly had called a press conference for nine o'clock that morning to announce that they would be filing against Stella in the death of her parents. The day before she had bought a new dress, and the lightweight fabric hugged her body like a second skin. The skirt was hemmed several inches above the knee in the latest style, and Holly was wearing sheer black nylons and spike heels.

When she arrived at the D.A.'s office that morning, though, she was surprised that she didn't see the remote vans from the TV stations parked out front. She preferred to address the media on the front steps leading into the building instead of using her cramped office. She stood there a few moments, glancing up and down the street, thinking they would pull up any second. But the August sun was already beating down on her, the temperature rising by the second.

"Screw this," she said, fearful her makeup would run and she would end up with perspiration stains on her three-hundred-dollar dress. Heading directly to Minor's office, she poked her head in the door. "Where is everybody? It's almost nine, and no one is out there. Besides, it's hot as a bitch already. Maybe I should hold the press conference in your office instead."

"Called off," he mumbled, his head down as he shuffled through some paperwork on his desk.

"What did you say?" Holly said, her eyes widening.

"I said the press conference has been called off."

"Who called it off? Everything was set."

"Jack Fitzgerald," Minor said, looking up. "He doesn't think we have a case. Besides, Growman flew down here himself and threatened to fight us every inch of the way. Dallas is at the top of the heap right now in stats, and Growman has a lot of influence. Guess Fitzgerald doesn't have the guts to take on a fight these days."

Holly shook her head as if to clear it, her blond curls spilling over onto her face. "Fine," she said, tossing her hair back from her forehead. "I told you this was never going to fly. To be perfectly honest, I'm relieved. I felt terrible doing this to Stella. My guess is Randall is the guilty party, anyway. We should drag his ass into court instead of going after Stella."

Minor was preoccupied and not listening. He shoved a file to the edge of his desk. Prosecuting an unknown like Tom Randall for a sixteen-year-old crime was small potatoes, and as far as Minor was concerned, the Cataloni case should now be closed and forgotten. "I'm giving you the Wesley matter," he said, rubbing his eyes. "McCarthy can't handle it. He's got too much to handle with the Bramford homicide."

"What do you mean?" Holly exclaimed. "I was supposed to handle Bramford. I did all the preliminary work on it. I've been putting it together for months now."

"Look," Minor said, setting his paperwork aside, "I reassigned it because I thought you would be buried under this Cataloni thing. There's no way you could have handled both cases simultaneously. The Cataloni case is a double homicide."

"But I'm available now," Holly argued, her voice cracking. "You promised me that case, Frank. I don't want Wesley. It's not even going to trial. His attorney is already trying to negotiate a plea agreement."

"So?" Minor said. "It still goes down as a conviction. It'll raise your stats."

"That's not the same and you know it," Holly snapped. "Aren't you the one who told me just the other day that I needed to bring in a big case? Wesley's not big. By next week, it will probably be resolved. Craig Bramford is a cop, for Christ's sake, a cop who murdered his wife and kid. That's the case I need right now."

Minor glared at her, pushing the file even closer

102

to the edge of his desk, a gesture meant to let Holly know that his decision was final. She could complain all she wanted. Once he made up his mind, he never reversed himself.

Holly glanced at the file and then thrust her chin out in defiance. "You can't do this to me," she insisted. "I have more seniority than McCarthy. I'll take it to Jack Fitzgerald. I'll file an official grievance."

Minor's private line was ringing. "Take it to anyone you want," he finally said, picking up the phone. He had long ago learned that Oppenheimer would walk all over him if he let her. No one got the better of Frank Minor. "Now if you'll excuse me—" he said, holding the receiver to his ear.

Holly stormed out of his office, bumping shoulders with another D.A. in the hall and refusing to answer when he spoke to her. Walking at a fast pace, she made it halfway down the corridor when she stumbled and fell sideways against the wall. She generally didn't wear heels this high. After being a police officer and getting used to comfortable shoes, she brought out her spike heels only when she wanted to make an impression. "Fuck," she said, as she saw that the heel on her right shoe was broken. Removing it and carrying it in her hand, she hobbled past the door to her office and walked straight out of the building, her face twisted in an ugly, bitter grimace.

Stella decided Mario must have spent the night with his girlfriend. She was eager to tell him the good news before she left for the airport, however, so she felt she had no choice but to wait.

While she was sitting in the apartment with nothing to do, she put in a call to Growman, but his secretary said he had taken the morning off to spend time with his daughter before she returned to college. She finally reached Sam and he offered to pick her up at the airport. Stella told him she would arrive on the afternoon shuttle.

Once she concluded her phone call, Stella roamed around her brother's apartment, making beds and straightening things up. Cracking the door to his darkroom, she peered inside, sniffing the pungent odor of chemicals. She was about to leave when she saw something on his workbench in the dim light. It looked as if Mario had spilled a sugar packet out on the bench, and Stella knew it would attract ants if she didn't clean it up. She went to the kitchen for a sponge and returned. Without thinking, she pressed her finger into the white substance and gingerly brought it to her mouth. The next moment her muscles stiffened. "You little shit," she said, realizing the white powder wasn't sugar. It was cocaine. Good cocaine too, she thought, feeling her tongue go numb from the minuscule amount she had tasted. Mario had had problems with drugs, but that had been years ago when he was still in his teens. It made Stella furious to know he was using again.

No wonder Mario had gone out the night before, she thought, angry and disappointed. If he was heavily into coke, he probably couldn't sleep. She felt a grim sense of satisfaction as she sponged up the costly drug. She then started flinging open the cabinets, determined to find her brother's stash and flush it down the toilet. When she didn't find it in the darkroom, she systematically searched the apartment. She found nothing and as it got closer to one o'clock, she knew if she waited any longer she would miss her flight.

Scribbling a note for Mario to call her in Dallas as soon as he returned, she left it on the kitchen counter. Grabbing her purse and cosmetic case, she rushed downstairs to her rental car and drove off.

Stella boarded her two o'clock flight on time, but the plane failed to take off. After the passengers were strapped in their seats for takeoff, the stewardess's voice came over the loudspeaker announcing the flight would be delayed. After waiting on the runway for over thirty minutes, the plane finally departed and Stella arrived in Dallas late, wondering if Sam had given up and gone home.

Damn airlines, she thought as she disembarked, still seething over what she had found in Mario's darkroom. When he called, she was going to ream him out good. She had devoted too much of her life to him to see him destroy himself this way. Besides, she knew cocaine was one of the most dangerous and unpredictable of all drugs. Even teenagers sometimes dropped dead of a heart attack when using, and she wasn't about to bury the only surviving member of her family.

Because the plane was small, it didn't pull up to the gate. Shielding her eyes as she stepped out into the bright afternoon sun at Love Field

Airport, Stella spotted Sam standing behind the security railing, a young boy in front of him with a bouquet of white lilies clutched in his hand. Sam had brought Adam, his twelve-year-old son. The wind was gusting and Stella held the right side of her hair flush against her cheek, not wanting the boy to see her scar and become frightened. But her nervousness soon dissipated. Seeing the boy standing there, so fresh-faced and young, she was reminded of Mario when he had been that age. Smiling and waving, she carefully navigated the narrow steps leading down from the plane, wanting to appear poised and confident.

As soon as Stella reached the bottom of the ramp, however, two men in business suits stepped in front of her. "Stella Cataloni," one of them said. "Are you Stella Cataloni?"

"Yes," she said. Had something happened to Mario? Had he been in an accident or overdosed on drugs?

The man flipped out a badge and flashed it in her face. "U.S. Marshal's Office," he said. "We're going to have to place you under arrest."

Stella stiffened in shock. Then she realized Fitzgerald might not have informed the right people that he was calling it off. "There's a mistake here," she said, her gaze darting over to Sam and his son. "They were going to file charges against me but they decided against it just this morning. I guess no one got around to telling you guys. Are you stationed here in Dallas, or did they send you all the way from Houston?"

"We're in the Dallas Marshal's Office," he said. "I'm sorry, but it's better if you go peacefully. We don't want any problems, miss. We're only trying to do our job." He reached in his wallet and pulled out a plastic card, proceeding to read Stella her rights. "You have the right to remain silent. You have a right to have an attorney present during questioning. If you cannot afford an attorney, one will be . . ."

Stella tuned out the words. The other officer had walked behind her and was pulling on her arm, the steel handcuffs jangling in his hand. She twisted away, on the verge of panicking. She couldn't let them handcuff her and cart her off in front of Sam and his son. "Didn't you hear me?" she shouted, the sound of the nearby jets reverberating in her ears. "They called it off. Call Jack Fitzgerald at the Houston D.A.'s office and he'll confirm it for you."

Sam was grimacing. Stella watched as he said something to his son and then tried to walk through the opening in the fence leading to the plane. A security officer for the airline stopped him, though, and Stella saw the sign that said the area was restricted to passengers only. Sam returned to stand next Adam, both their fingers laced now into the wire-mesh fence.

The two marshals exchanged somber looks, then took up positions on either side of Stella. Within seconds, they had her hands cuffed behind her back and were escorting her across the runway. "Please don't do this to me," Stella cried. "Just take the handcuffs off. I'll go with you. I won't make a scene. My friends are here. I'm not a criminal. I'm a district attorney. This is all a horrid mistake."

"I'm sorry," the taller of the two men said. "It's the rules, you know. Every prisoner has to be cuffed."

Stella dropped her head in shame. As she passed through the security gate, she heard Sam's voice, but she couldn't force herself to look at him. The two officers led her through the crowded terminal, and Stella heard people's comments when they saw the handcuffs. "What did she do?" an alien, detached voice said. "Do you think she's that woman who murdered her children over in Addison?"

"You know what, Mabel?" another voice said. "I think she's that district attorney, the one that was on TV so much."

"You're right," the other woman said excitedly. "Good lord, she looks just like her. What in the world did she do?"

Each word was like a knife plunging into Stella's side. Her heart was pounding like a giant fist inside her chest, her clothes soaked with perspiration. Her mouth was so dry, she couldn't find enough saliva to swallow.

Planting her feet and pulling against the men, Stella said in a hoarse voice, "I want to see the warrant. I have a right to know what I'm charged with."

Stopping on the mat for the automatic door leading out to the street, one of the men whipped out a sheet of paper. "You're charged with one count of homicide, ma'am," he said, pausing as he read through the particulars. "According to this document, you shot and killed a man by the name of Thomas Randall, one of the state's prime witnesses in an arson case. Crime only went down this morning." He paused and exchanged glances with the other marshal. "Seeing they moved this fast, Harry, I'd say this lady's in one heck of a lot of trouble."

Stella had heard nothing past the name Randall and the charge of murder. Her brother's face flashed in her mind, along with an image of the white powder she had found on his workbench. Had he used cocaine to give himself the courage to commit murder? Stella felt her entire world shattering. Black spots danced in front of her eyes. Why had Mario done it? Fitzgerald had been ready to drop the charges. How could her brother have acted so impulsively? As the automatic doors opened and shut repetitively, Stella felt as if she were sinking into a dark, bottomless hole. Everything suddenly went black and her body slumped in the men's arms.

"Damn women," the man named Harry said. "They always fucking faint. Get a good hold on her," he said, "and let's get the hell out of here. I promised my wife I'd be home for dinner."

Supporting Stella under the armpits, her body limp and her head wobbling, the two marshals dragged her through the automatic doors across the rubber mat, and over the concrete curb.

When Stella came to, she saw the door to the police car, then felt a hand on her head as she was pushed inside. Looking back at the terminal, she spotted Sam and Adam peering out from behind the glass of the automatic door. They watched as the officers circled to the front of their police car, gunned the engine, and sped off.

chapter

FIVE

By six o'clock that evening, Stella was inside in the Lew Sterrett Correctional Center in downtown Dallas, one of the bleaker presentence facilities in the state.

As soon as the booking officer offered the customary phone call, Stella contacted Growman, asking him what she should do and what he had heard regarding Randall's death. "I haven't heard anything," he said, stunned at the news of her arrest. "Look, I know a crackerjack attorney in Houston," he said a few moments later. "His fees are high, but he's one of the best defense attorneys in town. His name is Paul Brannigan and I'll get in touch with him right away. Just stay cool, Stella. This has to be some type of crazy mix-up, particularly if Fitzgerald called you this morning and indicated they weren't pursuing the case."

"Didn't you hear me?" Stella shouted, speaking from a pay phone in the booking area. "Tom Randall was shot, murdered. It must have happened sometime this morning. Fitzgerald just hadn't been notified yet when he called me."

"Where were you when Randall was killed?" Growman asked. "If this isn't a mistake, establishing an alibi is your first priority."

"How do I know?" Stella snapped back. "Until the medical examiner establishes a time of death, how can I possibly provide an alibi? I could have been on the plane, Ben."

"You were with Mario, though?" Growman said. "Right? You told me you weren't going to stay in a hotel. If Mario was with you the whole time, you shouldn't have a problem."

Glancing back over her shoulder at the booking officer, Stella felt her breath catch in her throat. Should she tell Growman the truth, that Mario had gone out sometime during the night and never returned? Tell him she was terrified that her own brother might have been the one who had shot and killed Randall? The night before, Mario had been distraught and angry, certain his sister was about to face murder charges. Had he decided to help her by eliminating the state's only witness?

Of all the crimes the court handled, Stella knew the murder of a vital witness was one of the most serious. Killing a witness put the entire system on edge. Whereas the wheels of justice normally moved at a snail's pace, when something like this occurred, events moved at the speed of sound. Warrants were cut in hours. Every police agency in the state was placed on alert.

"They say they're holding me for the Houston authorities," Stella told him. "God, Ben, they're going to ship me back to Houston. Until I appear in their court for arraignment, I can't even post bail. They're going to lock me up in a jail cell."

"Settle down," Growman said, although his own voice was shaking. "We're going to get to

111

the bottom of this right away. I'll assign Brenda Anderson to it immediately. If I have to," he added, "I'll send her to Houston and let her set up shop there."

Stella looked up to see the booking officer tapping the face of his watch and motioning that it was time for her to get off the phone. "I have to go," she said. Once she had hung up, she pleaded, "I have to make one more call. I need to speak to my brother. Please, it's urgent. You can't lock me up until I talk to him."

"Sorry," he said, "we need to get you printed and processed."

The officer led her to another section of the booking room to roll her prints when Stella suddenly stopped short, a startled expression on her face.

Carl Winters was standing in the far corner of the booking room, leaning against the wall.

"So, we meet again," he said, his eyes narrow. He stepped up close and leveled a finger at her chest. "This time you're not going to walk away, lady. This time you fucked up big time."

Stella's eyes burned right through him. She wanted to smack Winters across his fat face. Then again, antagonizing the detective was definitely not in her best interest. "When are you taking me back to Houston?" she said instead, forcing a mild tone.

"Well, I don't know," Winters said, wanting to watch Stella squirm. "Could be tomorrow. Could be next week. Dallas is a right fine town, and I might want to take in some sightseeing."

Stella's jaws locked so hard in anger, she heard

front of a thick metal door until a guard saw them and buzzed them through. At that point he handed her over to a female correctional officer, a short, squat woman of maybe twenty-five, with blond hair pulled back and fashioned in a long french braid.

Stella's heels tapped on the tiled corridors as she was moved from one section to another. "I'm a district attorney," she blurted out.

"Oh, really?" the woman said, laughing. "Well, I'm really the mayor but don't tell anybody."

Stella followed behind her to a large holding cell where several other women were waiting. "Can't I be placed in a cell by myself?" Stella pleaded. "I'm a district attorney, I swear. Check the booking sheet. I could have prosecuted some of these women. One might recognize me and try to kill me."

"Humph," the jailer said, eyeing Stella suspiciously. "You making this up?"

"I swear," Stella said.

The woman jerked her arm and led her back through another maze of corridors. Then she stopped at a small window and stuck her head inside. "Hey, Lucy, check the booking sheet on this inmate. She claims she's a district attorney. If she is, she should be in protective custody, not in the main jail population."

When the woman confirmed what Stella had told her, the jailer asked what the charges were. Then she turned around and gawked at Stella. "Who did you murder? Was it your husband?"

"No," Stella mumbled. "They're trying to say I killed a man named Tom Randall."

"Well, I'll be damned," the woman said. "Come on, we're putting you in the infirmary. All the cells in the protective-custody wing are occupied. We've got a lot of crooked cops right now."

"I'm innocent," Stella said as they were walking.

"Then you'll be in good company," the woman said. "Everyone in here is innocent."

Stella managed to talk the female guard into allowing her another phone call before depositing her in her cell. As soon as Brenda Anderson came on the line, Stella asked if she had spoken to Growman. When the woman acknowledged that she had and was preparing that moment to fly to Houston and begin her investigation, Stella started rattling off a list of things for her to do. "We need to find out where Randall has been all these years and why he suddenly decided to return to Houston. Run him through NCIC, as well as the Texas system, and see if he committed any other crimes while he was outstanding." Knowing she didn't have much time, she was speaking fast, her words running together. "If you're sneaky, you might be able to get to Randall's wife and find out names of his friends and associates." She sighed, and pressed her fingers against her forehead. "I didn't kill him, Brenda, but in order to clear myself, I guess we're going to have to find out who did."

Brenda Anderson felt terrible for Stella. Of all

the prosecutors she worked with, Stella was her favorite. She was demanding, but always appreciate of Brenda's efforts. The two women had worked late almost every night during the Pelham trial. Larry Kominsky would get tired and go home around eight o'clock, leaving Stella and Brenda in the conference room alone. With only Stella to contend with, Brenda had found herself opening up, and their discussions of the Pelham case became sprinkled with bits and pieces of their personal lives.

After reaching the rank of sergeant at the Dallas Police Department, a remarkable accomplishment for a woman police professional in the Southwest, let alone a woman of color, Brenda had taken a leave of absence and obtained her master's degree before transferring to the D.A.'s office as an investigator. Tall, reserved, and efficient, with enormous brown eyes and luscious lips, she dressed conservatively, giving her a neat, professional appearance even though it hid her considerable curves. Brenda's claim to fame, though, was not her shapely body, but her mastery of sophisticated technology. She never went anywhere without her portable computer, her fax, and her modem.

Brenda had worked since she was a child to perfect the skills she now possessed. A soft-spoken intellectual, her father had been employed as a computer programmer for almost twenty years, back in the days when most African-Americans had never even seen a computer, let alone mastered one. Her mother was a schoolteacher, and a tireless worker. She sang in the choir at their church, and every Saturday she could be found in the ghetto dispersing food to the homeless. When people raved about her technical abilities, Brenda Anderson always gave credit to her father. But overall, it was her mother who had instilled her with the necessary drive to succeed. "Keep your nose to the grindstone, baby," she'd always told her. "If you don't, you'll never beat the odds and get ahead in life."

"I have a friend in Houston," she told Stella, "an investigator I was involved with for a brief period of time. We were both assigned to the Watterman case several years back. You know, our agencies collaborated on that one." She paused to look up at her computer screen. "I just got off the phone with him. The police have a witness, Stella. His name is Victor Pilgrim."

Stella was shocked. "What did he see?"

"Enough to get you arrested," Anderson said. "Other than that, I don't have any idea. My friend wouldn't say."

"Have you checked him out?" Stella asked, knowing this could fall either way. Because she was innocent, it was difficult to believe a witness could be damaging, but then she didn't know what she was up against.

"I'm doing that now," Brenda said, computer keys tapping in the background. "I didn't get much from his driving records, just his age, description, address. He's forty-seven . . . lives in Galveston. He appears to be a city employee. Wait," she said, "I've been waiting to go on-line, and I just got through. I know how to access the city's personnel files in Houston."

"How?" Stella asked. Computers and on-line systems were intriguing to her, but she had never found the time to become proficient.

"You can get into anyone's files," Anderson told her. "If you know what you're doing, you can even get into DOD files. You know, Department of Defense." She was quiet for a few moments, waiting for the answers to her queries to flash on her computer screen. "Okay," she said, "here it is. Shit, he's an ex-cop! He used to be with the Houston P.D."

"Good God," Stella gasped, "Winters is trying to frame me."

"What makes you think that?"

"He's been after me all these years," Stella said. "Maybe he got tired of playing by the rules." The female jailer was chatting with another guard, but glancing over at Stella and motioning that it was time to conclude her phone call. "Check records and see if this Pilgrim guy ever worked under Winters."

"That's going to take some time, Stella," Anderson said. "I know how to get into the city's personnel system, but the police department's records may not even be computerized, particularly those listing job assignments and performance reviews. Internal Affairs usually keeps a tight lid on that kind of stuff."

"You have to find out what he saw," Stella said. "If this Pilgrim guy claims he saw me shoot Randall, we'll know for sure it's a setup."

"I'm leaving on the next shuttle," Brenda said. "I'll do my best, Stella. Try not to panic. We're going to get you out of there. Growman's behind you all the way, as well as everyone else at the agency."

Before Stella could say anything else, the guard walked over, snatched the phone out of her hands, and replaced it in the cradle.

Later that evening, the same blond guard opened the door to Stella's room in the infirmary and told her she had a visitor. Stella had been pacing back and forth and slapping the walls, desperate to get out of the tiny cubicle. As she walked behind the guard, the inmates whistled and tossed out profanities. "Hey, D.A.," a female voice yelled, "how do you like being behind bars? Isn't much fun, is it? Fucking bitch."

The guard just looked at Stella and shrugged. "News travels fast inside a jail facility. You better watch your back, Cataloni. From what I can tell, you don't have a lot of fans in here."

The woman indicated that Stella should take a seat in one of the glass-partitioned cubicles. Her body stiffened when she saw Sam staring at her through the glass.

Sam picked up the phone. "This is terrible, Stella," he said. "I tried to find out what's going on, but the jail won't tell me a thing."

"That's because you're not representing me," Stella said. "Next time, tell them you're my defense attorney and they'll let you see me in an interview room."

"What in God's name happened?" he asked. "I thought you said this Randall thing had been cleared up. Isn't that what you told me when you asked me to pick you up at the airport?" He stopped speaking and buried his head in his hands. "I felt so helpless out there today. I wanted to do something, but I was powerless. I had to just stand there while—"

Stella tuned his voice out. Her face was burning in shame as she recalled how Sam's son had watched as they handcuffed her and marched her away. That was the end of that, she thought sadly; Sam might be here now, but he wouldn't be around much longer. No father would want an accused murderer hanging around his kid.

When they had both composed themselves somewhat, Stella explained what had transpired and what she had learned thus far. "Murder?" Sam exclaimed, his face ashen. "You're going to need money for an attorney. I'll call Brad as soon as I leave and see what funds he can raise."

"Thanks," Stella said, her eyes misting over. "I'm so sorry your son had to be there today, Sam. I was hoping he'd like me, you know. How can he ever respect me now?"

"Forget it," Sam said softly, mustering up a smile. "Just worry about yourself, Stella. Is there anything I can do? Anything I can get for you?"

"Yes," Stella said. Behind her a recorded voice came over the loudspeaker, advising that visiting hours would be over in five minutes. "I've been trying to reach Mario, but I can't find him. I don't want him to hear about my arrest on television. Can you try to get through and tell him what's happened, see if he can call me here at the jail?"

"Certainly, Stella," Sam said, waiting while Stella pulled out a piece of paper with her

121

brother's number on it and placed it in the metal bin.

"And clothes," she said. "When I get to Houston, I'll need some fresh clothes for the court hearing. Also, could you check my—"

Just then a male guard appeared in the door behind Stella and barked in a loud, abrasive voice, "Move it, Cataloni. Didn't you hear the announcement? Visiting hours are over."

Sam leaped to his feet, placing his palms against the glass. "Can you give us a fucking minute here?" he shouted. "At least let the woman finish her sentence."

"I've never heard you curse before," Stella said, surprised at the fierceness she saw in his eyes. The guard walked over and placed a hand on Stella's shoulder.

"Oh, yeah?" Sam said, giving the guard a scathing look. "There's a lot of things you haven't seen me do. What were you saying, Stella? Don't let these goons push you around. You have rights, you know, even if you are a prisoner."

At the jailer's insistence, Stella slowly stood, depositing the phone in the metal bin. Sam might be an attorney, she decided, but he had a lot to learn about being in jail.

When Carl Winters appeared the next morning to transfer his prisoner to Houston, he had a thick stack of newspapers in his arms and a smug smile on his face. Stella stepped into the holding pen and stuck out her hands, waiting for Winters to cuff them. Instead, he flashed the front page of the *Dallas Morning News* in her face. "I got us some reading material for the plane. Recognize anyone?"

Stella gawked at the headline, "D.. IN PELHAM CASE ARRESTED FOR MUDER." Underneath the header was a picture of Stella, taken on the last day of the Pelham trial, her hair pulled back in a ponytail and her scar clearly visible. When she tried to read the rest of the text, Winters snatched the paper back and snapped on the handcuffs.

Stella was booked into the Central Jail on Franklin Street, the facility used to house female inmates, one of the four detention facilities located in the Houston system. Although she was processed at noon, she was told she wouldn't be arraigned until the following afternoon. She asked to make a phone call, and finally reached Mario at his apartment. "I've been arrested," she said. "Someone killed Tom Randall."

"I heard the news over the radio," Mario answered, the line falling silent. "I tried to call you in Dallas as soon as I heard," he said a few moments later, "but they told me you weren't there anymore. I've been frantic, Stella."

"I don't want to talk over the phone," she said. "Visiting hours are at eight tonight. You damn well better be here."

"What does that mean?" Mario said. "Why are you taking that tone of voice with me? What did I do?"

"You know," Stella hissed, keeping her voice low so no one could overhear.

"No," Mario said, "I don't know. If there's something going on that I should know about,

Stella, why don't you just tell me? Why make me wait until tonight?"

"Just be here tonight at eight," she said. "Winters is pressing me for a statement, and I have to talk to you first." She paused and then added, "You didn't come home, Mario. I have to know where you were and what you were doing when Randall was shot. Don't think you can lie, either. No matter what you did, I have to know the truth. I found the cocaine in the darkroom." Stella didn't wait for her brother to respond. She hung up the phone and motioned for the jailer to take her to her cell.

"I can't take your case."

Paul Brannigan, the attorney Growman had recommended, appeared at the Central Jail the following morning, asking that he be allowed to see his potential client face to face instead of behind glass. In his mid- fifties, the man was a character, a little too flamboyant and eccentric-looking for Stella's taste. But Growman had given him a glowing recommendation and she trusted him implicitly.

The attorney strolled in wearing a Western-cut suit, cowboy boots, a string tie, and carrying a battered leather attaché case that had to be twenty years old. His hair was a dark, artificial shade, which Stella assumed was the result of hair dye, but it looked as if he had colored it with black shoe polish. Over his lip was a preposterous handlebar mustache, the kind Stella had seen only in old movies. "What do you mean you can't take my

124

case?" Stella said. "Didn't Growman tell you how important this case is, who I am?"

"I'm in the midst of something else right now," he told her, twirling the ends of his mustache. "I didn't say I wouldn't represent you eventually, so don't get your pretty little face all twisted like that. I just can't step in on such short notice." He paused, thinking. "Now if I was in your shoes, I'd go pro-per, you know, represent myself. At this stage in the proceedings, it's pretty routine and you are an accredited attorney. All you're going to do is enter a plea of not guilty, anyway." He laughed. "Shucks, what do you need a high-priced gunslinger like me for? You're the gal that's been on everyone's TV lately."

Stella agreed with his reasoning, knowing the arraignment would be routine. Their discussion moved on to his fees should she decide to bring him on board for the remainder of the proceedings. When Brannigan stated his terms, however, Stella was taken by surprise. "Fifty thousand?" she said. "You want fifty G's just to look at my case? That's almost as much as I make in a year."

"Well, yes," he said, "this here is a homicide case. I have to hire investigators, set aside my other clients' needs, exhaust a great deal of time preparing and doing research, grant interviews with the media. Sweetheart, I have to tell you," he continued, "if this here case goes to trial, fifty thousand will only be the beginning."

On this depressing note, Stella concluded her meeting with Brannigan. As soon the guard came to escort her back to her cell, she allowed her to place a collect call to Sam from the pay phone located in the corridor near her cell. In Houston, high-profile inmates like Stella were housed in what they referred to as segregated cells. Once Stella had seen her cell, she realized what a segregated cell meant: no windows, no bars where other inmates could look inside, and a space that wasn't much larger than a chicken coop.

How could she ever raise enough money to hire an attorney? The money she had saved over the years had disappeared from their bank accounts, thanks to Brad, and Stella had no resources other than her monthly income. With mortgage payments, insurance, and Sam's legal fees, she had very little left over at the end of the month. She might be able to represent herself at her arraignment, she decided, but only an idiot would fail to hire appropriate representation should the case proceed to trial.

"What am I going to do?" she asked Sam, her nerves frazzled. "Did you talk to Brad, tell him what's going on? Is he trying to come up with the money? Not only do I need it for Brannigan's retainer, but I'll need money if they set bail."

Sam thought briefly of reminding Stella that he had warned her to fight for what was rightfully hers, that she might one day need the money her husband had managed to steal away. Beating a dead horse, however, was not his style. Finally he spoke, his voice strained and weak. "He's not being very cooperative," he said. When Stella pushed him to be more specific, he spelled it out for her. "I'm sorry, Stella," he said. "Brad says he doesn't have any money and that you can just sit in jail."

126

"Bastard," Stella mumbled under her breath. Once Sam had disconnected, she pressed her forehead against the dirty wall. A combination of odors drifted to her nostrils—disinfectant, body odor, human excrement. The smells seemed to be seeping from the walls. Behind her, one of the heavy steel doors that separated the quadrants dropped down and Stella jumped at the grating sound.

Of all the foul scents that assaulted her and turned her stomach, though, one was the most pronounced. Stella knew it wasn't coming from the old urine stains on the floor or the jail's kitchen where they prepared the slop they passed off as food. It was emanating from her own pores, being manufactured by her own body—the distinctive and pervasive odor of fear.

chapter

SIX

"State of Texas versus Stella Cataloni Emerson," Judge Lucille Maddox said, calling the case at precisely one o'clock that afternoon, her voice amplified by a small black microphone.

Stella felt a measure of relief that she had drawn a woman judge. Maddox had a reputation of being fair. Even though Stella realized Maddox would not be the trial judge, she could well preside over the preliminary hearing. By barring the media from today's hearing, Judge Maddox had already done Stella a favor.

Lucille Maddox was in her late forties with ash blond hair and fair skin. Stella had heard that she leaned toward leniency, another comforting fact. Texas had the greatest contingent of what people referred to as "hanging judges," jurists so hard-nosed that they sentenced every person who appeared in front of them to prison, and for as long as the law allowed. Stella had known for some time that if a person wanted to commit a crime, the place to do it was anywhere outside the state of Texas. The overcrowded Texas prison system had people serving outrageous and unjust terms from as far back as the 1960s. Among them were the scores of hippies and flower children still serving life sentences for possession of a few marijuana joints, an offense states like California had routinely punished with a slap on the wrists.

Another terrifying fact darted through her mind. If Fitzgerald's office decided to file on capital murder charges, an offense which carried the death penalty in Texas, Stella knew she could be executed. Prisoners on death row used to languish indefinitely, but no more. Executions now went on at Huntsville on a regular basis. The *Dallas Morning News* had run an article only a few weeks ago, stating that over eighty inmates had been executed since the state reinstated the death penalty. She couldn't recall if any of them had been female.

Accepting a copy of the pleading from the bailiff, Stella quickly scanned it. The D.A. had elected not to file on capital murder charges. As she continued reading, however, her relief was short-lived. She knew she would be charged in Randall's death, but she had never dreamed she would be prosecuted for her parents' deaths as well. But there it was in black and white, a charge of arson in the old fire as well as two additional counts of homicide. Her blood turned to ice and she stared over at Holly at the counsel table. So, she thought, Houston officials were going for the full boat. Mario might have been foolish enough to think Holly would stand up for her, but Stella knew now that whatever friendship they had shared was dead.

Without Randall's testimony, did the state really have a case? After giving it more thought, she realized that the D.A.'s office had no choice but to file in the arson case. If the people didn't establish that Randall's testimony was vital and damning, they would not be able to prove that Stella possessed a motive to kill him. Additionally, she recognized this as a prosecution ploy, one she had used herself on many occasions. By filing all the charges, even those the state might not be able to sustain, the prosecution awarded itself sufficient leverage to plead the case out and avoid the uncertainties of a jury trial. Fitzgerald would more than likely offer Stella a deal as things moved along, agreeing to dismiss the old charges in return for a guilty plea in the Randall homicide.

Would the state try the cases together? Stella wondered, seeing dollar signs flashing in front of her eyes. If not, it would mean two separate trials, and Brannigan would probably want a hundred thousand on retainer instead of fifty.

She had her answer all too soon. As the judge's voice rang out again over the microphone, Stella heard two separate case numbers being read and knew the cases would not be consolidated. The state would probably go forward with the old charges first, she decided, attempt to dispose of them, then move on to the Randall matter. This way, the state would have time to collect more evidence and prepare its strategy in the Randall homicide, as well as have ample time to discourage Stella from taking a chance that she might be found guilty of all the charges, thereby forcing her to settle the case by entering into a negotiated disposition or plea agreement.

Holly was poised and alert, having given Stella no more than a glance since she strode into the courtroom and took her seat beside Frank Minor. Her blond curls were slicked back with gel in a tight french twist, making her face appear hawkish and narrow. Instead of the new designer dress she had purchased for her press interview, she was wearing a severe black knit sheath, the skirt dropping to mid-calf. On her feet were a pair of clunky black shoes with low heels and laces, her overall look that of a dowdy school-teacher.

With a conviction on any of the counts alleged, either separately or collectively, Stella could go to prison for what might amount to the rest of her natural life. She decided Holly saw this as a somber enough situation to forgo making her normal fashion statement. In all the years she had known her, she had never seen Holly Oppenheimer dress so sedately.

"We will proceed with the arraignment at this time," Judge Maddox said. She looked directly at Stella without flinching, as if she were no different from any other defendant. "Ms. Cataloni, I understand you have no legal representation today. Is that correct?"

Stella's throat was dry. She looked for the customary pitcher of water on the table, but didn't see one. She swallowed before speaking. "That's correct."

"Will you be acting as your own counsel, then?"

"Yes, Your Honor."

"Fine," the judge said. "We will begin." She slipped her glasses on and started to read from the pleading. "Stella Cataloni Emerson, you have been charged by the People of the state of Texas with the crime of murder in the death of Thomas Randall, a violation of penal code section 19.03(a)(2), a felony in the first degree, filed as case H345672. How do you plead?"

"Not guilty, Your Honor."

"You have also been charged with the crime of arson, case number H378941, a violation of penal code section 28.02(a), a felony in the first degree. How do you plead?"

"Not guilty."

"Ms. Cataloni, you have additionally been charged with two counts of murder in the afore-mentioned case, a violation of penal code section 19.03(a)(2), both felonies in the first degree. How do you plead?"

"Not guilty, Your Honor."

"Lastly, you have been charged with two

131

counts of voluntary manslaughter, violations of penal code section 19.02(a)(1), case #H378941, a felony. How do you plead?"

"Not guilty," Stella said, realizing the prosecution had given the jurors a bail-out clause on the arson. If the state couldn't prove beyond a reasonable doubt that Stella premeditated her actions in setting fire to her house and causing her parents' deaths, the jury could still bring in convictions on voluntary manslaughter.

"Will you be retaining counsel in the near future, Ms. Cataloni?"

"Yes, Your Honor," Stella said. "That is, to the best of my knowledge I will."

"I highly recommend it," Judge Maddox said, dropping protocol for a moment. No responsible jurist would condone a defendant acting as her own counsel. "I realize you are an attorney, and a good one as well," the judge continued, "but in a case of this magnitude, you should be represented by competent and independent counsel. Surely you are aware of that?"

"Yes, Your Honor," Stella said crisply.

"If it is a matter of inadequate funds," the judge continued, "I can appoint a public defender to represent you."

"That won't be necessary at this time," she said, hoping her statement was true. She'd get a loan against the house, she decided. It was the only hope she had to come up with the cash she needed.

Holly offered a date for the preliminary hearing, and Judge Maddox asked Stella if August 20 was acceptable.

"Yes, Your Honor, that's fine," Stella said, realizing the date was only eight days away. The sooner the better. Then she added, "I'd like to make a motion for bail at this time. You should have a bail review completed by the probation department. I spoke with the probation officer last night at the jail."

The judge turned to her clerk, and the woman handed her the report. "Have you seen this document, Counselor?" she asked Stella.

"No," Stella replied. "I didn't receive a copy. I guess no one realized I was going pro-per."

The bailiff brought the bail review to the counsel table. When Stella saw the sum recommended, she gasped. A million dollars! She could never raise that kind of money. She took a deep breath, trying to calm down. At least the probation officer had recommended bail. On charges this serious, it was a miracle she had recommended bail at all.

"Ms. Oppenheimer," the judge said, "please state your agency's position on bail."

Holly stood, cutting her eyes to Stella and then back to the judge. "We don't concur with the probation officer, Your Honor. We ask that the defendant be held without bail. Ms. Cataloni has not only been charged in a crime involving the death of a state's witness, but in two earlier homicides as well." Holly paused, looking down at the notes she had stayed up all night to prepare. "For sixteen years Ms. Cataloni has managed to avoid prosecution on these heinous crimes—the brutal and senseless deaths of her parents. Why would we give her a chance to escape the consequences of this new homicide?" She looked up at the judge. "There's no question that this woman should be held without bail," she practically shouted, her voice carrying so well that she pushed the microphone aside. "To allow her to return to the community for even one day would be irresponsible, not to mention the danger she could pose to any additional witnesses the state might produce."

As soon as Holly took her seat, Stella pushed herself to her feet, still reeling from the accusations her one-time friend had made. Growman had been right, she thought. Holly was a formidable adversary. When she spoke, her voice was shaky. "Your Honor," she said, "I know this is a matter of bail and we are not here today to decide my guilt or innocence, but I am innocent of these charges and would like to take this opportunity to advise the court of this fact." She paused, not wanting to grovel but determined to stand her ground.

"I appreciate the People's position," she continued. "If I was the prosecutor on a case of this stature, I would demand that bail be denied just as Ms. Oppenheimer has done. But I beg the court to consider the circumstances, to respectfully point out that every case must be weighed on its own merits." Stella stopped and linked eyes with Judge Maddox. Then she sucked in a breath and slowly let it out, wanting to appear strong and confident. "I must be housed in a segregated cell at the jail," she said. "Unfortunately, I may have to act as my own counsel until my divorce is settled and the necessary funds become available to hire an attorney. That means that I must have access to a law library and other reference materials to prepare for my defense." Stella paused and cleared her throat. "Since I have been charged with the crime of arson, a highly technical crime in nature, in addition to the other charges, I must study and prepare even more intently. If I'm to be segregated from the main jail population, I will not have access to the law library, and therefore cannot prepare my defense." She elevated her voice. "I consider my incarceration under these conditions to be a violation of my constitutional rights under the Eighth Amendment, which prohibits cruel and unusual punishment. I have not been convicted of a crime, and yet I am suffering a more stringent and restrictive form of imprisonment than the majority of the inmates serving time at a prison facility, let alone a presentence facility."

Stella paused as she sensed a presence behind her. She smiled faintly as Sam seated himself in the front row. With her eyes, she thanked him for caring enough to get on a plane and fly to her side. Growman had not been able to free himself from his responsibilities, and Mario had never appeared at the jail. For all Stella knew, her brother had left town and her suspicions that he had shot Randall could be valid. She had tried to call him five or six times and no one had picked up his phone.

"Are you finished, Counselor?" Judge Maddox said.

"No, Your Honor," Stella answered, quickly refocusing her attention. "I'm virtually being held in solitary confinement due to no fault of my own. I also direct the court to consider that I have no prior criminal convictions to support a denial of bail. Up until today, I have been a contributing member of society, a defender of the very system where I now stand accused."

"Your Honor," Holly said, waving her arm toward Stella, "Ms. Cataloni is being housed in a segregated cell for her own protection. If she doesn't like it, then she can return to the main jail population."

Judge Maddox toyed with her pen as she thought over her next statement. "Ms. Cataloni has presented what I view as a valid argument," she said finally. "Returning this particular prisoner to the main jail population could put her in serious jeopardy. As it is clearly the responsibility of the bench as well as the county to keep those under our jurisdiction free from harm while they are incarcerated, the court will not allow Ms. Cataloni to be exposed to this type of danger."

While Holly grimaced and leaned down to confer with Frank Minor, Judge Maddox continued, "Is that all you wish to say, Ms. Cataloni?"

"No, Your Honor," Stella said, her legs so weak that she leaned against her chair to steady herself. "I beg the court to release me on my own recognizance, and I further feel that the court has no alternative but to honor my request."

The courtroom fell silent as the judge pondered her decision. She read through a few pages of the arrest report, going over the details of the crime and what evidence the state possessed. Then she looked up. "The defendant's request for O.R. is denied," she said. "Bail is set at fifty thousand dollars in case H378941, and fifty thousand in case H345672." Then she peered down at Stella. "There will be no ten percent privileges, Ms. Cataloni, just so we understand each other. I'm setting bail at a moderate sum based on your lack of criminal history and your standing in the community, but I want the full amount before you walk out the door."

Holly shot to her feet. "The People object, Your Honor. If you feel you must set bail, at least set it at an appropriate amount, an amount that reflects the seriousness of these crimes. To set it at only a hundred thousand is unconscionable." Frank Minor yanked on her sleeve, and Holly saw the dark look on Judge Maddox's face. Calling a judge's ruling unconscionable in an open courtroom represented a serious breach of protocol. When she resumed speaking, Holly's annoyance was in check, and her tone formal. "Your Honor, allow me to respectfully point out that these are murder charges. Not one, but three innocent lives have been lost. As to Mr. Randall, he was in my office only a few days ago. I was present when the defendant threatened to kill him. If I was out of line earlier, I beg the court's forgiveness, but I'm gravely concerned about this woman's release and the risk it might pose to other witnesses."

"I'm more than aware that these are homicides, Ms. Oppenheimer," the judge said, glowering at her. "Bail will remain as previously set."

Even though Stella had no idea how she would come up with the money, her spirits soared as she watched Holly and her co-counsel whisper to each other. She had won an important victory. She prayed it was the first of many.

The judge jotted down her notes in the file and then handed it over to the clerk. "The preliminary hearing on the arson and homicide counts will be held at nine o'clock on August 20 in this court-room. When we convene at that time, we'll select a date for the preliminary hearing on the Randall homicide. Is that agreeable to both parties?" Once Holly and Stella concurred, Judge Maddox looked out over the room and tapped her gavel. "This court is adjourned."

Until she came up with a hundred thousand dollars, Stella would be returned to the jail. As she was escorted out of the courtroom, she looked over at Sam, desperation in her eyes. "Don't worry, Stella," he called. "I'll call Brad again. We'll work something out."

Once she was back in her cell, Stella pulled out the yellow notepad she had purchased from the cart that came around each day, and began listing all the particulars she wanted to relay to Brenda Anderson. She had no choice now but to turn her attention to the old fire, since it would be the first crime she would have to defend herself against. Propped up on her cot, her head braced against the cracked plaster, she was writing when she heard a key turn in the lock. Looking up, she saw a woman's face peering in through the small glass window in the door.

A female jailer, this one with a gravelly voice and a face ugly enough to stop traffic, opened the door and stuck her head inside. "Come with me," she said.

"Where?" Stella said without looking up, adding the letters KAL to her list. Her top priority was to rule out any possibility of Mario being involved. She wanted Brenda to check on Mario's stewardess and see if she had still been in town during the hours Randall was murdered. She needed to know if the woman could substantiate her brother's whereabouts. She was fairly certain Mario had told her the woman flew for Korean Airlines. But she also realized she needed to file a discovery motion in order to find out what kind of evidence the prosecution possessed. She quickly added that to her list, then tossed the notebook down. "What do you want? Do I have a visitor?"

"Yeah," the jailer said. "Hurry up. I don't have all day here."

Stella followed her to one of the glass-partitioned cubicles. Her jaw dropped when she saw Brad. "Why are you here?" she asked, the phone pressed to her ear. "Were you in the courtroom?"

"I told you not to go poking around in the past," he told her, scowling. "See what you've done, Stella? You've stirred up a hornet's nest. You just couldn't let things alone, could you?"

Stella was tempted to hurl the phone at the window. Instead she said, "Is that why you flew down here? Just so you could gloat?"

"No, no," he said, his tone soft and placating now. "Even if you don't realize it, Stel, I care about you. No matter what happens between us, I'll always be here for you."

139

"Oh, really?" Stella shot back. "Sam said you told him I could just rot in jail."

"Well," Brad said, his face flushing, "I have to admit I was a little hostile when he called. The guy just rubs me the wrong way, you know, making all these crazy allegations like he thinks I'm some kind of crook."

Stella remained silent.

"So," Brad continued, smiling at her, "I had a nice long chat with my attorney this morning. I think I can free up the money you need, but he says I can't do it until we settle our financial affairs."

"What do you mean?" Stella said, jerking her head up. The scent of freedom drifted past her nostrils, and she was willing to do just about anything to make it real.

Brad removed a stapled stack of papers from his jacket and placed them in the metal bin. "Look," he said before Stella had retrieved them, "this isn't my doing, so don't jump all over me. If I could get my hands on the money any other way, I'd do it and get you out of here. My attorney says it has to be done this way. Weinstein froze all our assets, see, and until these forms are signed, I can't get my hands on a dime." He stopped and smirked. "Let me tell you, a hundred big ones is far from small change."

Stella read through the paperwork, trying to keep her anger in check. Brad was asking her to sign over everything they owned: all rights to his business, the house, the furnishings, whatever money had been present in their savings accounts, any and all equipment. Stella could

140

keep her BMW and her personal effects, and that was it. "This is blackmail," she said, shoving the papers back in the bin.

"You don't understand," Brad said. "The hundred grand I've got to put up for your bail was taken into consideration. My lawyer says this is more than fair. He even told me I was being overly generous." He paused and then added, "Remember, I owned the business before we even met, so that's mine fair and square."

"You didn't own the house, though," Stella argued. "Not only that, by law I'm entitled to a percentage of all monies earned in the business during the course of our marriage. Don't tell me after all these years all you earned was a paltry hundred grand. I know better, Brad. I'm not an idiot."

"Hey," he said, "I came here out of the goodness of my heart, out of the love we once shared. If you want me to leave, I'll go right now. I just couldn't stand to see you sit here in jail, but if this is how you—" He replaced the phone and was about to leave when Stella motioned for him to sit back down.

"I'm sorry," she said, backtracking. At present, Brad was her only chance to make bail. If it meant she had to kiss his ass to get out of jail, then she would have to do it, and do it well. "Maybe I'm being obstinate, Brad. Hell, maybe I'm even bitter. I mean, you did dump me for another woman." Her shoulders rose and then fell. "I do appreciate you coming, though. You know, it's nice to know you still care."

"Of course I care," he said. "You were just a

kid when I married you. When you used to ask me why I didn't want to have children, what did I always tell you?"

"I was your little girl," she said, meeting his eyes and then quickly looking away.

"I tried to give you a good life," he continued. "I even tried to help raise Mario. I don't want to cheat you. I'm here to help you. Even if we go our separate ways, I want us to always remain friends."

"You did a lot for me, Brad," Stella said. "I didn't mean for my job to come between us. I only wanted to make a name for myself, have something I could feel proud of. You had your business, you know. Was I really that bad?"

"Nah," he said, shaking his head. "I guess turning fifty a few years back made me a little crazy. I just wanted to kick up my heels before I ended up six feet under, have a few laughs, a little fun. All this career stuff, setting the world on fire, well, that's fine for you, Stella, but for me, it's a thing of the past."

Stella's anger flared. Why did he always say the wrong thing? Kick up his heels, huh? Had he really ended their fifteen-year marriage for such a childish and self- serving reason? What? So he could chase girls and prove he was still a desirable man? And he had the balls to ask her to sign over everything they owned so he could have enough money to carry out his plan. Was he going to move his blond bimbo into her house and toss her out on the street? "Give me a pen," she said, wanting to get it over with before she backed out. "But promise me you'll post the bail money right

142

away. Can you get it here by tomorrow morning?"

"As soon as you sign," Brad said, reaching in his pocket for a pen, "I'll get the bank to release the funds and wire them straight to the jail. Then I'll see if I can dig up some more money so you can get yourself a real good attorney, someone with enough smarts to get you out of this mess."

Stella picked up the pen and was about to sign the forms when the jailer stepped up behind her. "I'll be finished in about five minutes," she said, glancing through the papers and seeing that her signature was required in several different spots.

"Well," the woman said, "if you go with me, you can finish your conversation outside. Your bail's been posted."

Stella looked at Brad and then back to the guard. "You must be mistaken. We're making arrangements to get my bail posted right now."

"I've got the release form right here," the woman said, waving a piece of paper in Stella's face. "But hey, you want to stick around, be my guest."

"Are you certain?" Stella said, dumbfounded. "Who posted my bail?"

"Don't say on the form," the woman said, a bored expression on her face.

Stella placed the unsigned forms in the bin and passed them back to Brad. "Wait," he said, "what are you doing? These aren't signed. You said you were going to sign them. Who put up your bail? Don't forget, Stella, you'll need money for your attorney."

"I guess I don't need to sign my life away after

all," Stella said, a smile playing at the corner of her lips.

Brad sprang to his feet, dropping the phone and yelling through the glass, his hot breath smoking a circle. "You're making a mistake," he shouted. "I'm not coming back here again. You just burned your bridges with me, you ungrateful little bitch."

"Fuck you," Stella mouthed. Brad might not be able to hear her through the glass, but she found the moment immensely gratifying. Standing, she let the jailer lead her away.

It took Stella approximately fifty minutes to be processed for release. She walked out of the jail into a bright afternoon sun, relishing its warmth against her skin. She was about to head down the steps to the street, thinking she would have to call a cab to take her to the airport, when she saw Sam waving at her from a car parked at the curb. Racing down the steps, she leaped into the passenger seat and grabbed him in a bear hug. Her arms were so tight around his neck, he had to pull them off to keep from being strangled. "You posted my bail," Stella exclaimed. "How can I ever thank you? This is the sweetest thing anyone has ever done for me."

Sam smiled. "I'm sure you'll find a way, Stella. I couldn't let you stay in that awful place." He momentarily looked away. The attorney was far from poor, but he wasn't prone to part with his money, particularly to assist someone he had known only for a short time. He had his son's future to provide for, and after losing his wife, he always made certain he had money stashed away should anything ever happen to him. All night long, he had anguished, unable to sleep, wanting to disentangle himself from Stella and her problems. When the sun came up, however, he had jumped on the first plane to Houston. Then when the judge had set bail, he'd marched to the jail and promptly paid.

While Sam sorted through his thoughts, Stella leaned back in the seat and inhaled the fresh air floating in from the window. It was hot and humid, but she didn't care. She had never smelled anything more wonderful in her life. As she filled her lungs with oxygen and then slowly let it out, she felt a rush of adrenaline. She was filled with joy, overwhelmed with relief. It didn't matter that her freedom might be short-lived, that depending on how the preliminary hearing turned out, her bail could be revoked and she could be returned to the jail for the remainder of the proceedings. Right now she was free, and the taste of freedom was exhilarating. Stella felt like she was drunk on fine wine. Her stomach purred, her skin tingled, and Sam's aftershave floated past her smelling lemony and delicious.

"Let's go to a hotel," she said. "We'll get naked and celebrate my release."

"Please, Stella," Sam said, scowling, "I don't want you to think that because I posted your bail, you have to grant me sexual favors."

"I know that," Stella said, flicking her wrist at him and smiling. "I'm not doing it for you, anyway, I'm doing it for me."

"Oh, really?" he said, smiling back. "How's that?"

"The other night," she said, her tongue flitting over her upper lip, "you played my body like a violin. I never dreamed you were so talented."

"Hmmm," he said, obviously pleased. He pulled Stella closer and gave her a quick kiss. "I'm always glad to oblige," he said playfully, twirling a strand of her hair. "I mean, a fellow works hard to perfect that kind of skill. When you told me to leave so suddenly, I got to thinking I might have been a little rusty."

"Not at all," she said. "You were great. With all this time on my hands, I remembered every second of that night. It kept me going while I was in that miserable stinkhole."

"Well," he said, cranking the engine and smiling over at her, "if you insist, I think there's a motel right down the block. It's not fancy, though. Are you sure you don't want to go downtown to a first-class hotel, maybe the Omni or the Ritz-Carlton?"

"I've been in jail, Sam," she said. "Right now, Motel 6 would seem like a palace."

Sam took his hands off the steering wheel and faced her again. "Maybe we should go and have a nice dinner somewhere instead. Then later—"

Stella leaned over close, her hand brushing over his crotch. Rubbing her breasts against him, she whispered in his ear, her voice breathy and sexy, "Play it again, Sam."

The next moment they were speeding down the road in search of the nearest bed.

chapter

SEVEN

The room was small and tawdry. With a torn chenille bedspread and limp, worn sheets, it reeked from bug spray. Stella nonetheless felt the motel room was an improvement over the jail.

As soon as she stepped out of the shower with a towel wrapped around her and walked into the other room where Sam was waiting on the bed, he reached out and snatched the towel away.

"Don't, Sam," Stella said, frowning as she grabbed the towel back and quickly covered her body. "I thought you said they had black-out drapes in this room. Why's there so much light?"

"They do have black-outs," Sam responded. "They just won't close. Something's wrong with the curtain rod, I guess. Besides," he continued, "I want to look at you."

Stella's chin went up and her back became rigid. "You only think you want to look at me," she said. "Trust me, Sam, you don't."

A stream of light was pouring in from the crack in the drapes, and Stella realized she was standing in the center of it, almost as if she were being illuminated by a spotlight. She moved several feet back into the shadows.

"Don't be self-conscious," Sam said. "I've already seen the scar on your face, remember. It

147

isn't that bad, Stella. With the way you wear your hair, it's not even noticeable."

"You think that's the only scar I have," she told him. "It's not, Sam."

"So," he said, maintaining their eye contact without flinching, "whatever it is, I can handle it. You look fine to me. You're beautiful, Stella. I don't know why you don't realize it. Everyone else does."

When she began speaking, her voice was a low monotone. "Handicapped people are very resourceful, Sam. Girls with deformed hands learn to wear long, ruffled sleeves to cover them. Boys with no ears wear caps with flaps. People with atrophied legs learn to cover their lower extremities with blankets." She stopped and cleared her throat, her eyes glistening with tears. "I've spent months in burn units, seen people with injuries so horrifying and disfiguring that I couldn't understand why the doctors kept them alive." She sighed. "I guess the will to live is so strong, the fear of death so overpowering, that thousands of these poor people go out into the world every day, accepting people's stares and careless remarks. But I'm not like those people," she told him. "I can't function if I know the person I'm with sees me as deformed."

"Come here," Sam said, a look of tenderness softening his face. "I didn't mean to make you uncomfortable. I'll never again ask to see your body. I promise." He held his arms out, beckoning her to come to him.

Stella slid into the bed, pulling the sheet up over her and resting her head on Sam's chest.

"I'm sorry," she said. "I guess I ruined our cele-bration."

"Listen to me," he whispered. "Don't talk, just listen. I know something about scars. When a person dies of cancer, they don't just die. They cut you away a little at a time. Liz underwent a double mastectomy before they realized the cancer was terminal. Do you think I no longer found her attractive? Do you think for one minute that her scars disgusted me or horrified me?" He softly stroked Stella's hair as a parent soothes an overwrought child, his voice strained with emotion. "She was as beautiful to me when she died as she was the day I married her. I didn't fall in love with her skin, her breasts, her hair, her various parts and components. Beauty isn't superficial, Stella. Beauty comes from inside." He drew in a deep breath. "Real beauty comes from the heart. When you look at someone, you're only seeing a reflection of the person inside."

Stella felt Sam's chest rising and falling. Even though his words were comforting, she sensed something else, something no words could ever capture and identify.

He understood.

At that moment, Stella truly believed he could accept her, even give her the type of love she had always longed for and had never been able to find with Brad. But could he really understand the bitterness she carried in her heart, more ugly and repulsive than any scar? "I went to a shrink," she said. "It was years ago, not long after the fire. I wanted to remember, you know, but I just couldn't. It was a woman psychiatrist and I let her hypnotize me, hoping I could remember what happened the night of the fire."

"Did you?" he said. "Were you able to remember?"

"Some things came back," she said, "but they were like snapshots, sort of frozen images that I must have plucked out of the chaos of that night. Either that, or the memories were planted by my therapist and were not real at all."

"Why do you say that?"

"I saw my father's face," Stella said, her voice quavering. "He had this terrified, anguished look, and then I saw something flashing in his hands."

"Go on," he said.

"I don't know what I saw," Stella said, her words mumbled against Sam's chest. "At first I thought it was a knife, but it was too big to be a knife. And it wasn't chrome or shiny like a knife. It looked dark and rusted, like some kind of gardening implement or a tool of some kind. I saw my father holding it up in the air, as if he were about to bring it down on my head."

"Do you think your father set the fire, Stella?" Sam asked, shocked at what she was implying.

"No," Stella said, lifting her head up, "my father would never have done something like that. He loved me. We were very close. Like all the Catalonis, he had a temper and occasionally got carried away, but until the night of the fire he never once struck me. He was just a basic man, a workingman, you know, a man who believed in the family, the value of life."

"You mean he wouldn't let you have the baby aborted?"

"Yes," Stella said, her features becoming hard. "I know it had to be Randall. He wanted to get rid of me, get rid of the baby. He was immature and selfish, the big football star. When my father insisted he marry me, he became terrified that his life would be ruined. He must have just reacted and set the fire, wanting to make it all go away."

"What else do you remember?"

"Nothing," Stella sighed, falling back on the pillow. "The shrink tried to tell me that I couldn't remember because it was my father who set the fire, that my father had been molesting me, possibly even fathered my unborn child. She said the realization of this was more than my mind could handle. Therefore, every time I went back in time to the night of the fire and saw my father's face, my mind simply shut down."

"Do you think she was right?"

"Absolutely not," Stella said, staring up at the cracks in the ceiling. "See, I recall almost everything that happened before the fire. None of those memories seem to be impaired. How could I forget something as sick as my father molesting me? If he'd fathered my child, I doubt if a pregnancy would have resulted from a single incident, so that means it had to have been going on for some time. It just didn't happen, Sam," she said. "I've never once felt anything but love and admiration for my father. Even when I recall the image of him holding something in his hands, it's frightening, but I'm certain he wasn't trying to hurt

151

me." She stopped speaking and fell silent. Some-time later, she said, "No one will ever convince me that my father set the fire."

"Don't talk about it anymore," Sam said, softly stroking Stella's breasts under the sheet. "Some-times it's better to let the past go."

"I can't do that, don't you see?" she said, sniffing back tears. "They're going to put me on trial for killing my parents. I have to be able to reconstruct that night, be able to tell them what really happened and who was responsible. It's the only way I can clear myself."

"But Randall set the fire," Sam said, somewhat confused. "Isn't that what you've said all along?"

"Yes," Stella said, "but I'm not one hundred percent certain. And Randall is dead, Sam. Making him the scapegoat will appear too conve-nient to the jury, particularly since they'll know that I'm accused of killing the bastard."

As an attorney, Sam was beginning to under-stand Stella's predicament. "The more dirt you throw on Randall," he said, "the more you estab-lish a motive why you might have killed him."

"That's precisely what I mean," she said. "Whatever I testify to in that courtroom, or let's say I don't testify and merely present evidence that Randall set the fire, it's all fair game. Reporters can print whatever they want, whatever they hear, anything they see or suspect happened that night. They'll paint me as the cruelest person alive because that's the story the public is clam-oring for, the kind of story that sells newspapers. Potential jurors in the Randall homicide will read that shit and be prejudiced by it before they even get their jury summons in the mail."

"That happens with any criminal case," Sam said. "Whenever there's any notoriety, you always have a problem finding an impartial jury panel, but it doesn't mean it can't be done."

"But the more circumstantial a case is," she argued, "the more important public opinion becomes." Stella heard someone insert a key in the door next to them, and her ears pricked at the metallic sound. "My strongest memory was not something I saw, Sam, but something I heard," she continued with greater intensity. "It was a clicking noise, broken by a different sound, sort of metallic and abrupt, then followed by another clicking noise identical to the first one. Not long after I heard this, I realized my bed was on fire, and I smelled this awful, pungent odor that had to be my skin burning." Stella bolted upright in the bed, placing her hands over her face, without realizing that she was mimicking the exact movements that she had made the night of the fire. "If I could only identify that sound, Sam. I know that's the key."

"The arsonist had to set the fire somehow," he said, thinking. "The clicking noise you heard was probably a cigarette lighter."

"I've considered a lighter," Stella said. "I've listened to dozens of lighters, though, and the sound I heard that night is different, more distinctive, more metallic."

Sam continued stroking her beneath the covers, his hands roaming over her breasts, down her stomach, and drifting lightly over her thighs.

Stella pushed his hands away, and tossed the sheet aside. Then she got out of the bed and stood beside it. Without speaking, she moved her legs apart and watched as Sam's gaze fell to the scars on her inner thigh.

Of all the injuries Stella had sustained, the ones on her thigh had been the most devastating. The flames had burned away so much of her flesh that she had required numerous skin grafts. Even now, it looked as if someone had taken a ice cream scoop to her leg. Glancing at her shadow on the opposite wall, she saw how uneven her legs appeared and shivered, knowing Sam could see the same thing.

Sam didn't blink or recoil. He only sighed, the air leaving his lungs with a faint whistling sound. Stella turned around and walked to the bathroom, letting him see the white squares on her buttocks and upper back where the surgeons had removed the skin for the grafts. Now that he had seen her, could he ever make love to her again?

Glancing in the bathroom mirror, Stella blew her nose, and then returned to the bed. Sam didn't speak, but he held Stella tight against him. After an unknown period of time had passed, they slowly began making love. The experience was so emotionally charged, their feelings for each other so genuine, that when Stella finally cried out in pleasure, Sam broke down and wept. "Oh, Sam," Stella said, "look what I'm doing to you."

"Since Liz died, I've been so empty," he said, using the sheet to dab at his eyes. "I've been with other women, but I never felt anything. It was like I was dead inside. I went through the motions, but that's all they were, motions, gestures, a brief shot of pleasure. I've never felt I was making love to these women. It was sex, plain and simple. You've convinced me that I'm still alive, that I can feel again."

Sam had moved to the edge of the bed. Stella crawled over and held him from behind, rocking him back and forth in her arms. Hours passed in the now dark room and neither of them made a sound. Sam finally shut his eyes, and they both fell asleep.

At nine o'clock the following morning, Stella drove Sam to the airport to return to Dallas. She had decided to stay in Houston. Brenda Anderson was already entrenched at the Holiday Inn making inquiries, and Stella wanted to start feeding her leads. Sam had insisted that she keep his rental car rather than renting another one under her name. Dropping him off at the curb, she got out and embraced him. "It's going to be okay," he reassured her. "You're going to get off, Stella. I'm certain of it."

"It's not that, Sam," she said. "It's just that last night went so fast."

"We'll have other nights, Stella."

"We better," she said, kissing him quickly and then circling around to the driver's door. As she drove off, she watched him in the rearview mirror. He looked so handsome in his pinstripe suit, standing there with his briefcase and duffel bag. She wanted to throw the car in reverse and go back for him, beg him to stay with her. Instead, she floored the car and sped off. She had work to do. If she didn't clear herself, she would lose him. She couldn't let that happen.

When she was first arrested, Stella had anguished over what people would say, how her predicament would affect her career, her standing in the community, any chance that she could ever run for public office. Brad had always told her she didn't understand about life, that she didn't recognize the things that were truly valuable. Stella knew now that her husband had been right. A loving relationship was far more important than winning a case or rising a few more notches at the office. She could win all the cases in the world, and her success would never compare to the way Sam made her feel. In many ways, Stella knew she had taken Brad for granted, that she had neglected their marriage until he turned to another woman. She couldn't go back and change the past, but she could fight for her future. Squinting into the bright morning sun, she vowed to use every skill she possessed. She would bury Holly Oppenheimer in a blizzard of paper, filing every motion the law allowed. Glancing in the rearview mirror again, she brushed back her hair and examined the scar on her face. She'd suffered enough punishment. She wasn't about to go to prison for a crime she didn't commit.

The situation with Mario filled her with fear. Instead of going to the Holiday Inn to confer with Brenda Anderson, she drove straight to Mario's apartment. Seeing his car in his assigned parking spot, she raced up the stairs and pounded on his door. When she heard footsteps approaching from inside, she moved to the side so Mario couldn't see her through the peephole.

"Who's there?" he yelled through the door.

Stella remained silent, reaching her arm over and knocking again, then stepped back to her previous position.

"I can't see you," Mario said. Finally curiosity got the better of him and he flung the door open.

Stella stepped out of the shadows. Mario stepped back inside and tried to close the door in her face. "Don't you dare," Stella shouted, pushing her way in despite his attempts to bar her way.

"Why are you doing this?" Stella asked him. "Why are you avoiding me? You didn't even come to see me at the jail."

"I knew you were going to blame everything on me," he said, refusing to look at her. "You always blame everything on me."

"I do not," Stella said, her voice booming out over the room.

"Yes, you do," Mario yelled back. "It's always been my fault that you got burned. I've heard you say a dozen times that you wouldn't have been burned if you hadn't gone back down the hall to get me. Sometimes I wish you'd just left me there."

"That isn't true," Stella said, walking around in a small circle. "You're just throwing this shit at me to avoid the real issue. Where were you when Randall was shot? Tell me, Mario. I have to know and I have to know right now."

"I spent the night with my girlfriend, Stella. I wasn't aware that constituted a capital offense."

"Which girlfriend?" she said. "The stewardess?"

"You really think I'm responsible for Randall's death?" he said, shaking his head.

"Well," she said, stepping closer, "are you? If you are, why don't you admit it? Then I'll know what to do."

Mario tried to walk off. Stella stepped in front of him and seized him by the shoulders. "I'm going to start digging into Randall's death," she said, shaking his shoulders the way she used to when he was a kid. "I'm going to dig and dig until I get to the truth. Is that what you want, Mario? Do you want me to find out the hard way? Uncover things that might put you in prison? Do you want me to launch an investigation against my own fucking brother?"

Mario wrenched away. "I didn't do it," he insisted, a pouty, childish expression on his face.

"What about the cocaine?" she said, refusing to let up. "How long have you been using?" She suddenly noticed how small his pupils were, and at the same time, saw what she had failed to see before—the telltale redness and irritation around his nose. Her eyes took in the room and she suspected he had been holed up in the apartment for days. The ashtrays were spilling over with cigarette butts, beer cans had toppled over onto the carpeting, and she spotted several rolled-up dollar bills and a razor blade on the coffee table. "You're high now, aren't you?" she snarled. Lashing out with her hand, she slapped him across the face. "How could you do this?" she screamed. "After all I went through for you, how could you poison your body with drugs?"

Mario was no longer defensive. His anger fueled by cocaine and years of guilt, he knocked Stella off her feet, watching as she slammed back into the wall, then slid in a heap to the floor. Snatching his keys off the coffee table, he stormed out of the apartment.

chapter

EIGHT

Stella stood in the shower, letting the icy water splash over her face. She had arranged to meet Brenda at the Holiday Inn at noon, but called and asked her to come to Mario's instead. The humidity in Houston was so oppressive that by the time she'd finished putting the apartment in order, her clothes were sticking to her body and she was drained and miserable.

Mario would return, she hoped, and this time she would try to deal with his problems in a rational manner. Pressing her forehead against the cool tile, she realized she would have to get him professional help. One of the reasons she had encouraged him to move back to Houston three years ago was that the lifestyle was somewhat slower. Dallas was notorious for its flashy nightclubs and fast-paced social scene. A handsome bachelor like Mario could easily get caught up with the wrong crowd. Had he been using again even before he left Dallas? Had she been so immersed in her work that she had failed to see it?

In his drugged-out state, had her brother shot and killed Tom Randall?

Stella felt herself shivering. She turned off the water and got out of the shower, quickly dressing and setting up her paperwork on the kitchen table. A few moments later, the doorbell rang and Stella admitted Brenda Anderson into the apartment.

Dressed in a pair of baggy jeans and an oversized sweatshirt, Brenda wore her hair loose and free, her face devoid of makeup. This made her eyes seem somehow larger and more luminous, and she looked youthful and pretty, more like a college girl than the somber-faced, conservatively clad investigator Stella was accustomed to seeing at the courthouse. "I've never seen you with your hair down," she told her. "You should wear it this way all the time. It does something wonderful to your eyes."

"Really?" Brenda said, smiling as she fluffed her hair around her face. "Makes me look young, though, right?"

"What's wrong with looking young?"

Once the pleasantries were concluded, the two women got down to business. Brenda set up her computer on the kitchen table, and Stella pulled out her yellow notepad, going over all the things she wanted the investigator to look into. Stella wrote out the discovery motion in longhand and waited while Brenda typed it on the computer, then hooked up her portable printer.

"Okay," Stella said as she shoved the papers into a manila envelope, "if you hurry, you can get these filed today. I'm hoping Judge Maddox will rule on them by tomorrow morning. I have to get my hands on the evidence from the fire as soon as possible. We don't have that long before the prelim."

"Stella," Anderson said, "we have to talk. I managed to get my hands on more information last night."

"What?" Stella said. "Anything we can use?"

"I went out to dinner with the investigator I mentioned," she said. "A few drinks, a few false promises, and I finally got him to loosen up and talk. Seems their witness saw a woman driving a white rental car with a Hertz sticker on the back, speeding away from the scene of the Randall homicide only moments after it occurred."

Stella's jaw dropped. "Repeat what you just said."

"Victor Pilgrim, the witness I told you about," Brenda continued. "He claims he saw a woman in a white rental car, a Hertz rental car to be specific. I don't know how damaging this is. I mean, according to my contact, the guy didn't see the woman's face. He's certain it was a woman, though, but what difference does that make? Think of all the traffic that must pass by that street. It was broad daylight and just seeing a woman is not going to amount to much."

Stella's heart pounded against her chest. "You're wrong," she said. "When I came to

161

Houston, I rented a white Chevrolet Caprice from Hertz. I returned it the day of the murder."

"Oh, boy," Brenda said, compressing in her seat. "What time did you return it?"

"I'm not certain exactly," Stella said, "but I think it was between one and one-thirty. You know, right before I got on the plane."

"The M.E. has set the time of death around eleven," she answered. "Can you account for your whereabouts from say nine in the morning to eleven?"

Stella shook her head. "I was here in the apartment, but I don't have anyone to verify it."

"Where was Mario?"

"Out," she said, somewhat guarded. "Where he was doesn't really matter, does it?"

"Shit," Brenda said, "what in the hell is going on? Was the rental car here the entire time?"

"As far as I know," Stella said, shrugging.

"It's too big of a coincidence," the investigator said, getting up to refill her coffee cup. "Someone must have known you were driving a white rental car. Either that, or Pilgrim is lying through his teeth."

"They're trying to frame me," Stella exclaimed. "Didn't I tell you the other day that they were setting me up?"

"Who?" Brenda said. "Randall is dead. If anyone wanted to harm you, wouldn't it be Randall?"

"The police," Stella answered, her lips so stiff they barely moved.

"No way," Brenda said. "I don't see it. Why would the police want to frame you?" She waved

162

her hand in the air. "You've lost me, Stella. None of this makes sense. Winters might have a hard-on for you, but I doubt if he'd risk his pension just to nail you. Besides, I get chapped over all this police corruption and how everyone thinks we're a bunch of crooks nowadays. I've never met a crooked cop and I've been in this business a long time."

"It's not just Winters," Stella explained. "My uncle was a captain at the Houston P.D. until he retired six months ago. His full name is Clementine Cataloni, but he goes by Clem. He's always believed I set the fire. He despises me, Brenda. Maybe he's conspiring with Winters to put me away. Pilgrim could be their point man, don't you see?"

Brenda stood, placing the envelope Stella had given her in her briefcase. She knew how desperate Stella must be, but she found her conspiracy theory unreasonable. Trying to console her, she said, "You may think what's going on right now is frightening, Stel, but my mother always taught me that everything happens for a reason. Not only are we going to get you off, we're going to get to the bottom of this once and for all."

"I hope so," Stella said, smiling weakly.

"Oh," Brenda said, "you asked about Pilgrim's personnel files. I printed out what I found. Maybe you'll find something interesting." She handed the paperwork to Stella. "Look at the time. I'd better run. If I don't get to the courthouse right away, the clerk's office will close for the day."

Once she had left, Stella read through the infor-

163

mation, seeing nothing noteworthy. She was about to set it aside when she noticed a sheet listing Pilgrim's current status on the city payroll. Seeing the letter "D" listed in a column, Stella realized Victor Pilgrim must have retired on disability. There was nothing in the file to indicate he had ever worked under her uncle or Carl Winters, though. As Brenda had informed her earlier, they would have to get into the police files to obtain that type of information, and thus far Brenda had been unable to do so.

Deciding to give the material one more pass, Stella went back to Pilgrim's original job application. He had not started his career with the Houston P.D. as they had first suspected, but had transferred from the Sheriff's Office in San Antonio only a few months prior to his injury. She read through the various individuals he had listed as references, seeing nothing that caught her eye. In the section that listed organizations and special awards or degrees, she finally saw something. Victor Pilgrim had once held an office in the Knights of Columbus.

"Okay," Stella said, her voice echoing in the empty room. Clementine Cataloni had long been active in the Knights of Columbus. If she were the victim of some type of conspiracy, a certain pattern would surface linking the conspirators. Pilgrim, Winters, and her uncle all had the Houston P.D. as a common denominator. Now she had added the Knights of Columbus, at least where Victor Pilgrim and her uncle were concerned. If she remembered correctly, her uncle had once been the top dog in the Southwest region. It wasn't much, but at least it was a start. Grabbing her purse, Stella gritted her teeth and headed for the door. It was time to pay the Grand Wizard, or whatever they called him, a little impromptu visit.

Driving the red Ford Fairlane Sam had rented, Stella turned into the driveway and made her way up a private paved road that led to her uncle's sprawling estate near Rice University. Seeing the two-story white colonial and its elaborate terracing brought back memories of her childhood, riding in the backseat of her family's battered station wagon. Every time they went to visit her aunt and uncle, her father had given Stella a lecture about the American dream and why his own father had immigrated to the United States from Sicily when he and his brother were children. She recalled how her father had always called her aunt and uncle their rich relations, bragging about how his brother had taken his modest income at the police department and parlayed it into a small fortune. Stella's uncle had at one time owned a pizza parlor, as well as a dry cleaners, and numerous parcels of commercial real estate.

Her father never matched his brother's success, however, no matter how hard he worked or how much he scrimped and saved. He'd taken the only job he could find that would guarantee him a steady income. He became a building inspector for the county.

Around the time of the fire, the brothers had a falling-out. Stella had always assumed her father's failed attempt to mimic his brother's success had made him bitter and envious. Stella and her brother were no longer allowed to mention their uncle's name aloud in the presence of her father.

What exactly had transpired between the two men, Stella would never know, but she did recall her father making statements to the effect that his brother had abandoned the old ways and values. Only a few days before the fire she heard him call his brother a "no- good, two-bit crook," going on to say that he was a disgrace to the Cataloni name.

Due to the bad blood between her father and his brother, Stella had been surprised that her uncle had been so distraught over her father's death. She could never forget the first few days following the fire, though. Her uncle had come to the hospital to see her, ravaged by grief. Carl Winters had been present as well, and after taking her uncle outside the room to speak privately, her uncle had flown into an uncontrollable rage, causing the detective to have to subdue him.

Drugged and bandaged, her parents dead, her unborn child lost, Stella had listened as Carl Winters read her her rights, then told her she was being charged with murder in the deaths of her parents.

"God," she said, trying to push back the horror of those awful moments. Instead of defending her, her uncle had turned against her. If anyone should be out for blood, she told herself, it should be her, not her uncle or Carl Winters. Her eyes dampened with tears, but she would not allow herself to indulge in self-pity. The past was the past, as Brad had always told her. She had to deal with the present if she wanted to survive.

Glancing in the rearview mirror before she got out of the car, Stella made certain her hair was positioned correctly to cover her scar, then exited and headed up the concrete walkway, bordered with blooming shrubs, to the front porch. Inhaling the scent of roses and gardenias, she rang the bell and waited for someone to come to the door.

Clementine Cataloni flung the door open and saw Stella on the porch. "What do you want?" he said gruffly. "I thought you were in jail."

Stella had forgotten how much he resembled her father. For a moment, she was speechless. "I made bail," she said. "I thought you'd want to see me since I'm in town. I mean, you are my uncle, and I wouldn't mind seeing Aunt Sarah after all these years."

"Oh, yeah?" he said, his lip curling. "Well, you were wrong. We don't need your type around here." He stepped back and had started to close the door when Stella grabbed the doorknob.

"Whether you believe it or not," she said, "I didn't set the fire, and I certainly didn't kill Tom Randall. You're my damn kin," she continued, her voice rising. "Seems like you'd want to stand behind me. If for no other reason, out of respect for my father."

"Tell it to the judge," he said. "I don't have time to listen to your lies. How did you get to be a D.A., huh? Don't those people do background checks? Didn't they know they hired a murderer?"

"You've never listened," Stella yelled at him. "Maybe if you'd taken the time to listen to my side of the story, you would have realized that I didn't do it. The very least you could have done was to try and help Mario, give him a home." She paused and took a breath. "But no, you didn't even do that. You took him in for a few days and then washed your hands of him. You believed that stupid buffoon, Winters, and all his sick lies. Mario and I weren't sleeping together, any more than I was sleeping with Dad."

"You and your brother," he said, shaking his head. "How could you disgrace this family with your sick perversions? You're not Catalonis."

"If I hadn't married Brad Emerson," Stella continued, her voice fierce, "my brother would have ended up living with strangers."

"Get off my property," Clem Cataloni shouted, perspiration popping out on his forehead. "If you don't, I'll call the station and have you arrested for trespassing."

"What happened between you and Dad?" Stella said, lowering her voice. "I remember you being really close at one time. He used to look up to you, admire you. What went wrong?"

The change of subject brought him up short. "Your father was a good man," he said, momentarily setting aside his anger. "He was a simple man, though. He never understood what it took to make it in this country. I know one thing," he said, his eyes narrow again. "Tony didn't deserve the fate he met, what you did to him. Not even a damn dog deserves to be burned alive."

"Did Victor Pilgrim work for you?" Stella said,

stepping forward into the doorway, far enough so that she could see the inside of the living room and the hall leading to the kitchen and dining room. She spotted the plaque on the wall from the Knights of Columbus, right next to the glass case that housed his gun collection. Inside were several high-powered rifles, along with a dozen assorted handguns. "Were you in the Knights of Columbus together? You know," she said, "you and Victor Pilgrim?"

"You fucking slut," he shouted. "Get your lying, murderous ass off my porch before I get my gun after you. Coming here like this, asking me—"

Before she could say anything else, her uncle shoved her out of the way and slammed the door in her face. Instead of becoming enraged at how he had treated her, though, Stella felt a rush of adrenaline. He might not have confirmed it with words and it was in no way proof of anything illegal, but she left convinced that her uncle and Victor Pilgrim knew each other. Just how well was something she'd have to find out. And the way things were shaping up, she'd have to find out fast.

Heading down the walkway to the car, she broke off a gardenia and held it up to her nose. If the state's primary witness was connected to a powerful man like her uncle, she knew there was no one she could trust in the Houston area, no matter what kind of badge they carried or what kind of promises they made. Being a cop was like belonging to a secret society, and as a captain, her uncle had wielded considerable power among the many men he had commanded. That he had retired meant nothing. Once a cop, always a cop. Loyalties were as strong and unfailing as the blood bonds of large families.

Reaching the car, she glanced back at the house. Through a crack in the drapes she saw her aunt's face peering out. The woman would be her trump card, she decided. If she couldn't find out what her uncle was up to through other sources, she might be able to extract information from his wife. A moment later, she saw her uncle's face flash in the window and grimaced as he grabbed her aunt by the shoulder and roughly pulled her away. Angry, loud voices followed. Stella had no doubt that her uncle was making his position perfectly clear. So much for her trump card, she thought. Crushing the gardenia in her fist, Stella tossed it on the ground, leaped into her rental car, and took off.

With her legs on top of her desk, Holly took a bite of pizza and then tossed the rest back in the box. "That was disgusting," she told Carl Winters. "I can't believe you talked me into eating it."

The older detective was sprawled in a chair next to Holly's desk. Unlike Frank Minor's office, her work space was far from plush. With her own money she had purchased an oak bookcase to hold her law books and periodicals, and the county had assigned her three vinyl and chrome chairs. Instead of displaying her less than prestigious law degree, the walls were covered with framed Salvador Dali prints. The pictures on her desk were studio portraits of her ten-year-old daughter in a variety of elaborate dresses. Winters glanced at one and decided that the child must resemble her father. Her face was round and her hair dark, her lips full and pouty, not narrow like her mother's. "Cute kid," he said, picking up one of the pictures and then setting it back on the desk.

"Spoiled rotten," Holly said, glancing at the photo and then over at the detective. "I spend more money on her clothes than I do on my own."

"Do say?" he said. In her customary mini-skirt, the district attorney's legs were like a flashing neon sign and Winters couldn't stop himself from gawking. "Why'd you wear that long dress the other day in court?" he said. "Damn, woman, it's a sin to hide those legs."

"Really?" Holly said, rubbing her hand back and forth on her thigh and causing her skirt to slide up several more inches, then just sitting there and letting Winters feast to his heart's content. Finally she set her feet on the ground and faced him. "Frank Minor thinks he can dictate what I wear now," she said, grimacing. "He wants me to wear my hair tied back and granny dresses. He even insisted that I go to some old-timer's store and buy a pair of lace-up shoes like the damn nuns wear."

"Why?" Winters said, chuckling at Holly's intensity. Even though he enjoyed seeing her legs, he didn't think clothing was something to get all worked up over.

"Minor's an idiot," Holly snapped.

Winters laughed louder. "Other than that—"

"He thinks I'll make a better impression on the jurors," she continued, focusing on a spot over his head. "He wants me to appear more conservative. Since Stella is a woman and we worked together in Dallas, he doesn't want the jurors to think my motive for prosecuting her is based on female jealousy or professional rivalry. You know, now that Stella has made a big name for herself with the Pelham case, every prosecutor in the state is supposedly green with envy."

"I see," Winters said slowly. Holly had some type of tank top on under her navy blue jacket, and now that her jacket was unbuttoned and she was leaning forward, he caught a glimpse of the top of her breasts. Creamy skin, luscious mounds. Before he could get his lust in check, Holly stood, circled behind him, and began massaging his neck and shoulders.

"Feel good?" she asked, pressing her chest into his back.

"I'll give you an hour and a half to stop," Winters said, trying to appear nonchalant while his heart was doing a tap dance inside his chest. He hadn't had sex with a woman in over ten years. Until today he had thought these feelings were dormant. Long way from dormant, he thought, closing his legs so Holly didn't spot his erection.

Her hands suddenly stopped and she returned to her desk. Winters experienced a letdown, then quickly asked himself what he had expected. He was an old goat and she was a pretty young woman. He wasn't so stupid that he didn't know

172

when he was being toyed with, but the look in Holly's eyes was all business now. Whatever had passed between them was no longer present. "Is the report in on the gun yet?" he asked, yanking his collar away from his neck.

"Not yet," she said. "The lab's been snowed lately, so I guess we'll have to wait."

"Ain't gonna find anything," he told her. "To tell you the truth, it's puzzling that she left the gun at the scene at all. Stella Cataloni's too smart to leave her prints on the murder weapon, though, so don't bank on that one."

"Maybe," Holly said, dumping the pizza box in the trash, "and maybe not. She blew this guy away in broad daylight. That's a long way from smart, Carl. Particularly since she threatened him in front of witnesses. We're talking a desperate, irrational woman here."

"Did she think she could get away with it?" Winters asked.

"Of course she did," she answered. "No one kills someone thinking they'll be caught. Stella used to be different. You know, she was feisty and temperamental, but at the same time, somewhat reticent, probably because of the scars. Since the Pelham case, though, she's developed a king-sized ego. I'd probably have a swelled head too if someone as influential as Growman endorsed me on national television." She smiled, her eyes filled with mischief. "Guess Stella can kiss that prospect good-bye, huh? I guarantee she'll never win an election in this state."

"She could be acquitted."

"Not on your life," Holly said, fixing him with

a determined look. "Besides, it doesn't matter. Once you get this much dirt on you, you never come clean."

"With so much going for her," Winters said, "why would she do it? You know, kill someone."

Holly wondered the same thing, but she wasn't about to let doubts slow her down. "How the hell do I know? I guess she thought Growman and his people would get her off, keep us from prosecuting her." At the mention of Growman, her mouth tightened. "Let me fill you in on what I found out today."

"I'm all ears."

"Okay," Holly said, springing to her feet, "I called Hertz and found out Stella rented a car meeting the description that Victor Pilgrim gave us. She rented it the day before the murder and returned it a few hours after someone plugged Randall. I need you to go over there and pick up the original rental receipt and a copy of the charge slip bearing her signature. Also, tow the car to the lab and have them examine it. Even if Hertz rented it to someone else, there might be blood evidence or something else valuable inside it. Make certain you have the lab use the infrared scanner as well. They might pick up traces of blood that can't be seen with the naked eye. We need everything we can get our hands on for the Randall prelim."

"No problem," Winters said. "Are we going to put her in a lineup and see if Pilgrim can identify her?"

"Not now," Holly said. "He claims he couldn't see the woman's face that well, so why do the lineup? If he fails to identify Stella, she can use this to prove her innocence. We can't afford to make any mistakes."

"If Pilgrim knows it was a woman," he said, "then he had to have seen her close enough to identify her. I can get together a photo lineup if you want. That way, if Pilgrim fails to make a positive ID, no one will know."

"I already tried that," she said, tossing a paper clip across the room. "Pilgrim refused. He insists he can't identify the woman. What do you want me to do, Carl? Call the man a liar to his face? He's the only witness we have right now. Besides, he's an ex-cop. If he says black, it's black." She picked up some papers and read through them. "He said he could tell it was a woman because of the long hair. He doesn't know anything other than that. Do you know this guy, by the way?"

"Yeah," he said, "but I haven't seen him in years. Want me to speak to him? Maybe he can improve the description?"

"Just cool it for now," Holly advised. "If you press him, he could bail out and leave us high and dry."

"What I don't understand," the detective said, "is why you decided to try the old case. With Randall dead, you'll never prove it."

"Who knows," Holly said, "we might come up with another witness. Maybe not by the prelim, but before we get to trial."

"Who?" Winters said. "Hell, everyone who was inside that house is dead now."

"Not everyone," Holly said, a devious smile on her face.

Winters shook his head. "You've lost me."

"Stella's brother isn't dead," she said. She reached over and thumped him on the thigh. "Shit, Carl, I thought you knew this case like the back of your hand. Mario Cataloni is a bird's nest on the ground."

"Nah," he said, "you're dreaming. He'll never incriminate his own sister. Those two are tight. Captain Cataloni told me all about them."

"Well," Holly said, "we'll just have to wait and see, then. For right now, get me that rental car receipt, and advise your people to round up all the evidence on the old case. Stella filed a discovery motion today, and Judge Maddox has already signed it. Call her and tell her to meet us at the P.D. tomorrow at one o'clock if she wants to physically inspect the evidence."

The thought of a suspect pawing through vital evidence riled the detective. "Have you gone over the evidence already?" he asked. "I mean, how do you see the case?"

"Of course I've reviewed the evidence," she told him. "It's not the worst case I've ever tried, and it's not the best. We're going to get Randall's taped interview admitted into evidence, so that should fill a lot of holes."

"Can you do that?"

"I'm fairly certain Maddox will rule it's admissible," Holly said. "We would have a problem if the guy was still alive and we couldn't find him, as whatever we presented would be classified as hearsay. Now that Stella blew him away, though, his statement is directly linked to the crime and goes toward motive."

"Sounds good," Winters said, standing to leave.

"Don't forget to call Stella," Holly reminded him.

"Where is she?" he asked. "I can't call her if I don't know where she's staying. For all I know, she went back to Dallas. I don't think the court put any restrictions on her release."

"Where do you think she is? She's staying at Mario's place. Here," she said, scribbling down a number and handing it to him.

Winters wondered what the prosecutor had up her sleeve. One glance at her face, however, and he knew it was no use to ask. When she was ready to tell him, she would. "It's funny," he said, rubbing his chin. "I thought you and Stella were buddies. I never dreamed you'd be willing to prosecute her. Isn't that what you told me when I first approached you and asked you to reopen the case? That the woman couldn't be guilty because she was your friend."

Holly's feet were back on her desk. She craned her neck around to look at him. "I'm friends with the people I need to be friends with," she said. "I thought you knew that, Carl."

After taking a quick swim in the cool blue eyes of Holly Oppenheimer, Carl Winters no longer needed a cold shower. Women just weren't the same as they used to be, he decided, tipping his Stetson before he stepped through the door.

chapter

NINE

When Stella got up the next morning, she was hoping that Mario had returned. Seeing a few cigarette butts in the ashtray that she knew hadn't been there the day before, she decided that he must have come home sometime during the night, and then left again before she had awakened. Stella was deeply concerned. Like all siblings, they'd had their share of arguments over the years, but they had never stayed angry at each other. Was it her fault? Had she been wrong to accuse him? As she was beginning to see her uncle in a more sinister light, she was feeling guiltier over the way she had handled the situation with Mario. His drug use was something she couldn't overlook, though, and she had decided to stay in his apartment. When he came back, she would try to talk him into entering some type of treatment program.

While she was in the kitchen making coffee, Brenda Anderson called. "I want to go to the P.D. with you," she told her.

"Fine," Stella said, holding the phone between her ear and her shoulder while she filled the coffeepot with water. "But why? I personally feel your time could be better used elsewhere. Have you thought of a way to get to Randall's wife?"

"Not yet," Brenda said. "Listen, Stella, I didn't sleep much last night. I've been thinking this through, and I think I have something that might work in our behalf."

"What?" Stella asked, setting the coffeepot down.

"You told me the other day that you would have to reconstruct the night of the fire to find out what really happened, right?"

"Right," Stella said.

"Well, there's a new technology we might want to take advantage of. It's called C.A.D., computer-assisted design. Do you know what I'm talking about? They've been using it to re-create crimes in the courtroom. Some people refer to it as forensic animation."

"I think so," Stella said. "They used it not long ago in a case in San Francisco."

"Right," Brenda said. "But they've used it in other cases as well. It's not easy, Stella. This is very time-consuming stuff. I'll have to contract with an outside computer lab, but I think I can get Growman to bill it to the county, with the understanding that you'll eventually reimburse them."

"Explain it to me," Stella said, pulling up a chair by the phone and taking a seat.

"First," Brenda said, "we'll begin by reconstructing your old house to scale, using the exact dimensions. That means I'll have to get my hands on a set of plans. Hopefully, when they built the house they had to submit the architectural renderings or at the very least, a detailed floor plan. Don't they have to do that to get building permits from the city?"

"My father was a building inspector," Stella said. "He built the house himself. I'm certain you'll find a set of plans on file. He was very meticulous about that type of thing."

"Okay," Brenda told her. "Once we input the dimensions of the house into the computer, we'll take all the evidence and have an independent lab analyze it, tell us what we've got. You know, basically identify it. Then we'll input that information as well. What we're going to do is show the court the house, the people who were inside when the fire broke out, and actually re-create the crime itself. Then we'll know if Randall's statements were truthful. If it's not physically possible for the crime to have happened the way Randall said, you could be exonerated." She paused and took a breath. "Not just on this case, Stella, but in Randall's death as well. If we can prove he lied, that Randall is actually the guilty party, then the state will no longer have a motive for why you supposedly had to kill him."

"Slow down a moment," Stella said, her mind spinning. "How can you re-create the fire? This is on a computer, right?"

"Yes," she said. "But, Stella, you have to see it. It's very lifelike. Just like we will re-create the people who were inside the house that night, we'll also create most of the furnishings. We'll go by old pictures, if we can find them, and of course, information obtained from you and Mario."

"All of our photographs were destroyed in the fire," Stella said. "The only one who might have

180

pictures of my parents and the inside of the house would be my uncle. And he'll never cooperate with us."

"We'll subpoena them, then," the investigator said.

"That could work," Stella said.

"We'll use everyone's exact body weight and height," Brenda continued. "When we get the stage set and the actors ready, we'll set our creation into motion, re- creating the fire itself. Wherever the arson investigators think it started, for instance, we'll start our computer- generated fire. Then we'll feed every possible statistic on the nature of fire into the computer, as well as what type of materials were inside the house. This way we can predict how the fire advanced and what part of the house would have burned next. We should be able to tell where the bodies would have fallen, which of your parents died first, where you and Mario were in the house when it happened, and then explain how you got burned. Don't you understand?" she said. "It will be as close as you'll ever get to reliving that night. When we're finished, you'll finally know the truth."

"You're certain this is going to work?" Stella said, twisting a dish towel in her hands. She'd waited so many years to know the truth. Was it possible that they could actually re-create the exact sequence of events?

"I'm convinced of it," Brenda answered. "That's why I want to go down with you to view the evidence and take pictures. If we're going to do this, Stella, we have to get started immediately or we'll never get it done in time."

"I'll meet you at the P.D. at ten o'clock sharp," Stella told her, glancing at the clock and seeing it was already after nine. "I'm getting in the shower right now."

When Brenda Anderson showed up at the Houston P.D., her hair was tied back and she was dressed in a tailored beige pantsuit. Stella arrived a short time later and found Holly and Detective Winters waiting with Anderson in front of the evidence room.

"You're lucky," the officer told Stella when she stepped up to the window and presented the court order. "Winters over there hauled in almost every piece of junk left in that house. I've been trying to get rid of it for years. If I even move a box, he has a frigging cow. You know how much room this kind of shit takes up?"

"Can you put it in a separate room for us?" Brenda asked, wanting to examine the evidence without Holly and Winters looking over her shoulder.

"No way, man," the officer protested. "It'd take all week to move this stuff. You'll have to do your thing in here. I'm not breaking my back. If you want it moved, you'll have to hire someone."

Brenda smiled at him. "Ah, come on," she said, "be a sport. There can't be that much stuff to move."

"You don't understand, lady," he said, frowning. "This department has more people on disability than any other department in the state. Hell, the city manager told us the other day that the pension fund is almost bankrupt. You hurt your back around here and you're fresh out. Kind of know what I mean?"

"I guess we'll have to make do, then," Brenda responded. When she looked over, Stella had an excited look on her face. "What's up?" Brenda whispered. "Did I miss something?"

Stella shook her head. Something was floating around in her mind, but as yet, she had no way of knowing if anything would come of it.

The officer led them to the back of the large room, crammed to the ceiling with boxes and paper evidence sacks, all cataloged and numbered. Winters and Holly followed and watched as Brenda and Stella started opening the packages and picking through the contents.

At first, it looked like nothing more than a bunch of charred rubble, but Stella soon realized she was holding the shattered pieces of her family's life. Picking up a plastic bag containing a metal Tonka truck that had belonged to Mario, she had to fight back tears as she turned the small toy over in her hands and stared at it through the plastic. Then she spotted something that looked like a marshmallow roasted over a campfire and realized it was the rubber tip off one of her batons. She remembered how she used to march down the football field, high-stepping to the band in her short uniform, tossing the baton in the air and then praying she would be able to catch it. Her fists clenched shut, her fingernails digging into her palms. The days when she could expose her legs were gone. She glanced over at Holly's short skirt and heard her laughing at something Winters had said.

Stella exploded. "How could you do this to me?" she shouted. "I thought we were friends. If this is the way you treat your friends, I'm just glad I'm not your enemy."

"It doesn't look like you're suffering," Holly said, crossing her arms over her chest. "You made bail. You're not in jail. What? Did Growman put up the money for you?" She moved closer. "Are you his little pet now, Stella? I saw you on TV, how you were looking at each other. Don't tell me you're not fucking him, because I know better. That's how you got him to endorse you, isn't it?"

Stella dropped the plastic bag containing the charred piece of rubber from her baton. "Is that why you're doing this to me, because you think I'm having an affair with Growman?" Sam had made a similar statement, and Stella found it baffling. "I'm not sleeping with him," she told her. "You're still bitter because Growman demoted you, forced you to resign. Don't you think it's time you let it go?"

"You're damn right I'm bitter," Holly shot out. "By rights, I should be in your shoes right now."

Stella laughed. "I'd gladly change places with you."

"I didn't mean now," Holly said, realizing how silly she sounded. "Forget it, okay. Just forget it. Sort through your stupid evidence. I have to get back to work."

Once Holly marched past her, Stella started checking the items in the room against the inventory list, trying to make certain everything was accounted for. A few moments later, Brenda appeared at her side. "Look at this," she said. "I have no idea what it is, and the evidence sack doesn't say where it came from."

Stella looked down at what Brenda was holding and saw a plastic bag containing what appeared to be melted chips of metal. Brenda turned to Winters. "Do you know anything about this?"

"I know where it was found," he said, "but the lab couldn't make anything out of it. Those chips could have been anything, see. Once the metal melts like that, it's impossible to tell."

"Where was it found?" Brenda asked.

"In the basement," Winters said. "At least, we think it was the basement. Because the first floor collapsed, it made it difficult to tell."

Deciding to go over the list with greater scrutiny later, Brenda spread all the evidence out on the floor and started snapping pictures. When she was finished, she helped the evidence clerk place it back in the proper sacks and containers.

She motioned to Stella and they left, stepping past the detective without speaking. "Why were you so curious about those pieces of metal?" Stella asked. They were standing on the front steps of the building now and the summer sun was as intense as an oven. "They were so small, how could they be important?"

Brenda popped the roll of film out of her camera, placing it in her pocket to drop off for developing later. "Sometimes it's the little things," she told her, smiling. "You heard a metallic sound that night, right?"

"Right," Stella said. "And the stuff we saw back there was metal."

"Exactly," she said. "Now all we have to do is put Humpty-Dumpty back together again."

They headed off in separate directions, agreeing they would meet for dinner at the TGIF restaurant not far from Mario's apartment. It was one of her brother's favorite haunts, and Stella was hoping they might find him there.

By seven o'clock that evening, Stella's concerns for Mario had reached the breaking point. She called the hotel, and asked Brenda to check the computer and see if her brother had been arrested. "No problem," she told her, asking Stella for his date of birth while she went on- line and entered the Houston system. "Whoops," she said a few moments later.

"Damn," Stella said, grimacing, "I knew it. He's in jail, right?"

"No," Brenda said, "hold on, I have to pull up another file. He isn't in jail now, but he was arrested six weeks ago for possession of a controlled substance. According to this, the drug was cocaine. The arrest shows on his rap sheet, but there's no disposition listed."

"That means the case is still pending?" Stella said, a hand over her chest. "He'll go to jail if he's convicted." She could see her problems multiplying right before her eyes. She didn't have enough money to hire an attorney to represent herself, let alone hire one for Mario.

"Either that," Brenda said, "or the D.A.'s office didn't follow through and file the case.

They could have dumped it for some reason. You know, maybe the stuff he had on him was tested and determined to be something other than cocaine. That happens now and then."

"We need to find out who handled it at the D.A.'s office," Stella said, not willing to tell her what she had found in Mario's darkroom. "Can you get in touch with your friend? You know, your contact down there?"

"If I hurry," she said, "I might still catch him at the office."

"Do it," Stella said. "I have to know what's going on with my brother. You may not think this is related to Randall's death, Brenda, but there's a possibility that it is."

"Just meet me at the restaurant," Brenda told her. "I'll get on the phone right now."

Clem Cataloni's footsteps were heavy as he made his way down the corridor at the Houston Police Department. Dressed in a plaid shirt and tan slacks, his skin was burnished from the sun, but underneath, it had a sickly yellowish cast. Holding his hands out in front of him, he saw his fingers trembling and quickly dropped his hands back to his side. "Hey, Captain," a uniformed officer said, coming up behind him, "did you get the invitation to Smitty's birthday party?"

"Uh, yes," Cataloni said, although he couldn't recall. He spent a few minutes playing with the man's name, trying to place him. Smitty Barnes, maybe, he told himself. Between his contacts in the Knights of Columbus and his friends at the P.D., hardly a week went by without some sort of invitation. At the moment, though, parties were the last thing on his mind. "Got to check my schedule first."

"Gonna be a good one, Captain," the man said, smiling. "Rogers hired a stripper. I know it would mean a lot to him if you could come."

"I'll let you know," he responded, continuing down the hall to Carl Winters's office. Before he reached the door, another man interceded.

Dressed in a dark suit, a withered white shirt, and a red- and-black-striped tie, Chief Earl Gladstone stopped and pumped Cataloni's hand. "I was just going to my office to call you."

Clem Cataloni scowled. Had something happened in the case against his niece? Was this the reason Winters had called and asked him to come down? Stella appearing on his doorstep had unnerved him. After her stint in jail, he had expected a broken and terrified woman. Stella would never break down, he now realized. She was a Cataloni in every sense of the word.

Seeing his niece had brought back many painful memories: his childhood in Sicily, his older brother looking out for him, riding their bicycles down the cobblestone path to town each day. For years after his brother's death, Cataloni had been plagued by nightmares. The dreams were always the same. He was standing on his brother's front porch, begging him to forgive him. Just when his brother smiled and reached out to him, his body erupted in flames. It had been years since he had last experienced the dream, but last night it had returned. He had awakened in a cold sweat, certain his brother was standing by the bed.

"Are you okay, Clem?" the chief asked, sensing something was amiss. "I guess this thing with your niece has been difficult."

Removing a handkerchief, Cataloni wiped his face and neck. "It's the blasted heat," he said. Forcing a laugh, he added, "Are you trying to cut corners by cutting back on the air-conditioning, Earl? It must be eighty degrees in here."

The chief ran his fingers through his salt-and-pepper hair, an impish expression on his face. "Maybe you can give me a hand on the new budget proposal," he said. "You used to be a wizard at this stuff. I thought—"

"Call me next week," Cataloni said, stuffing the handkerchief back in his pocket. "I've got some things to take care of right now."

"No problem," the chief said. "How's Tuesday?"

"Fine," Cataloni said.

Seeing the door to Winters's office, Cataloni stepped inside. The detective had his Stetson off, and his legs were propped up on his desk. For a few moments, Cataloni was taken back. He seldom saw the detective without his hat. Other than a few sickly fringes that circled the lower half of his skull, Winters was completely bald. Without the hat, the detective looked tired and worn. Before long the old brigade would be gone, Clem thought. Who would right the wrongs? The kids they hired today didn't know what it meant to be a cop. To them, it was only a job. He found it sad. "You called," he said.

"Yeah," Winters said. "I stumbled across something interesting." Opening a drawer and removing a small paper bag, he dumped the contents out on his desk. "The investigator from Dallas spotted these metal pieces when she was going through the evidence. I thought we had checked them out years ago, but I guess I must have been mistaken. They're not mentioned in any of the original reports."

"Tell me about this investigator," Cataloni said, anger coursing behind his eyes. Stella was not the average murder suspect, which complicated matters considerably. Not only was she a crackerjack attorney, she was respected enough by her agency that they had even provided her with her own investigator.

"Name's Brenda Anderson," Winters advised, adjusting his body in his chair. "If you want to keep your eye on anyone, this is the gal to watch. She's sharp, Captain. She could blow this case apart."

Cataloni opened his hand to pick up one of the pieces. When he saw his fingers trembling again, he closed his hand into a fist. "You took these out of the evidence room?"

"Well," Winters chuckled, "let's just say I borrowed them."

"You fucking moron," he shouted. "Now that we finally have the situation in hand, you're going to compromise the entire case. Get this stuff back in the evidence room. Does anyone know you took it?"

"Don't you even want to look at them?" Winters said. He started arranging the metal pieces into some type of order. "See," he said, "they spell something, but I haven't been able to figure out what it is yet. If Anderson's hot for them, though, they must be important." He stopped fiddling with the pieces and looked up. "Maybe this is the key, you know."

"The key to what?" Cataloni said, standing stiffly in front of Winters's desk.

"The key to identifying the killer."

Cataloni leaned forward and swiped his forearm across Winters's desk, knocking the chips onto the floor.

"Aw, shit," Winters said. "Now I'll have to pick them all up. Why'd you do that, Captain? If you give me enough time, I should be able to figure out the writing."

"We know who the killer is," Cataloni said, slamming his fist down on the desk. "A few fragments of metal won't exonerate Stella, but if they catch us tampering with evidence—"

Winters was hurt. He puffed out his cheeks, then slowly exhaled. After his wife had passed away, the detective had turned to alcohol to ease the pain. One rainy night he was called out on a homicide after a night of heavy drinking. He'd driven through a red light and broadsided a car in the intersection, injuring several people. Clem Cataloni had stood beside him when everyone else in the department had turned away. The captain had appeared in front of the police review board, getting them to agree to a week's suspension and supervised treatment in lieu of Winters's dismissal. Week after week, Cataloni had shown up on Winters's doorstep to drive him to the mandatory AA meetings. A long time had passed, and for all he knew, Cataloni had forgotten about those days. But Carl Winters wasn't one to forget. If he could hand his friend his brother's killer, he would be able to settle the score. "I just thought—"

"You don't have the brains to think," Cataloni said, still seething. At the door, he paused, letting the anger go. "Just do your job, Carl," he said softly. "I appreciate your efforts, but we can't step out of line here."

Not only was the popular restaurant packed with people, but the noise level was deafening. Everyone seemed to be talking at one time: dishes clattered, glasses tinged, music blasted. Stella looked up and grimaced at the crowded bar, located on a raised platform overlooking the dining area. She hated places like this, but her brother frequented them on a regular basis. He'd told her more than once that this restaurant was the perfect place to pick up girls.

Pushing her way to the bar, Stella ordered a gin and tonic from the female bartender, a tall brunette with broad features and arms laced with sinewy muscles. The restaurant had a carnival feel to it, with the employees wearing referee--style shirts, suspenders with dozens of buttons pinned on them, shorts, and knee socks.

"Hey, you're that district attorney," the bartender said loudly. "I saw your picture in the paper just this morning. Aren't you in a lot of trouble or something?"

"Yes," Stella said, wishing she could sink

through the floor and disappear. She glanced over her shoulder and saw a man staring at her, as if he too had recognized her.

Once Stella got her drink, she plucked some bills out of her wallet, placed them down on the bar, and quickly got lost in the crowd. She had learned her lesson, she decided. After tonight, there would be no more dinners in restaurants. Mario wasn't here, and as soon as Brenda showed up, Stella was going to suggest they pick up something and eat it at the apartment. Either that, or order room service at Brenda's hotel.

She looked around for an open table. No seating was provided in the bar area, only high tables for customers to set their drinks on. Stella had already asked the hostess to seat her in the dining room section, but the girl had refused. The management evidently had a rule that all members of a party had to be present before anyone would be seated. Deciding there was no such thing as an open table, Stella nudged her way to the very back of the bar, taking a spot near the railing where she could keep her eye on the front door.

Thirty minutes passed, and still Brenda had not appeared. Stella's drink was gone and she wasn't about to order another one. Sandwiched in between two men in business suits, she was wearing a long flowered skirt and a lightweight knit top. She never went to bars by herself. She felt self-conscious and silly. Why would anyone want to come to a place like this? Just for the privilege of standing around elbow to elbow like a bunch of sardines?

"How are you fellows doing?" Holly said, slipping in between Stella and the two men and slapping her beer bottle down on the table. "You already met my friend over here?" she said, tilting her head toward Stella.

Stella was flabbergasted. "What are you doing here?"

"This is my town," Holly said flatly. "Guess I could ask you the same thing."

Stella tried to make her way through the people, but Holly pulled her back to the table. "Come on, Stella," she said, "don't run off. Hang around awhile. Let's talk, you know. If you want to settle this, I might be able to approach Minor and work something out. Why put yourself through a trial?"

"Let me go," Stella said abruptly. "I have nothing to say to you."

"I don't think that's true," Holly said, taking a slug of her beer. "Don't you have some unanswered questions about your brother's illegal activities? I thought you were interested in Mario's court case."

Stella was instantly wary. "What are you trying to say?"

Holly said, "What do you want to know?"

Stella looked over her head, and saw Brenda Anderson moving through the crowd of people. Without taking her eyes off the men, Holly leaned closer and whispered in Stella's ear, "The short one isn't bad-looking. What do you think? Think I should make a move on him?"

Stella recoiled just as Brenda appeared at the table. "She's the D.A.," the investigator said, pointing at Holly. "Don't you know what they're doing, Stella? They're holding the charges over your brother's head, trying to get him to turn state's evidence and testify against you in the death of your parents. The cops arrested him for simple possession, but he had enough coke on him to classify it as possession for sale. Your brother's facing a prison sentence, not a jail sentence."

"Not if he cooperates," Holly said, running her tongue over her lower lip. "What do you think he'll choose, Stella? His own neck or yours?" Leaving the question hanging in the air, she disappeared into the crowd.

Stella stood there in shock, trying to sort through what she had heard. "I'm sorry it went down this way," Brenda said. "I guess it's my fault. My contact is a bastard. Maybe it's why I never gave in and slept with him."

"Did you tell him you were meeting me here?"

"Yeah," Brenda said, jerking her head to the side. "I didn't think he'd run straight to Oppenheimer, though. Evidently, I'm not such a good judge of character." She looked over at Stella. "I feel terrible. I made a wrong turn on the way over, or I would have been here sooner."

"What am I going to do?" Stella said, a dazed look in her eyes. "Holly knew about this all along, didn't she? Mario was her ace in the hole."

"Looks that way," Brenda said. "Your name's fairly distinctive, Stella. Once the D.A. decided to file against you, someone in their office must have brought Mario's case to Holly's attention.

She then decided to prosecute it herself, knowing it could give her leverage. Pretty shrewd."

Stella was livid. "She told me she ran into Mario at the gym several weeks back. I guess that was a lie. She probably had him come down to the courthouse so she could coerce him into testifying against me." She paused, not wanting to place the blame on Mario. "When Mario knew her, Brenda, Holly wasn't the same as she is now. He met her at a birthday party for Growman that we threw at the office, back when Holly and Growman were still on good terms."

"Holly knew your brother from Dallas?" Brenda asked, a fluttering of concern in her stomach. "Why didn't you tell me they knew each other?"

"I never thought my brother's future would fall into the hands of the person prosecuting me for murder," Stella said. She saw something that caught her attention on the first level of the restaurant. For a second, she was certain it was Mario, but when the man turned and faced her, she realized she was mistaken. She dropped her head and tried to regain her composure through silence.

"You need to talk to your brother, girl." Brenda popped an ice cube in her mouth, then crunched it loudly with her teeth. "I mean, a serious talk. I don't like the way things are shaping up. If your brother cuts a deal—" She stopped speaking and looked around for the waitress. "This place is a zoo. Wait here, and I'll go get our drinks at the bar."

"I don't want to stay here," Stella said.

"We'll go somewhere else," Brenda answered, "but let's have a drink first. I think we both need it."

Stella stepped back closer to the railing. It seemed as if Brenda was gone forever. She was tempted to find her and tell her to forget the drinks when suddenly she felt something stinging her calves. The next moment, the distinctive odor of smoke rose to her nostrils. "Help me!" she shrieked, her hands clawing frantically at her thighs. "My skirt's on fire."

Stella's eyes were wide with fright. Trapped between the table and the open railing, she shoved the table hard, causing it to tumble forward and strike the two men in the back. "I'm on fire," Stella screamed. "God, help me. I'm on fire!"

"Shit," Brenda shouted, seeing the commotion and Stella trying to leap over the table. Smoke was billowing out all around her, and the hem of her skirt was engulfed in flames. Unable to think of anything else, Brenda raced over and tossed her drink in the direction of Stella's skirt. "What the—" Then she realized the material was still burning. All of the other drinks had spilled when Stella knocked over the table. Brenda had to find something else to put out the fire.

Wild-eyed and terrified, Stella darted through the crowd and then tripped over someone's feet and fell, landing face first in front of the bar. "Put it out," she yelled frantically. "Oh, God, please, put it out." She was rolling around on the floor, sobbing uncontrollably, slapping at the burning fabric with her palms in a desperate attempt to put out the flames. People gawked and stared, but no one attempted to do anything.

Like a linebacker, Brenda used her shoulders to knock people aside. Then she leaped onto the bar and grabbed the hose the bartender used to make drinks, squirting soda water at Stella until the flames were out.

"What happened?" Brenda said, dropping down on her knees next to her.

"I don't know," Stella cried, covering her face with her hands. "I was just standing there, and my skirt burst into flames."

"Let me see how bad it is," Brenda said, reaching for the seared hem of Stella's skirt.

Stella grabbed her hand. "Don't touch it," she said. "Please, Brenda, you'll pull the skin away with the fabric."

People were gathering around them, and Brenda felt hemmed in by a sea of legs. Removing her shield from her pocket, she quickly flashed it. "Get back," she shouted. "This is a police emergency." Once the onlookers stepped a few feet away, she leaned down and spoke to Stella again. "I have to know if you need an ambulance. Please, Stella, let me look at your legs."

"No," Stella said, her eyes enormous, "it's all burned. I know it. I can feel it. What if they have to amputate my legs? God, I'm so scared." She squeezed the investigator's hand.

"Your skirt must have drifted through the railing," Brenda said, her voice soft and consoling. "The person sitting at the table beneath you must have been smoking a cigarette and accidentally ignited your skirt. There have been several recent lawsuits over this kind of fabric. It's highly flammable." She waited until Stella's breathing slowed, and then without asking, gently lifted the hem of her skirt and peered beneath it. "Look, Stella," she said, "it's not much worse than a bad sunburn. You'll have some blisters tomorrow, but it's not serious."

"You're certain?" Stella said, her voice shaking. "Don't lie to me. Please, Brenda, if it's bad—"

"I promise," Brenda said, pulling on Stella's hand. "Come on, let's get out of here."

Once Stella was on her feet, the investigator placed an arm around her waist and walked her down the steps to the restaurant level, her eyes darting over to the empty table beneath the railing where Stella had been standing. She flagged down a passing waitress. "Do you remember who was sitting at that table a few moments ago?"

"No one," the girl said. "See, it's not even set up. That's the table we use to work on the seating charts."

"You didn't see a blond woman over there?" Brenda asked, searching the people's faces at the various different tables on the ground level. "She was in the bar area and we thought she left. It's possible she took a table down here instead."

"If she did," the girl said, "I didn't see her. There was an older man, but he wasn't really sitting at the table. He was just standing over there by the railing."

"What did he look like?"

The girl wiped her hands on her apron. "I

don't remember. I think he had on a navy blue shirt, but I might be mistaken."

Brenda thought of Clem Cataloni. "Did he have black hair? Was he short, tall?"

"Look," the waitress said, "I have customers waiting. I don't remember anything else. I'm not even sure about the things I told you. We see a lot of people in here."

Brenda continued walking with Stella until they were outside the restaurant. "Houston," she said, letting her shoulders fall, "is definitely not my favorite town."

"You don't think Holly did this, do you?"

"I don't really know," Brenda said, shrugging. "She's a mammoth bitch, all right. But setting your skirt on fire? I don't think even she would stoop that low. Like I said, it was probably an accident."

Did Holly's vendetta against her center around Growman? Stella wondered, still weak and terrified. Holly had accused her of being Growman's new pet that afternoon at the police department. Was the D.A.'s endorsement of Stella's future candidacy what had spiked Holly into a frenzy? Enough so that she would make an attempt to set her on fire? "Should we file a police report?" Stella asked, taking several deep breaths as she tried to calm down.

"We could," Brenda said. "I think it's a waste of time, though. There's nothing they can do, Stella. They could try to lift prints from the table, but dozens of people probably sat at that table today. How could we distinguish one set of prints from the other?"

"Maybe Mario did it," Stella suggested, favoring the known over the unknown. "He could have come in and seen me, then become angry that I was hanging out at his favorite restaurant, trying to track him down."

Brenda tilted her head. "You really believe he would do that? Just because you were looking for him? Think about what you're saying, Stella."

"People on drugs do irrational things," she answered.

"No shit," Brenda said.

Stella fingered the scorched hem of her skirt, then dropped her hands to her sides, forcing herself not to think about it. "Did you ever find out about that stewardess?"

"I think you gave me the wrong name. Korean Airlines doesn't have a Kelly Murietta on their payroll."

"Let's go to Mario's house and see if her name and number are in his address book," Stella told her. "I think I saw it in his bedroom this morning."

"You're worried about Randall, right? You think your brother may have shot him to protect you."

"Anything can happen," Stella said, starting to shiver again. "Look what happened tonight. You really think it was an accident?"

Brenda shook her head. "This was no accident. This was deliberate." She met Stella's eyes. "What is the one single thing that frightens you above everything else?"

"Fire," Stella said, without a moment's hesitation. "You think someone wanted to scare me then, frighten me into backing off? But why? Because we've been dipping into the evidence on the old fire?"

"Exactly," Brenda said. "Like I told you before, everything happens for a reason. We know more now than we knew before this happened."

"What?" Stella asked, wrapping her arms around her chest. "You mean, what we found out about Mario?"

"No," Anderson said, glancing behind her and scanning the cars in the parking lot. "We must be getting close, Stella. When someone does something this rash, you know you're moving in the right direction."

"The right direction, huh?" Stella said. "What should we do now?"

"Move faster," Brenda said.

chapter

TEN

As soon as they reached Mario's apartment, Stella left Brenda in the living room and retrieved her brother's address book from the nightstand in his bedroom. "What name did I give you?"

"Kelly Murietta," Brenda said, sitting Indian--style on the floor.

"Okay," Stella said, taking a seat on the sofa and picking up the phone, "I found a Kelly

Muriel, so that must be it. I'm calling her right now."

The phone was picked up on the second ring. "Yes," a woman's voice said.

Stella identified herself and asked her when she had seen Mario last. "Not for months," the woman said. "We had an argument. I'm not seeing him anymore."

"Are you certain?" Stella said, her hands trembling on the phone. "The night I'm referring to is Wednesday of last week. He told me he was with you, that he spent the night with you."

"He lied," the woman said. "Believe me, with Mario, a lie comes easier than the truth. Is he really your brother?"

"Yes," Stella said.

"You better get him some help, then," she said. "He's in over his head. The man's into nose candy. It's the reason I won't see him anymore. I don't want anything to do with that shit."

Before Stella could say anything else, the woman had hung up.

"This is serious," Stella told Brenda. "If Mario wasn't with this woman, where was he?"

"Guess we'll have to wait for him to tell us," Brenda said, pushing herself to a standing position. Seeing Stella's shoulders shaking, she walked over and put her arms around her. "It's going to be okay. I'm sure your brother didn't do it. He's just messed up with drugs, sweetie. Happens in the best of families."

"Do you have any brothers or sisters?" Stella asked, dabbing at her eyes with a Kleenex.

"No," Brenda said, taking a seat next to Stella

on the sofa. "My parents didn't think they could afford to send more than one kid to college, so they only had me. But I have plenty of cousins with drug problems, Stella. It's the world we live in today. Everyone is looking for a quick fix. No one wants to deal with reality anymore."

For a long time Stella was too despondent to move. Brenda insisted on spending the night with her, and Stella finally mobilized herself to go get some blankets. She offered to change the sheets on Mario's bed and let the investigator sleep there, but Brenda said she'd just as soon sleep on the sofa. That way, she said, she could keep an eye on the front door. "If Mario shot Randall," Stella said, handing her the bedding, "he did it to protect me."

Brenda unfastened her shoulder holster, removed her revolver, and then placed them both on the coffee table. "It doesn't matter why he did it," she said, pulling out her shield and tossing it with the rest of her stuff. "No one's going to give him a medal. I don't want to make you feel worse than you already do, but murder is murder."

"Yeah," Stella said, shuffling off down the hall to the guest room. A moment later, she returned. "Don't shoot my brother," she cautioned Brenda. "He may sneak in during the night. I'm almost certain he was here last night. I found cigarettes in the ashtray."

Brenda reached over and picked up her gun, checking the ammo and then placing it back on the table. "Did you save the butts?"

"No," she said. "Why would I do that?"

The investigator's eyes expanded. "Maybe the person who was prowling around in here last night wasn't your brother."

Stella's skin turned cold and clammy. She glanced at Brenda's gun, then rushed out of the room, hoping the investigator was a light sleeper.

In the bathroom, she removed her clothes and doctored the burns on her calves with antiseptic cream. Once she was finished, she yanked all the hair back from her face and stared at the abraded scar tissue by her ear. "What more can they do to me?" she said, picking up the plastic drinking cup and hurling it at the mirror. Feeling her calves smarting from the burns, Stella knew she could be set on fire again, and the thought filled her with terror. Someone had tried to hurt her tonight. Would the person who set her skirt on fire come back tomorrow, next week, next month? "Just kill me," she said to her mirror image. "I'd rather be dead."

When Stella got up and went to retrieve the newspaper the next morning, she found a messenger had dropped the information she had requested on Mario's doorstep. After her trip to her uncle's house, Stella had called and asked for a roster of members for the Houston chapter of the Knights of Columbus. She'd told the person on the phone that she was organizing a charity affair through the mayor's office and needed the names and addresses of their members for the guest list.

By six o'clock, Brenda Anderson had showered, run down to the store for doughnuts, and connected her computer and modem up in the kitchen by tapping into Mario's phone line. As on the day before, they were using Mario's butcher block table as a work station. "Okay," Stella said, still in her bathrobe, "while I get dressed, go through this roster and see if Carl Winters's name is listed."

"Why?" Brenda asked, tilting her head. Pictures and papers were spread all over the table, and the investigator was trying to compare the evidence they had seen in the police evidence room with what was listed on the inventory sheet. She wanted to make certain nothing had disappeared during the sixteen years since the fire, particularly evidence that might provide proof of Stella's innocence.

"I'm trying to link up conspirators," Stella said, seeing Brenda giving her a curious look. "Please, humor me on this one. I know Winters and my uncle knew each other from the department. It's more than that, Brenda. I have a hunch and I want to follow through on it. It could be more significant than you think."

By the time Stella had showered and dressed, Brenda had run the list of men through the computer and had a printout ready for her to review. "Okay," she said. "Winters doesn't show up on the roster, but I did some other comparisons just for the hell of it. Out of the local chapter of Knights of Columbus, fifty-five men are ex-cops. Pretty high ratio since their membership is only about two hundred strong, half of them listed as inactive." She handed the list to Stella. "I've heard they're pretty heavy drinkers, but I

206

never considered the Knights of Columbus to be a sinister organization. What gives, Stella?"

"You said ex-cops?" she exclaimed, a flurry of excitement in her voice. "Victor Pilgrim is an ex-cop. That's our common denominator. What else can you find out? Were the men all retired from the Houston Police Department or did some of them come from the sheriff's department?"

"The computer's searching for that right now," Brenda said, glancing at the screen. "Shit," she said when the response came through, "this is going to be harder than I thought. These men came from all over the state, but you're right, they're all former officers from the Houston PD."

"Well," Stella said, bracing her head in her hands, "I guess that doesn't really mean anything."

"Maybe it does," Brenda said, reading the information directly off the computer screen. "Hardly any of these men were on active status for longer than six months to a year before they were retired. You might stumble across one or two men with backgrounds like this, but not a whole group of men." She looked over at Stella and smiled.

"You really think we have something, then?" Stella said.

"Hold on," Brenda said as her fingers flew over the computer keys. "I'm still checking." She hit the enter button and waited for the computer to respond. A second later, she looked up at Stella. "See this," she said, pointing at the screen, "thirty-one of the fifty-five men are listed as permanently disabled on the city payroll. That means they're receiving full pension benefits. They must have all been injured on duty. Not only that, they were all injured on duty within a time span of six months to a year. I'd say that's a little strange, don't you think? I mean, a bunch of ex-cops belonging to the same organization is interesting, but not anything to jump up and down about. But ex-cops who are also disabled, well, that's more unusual. It's even more intriguing when you consider that Pilgrim was retired on disability as well."

"Are you sure these men are listed as disabled?" Stella said, trying not to leap to conclusions. "I mean, they would still be eligible for disability even if they suffered a heart attack or a stroke, right? They just had to be employed by the P.D. when it happened."

"True," Brenda said, rubbing her chin. "If you give me more time, though, I can probably find out what kind of disability they had, whether it was an on-duty injury or some kind of illness. You're right in one respect. Many of these men are far from youngsters, so they could have been classified as disabled due to an illness." She leaned back in her chair. "Why don't you tell me where you're going with this, Stella? Then I'll know what to look for."

Stella ignored her as she studied the printout. "I think I see a pattern," she said a few moments later. "They were all with other departments at one time, but they were all members of Knights of Columbus. For example, this guy here," she said, pointing to a name on the list, "was with the Dallas branch of Knights of Columbus, and was a deputy with the sheriff's department. He transferred to the P.D. in Houston, and within six months he was retired on full disability. Use him as your test case," Stella told Brenda, sliding the paper across the table. "Check records at the Dallas S.O. and see if this man was ever injured on duty and tried to claim permanent disability, even if it was later denied. If you come back with a positive, backtrack on all of them and check the departments they came from for the same set of circumstances."

"You think this is a scam, right?" Brenda said, arching an eyebrow. "Now I'm getting the picture. What made you think of this?"

"The other day when we were talking to the evidence clerk," Stella said, "he mentioned something about how many men they had out on disability. He said the pension fund was almost bankrupt. Do you remember?"

"Vaguely," Brenda said.

"Let me tell you how it might work," Stella continued. "The men file for disability with their respective departments, get turned down, meet Uncle Clem through the Knights of Columbus, maybe at some of their regional affairs and banquets. They talk over their problems, complain they've been turned down for disability, and Uncle Clem tells them he can get them hired here in Houston. Once they're on the payroll, he proceeds to push through their disability papers. He probably has a doctor helping him with the paperwork on the medical end of it."

"Even if you're right about the pension scam,"

Brenda said, "why would you think your uncle is involved?"

Stella smiled, tapping her fingernails on the table. "He has too much money for a cop. You should see his house, Brenda. My father thought he made all his money on a pizza parlor and a dry cleaners. Those businesses were probably only fronts, a way for him to launder the cash these men were paying him to get their pensions approved."

Brenda was getting excited. "You know what something like this might be worth? Most of these guys are receiving close to their full salary. When you're injured on duty and retire on full benefits, you make only slightly less than you did when you were working. That means these guys are getting paid for doing nothing, and not only that, they'll keep getting checks until they die."

"That's it, don't you see?" Stella said. "Over the course of their lifetime, depending on how old they are when they retire, we're talking about hundreds of thousands of dollars. Also," she added, "think of this. If these men aren't legitimately disabled, and obviously they aren't or they wouldn't have to pay my uncle to get them approved, they can take extra jobs and double their income. That means they could end up making more money this way than when they were cops, and no one's going to take a shot at them. On the outside jobs, they just keep a low profile and ask to be paid under the table."

"They don't even have to do that," Brenda said, leaning forward over the table. "Let's say they're injured for a bad elbow, making it impossible for them to draw their weapon and remain a cop. They can't perform their duties, so they're technically disabled. But they could be an accountant, a salesman, any number of other occupations and still draw a disability check for the rest of their lives. If they get paid on the books, they lose some of their pension, but only a small percentage."

Once she stopped speaking, Brenda's face fell. "This is fascinating stuff, Stella," she said, "but how does this relate to the fire? I'm not here to clean up police corruption in Houston. Growman instructed me to work on your case and nothing else."

"It may not relate to the fire," Stella told her, "but it could be connected to Randall's death. If Victor Pilgrim is a member of the Knights of Columbus and was also retired on disability, he's probably a beneficiary of my uncle's little pension scam. Therefore, my uncle could have orchestrated him stepping forward as a witness. You know, claiming he saw a woman in a white Hertz rental car leaving the scene of the crime."

"I see what you mean," Brenda said, staring at the cursor blinking on the computer screen. "For all we know, Pilgrim might owe your uncle money. Maybe he didn't have the whole sum, and your uncle took care of him anyway. All he did was call the debt due. But how did your uncle know you were driving a white rental car?"

Stella stood, too tense to remain seated. "Easy," she said. "He's got dozens of eyes and ears, remember? The entire Houston P.D. is at his beck and call." Was there really something to pursue, or were they just wasting valuable time?

Stella paced back and forth in Mario's small kitchen, going over in her mind what they had learned. Thirty-one men, all retired on disability after a brief period of employment, all members of the Knights of Columbus, all transfers from other departments. The more she thought about it, the more energized she became, the way she always felt when a case started to come together. In the early stages of an investigation, suspects and possible scenarios seemed to blink on and off like dots on a radar screen. Stella would look at them and see nothing. Then she'd examine them a week later, and see something entirely different. When the blinking dots moved closer together, though, an alarm always sounded. "Conspiracy," Stella said, as if she were issuing a proclamation.

"Okay," Brenda said. "I agree with you that something's going on. But even if your uncle is dirty, it doesn't mean he has anything to do with these killings."

For Stella, though, the puzzle seemed to be falling into place. She sat down, searching for the remaining pieces. "My dad was a straight shooter, Brenda. He decided my uncle was a crook only a short time before the fire. Maybe he learned about my uncle's scam and threatened to expose him."

"His own brother?" Brenda said. "You really believe he would do that?"

"Maybe," she said. "He was terribly jealous of my uncle. Clem seemed to have everything while my father was barely getting by." Her voice softened. "Our house, well, it wasn't much. My dad built it with discarded lumber he found on various construction sites. The walls were paper thin. I don't think he used drywall, because it was too expensive. The walls were made of reinforced plywood, I think, and the house wasn't insulated at all. During the winter, we froze to death, and in the summer months, the heat was unbearable."

"Didn't your father make a fairly good income as a building inspector?" Brenda asked. "The way you're describing it, you were dirt poor."

"He was behind the eight ball," Stella said. "He tried to imitate my uncle by opening up his own construction company, but all he did was run up enormous debts. He could never get the company off the ground. I don't think he had the necessary business skills."

"If your house was that poorly constructed," Brenda said, "no wonder it burned so fast." She stopped speaking and thought it through, trying to test Stella's reasoning. "Let's say your father did threaten to expose your uncle and your uncle tried to stop him, do you think he would be willing to kill an entire family to protect himself? The person you're describing would have to be enormously cruel to do something like that, particularly to his own relatives. Wouldn't he have realized his nephew and niece were inside that house, along with his sister- in-law? It's one thing to kill the person posing the threat," she added, "but it takes a real son of a bitch to risk the lives of an innocent woman and her two children."

"He could have hired someone else to do it," Stella said. She went over to pour herself a cup of coffee and refilled Brenda's cup as well. "Maybe my uncle had one of his police pals take care of it for him. Possibly he didn't intend to kill anyone, only scare my dad into backing off. Then something went wrong, and the fire got out of hand."

"Like someone tried to scare you off last night?" Brenda said, a tense expression on her face. She stood and disappeared into the other room, returning a short time later. She was carrying something in her hands, but took her seat, keeping the object concealed in her lap.

"What's that?" Stella said.

"Have you ever fired a gun?" Brenda asked.

"Never," Stella said, recoiling. "I hate guns. Besides, Brenda, I'd never be able to fire a gun at a human being."

"Once we get the court to hand over a copy of the Randall tape," the investigator told her, "I'm going to have to fly back to Dallas. I've found a lab in Dallas that's willing to create the program we need, but I have to work alongside them and help them to design it correctly. If you're going to stay here in Houston, you need protection." She placed a 9mm Ruger on the table, the gun striking the butcher block with a resounding thud. "This is from my personal collection. I want you to keep it." She picked up the gun and removed the clip. "It's fairly easy to use," she said, slamming the clip back in place and setting the gun in front of Stella. "All you have to do is point it and fire. I'll give you another ammo clip just in case you need it. There's fifteen rounds in every clip."

Stella shook her head. "I don't want it," she said. "I could never point that thing at someone and pull the trigger. Just the thought of it makes me sick."

Brenda's voice was loud and jarring. "If someone tried to set you on fire again, do you think you could pull the trigger? You know what it feels like to be burned. Could you suffer that kind of agony again? Maybe next time, Stella, they'll make certain you don't survive."

"I'd rather die than go through what I went through before," Stella said, touching the right side of her face.

Brenda said, "Take the gun, Stella. If what you suspect is true, and your uncle has been running a disability scam, the people you could be up against will definitely be armed. They're all ex-cops. Think about it." She grabbed a doughnut out of the box on the table and took a bite. Then she set it back on her napkin. "Your father and uncle were from Sicily, right? This little scheme of your uncle's smacks of the mob. Maybe your uncle was connected to one of the crime families out of Sicily and your father didn't realize it."

"That's ridiculous," Stella said. "They were both children when they came over here."

"What about your grandfather?" she asked. "If he was involved in organized crime in Sicily, your uncle could have gotten his feet wet as a young man. Don't kid yourself, Stella. These people start early. Who was the older of the brothers?"

"My father," Stella said. "I think that's why he became so envious of my uncle's success."

"Well," she continued, "have you ever thought of the possibility that both your father and uncle were involved in this scam together, both of them connected to organized crime? You know how many people bribe building inspectors?" She stopped and sighed. "A building inspector and a police captain. Shit, Stella, can't you see how valuable these occupations could be to the Mafia?"

"My father wasn't a wiseguy," Stella said, finding the mere thought preposterous. "He was about as far from a criminal as a person can get. He was a simple man, a workingman, just trying to raise his family and give us a decent life. If he had been a gangster, don't you think we would have lived in something nicer than a shack?" She laughed. "You've been watching too many old movies, Brenda."

"It's your neck," Brenda shrugged. "But if you stay here in Houston, you better have a way to protect yourself. I feel certain your life is in danger. Last night was just a tease, a little wake-up call. Someone wants to give you a taste of what you can expect if you don't stop digging."

"I don't want the gun," Stella said, pushing it back across the table. "If I ever get out of this mess, I want to build my political platform on this very issue. I can't very well tote a gun around and claim I'm a gun control advocate."

"You'll never get elected in Texas on a gun control platform," the investigator said.

"I'll probably never get elected, anyway,"

Stella answered, disappointment etched on her face. She wasn't one to throw her hands up and quit, but in this regard, she knew her dreams were light-years from reality. Even if she were completely cleared, she would always be "that Stella Cataloni"—the prosecutor who had been charged with murder.

"If you won't take the gun," Brenda continued, "then you'd better get out of Houston. As long as you stay in this town, you're a sitting duck."

"I'll go back to Dallas, then," Stella said. She went to pack her things, leaving the gun on the table.

At one o'clock that afternoon, Stella appeared for an evidentiary hearing in Judge Maddox's courtroom. Brenda had insisted that she get the court to release a copy of the Randall tape, along with the melted metal samples they had found in the evidence room.

"Your Honor, I don't have a problem with the Randall tape," Holly Oppenheimer responded once Stella had set forth her request, "but why do they need a few pieces of metal? We're conducting tests on these items as we speak. I sent them to the crime lab just this morning. What am I supposed to do? Abandon our tests and just hand over anything they want?"

"The prosecution has had these samples in their possession for sixteen years," Stella argued, "and they still haven't been able to identify them. The law affords the defense the right to conduct independent testing. If we don't acquire these samples immediately, we won't be able to conclude the tests prior to the prelim next week."

They argued back and forth for the next thirty minutes before Judge Maddox finally issued her ruling. "I think Ms. Cataloni has made her point," she said. "The People have been in control of the evidence and have had ample opportunity to conduct any number of tests should they have desired to do so. The evidence in question will therefore be transported to the lab Ms. Cataloni has designated on Thursday of this week, to be returned the following Tuesday. As to the Randall tape," she continued, "I would assume a copy of it could be made available today. Is that correct, Ms. Oppenheimer?"

"Yes, Your Honor," Holly said, slapping back in her seat.

Brenda Anderson slipped in the back door of the courtroom and quietly made her way to the counsel table. Taking a seat next to Stella, she leaned over and whispered in her ear.

Stella sprang to her feet just as the gavel was about to come down. "Your Honor," she said, "a serious discrepancy has just been brought to my attention. One of the metal pieces has disappeared. It's listed on the inventory sheet, but no longer physically present in the evidence room." She pointed at Holly. "Ms. Oppenheimer is purposely trying to sabotage any tests we might conduct. If the missing evidence isn't located by tomorrow," she said, "I shall have to ask the court to continue the prelim to a later date. We have to be able to examine the evidence in order to prepare a proper defense."

"Are you aware of this problem?" Judge Maddox asked Holly, a scowl on her face.

"This is a sixteen-year-old case, Your Honor," Holly said. "The defense knows perfectly well how difficult it is to control a large quantity of evidence for so long. They're using this as a ploy to buy additional time and delay the court proceedings." She glanced at Stella and snarled, "We resent the implication that a member of the prosecution team would purposely tamper with evidence. Ms. Cataloni can't make allegations like this without proof."

"Settle down, Ms. Oppenheimer," Judge Maddox said. "Why don't we handle it this way?" She jotted some notes in the file and then rendered her ruling. "A complete and thorough search of the police evidence room is hereby ordered to locate the missing evidence. This search shall be conducted immediately and the results made available to this court by nine o'clock tomorrow morning. If the evidence isn't located, I'll consider the defense's motion for a continuance at that time."

"There's no way we can comply with this order," Holly shouted. "It could take weeks to sort through all the items contained in the evidence room. The sample they're referring to is only a little larger than a thumbnail." She dropped her voice and continued, "There's no way to arrive at a positive identification, Your Honor, no matter how many tests they plan to conduct. The metal pieces have been already examined at an earlier date and described as an aluminum alloy. Due to the intense heat inside that house, the metal is melted and unrecognizable. There's no way to tell what type of object this metal came from, therefore, the defense's request is invalid."

"But your agency is testing this material right now," Judge Maddox said. "Isn't that what you said, Ms. Oppenheimer?"

"Well, yes, Your Honor," Holly said reluctantly, realizing she had talked herself into a corner, "but these are only perfunctory tests. We don't anticipate discovering anything earth shattering. The object is probably something innocuous like a piece of cookware or an aluminum teapot, not exactly the type of evidence Ms. Cataloni needs to prove her innocence."

"My ruling stands," Judge Maddox said abruptly. "This court is adjourned until nine o'clock tomorrow morning."

As soon as they got out of court, Stella and Brenda Anderson picked up a copy of Randall's taped statement from the D.A.'s office, then rushed back to Mario's apartment to play it. After the tape clicked off, Stella shook her head in disbelief. "If Randall had only told this story sixteen years ago," she said, "he might still be alive today."

"What do you mean?" Brenda asked.

"When Carl Winters first contacted him after the fire, he didn't mention seeing my father arguing with an unknown man in the front yard. Don't you see, Brenda?" she said. "This person must have been my uncle. Randall even heard my father call the person a crook, and my dad had started calling my uncle a crook right before he died. This confirms everything we talked about this morning."

"Possibly," Brenda said, a look of concern on her face. "It also confirms what I've been trying to tell you. You're in danger, Stella. I've been making inquiries into your uncle's affairs all day, calling and faxing all the various police departments throughout the state, asking specific questions as to why these men decided to transfer to Houston, and whether they ever tried to claim disability. How long do you think it will be before someone puts two and two together and alerts your uncle? Police officers are very clannish. If he doesn't know already, I guarantee he'll know by tomorrow or the next day."

"He killed Randall, see," Stella said. "He must have got his hands on his statement through his connections at the police department. Then he became terrified that I'd figure it out once I heard Randall say he had seen my father arguing with someone that night on the lawn. So, he shoots Randall, thinking that will put an end to it. The state no longer has a witness, and therefore no reason to reopen the case. His nasty little secrets stay buried forever."

"Why did he have Victor Pilgrim step forward, then?" Brenda countered. "Once he gave the state another witness, he erased what he had accomplished by killing Randall."

"How do I know?" Stella snapped, tense and irritable. "Maybe he did it just to make certain I took the fall for Randall's death. He's always believed I killed my father."

"I just think there's more to this than meets the eye," Brenda said. "If you could just remember the night of the fire, I'm certain you'd recall something significant. Maybe you saw the killer himself and that's why you suppressed it."

Stella's head was spinning. Was it possible? When she tried to think back to the night of the fire, it was as though a wall came down and there was no way she could pass through it. "There's no use discussing it," she told her. "I can't remember. I've tried for years and I just can't."

Brenda said, "I have an idea. It's a little radical, but it might work. We have to circumvent your memory somehow and get you back to the night of the fire, tap directly into your subconscious. It's all there, Stella. All we have to do is find a way to get to it."

"I've already been hypnotized by a shrink and it didn't help. All I recall is the clicking noise I told you about and seeing my father's face when he raised something in the air."

"You need something to stimulate your memory," the investigator continued. "If I could put you inside that house again, re-create the fire exactly, it might all come back."

"Well, you can't do that," Stella said, flicking her fingernails.

"Yes, I can," Brenda said. "I picked up the plans for the house today. I've already faxed them to Oracle Laboratories in Dallas. I have the coroner's reports, the arson investigator's findings, the police reports, and photographs of the evidence collected, everything but the missing pieces of metal. I know where the bodies were

222

found. All I need from you, Stella, is a description of the furnishings and how they were positioned in the house, along with some snapshots of your mother and father."

"I don't know what you're talking about," she said.

"Okay," Brenda said, "we're planning on re-creating the crime by using forensic animation. Meaning, the jurors will see a partial depiction of what occurred that night, but without the feeling that they are actually present. They'll just see a computer-generated program, similar to an animated videotape. With a little extra effort and the right equipment, we can take it to another level." She stroked the side of her face, hoping she wasn't promising too much. Something this complex normally took months. They didn't have months, but with the right people, she believed it could be done. "I can put you in a virtual reality environment at the lab, and it will be almost identical to reliving that night. It could be terribly traumatic, Stella. Do you think you can handle it?"

"This is all on a computer, right?" Stella said, not understanding why Brenda was making such a big deal. "I mean, you're not going to set me on fire, so I can't see how it could be so traumatic."

"Good," she said, "let's get busy right now." She pulled a yellow pad out of her briefcase and placed it on the table. "Start by telling me everything you remember from the night of the fire. Oh, and I need those photos."

"I don't have them," Stella said. "I told you everything was destroyed in the fire."

"I'll see what I can do," Brenda said. "I'll start working on that aspect of it today. As soon as the hearing's over tomorrow morning, we'll fly back to Dallas and make all the arrangements."

The house was located in the Bellaire section of Houston. It was constructed out of red brick, and the yard was shaded by mature elms and cedars. At nine o'clock that evening, the front of the house was dark, and from all appearances, no one was home. The only light burning was in the master bedroom, located at the rear of the house.

Holly stepped out of the bathroom, a towel wrapped around her wet hair. Dressed in a transparent lace negligee, she snapped at the man in the bed, "I told you to go. My ex-husband is bringing Tiffany home any minute. I don't want him to see your car in the driveway. He doesn't like me to entertain men when my daughter is in the house."

The man was resting face down on the bed. His skin glistened with perspiration, his back and arms solid muscle.

"Are you deaf?" Holly shouted. "You promised you'd be gone by the time I got out of the shower. Why are you still here?"

He groaned, rolling over onto his back and staring up at the ceiling. "We have to talk," he said tensely. "I can't do what you want, Holly. There's no way I'll testify against my sister."

Her face hardened. "You'll do exactly what I say," she said. "If you don't, the only person you'll be fucking is your cellmate at Huntsville."

She threw her head back and laughed, a sinister, grating sound that caused Mario to flinch. "Correct that, okay?" she said. "They'll be fucking you, sweetie. You'll be on the receiving end."

"God," he said, rolling over and burying his face in the pillow, "how did I ever get involved with a bitch like you?"

Holly strode to the bed and smacked him on the buttocks. "A bitch, huh?" she said. "I might not seem like such a bitch after those hairy cons get a look at this tight little ass of yours. You'll be the belle of the ball, Mario."

"You're despicable," he said, leaping to his feet and grabbing his pants off the chair. He stepped into them and yanked up the zipper. "All you care about is your fucking career, making a big name for yourself at Stella's expense."

Holly leaned into his face. "And you, Mario?" she said, grabbing a handful of his chest hair and pulling on it. "What do you care about? A little coke and you're in hog heaven. How are you going to get to heaven in prison?"

Mario knocked her hand away. "I'll take my chances with the judge," he muttered, his chest heaving. Then he looked out over the room. "I don't have a bad record. This will be my first felony conviction. The only other time I was arrested, I was a juvenile, so they'll probably just put me on probation."

"Hey," she said, "if you want to roll the dice, be my guest. They don't like drug dealers in Texas, though," she added. "I can almost guarantee you'll go to prison. Besides," she said, "I'll argue for prison. I always get what I want when I set my mind to it. I got you, didn't I?"

Mario grabbed his shirt and shoved his arms into the sleeves, his face flushed with rage. Finally dressed, he stormed out of the room, made his way through the house, then jumped in his Corvette and roared off.

chapter

ELEVEN

When Sarah Cataloni came to the door, she opened it only an inch. "What do you want?" she said.

Brenda Anderson flashed her shield. "D.A.'s office," she said, hoping the woman didn't notice the city insignia for Dallas. "We need your help. Do you mind if I come in?"

"My husband isn't here now," the woman said, hiding her body behind the door. A small woman, with dull brown hair and a heavily lined face, she eyed the visitor on her porch with suspicion.

"Perhaps you can help us, then," Brenda said. She had to get Stella's aunt to drop her guard. "What we're looking for are some snapshots of Stella Cataloni's parents. We need them for the trial."

"Why do you need pictures?" Sarah asked. "The poor people are dead."

"Ah," she said, "we want them to show the

226

jury what they looked like. You know," she continued, "that way the victims seem more real to them. It's particularly important when a case is this old."

"I don't have any pictures," Sarah said, trying to close the door. Brenda wouldn't let her, though. She put her foot inside the threshold. "Clem threw them all away. They upset him too much."

Guilt, Brenda thought. The man was so guilty, he couldn't stand to look at his brother's face. "Do you know any other relatives who might have pictures?"

"Maria has pictures," she said. "She lives in San Francisco. She's my husband's first cousin. Would you like me to get her address?"

"Yes, please," Brenda said. "And her phone number as well."

Sarah Cataloni disappeared inside the house and then returned a few moments later. "I don't think Stella is guilty," she said. "Do you know where she is, Officer? Clem told me she made bail."

"Of course," Brenda said. She tried to maintain the same detached demeanor, but it was hard to quell her excitement. They had their first major witness, and Brenda had snatched her right out of the enemy camp. On the witness stand, every word out of Sarah Cataloni's mouth would be solid gold. "Is there something you want me to tell Stella?"

Sarah sucked in a deep breath and then slowly let it out. "It was so awful, you know. My husband's a fair man, but as in many families, there were problems. Clem and his brother were estranged at the time of his death. There was a great deal of animosity between them."

"I see," Brenda said slowly. "That doesn't explain Captain Cataloni's belief that your niece killed her parents. If you know something—"

Sarah brushed a few wispy strands of hair off her face. "Young people have few regrets," she said, staring deep into Brenda's eyes. "When you get a little older, perhaps you'll understand. When you blame yourself, or you're torn up over something you didn't say or do, it's the worst pain imaginable."

Brenda nodded, but remained silent, fearful anything she might say would stop Sarah from continuing.

"Well, what I'm trying to say," Sarah continued, "is a person must eventually find a way to relieve themselves of this burden. My husband could not right the wrongs with his brother, so he transferred his guilt to someone else. When Tom Randall said Stella was responsible for setting the fire, Clem believed him." She paused, a birdlike hand appearing on the edge of the door. "He believed it, you see, because he wanted to believe it."

If only I had brought a tape recorder, Brenda thought, knowing Stella's aunt could recant her statements once she got to court. They would have to subpoena her right away, she decided, and depose her under oath.

"Wait," Brenda said, seeing Sarah closing the door, "didn't you want me to give a message to Stella?"

For several moments, Sarah was deep in thought. To Brenda, it seemed as if she had waited many years to say what she was about to say. "Tell Stella I'm sorry things ended up this way," she said, "and that I do care about her. After the fire, I wanted to take Stella and Mario in to live with us, but Stella's wounds were too severe, and of course, Clem wouldn't hear of it. We *did* take Mario for a few days. That poor boy," she said, her eyes misting over. She stopped and composed herself, dabbing at her eyes with her fingers. "There's no use discussing it now. We had another young man staying with us back then, a foster child who was very troubled. It didn't work out."

Just as she was handing Anderson the paper with the address and phone number on it, a man with a scowl on his face appeared behind her and snatched it right out of her fingers. Brenda repeated the phone number several times in her mind, committing it to memory.

"Who are you?" Clem Cataloni said. "What are you doing at my house, bothering my wife this way?"

"I'll just be going," Brenda said, turning to head back down the steps.

"Come back here," he shouted. "I want to see your identification. You're not with the Houston D.A.'s office. Stella sent you, didn't she? You're the damn Dallas investigator. What kind of underhanded—"

Brenda glanced back over her shoulder, but she didn't stop. Cataloni was on his porch now, and she saw a bulge under his knit shirt that she knew was a handgun. Firing up the engine on her rental car, she sped away, leaving a streak of rubber on the asphalt driveway. Clementine Cataloni might not be a mobster, as Stella kept insisting, but Brenda had no difficulty now casting him as a killer.

After grabbing a quick dinner at a fast-food restaurant with Stella and advising her of what she had learned from Sarah Cataloni, Brenda headed off to her hotel room to continue compiling all the details Stella had given her on the fire, and to see if she could get in touch with Stella's relative in San Francisco and obtain the necessary photos. They could proceed with or without them, she told Stella, but she wanted the program they created to be realistic. The photographs would help.

Stella returned to Mario's. She called Sam the moment she stepped through the door. "How awful," he said, once she had relayed the latest developments. "You mean your uncle was committing crimes while he was a police captain?"

"It's more than just the pension scam," Stella told him. "We suspect he may have started the fire to keep my father from exposing him. Then he shot Randall so they wouldn't reopen the case."

"You could be next, Stella," he said, his voice edged with fear. "When are you coming back? I can't just sit here and worry about you. It's driving me crazy."

"Don't worry about me," she said. "Brenda's

with me all the time. Besides, I've decided to fly back tomorrow afternoon."

"I've missed you, Stella," he said softly.

"I've missed you too."

Stella hung up and went to take her clothes off in the guest room. Suddenly she stopped and remained perfectly still. Someone was inside the apartment. She heard footsteps coming from the direction of the living room. Panicked, she ran to the laundry room off the kitchen, shutting the door and locking it behind her. Then she remembered her skirt catching fire and realized the intruder might try to set a fire in the apartment. Afraid she would become trapped inside the small room, she cracked the door and peered out.

Mario was walking down the hall. "You scared me to death," she cried. "Why didn't you say something when you came in? Don't sneak up on me like that."

"This is my apartment, remember?" he said. He continued down the hall and then stopped, turning back around to face her. "What are you scared of, anyway? You're not scared of me, I hope."

"No," Stella said, her heart still racing. She went into the bathroom and splashed cold water on her face. Mario followed her to the door, and she saw him in the mirror. "I'm sorry about the things I said the other day. You know, accusing you of shooting Randall and all. I think I know who's behind this, Mario," she told him. "Not just Randall's death, but the fire as well."

"Who?" he said.

"Uncle Clem," she said. "I've been working

with Brenda Anderson all day. She's the investigator from Dallas Growman sent down. Do you want to hear what we found out?"

Mario grimaced, a whiff of Holly's heavy cologne drifting to his nostrils. "Can't I take a shower first?"

"Whatever," Stella said, annoyed that he had waltzed back in as if nothing had ever happened, seemingly more concerned about his shower than listening to what she had to say. Leaving him standing in the hall, she headed to the living room and flopped down on one of the white sofas. Mario trailed after her, though, and stood just inside the entrance. "Does this mean your shower can wait?" she said. "I mean, I wouldn't want to impose on you or anything."

"Go ahead, Stella," he said. "I'm listening."

Mario slouched on the sofa across from her, stretching his long legs out in front of him. Once Stella had finished outlining the day's events for him, she said, "Brenda checked with the other departments these police officers were with before transferring to Houston, and they all applied for disability before they put in for a transfer. In each instance they were turned down. They arrive in Houston, work six to eight months, and bingo, they're retired on full pension."

What his sister was saying made sense, but Mario knew his uncle would not fall easily. He recalled the time he'd spent at his uncle's house while Stella was still hospitalized from her injuries. Finding the atmosphere at his uncle's unbearable, Mario had climbed out of his window one night in an attempt to escape and find his sister. He'd only made it a block before his uncle had found him. Walking down a dark sidewalk at three in the morning, Mario had heard a car engine, and then a few moments later, found himself staring down the barrel of his uncle's shotgun. "Get in the car," his uncle had shouted. "I'm not about to raise a juvenile delinquent. You live in my house, you follow my rules. If you don't, I'll make arrangements for you to spend some time in juvenile hall."

Mario closed his eyes and tried to look at it objectively. It was one thing for Stella to stand accused of a crime she didn't commit, but she was turning the tables now and pursuing a man he felt certain was dangerous. Knowing his uncle, Mario decided he probably feared incarceration less than he feared public exposure. If he had killed his own brother to keep him from exposing him, he would not hesitate to silence Stella. "Can you prove this?" he asked. "If you can't—"

"Of course we can prove it," Stella said. She looked down at her hands nervously. "Well, maybe I'm being overly optimistic. We can prove the men applied for disability and were turned down, that they were all members of the Knights of Columbus. We know they're all classified as disabled now. Proving Uncle Clem arranged it all is something else, though. Brenda Anderson is checking, trying to see if the same doctor handled all the medical exams." She sighed. "Of course, even if it was the same doctor, we'll still have to connect him to Uncle Clem somehow."

"So, you don't have shit," he said, tossing his hands in the air. "What? Are you going to run over there and accuse Uncle Clem now? That's what you did to me. The only difference is Clem will shoot you."

"I said I was sorry," Stella said, downcast. "Can't you accept my apology? I've been under a lot of stress."

Mario gave her a scathing look.

Stella's face softened. "I love you, guy. We've always been a team. I got frightened when you didn't come to the jail to see me. I was certain you were trying to hide your involvement in Randall's death."

"I spent that night with my girlfriend," he told her, pulling his cigarettes out of his pocket and lighting one. "I told you that already."

"The stewardess?" she said.

"Yeah," Mario said, refusing to meet her eyes.

"What's her name?"

"Kelly," he said, flicking his ashes on the carpet.

Stella bristled. Should she confront him, tell him she knew he was lying? If she did, he would probably vanish again, and she didn't want that to happen. She decided to play along, hoping her brother's lies were related to his drug use and she could embarrass him into telling her the truth. "Is she in town now? We need to talk to her, make certain she remembers the dates and times you were with her. Sometimes people get things confused in their mind."

"I'm not accused of Randall's death," Mario said, puzzled. "Why do I need an alibi?"

"I don't know," Stella shrugged. "I just think it's better to be safe than sorry. What if they exonerate me and then decide to go after you? With Uncle Clem involved, there's no way of knowing what's going to happen. If he bombs out trying to pin it on me, maybe he'll try to pin it on you."

"It doesn't matter," Mario said, stabbing his cigarette out in an ashtray. "For all I care, you can tell them I killed the bastard. I'm going to prison regardless."

Mario started to walk off, but Stella called him back. "I'm sorry," she said, "but when you get involved with drugs, you have to anticipate something like this will happen. Brenda said you had more than just a little coke on you. She thinks they're going to file on possession for sale. That means you had to have a substantial quantity. Are you dealing drugs, Mario?"

"No," he shouted. "There you go again. Every time I see you, Stel, you accuse me of something else. I hear there was a murder in Hermann Park today. Are you going to accuse me of that as well?"

"Why did you have so much coke, then?" she asked.

"You know how it goes," he said. "Some of my friends like a little blow now and then, so I score for all of us. If we buy in bulk, we get more for our money."

"It's nice to know you're so frugal," Stella said.

"I'm not an addict," he pronounced emphatically. "I can quit anytime I want."

"Sure," she said, shaking her head. "And I'm not facing a murder rap."

"No, really, Stella," Mario insisted, "I'm not

addicted. I swear. I just get depressed sometimes, and the coke helps. I don't use every day. Sometimes I don't use for weeks at a time."

"What about Holly?"

He blanched, taken aback. "What about her?"

"Brenda Anderson thinks she's going to offer you a deal if you testify against me," she said. "Is that true?"

"What could I tell them?" he said, an anguished look on his face. "I didn't see anything. I don't know anything. I was asleep when the fire broke out. That's not exactly compelling testimony. Even if I do cut a deal, I don't see how it can hurt you."

"Don't be a fool, Mario," she exclaimed, realizing he might do exactly what Holly wanted. How could it be possible that Mario would turn against her? She'd always protected him, looked out for him, solved all his problems. Although everything she had done had sprung from her love for him, she realized now that she had done her brother a disservice. She had pampered him in his early years, and now he expected the world to do the same. Mario was looking for the quick fix, the rescue, anything that could keep him out of a jail cell. If he had to sell his own sister down the river to protect himself, he just might do it.

"Don't think for one minute they won't ask you to incriminate me," she said. "They'll dictate every word you say. Either that, or they'll get you up on the stand and get you confused, lead you around in circles until you say things you never intended to say."

"So I should just let them send me to prison, huh?" he said, his shoulders squared in defiance.

"I didn't say that," Stella snapped back. "You're not an attorney, Mario. You don't understand. Just by the mere fact that you're cooperating with the prosecution, you'll make me look bad in the eyes of the jury. You're my damn brother, for Christ's sake."

Mario's face flushed. "When you're in trouble," he said, "it's a big fucking deal. But it's fine for me to get shipped off to prison just so I don't make you look bad. What? Just because I'm not some hotshot attorney, my future doesn't count?"

"I'm on trial for murder, Mario," Stella said. "I don't think that's the same thing as a drug rap."

They both fell silent, tension coursing through the air. Stella didn't understand how their lives had taken such a drastic turn. Mario had been a successful photographer, while she had been at the height of her career. How could they be arguing about which one of them was in more serious trouble?

Mario took tentative steps toward her and then stopped. Stella saw the dark circles etched under his eyes, the unhealthy pallor, how terribly gaunt he was. "I don't want us to fight anymore," she said, the words catching in her throat. "I feel so alone right now. It's like everyone's abandoned me."

"Maybe you abandoned me, Stella," he said. "You know how many times you've come to see me since I moved back to Houston? What it is?

Once, twice. You're so busy with your career, it's as if I don't exist anymore. Every time I try to call you, I get some snooty secretary."

"I would have called you back," she said, sniffling. "All you had to do was leave a message. I can't pick up every call myself."

Mario was standing in front of her now. He extended his hand and Stella accepted it, letting him pull her to her feet. Before she knew it, she was in Mario's arms. "I'm sorry," she said. "I guess I did the same thing to you that I did to Brad. I was just so busy."

"It's okay," Mario said, pressing her head down onto his shoulder. "We're together now. Nothing's ever going to come between us again."

"Promise," Stella whispered.

"I promise," Mario said.

Stella strode into the courtroom for the morning hearing exactly at nine o'clock. She glanced over at the counsel table, expecting to see Holly, but the prosecutor had not arrived yet. Since no other hearings were scheduled on the morning calendar, the judge couldn't move to another matter, and everything came to a screeching halt. Stella hated watching a fully staffed court in limbo. With every tick of the clock, she saw another dollar of the taxpayers' money go out the window.

Judge Maddox leaned over and asked her clerk to call Oppenheimer's office. "Tell Miss Oppenheimer I'm about to hold her in contempt."

"She isn't there," the woman said a minute

later, replacing the phone in the cradle. "They claim she's on the way."

"I guess we'll recess, then," the judge said, standing to step down from the bench. Just then the back doors flew open and Holly marched down the aisle.

"Glad you could join us, Counselor," Judge Maddox said, snatching the file back from the clerk and retaking her seat. "Five more minutes and you might have been visiting the inside of a jail yourself. Your habitual tardiness must stop, do you understand?"

"Forgive me, Your Honor," Holly said, taking her seat.

Judge Maddox proceeded to call the case. Once they were officially on record, she said, "You were to produce the missing evidence, Ms. Oppenheimer. That's why we scheduled this hearing, in case you've forgotten."

"We can't find it," Holly said, glancing over at Stella. "We've searched the entire evidence room and it isn't there. Allow me to point out to the court that this was a very small item, and over sixteen years have passed."

"We can't proceed without seeing this evidence, Your Honor," Stella said, her voice loud. "I'd like to request a continuance at this time. Ms. Oppenheimer is withholding this evidence intentionally."

"I'll agree to a continuance," Judge Maddox said, "but I want to see you both in chambers." They selected a new date for the preliminary hearing and the judge exited the bench.

Holly and Stella reluctantly followed, passing

through the door behind the bench leading to the judge's chambers. Her office was well appointed and spacious. A large mahogany desk with a marble top faced out over the room, and a round conference table was situated in the far corner. The two women stood until the judge was seated, then took chairs in front of her desk. "I won't tolerate a hen fight in my court," she said. "Do I make myself perfectly clear?"

"Don't look at me," Holly said, kicking her leg back and forth. "She's the one tossing out all the accusations."

"Let me attempt to explain," Stella said, speaking softly. "This woman hates me, Your Honor. She has some kind of personal vendetta against me. It seems to be based on jealousy and professional rivalry. I'm not asking the court to do anything but assure me a fair trial, the same thing any defendant is entitled to."

"Baloney," Holly shouted, red-faced. "She's making it all up. The only goal I have is to convict a killer. If she wants to call that a vendetta, then I guess it's a vendetta. I call it doing my job."

"Perhaps another prosecutor should be assigned to this case," Judge Maddox said wearily. "This is a unique situation. I've personally never had a prosecutor before my court on criminal charges, and the two of you did work together at one time. That could be construed as a conflict of interest."

"You can't have me removed from this case," Holly said, standing and leaning over the judge's desk. "Conflict of interest, my ass. I don't care if she's Mother Teresa. What are we going to do?

Let all the criminals decide who they want to try their cases? She doesn't want me on this case because she knows I'm going to convict her." She pointed at Stella. "She's a cunning and devious woman, Your Honor. She knows the system like the back of her hand. She's trying to use this knowledge to her advantage."

"That's enough," Judge Maddox said, holding up a hand. "You've made your point, Ms. Oppenheimer." Her intercom buzzed and she picked it up, motioning for them to leave.

chapter

TWELVE

Sam was waiting in the baggage claim area at Love Field when Stella and Brenda Anderson arrived on the four o'clock shuttle. Brenda wanted to pick up her car. She had arranged a meeting with Ben Growman to explain what she hoped to accomplish with the forensic animation. As Brenda couldn't do it alone, it would be expensive, and she couldn't go forward without Growman's consent.

Once they had dropped Brenda off at her condo in Richardson, Sam scooted over in the seat and kissed Stella on the mouth. "I've been so worried," he said. "Can't you stay in Dallas now? After the incident with your skirt, I'd sleep a lot better if you were here."

241

"The prelim was continued," she told him, "but we'll have to go back if they produce the missing evidence. Brenda thinks it could be significant, so we want to conduct our own tests the minute they find it."

Sam pulled out into traffic, using the surface roads until he made his way to the freeway. "Isn't it just a piece of metal?"

"The question's not what it is, Sam," she said, her voice elevating in excitement, "it's what it might tell us. The original inventory list indicates some kind of writing or inscription was found on the pieces of metal. Brenda was able to make out a few letters, but without the missing piece we can't figure out what it says."

They went up the freeway ramp, but it was rush hour and traffic was barely moving. "Even if this piece is missing," Sam said, "didn't they record what the writing said somewhere else in the reports?"

"No," she said, "and that's peculiar. Except for the inventory list, the metal pieces don't exist. There's not one word about them in any of the reports we received. The D.A.'s office either failed to follow through when the case was first investigated, or someone purposely tampered with the evidence since my arrest." She grabbed his arm. "Don't you see, Sam? This might be something left behind by the killer."

"You mean someone other than Randall?"

"Right," she said. "Randall heard my father arguing with a man outside the house the night of the fire. The police think I killed Randall to keep him from testifying, but it could have been

242

the person who was arguing with my father. If this person set the fire, maybe he got wind of Randall's statements somehow and became spooked that the police would come looking for him. So, he kills the state's only witness, thinking it will prevent them from reopening the case. Let's say he knew there was incriminating evidence floating around, but it didn't matter as long as the case was in limbo. As soon as Randall reappeared, though, he knew there was a chance that I might talk them into reopening the case."

"These metal pieces are the incriminating evidence, right?"

"Yes," Stella said, watching a car edge past on her side. "Okay," she said as a thought came to her, "what if the killer left something inside the house that night? He could have lost a ring, a watch, an ID bracelet. All these years he's been holding his breath, praying no one would put it together."

"Wouldn't he think they'd go after you, Stella?" Sam said. "If he knew about Randall's statements, he'd know Randall implicated you. By killing him, he actually increased his chances that they would reopen the case and discover this incriminating evidence."

"He never thought they'd go after me," Stella argued. "I'm a district attorney, Sam. Who would ever think they'd prosecute a D.A.? I was shocked when they filed against me. Besides, the killer might not have known that I threatened Randall in front of witnesses two days before he was killed."

"Don't you realize what you're doing, Stella?"

Sam said, scowling at her. "You're doing exactly what this person doesn't want you to do. You're making a big stink over the missing pieces, trying to track down the mystery man. If this person killed Randall to keep this from happening, then he's probably gunning for you now."

"Possibly," Stella said, a slight tremor in her voice. "But I'm not going to back off, Sam. Don't you see? I can't. Finding the real killer is the only way to defend myself."

As they inched their way through the traffic, Sam gripped the steering wheel, released it, and then gripped it again. "I want you to stay with me, Stella," he said. "I don't want you staying in that house by yourself."

"Don't be silly," she said, mustering up a smile. "I'll be fine, Sam. If there's any danger, it has to be in Houston, not Dallas. I do need your help with one thing, though. I've got to raise the money to retain Brannigan." She turned her head away. "I'm going to call the bank tomorrow and see if I can get a loan on the house."

"That's not going to work," Sam said, shaking his head. "Brad is still listed on the title. Unless he signs the loan papers, they'll never approve it. Besides, if they know what's going on—"

"Here's what I want you to do," she told him. "Prepare a property settlement for my signature. Brad can keep everything except the house. I'll sign over all rights to the business, no questions asked and no additional accounting. He can even have my BMW if he wants it." She sucked in a breath. Giving in to Brad was not easy. "I'm desperate, Sam. I can't represent myself on a case like this. I'm too emotional right now and I'll make mistakes."

Having covered only a few miles in over thirty minutes, Sam steered the Mercedes to an off-ramp and parked on the surface road, deciding to wait until the traffic died down. "I can get you the money," he told her, turning sideways in the seat. "You don't have to do this."

"No, Sam," she said, "I can't take any more money from you. You already put up the money for my bail. As long as I appear in court and don't leave the country, you'll get the money back. Whatever money I spend on an attorney will be lost forever."

"So," he said, taking her hand, "it's only money. Let me help you, Stella."

"I can't, Sam," she said. "It isn't right. If you do what I say, everything should be fine. Brad doesn't have to come up with any cash. All he has to do is sign off on the house and I'll be able to get a loan against the equity."

"There must have been an accident earlier," he said, seeing the cars on the freeway moving at a faster clip now. Gunning the engine, he headed up the ramp again. "If you're certain you want to proceed this way," he said, "I can probably get the papers drawn up tomorrow."

"Good," Stella said, settling back in the seat.

Sam drove in silence awhile, thinking. "You definitely need an attorney, though. On that, I agree a hundred percent. Do you want me to talk to Brad, or would you rather do it yourself? You might make better headway with him, Stella."

"No," she said, remembering how she'd acted

when Brad had come to see her at the Houston jail. "If I approach him, we'll just end up fighting. He might not agree to sign over the house, Sam. If he refuses, at least try to talk him into co-signing on the loan with me."

"Do you really think he'd do that?" Sam asked. "If you're convicted, Brad would get stuck with the payments. If he was my client, I'd never let him agree to that type of an arrangement."

"Do the best you can," she said, shrugging. "I don't know what to tell you. Make something up. You have to convince Brad that I'll be able to repay the loan. Tell him you're certain I'm going to get off, that we've located new evidence."

Dropping the subject for the moment, Sam suggested they get something to eat. Stella was tired and eager to get home, so they stopped at a coffee shop for a quick sandwich. Once they were back in the car en route to her house, she looked out the window at the Dallas skyline and the glittering dome next to Reunion Arena. Inside the dome was a wonderful restaurant, but from a distance, it looked like a giant Christmas ornament. Stella couldn't help but wonder where she would be when the holidays rolled around. Closing her eyes and leaning back against the headrest, she didn't speak until she heard Sam's wheels crunching on the gravel in her driveway.

"I'd ask you in," she told him, "but I'm really beat. I want to get to the office early tomorrow morning, so I guess I should go to bed and try to get some sleep."

"I understand, Stella," he said, a tender look

246

in his eyes. "If you're up to it, though, I'd like you to come for dinner at the house tomorrow night. I want you to meet Adam."

"Adam?" Stella said, her stomach fluttering. "After he saw them arrest me, Sam? Do you think that's wise? What could he possibly think?"

"I want him to know the truth," Sam said. "Innocent people are sometimes falsely accused. Just because the police arrest someone doesn't mean they're guilty."

"What is this?" she said, defensive. "Reality 101?"

Sam pulled her gently into his arms, stroking her hair back from her face. "Give us a chance, Stella," he whispered. "We won't let you down."

She remained there for some time, her cheek pressed against Sam's jacket. It felt so good to have his arms around her, to know that someone cared. Finally she extracted herself, kissing him quickly on the forehead. Then she exited the car and made her way to the front door, disappearing inside the dark house.

Holly stormed into Frank Minor's office after her last court appearance of the day. "What do you mean I can't have an investigator?" she shouted. "This is the biggest case I've ever handled, and you're telling me I have to do all the work myself."

"We don't have anyone available," Minor said. "If I had someone, I'd assign them."

"We'll have to hire an independent investigator, then," she said, dropping down in a chair in front of his desk. "There are several good agencies in town, Frank. I'd rather use our own people, but if I have to, I'll settle for an outsider."

"We're already over budget this year," he said, tapping his pencil on the desk. "Harper may clear on his case by the time you get to the prelim. The prelim's been continued anyway, I hear."

"Only a week," Holly pointed out. "If I walk in there with what we have now, the case might not be held over for trial. Stella has an investigator. Growman lets her have anything she wants."

"If that's true," he said, chuckling, "then I suggest you get back to work."

"Screw you," Holly said. "I want that investigator, Frank."

Minor spun his chair around and gazed out the window. "I've been thinking about Randall's statement, particularly the part about the man he thought he saw arguing with Stella's father," he told her. "Her father was a building inspector. Who knows, there might be something there." Wheeling his chair back around, he added, "Check all the newspapers around the time of the fire and see what you come up with. Also, contact the building inspector's office and see what Cataloni was working on at the time of his death. Corruption in the building industry is fairly widespread. Maybe Stella's father stumbled onto something heavy and someone went after him."

Holly's jaw dropped. "What are you saying?" she cried. "That you think Stella is innocent?

Shit, Frank, if you think the woman is innocent, why are we prosecuting her?"

"I didn't say I thought she was innocent," he argued. "I just think we should cover all the bases. Do you want the defense to sandbag us with this kind of argument? Besides, in case you've forgotten, we're not here to put innocent people in prison."

"In case I've forgotten?" she said, incredulous. "This was your call, not mine." Minor was backtracking, giving her the impression that he thought they were making a mistake by going forward. Suddenly it all came together, and Holly's blood began to boil. "You amaze me, Frank," she told him. "You're looking for an escape route, aren't you? If Stella's cleared, are you going to make certain I take the fall for this fiasco? Well," she said, wrapping her arms around her chest, "I'm not going to stand for it. People are always dumping on me, and I'm tired of it. You're not going to hang me out to dry."

He laughed at her. When Holly got riled, she reminded him of a toy poodle. He occasionally felt an urge to see how far he could push her. "And just what are you going to do about it?"

Holly stood to leave. "Stella's guilty and I'm going to prove it," she said, her face set with determination. "This is my chance to make a name for myself. No one's going to take this away from me."

"Now that's what I'm looking for," Minor said, leveling a finger at her. "The killer instinct, Oppenheimer. I didn't think you had it in you."

"Think again," Holly said. She turned on her heel and marched out of the room, purposely slamming the door behind her.

"I need to see you in my office," Holly said, stopping at Janet's desk and then continuing on to her own. Janet stood, then picked up her steno book and pencil. Once they were both situated, Holly outlined Minor's concerns. "I want you to handle this research for me. Stella's been bombarding me with motions, so I don't have enough time to do it myself."

"Really?" Janet said. "That would be great, Holly. I could get a feel for what it's going to be like when I get out of law school."

Holly ignored her as she thought through what she wanted her to do. "You'll have to contact the building inspector's office and find out what Tony Cataloni was working on at the time of his death. Then you need to take it a step further and compile a list of the various people he might have come in contact with on job sites. Once you get some names, shoot them to records and check to see if any of them comes back with a criminal record." She tapped her pen against her chin. "That should be enough to satisfy Minor."

"God, Holly," Janet said, realizing the implications of what Holly had asked her to do, "we might be able to prove Stella's innocence if we find the man her father was arguing with." A dreamy look passed over her face. The thought that she might be the one to clear Stella was enormously appealing.

"Listen," Holly said, "you can get that stupid

look off your face, because Stella is guilty. All we're doing here is trying to discredit any defense tactics she may spring on us down the line. Get right on it," she concluded, picking a stack of papers off her desk.

"Can I look over what evidence you have now?" Janet asked. "It might help me to understand all the nuances in the case."

"Sure," Holly said. "Look over anything you want."

Janet walked to the door and then stopped. "I have several days of typing I haven't finished. You won't be able to get the motions filed, Holly. Who's going to handle my work?"

"You are," Holly answered without raising her head.

"Don't you want me to go to the building office in person, rather than handle it over the phone? They might be more cooperative that way. This goes back so many years, Holly. How do we know the building inspector's office still has that kind of information on file?"

"Use your free time," Holly said. She dropped her pen and looked up at Janet. "You have an hour for lunch every day. If you find something, work on it at home." Seeing the other woman's jaw drop at the thought of working without pay, she added, "If you do a good job on this, I'll write you a nice letter. You can use it to help you get into law school."

"What if they won't tell me anything?"

"There's always a way," Holly said, arching an eyebrow. She took in Janet's simple blouse and long skirt, her scraggly brown hair. The woman wasn't ugly, she thought, but she was terribly plain. Her forehead was too broad, her eyes too deeply set, and her fashion sense was appalling. Holly had ways to get what she wanted, particularly from the opposite sex. Janet Hernandez, she decided, would have to get the job done the hard way. "If they don't cooperate," she said, "tell them we'll get a subpoena. Before you do anything, though, get the *Dallas Morning News* on the line."

"Now?" Janet said, glancing at her watch. "It's after six, Holly. My husband's supposed to pick me up any minute. Don't you want to wait until tomorrow morning?"

"No," she answered, picking up the phone. "Go home, Janet. I'll make the call myself."

"I have to take you off the case."

Brenda Anderson and Ben Growman were seated in a booth at Cable's coffee shop not far from her apartment. Growman was sipping a cup of coffee, watching as Brenda wolfed down her hamburger. Once he had spoken, she choked on her food, and had to wash it down with her soda. "What are you saying?"

Growman looked out the window, deep in thought. "Someone called the *Dallas Morning News* and told them that you've been in Houston investigating Stella's case," he said. "Charley Abernathy called me a few minutes before I left the office, asking me who was footing the bill for your services."

"We can't do this to Stella," Brenda said, placing her palms on the table. "She needs me,

Ben. It's terrible. She's hardly eating. Wait until you see her. Her shoulder blades stick out in the back and her legs are as thin as toothpicks. The woman has it coming from every possible direction. Her brother's giving her problems, her uncle, Holly, Winters, and that doesn't count this mysterious witness who just happens to be an ex-cop."

His expression was flat, unreadable. "Do you think there's anything to her conspiracy theory?"

"There could be," Brenda said, "but it's too early to tell. If you give me more time, though, we might make some real headway. This afternoon—"

"I can't," he said. "If I don't put a stop to it, Abernathy says he'll do a story on how I'm expending the taxpayers' money to defend an accused murderer."

"Bastard," Brenda said, crunching her napkin in her hand. "Listen, Ben," she said a few moments later, "Stella's in tremendous danger, and I'm not referring to the possible outcome of the case. Didn't you hear about the incident with her skirt?" She also filled him in on Mario's arrest on drug charges, and how Holly was trying to coerce him into testifying for the prosecution.

Flagging down the waitress, Growman asked for a refill on his coffee, then took out his wallet to pay their bill. "My hands are tied, Brenda. We've done all we can do."

She wasn't about to abandon Stella. "I'll quit, then," she said. Brenda heard the words come out of her mouth, but had difficulty believing she had spoken them. She seldom asserted herself, and Growman had always intimidated her. The district attorney seemed to have a shield around him, and very few people other than Stella had ever penetrated it.

Dropping some bills on the table, Growman slid out of the booth. "You're being foolish," he said, yanking on the cuffs of his shirt. "You're a good employee, Brenda. I wouldn't want to lose you."

Brenda had competed against hundreds of candidates for her present position. If she resigned until Stella's legal problems were resolved, she would probably have to reapply and wait for another opening. How would she support herself in the interim? "Wait, Ben," she said, quickly scooting out of the booth, "I know how to solve the problem. I have three weeks' vacation coming, plus another three weeks of accumulated sick time. As long as I'm not being paid by the county, no one has anything to complain about. Right?"

Growman gave her suggestion some thought. "If that's what you want to do, then I guess I can't stop you."

"I'll call personnel tomorrow," Brenda said, sighing with relief.

The situation in Stella's office was worse than she imagined. Case files were overflowing her in-basket, her desk was completely covered in paperwork, and her secretary handed her at least twenty message slips when she walked through the door that morning. "Has Brenda Anderson called yet?"

"Yes," she said. "She wants you to meet her at Oracle Labs on Inwood Road at three o'clock. If you can't make it, she told me to let her know right away. She only has the use of the lab from three to five."

"Three's fine," Stella said. "Do you know where Growman is?"

"In his office, I guess," the woman said. "Want me to call and make certain he's there?"

"Please," she said, entering her office and collapsing in her chair. How would she ever catch up on her work? Scanning several files, she found her mind returning to her own predicament. If the charges weren't dropped by the prelim, Growman would have to consider replacing her. He really didn't have a choice. If she hadn't been in a supervisory position with the agency, he could simply reassign her cases until she returned, but the way it was, the work was simply stacking up. If they weren't careful, they would miss mandatory filing dates and dangerous offenders would go free.

She heard a noise and looked up, seeing Growman standing in front of her desk.

"I'm sorry for the mess, Stella," he said, running his fingers through his hair. "I've been handling most of your work myself, but it's been tough." He paused, staring at the files in her basket. "How bad does it look?"

Stella flicked the stack with her hand. "Bad, Ben. We're only talking a few days here. If I manage to bring Brannigan on board, maybe I can concentrate on my work until the prelim, but if I can't raise the money—"

"How much does he want?" Growman asked.

"He asked for fifty originally. Now that there's two cases, he'll probably ask for a hundred thousand on retainer." Stella laughed nervously. "Piece of change, huh?"

Growman winced in sympathy. "How is Brenda working out for you?"

"She's fabulous," Stella said. "I don't know what I would do without her. And, Ben—"

He was already leaving. He stopped and faced her.

"I can't thank you enough for all you've done," she said. Stopping to clear her throat, she continued, "By the way, you were right about Holly. She accused me of having an affair with you. I think she's jealous. It must be why she's been so hostile to me. When you endorsed me on television, she must have gone crazy."

"Holly's jealous of everyone, Stella," Growman told her. "If anyone else has so much as an extra crumb on their plate, she wants it. Not only does she want it, but she'll do whatever it takes to get it."

"It's funny," Stella said. "I never realized Holly was that type of person. You think you know someone, but you really don't. She's a complete phony, Ben. She's even trying to turn Mario against me."

"I heard," Growman said. "Anderson told me. Do you think there's any chance he'll cooperate?"

"No," Stella said, shaking her head. "Our relationship has been strained lately, but I think everything's okay now. Mario's just scared, Ben. I'm going to get him an attorney and see if we can't resolve his drug case. Then Holly won't have anything to hold over his head."

"Let's hope you're right," Growman said, continuing on through the doorway.

Stella pulled into the parking lot of Oracle Labs at three- fifteen that afternoon. She had worked through the lunch hour and managed to get the majority of the cases on her desk assigned. At least they would get filed, she thought as she opened the car door and stepped out into a furnace of stifling heat. Suddenly the humidity in Houston didn't seem so bad. When you went outside in Houston during the summer months, it felt as if someone had thrown a wet blanket over your head. The heat in Dallas was so searing that Stella's skin burned like a hot iron had been pressed against it. A lot of burn victims were sensitive to heat. Some of them even carried little portable fans around everywhere they went. It wasn't so difficult to figure out, she thought, as she headed across the parking lot to the building. Once the flames had licked at your skin, you never wanted to feel hot again.

Glancing at the drab gray building that housed Oracle Labs, she wondered why it had no windows. It looked like a fortress of some kind, the architecture stark and unappealing. "I'm here to see Brenda Anderson," she told the receptionist. She was seated at a curved marble console, a bank of computer terminals and security monitors in front of her. "She should be expecting me. Tell her Stella Cataloni is here."

The woman directed Stella to a grouping of

metal chairs. A few moments later, Brenda Anderson appeared. "We're all set up," she said, her face haggard. "We worked all night, but I think the program is fairly accurate. If we had more time, of course, we could add more details and take it to a higher level of reality." She stopped and glanced at Stella. "For the sake of time, I think it's better that we go with what we have. What do you think?"

"I guess," Stella said, following as Brenda led her through a maze of long corridors. She glanced through the glass partitions at banks of whirring computers and other sophisticated electronic equipment. Even though she was glad to be out of the heat, she found herself shivering in the cold building. "What do they do in this place? It's like a deep freeze in here. I don't think they even keep the morgue this cold."

"They keep it cool because of the equipment," Brenda told her. "In here," she said, opening a heavy steel door and holding it as Stella stepped through.

The room was enormous. Set up in individual work stations, the ceiling was two stories high, and Stella took in all kinds of wires and instruments that seemed to be suspended in thin air. With all the lights and cameras on tripods, it looked more like a television station than a computer workshop.

"This is the virtual reality lab," Brenda advised. "Here's what we're going to do. You're going to stand on that platform." She turned and indicated an area behind her. "You'll wear goggles, Stella. They have teleprocessors built into the lenses, so the images will seem similar to what you see on television. Instead of real-life images, however, the images you will see will be generated by the computer program we've designed specifically for this purpose. You'll also have sound. I'll be able to talk to you from the control room over there, and more or less guide you." She pointed to a glassed-in room, accessible via a stairway to the second level.

"What do you mean by guiding me?" Stella asked. "I'm not going anywhere outside this room, right?"

"Right," Anderson said. "But see the platform? It's a little like a treadmill. Once we get everything hooked up, it will move when you move, giving you the feeling that you're walking. It's all just a simulation, of course, but the more realistic we make it, the more you should remember about the night of the fire." A young man stepped up and Anderson introduced him. "This is Pete Frazer. He helped me develop the program, Stella. We have to pay for the use of the lab, but Pete offered his services for free."

"Thanks," Stella said, smiling weakly, "I really appreciate your help." Frazer appeared to be in his early to mid- twenties. With long hair and intelligent blue eyes, he was handsome and outgoing, well dressed and confident.

"I've heard a lot about you," he said, pumping Stella's hand. "I saw you on television during the Pelham case. You were brilliant. My fiancée's in law school and she's a big fan of yours."

Stella didn't answer. As her eyes roamed around the room, she began to get apprehensive.

"When Brenda told me about this, I didn't think it would be so sophisticated," she said. "From the looks of it, you've got more equipment in here than NASA. I won't get electrocuted, will I?"

"Nah," Frazer said, laughing. "Don't let all this stuff frighten you. Just relax and go with the flow. Think of it as a game if it will make you more comfortable. I know guys who'd give their right arm to play around in here. This is cutting-edge technology. Most of it isn't available to the general public yet."

Frazer led Stella to the platform, and handed her the goggles, while Brenda headed up the stairs to the control room. Once Stella slipped the goggles over her head, Frazer asked her to stand still while he adjusted them. "You should see a color grid," he said. "Can you see it?"

"Yes," Stella said.

"Stella, it's Brenda," a voice said in her ear. "Can you hear me okay?"

"Yes."

"The first thing we're going to do is walk you through the house," Brenda said. "If something isn't right, let us know so we can fix it. As far as the furniture goes, we have all the basic shapes and styles on file in the computer. Therefore, if something isn't right, we'll keep replacing it until we find something that fits. We'll do the same with the structure. I can move walls, doors, ceilings, whatever it takes to make it look like your house." She took a breath and then said, "Are you ready?"

"As ready as I'll ever be," Stella said. Her

hands were perspiring on the metal railing of the treadmill. The color grid disappeared and she suddenly saw the inside of a house. "I see it," she said. "It looks like my kitchen. It's fantastic, almost like I'm really there."

"Look at it really close," Brenda told her. "Is the window in the right place? The appliances?"

"Yes," Stella said. "The window was over the kitchen sink. Everything is perfect except the table. It was bigger and farther to the right."

"Hold on," Brenda said, quickly tapping the computer keys on the main console. "How's that?"

Stella was amazed. Right before her eyes the table changed. It was the same shape as before only now it appeared larger, and Anderson had shifted the image a few feet to the right. "The kitchen window had curtains," she added. "I guess I forgot to tell you about them before."

"What kind of curtains?" Anderson asked.

"Lace . . . white lace."

"Were they opened or closed the night of the fire?"

"I don't remember," Stella said.

"Okay," Brenda said. "Move around in the kitchen. Try walking over to the refrigerator."

Stella did what she said, moving her feet as if she were actually walking across her kitchen floor. It was an eerie sensation, real but not real. She felt as if she were suspended in another dimension. She reached for the handle to the refrigerator and gasped when it opened. Quickly closing it, she moved to the sink area and said, "Closed. The curtains were closed that night. At one point, I was standing at the sink next to my mother. She was rinsing off a head of lettuce."

Stella emitted a startled cry when the image shifted and she saw her mother's face. The body was robotic- looking and far from natural, but the face was identical. "How did you do it? This is the most amazing thing I've ever seen."

"I got the photographs from your cousin Maria in San Francisco. Looks good, doesn't it? If this doesn't jar your memory, Stella, nothing will."

Stella stared at her mother's kind face, wanting to reach out and embrace her. It was almost as if she had stepped to the other side and was looking at her mother's spirit. Because all their photos had burned in the fire, she hadn't seen her mother's face since the night she died.

"Where's Randall, Stella?" Brenda asked. "Try to think in the present tense from now on. When you hear my voice, try not to put a name or a face to it. Just think of it as the voice inside your mind."

"I don't know," Stella said. "Wait . . . I think Tom was in the living room. He thought he heard my father's car pull into the driveway, so he went to meet him at the door."

Brenda added the window treatments, wanting Stella to settle into the environment before they continued. Unable to find a predrawn image that was appropriate, she quickly sketched a pattern with her stylus and moved it into position. Then she motioned to the sound engineer. "Hit track one, Bill."

Stella stiffened as sounds filtered in through the earpiece. She heard what sounded like two men arguing in the distance, but she couldn't tell what they were saying. Focusing on the window, she could see figures standing outside on her front lawn. "I can see them," she said. "God, Brenda, I can see them. I completely forgot that the kitchen windows faced out to the front of the house. And the curtains were lace, so you could see through them even when they were closed. How did you figure it out?"

"From the architectural renderings," Brenda advised. "Don't ask any more questions, Stella. The only way this is going to work is if you convince yourself that what you are seeing is real, not fabricated."

"What *am* I seeing?" Stella asked, watching as the images on the lawn moved. "Isn't it just something you created?"

"Yes," Brenda said, sighing and glancing over at the sound engineer. "I hope this works," she whispered. "If not, we wasted a hell of a lot of time and energy." When the engineer merely shrugged, she turned her attention back to Stella. "Listen," she said, "we put the men out on the lawn and, yes, what you're hearing is a sound track, but if you let your mind go, you may see something other than what we've created. Am I making myself clear? Let us decide what you're actually seeing. All I want you to do is react."

Stella blinked several times, then stared at the window, trying desperately to recall what she had seen that night. "It's not working," she said at last. "I don't remember anything. I told you I couldn't remember." She was reaching up to remove the goggles when Brenda began speaking again.

"Give it some time," she said. "Take some deep breaths and relax. Let your mind drift. It has to come naturally, Stella. You can't force it to happen."

Five minutes passed, then ten. Finally, Stella thought she heard her mother's voice. "All the plans I had for you," she was saying. "You can't enter the Miss Texas pageant after you've had a child. If you'd only waited, Stella. Why did you have to have sex with this boy?"

In the background, Stella heard the men's voices again. "You can't do this," a man said, his voice loud and strained. Then she heard only fragments of sentences and disjointed words. "Tomorrow . . . more money . . . I promise . . . make it worth your while . . . please." Her father had a pronounced Italian accent and even though the voice sounded familiar, Stella knew it wasn't her father who was speaking.

"Stella," Brenda said softly, "what's happening?"

"The man's talking. He's pleading with my father. I don't know why. More money, he keeps saying. If you just wait, I'll get more money." Stella shut her eyes and listened, trying to conjure up the voices again inside her mind. "My father's telling him no, telling him to go away, calling him names."

"Who's the man, Stella? Can you see his face?"

"No," Stella said, her eyes still closed, "but I recognize his voice. I just can't place it."

"Hit track two," Brenda said to the engineer. "Quick."

Stella heard another voice. "Hello," the man said. "Who is this? If you're there, speak up." The same words were repeated several times before Brenda started speaking again. "Is that the voice, Stella?"

"I don't know," she said. "It's similar but not the same. I need to hear him say the same words in order to be certain."

Brenda removed her headset and tossed it down on the console. "This was the best I could do," she told the sound engineer. "I doubt if I can get Clementine Cataloni to record a script for me. All I did was call him up and record the phone call."

"We could do a voice match," the man offered.

"From what?" Brenda asked, frustrated that they weren't making more progress. "The voice we're matching it to is in her mind, Bill. How would that work?"

"Hey," he said, "I'm just trying to help. No one even told me what we're doing here."

Putting the headset back on, Brenda told Stella that they were going to move forward. If they had to, they could always go back to the kitchen and try again later. "I'm taking you to the living room now," she said. "How does it look?"

"Good," Stella said. "I mean, we didn't have a chair like that, but I guess it doesn't really matter. It's in the right place."

"This is where your father and Randall fought, right?"

"Right, and I got punched in the stomach."

"After the fight, what happened?"

"Tom left by the front door. I went down the hall to my room."

Brenda tapped the keyboard on her computer console and Stella found herself walking down a hall. Seeing an open doorway, she stepped inside and saw an exact replica of her room. The bedspread was the same pink- and-white pattern. Her dresser was in the right location, the bowl of matches on top of it just the way Randall had mentioned.

In one corner of her room, she saw several batons, and what looked like a majorette uniform on a hanger. She laughed, thinking Brenda had misjudged her. Back then, she had taken care of her room about the same way Mario took care of his apartment. Whenever she removed her uniform after a football game, she generally dropped it on the floor. Stella's mother used to make fun of her, saying she had an affinity for stacks. She always kept three or four piles of clothes and other personal articles scattered in various spots throughout her room. She only had one chest and the closet was so small, Stella could never find enough room to hang up her clothes.

Stella closed her eyes and let her mind drift far into the past. She saw herself walking with the other majorettes after a football game, laughing and joking. Her best friend, Kathy, kept bumping into her as they walked. Another girl came up behind her and hugged her. Stella felt as if she were watching it all from somewhere above. A happy, expectant face suddenly looked up, and she knew she was seeing her girlhood image.

Tears gathered in her eyes. She felt as if a boa constrictor had wrapped itself around her heart. She knew the exact night she was remembering— the night Tom Randall had taken her to the lake and they had made love for the first time. Go back, she told her image. You don't know what's waiting for you. For the thrill of this one night, you'll have years of pain and agony. You'll never feel safe again. You'll never see your parents again, your keepsakes, your home.

"Look at this," her girlhood image said, tossing the baton high in the air. She watched as the image twirled around and caught the baton between her legs. Her legs were tan and perfectly shaped, the skin smooth and luxurious. "I'm going to ask Mrs. Fisher if I can use it during next week's game."

Because there were no family pictures left after the fire, Stella had forgotten what she looked like without the scars. The face she saw in her mind was so perfect, so unmarred, that it almost took her breath away. Was it really her? Was the beautiful young woman she saw, so full of promise and hope, still locked somewhere inside of her?

Stella opened her eyes. The computer-generated images seemed to come alive and shift in color and shape, until she was seeing the real objects and furnishings instead of the ones Brenda had created. Suddenly it all seemed completely real, and vivid memories flashed in her mind. Her palms began sweating profusely. Fear engulfed her. She pressed both her hands into her abdomen and grimaced in pain.

"What's happening, Stella? Can you tell me?"

"Tom just came in and locked the door," she said. "My father hit me, and I'm afraid he'll come and hit me again. My stomach hurts. It's cramping terribly. I'm so ashamed. I've let my parents down. I've let everyone down."

"Where did Tom come from?" Brenda said, making some adjustments on her computer. "Didn't he go out the front door earlier?"

"He says he got in through the basement window," Stella said, her voice trailing off. "I've got to lie down. I don't feel good. I'm dizzy."

"She's into it now," Brenda told the engineer, moving the microphone away from her mouth. "Thank God, we finally got her to suspend reality. Now we might be able to accomplish something." Pulling the microphone back into place, she spoke to Stella again, her voice a controlled monotone. "Are you on the bed?"

"Yes," Stella said, sounding younger and more tentative than before. "Tom's talking to me. He's next to me on the bed. I'm angry at my father because he hit me. Tom says he's an asshole and that we should stay at his parents' house until Daddy cools down. He says I have to have the baby aborted, no matter what my father says. Tom says his parents will help us."

"Can you hear your father?"

"I don't hear anything," Stella said. "Tom's asleep on my bed. As soon as we're certain my father's asleep, we're going to sneak out the window. I'm sleepy too, though. I feel cold, really cold. I'm so cold, I'm shaking. My head's swimming and I'm afraid I'm going to pass out.

There's something wet and sticky between my legs, but I'm too tired to go to the bathroom."

Holding her hand over the microphone, Brenda whispered, "Let's leave her alone for a while. Let her go down to a deeper level. She had a miscarriage that night. That must be what she's referring to." She looked through the glass at Stella, thinking how sad it was that a young girl had to suffer through such an ordeal. "Load up the other tracks now, Bill," she said. "When I give you the signal, cut immediately to track three."

They both watched Stella from the control booth. She was standing ramrod straight on the treadmill, not a muscle in her body moving. Anderson filled her coffee cup from a pot behind her and then resumed her position at the control panel. After sipping her coffee, she pointed a finger at the sound engineer and the prerecorded sound track began playing. First there were a series of metallic clicks lasting a little over a minute. "Do you hear the clicking sound, Stella?"

"Yes," Stella said, her voice a tense whisper.

"Can you tell what it is?"

"No," she said.

"Where is the noise coming from?"

"Under my bed somewhere."

"Are you on the bed now?"

"Yes," Stella said. "I'm scared. I have to get out of here. My heart's beating so fast, I can't breathe. Something's wrong, really wrong."

"Go to track four," Brenda told the sound engineer. "We're about to get into the good stuff."

A crackling, popping sound came on, recorded from an actual fire. Brenda had added the sound of running footsteps in the hallway, thinking Stella's family would have either heard or smelled the fire before she awoke and tried to escape from the house.

Just then Stella started shrieking, the sound so high- pitched that Anderson almost jerked the headset off. "My bed's on fire," she screamed. "Someone's at my door trying to get in. Oh no. Oh no. Help me. Someone has to help me. I'm so scared."

"Who's at the door, Stella?"

"I don't know. I have to get out. I'm on fire. I'm burning. My face. Help me. Someone has to help me." Stella was running on the treadmill now and perspiration was dripping from her face, her blouse already soaked and clinging to her body.

"Where's Randall?"

"I don't know," Stella shouted. "Get me out of here. Please, help me. Oh, God, no, I'm burning." She began coughing and choking. "The smoke. There's too much smoke. I can't breathe. My chest is burning and my eyes sting."

"Where are you now, Stella?"

"I can't get out. The door won't open. Someone's beating on it, but it's stuck."

Brenda shook her head. She didn't know whether to stop or continue. Stella was kicking out with her feet, and Brenda was afraid she would trip and hurt herself. She decided to let it go a few more minutes, hoping they would discover something definitive. If they did, it would make Stella's suffering worthwhile.

"It's my dad," Stella cried. "He has an ax in his hands and there's this awful look on his face."

Brenda tapped a few keys on her console, inserting Stella's father into the scene, his face created from the old photographs.

"Where is he, Stella?"

"He busted the door down. He's grabbing me, screaming at me. He keeps saying my name and crying, "No, no, my beautiful daughter." There's smoke everywhere and I can't breathe. My dad's coughing too. He says we have to get out of the house."

"Can you hear anything else?"

"I have to get Mario, but my dad won't let go of me." Stella was moving her hands back and forth in front of her face, swatting at thin air. "My dad . . . he fell down. He can't get up. I keep pulling on him, but he can't get up. I don't know what to do. God, help me. He's too heavy. I can't lift him. Where's Tommy? Tommy, help me."

Brenda waited until Stella fell silent. Then she prompted her again. "What are you doing now, Stella?"

"I'm in the hall," Stella said. She was panting as she jogged on the treadmill. "I'm going to get Mario. My dad told me to get Mario. He said he would go upstairs for my mother."

"Is your father conscious now?"

"Yes," Stella said. "He choked on the smoke, but he got up. He's okay. He's going for my mother."

"Where is he? Can you see him?"

Stella's head turned, as if she were looking behind her for her father. "The fire's there now. I can't see him. Too much smoke. I don't know what to do. My dad's screaming, but I can't get to him."

"Where are the flames?"

"Right behind me," Stella panted. "I can't go back. There's a huge ball of fire leaping out of the door leading to the basement. I can't hear my dad anymore. I don't know if he went upstairs or the fire . . . I can't think about it. I have to get Mario."

"Is Mario calling for you?"

"I'm in his room, but he's asleep. I keep screaming at him but he doesn't hear me. I'll have to carry him."

Stella leaned forward at the waist, then a moment later, she stood and held her arms in front of her as if she were carrying something heavy. Several times, her knees compressed and she fell to the treadmill, then quickly scrambled back to her feet. Her mouth was open and she was gasping.

Brenda moved the microphone away, speaking to the engineer. "You have no idea what you're seeing."

"Oh, yeah?" he said.

"This woman was severely burned," she told him, "but she managed to find the strength to carry her brother out of that house. You're seeing raw courage, Bill. Take a good look at it, because there's not much of it around these days." She pulled the mike back to her mouth, knowing she would have to put a stop to their reenactment any second. "Where are you now, Stella?"

"Kitchen door. I hurt so bad, but I can't stop. The door handle's burning my hands." From the control room, Brenda could see Stella's body trembling. "There's this terrible sound. It's like a wolf howling or a hurricane. Mario's completely limp. I can't get him to wake up and help me. Everything seems to be shaking and moving. We're going to die." Stella placed her hands together in a praying position, but her words were too soft to be picked up by the microphone.

They watched as Stella reached out with her hand, grimaced and then stumbled forward, collapsing on the treadmill.

"Are you okay?" Brenda said. "Did you trip?" When Stella remained prostrate on the treadmill, she realized something was terribly wrong. "Shit," she said, hitting the toggle switch for the P.A. system in the lab. "Pete, quick. She must have fainted." Yanking the headset off, she left the control room and rushed down the stairs to the main level, afraid that Stella might be having a heart attack.

Before Anderson could get to the main floor, Frazer swept Stella up in his arms and carried her to a sofa in a far corner of the room. "Get some wet paper towels," he said to one of the technicians, bending down to place his head against her chest.

"Is she breathing?" Brenda said, squatting down beside Frazer and Stella with an anguished look on her face. "It was too much for her. I shouldn't have made her do it."

"She's breathing," he said. "Her heart's beating pretty fast, but I think she's okay. That was a scary scene. I think she just got spooked and blacked out."

Brenda took the towels from the technician and wiped Stella's face with them. A few moments later, her eyes opened and she looked around in a daze. "What happened?"

"You fainted," Brenda said. "How do you feel?"

"Awful," Stella said, trying to sit up. She peered up at Frazer. "This was definitely not a game. If your friends think it's fun, they need to have their heads examined."

"Don't get up yet," the investigator told her. "Just rest a few minutes. Do you remember what you saw before you fainted?"

Stella was staring at the ceiling, her chest rising and falling, her arms and legs splayed out around her. For a long time she didn't answer. "Yes," she finally said. "I saw hell, Brenda. You took me straight to hell. I'm just glad I found the way back."

chapter

THIRTEEN

Stella blamed her fainting spell on the fact that she had skipped lunch. Once she had rested, Brenda took her down to the snack bar in the building and bought her a sandwich and a soda. "I probably shouldn't have done this without a doctor or a psychologist present," she said, as they seated themselves at a table in the back of the room. "I'm sorry, Stella. I told you it might be traumatic, but I guess I didn't realize how painful it would be."

"It's okay," Stella said, taking a bite of her sandwich and then washing it down with the soda.

"You haven't been eating enough," Brenda said. "You can't run on pure determination, you know. A little food now and then makes a world of difference."

"Really, Brenda," Stella said, "I remembered more than I ever have. It was frightening, but it answered a lot of questions." She laughed. "I guess I can say all this because it's over. You'll never get me to put those goggles on again. I can promise you that."

"Tell me what you learned," Brenda said, leaning forward over the table. "I feel like shit

275

right now for putting you through this. My only hope is that we accomplished something."

"We did," Stella said, pushing her plate away. "As I told you, I could recall seeing my father's face, but all these years I thought he was still angry at me. Now I know what happened." Her eyes glazed over. "When the fire broke out, he must have come to get me but Tom had locked the door from the inside. The object in his hands was an ax. He broke open the door, and then he saw me. You know," she said, blinking, "he must have seen that I'd been burned. That's why he had such a horrified expression on his face."

"I see," Brenda said, wishing Stella had recalled more about how the fire had started.

"That alone makes it worth it," Stella continued, her voice heavy with emotion. "For sixteen years I thought my father was trying to kill me, hit me over the head with something. I guess I even wondered if he was the one who set the fire. That's probably why I suppressed everything."

"The most important thing is the man on the lawn," Brenda said. She was pleased that Stella had found a degree of peace over her father's role in the tragedy, but their primary goal was to solve the crime. "You said you recognized the voice. Was it your uncle? The voice I played for you was Clem's."

Stella's eyes came alive. "It has to be, don't you see? If I recognized the voice, then it had to be my uncle. Who else could it have been?"

"Randall said it might have been the

neighbor," Brenda said. "You'd recognize the neighbor's voice, wouldn't you?"

"It wasn't the neighbor," Stella said, shaking her head. "I'm almost positive, Brenda. The guy who was always complaining about our dog had a deep, raspy voice. He was an older man and a heavy smoker. If I remember right, he was from Arkansas originally and he had an accent. Real country, you know."

Brenda dropped her eyes. "None of this may be valid, Stella. I'm sure you've heard of false memory. By putting the men on the lawn and all, we may have caused you to create a scenario to go along with it, but that doesn't mean it really occurred that way. Your mind could have just responded to the clues we gave it, letting your imagination do the rest."

"No," Stella said, "I really remembered, Brenda. It's all coming back now. The only thing I'm still confused about is the clicking noise. I think I was partially asleep when I heard it."

"What about Randall?"

"What about him?"

"Once the fire broke out, you couldn't tell us where he went."

"He probably dived out the window," Stella said, squeezing her soda can until it dented. "He certainly didn't stick around to help me or my family. All he was concerned about was saving his own neck." She stood and deposited her trash in the can by the door. Brenda stood as well, and they walked together to the elevator.

"What I don't understand," Brenda said, once they had exited the building, "is why Randall didn't tell the police about the man on the lawn when they first contacted him after the fire."

"My uncle could have gotten to him first," Stella said, squinting in the sunlight. "Maybe he paid Randall to leave town and keep his mouth shut. When he came back to Houston and decided to tell the truth, my uncle could have become enraged and shot him. You know, as much out of anger as fear that something would come of it. My uncle's a tough customer, Brenda. If he paid Randall to keep quiet, he wouldn't be pleased to hear that he'd violated their agreement."

"This sounds like Mafia stuff, Stella."

"I told you my uncle wasn't in the Mafia," she said, laughing. Then she fell serious again. "He might have used similar techniques, though, to control people. If we're right about the pension scam, I guess he was running his own little crime game." Something else occurred to her and Stella's eyes flashed. "I'd bet my right arm that Victor Pilgrim was involved in this pension thing. I don't believe for a minute that he actually saw a woman in a white rental car. I think the statement he gave the police was fabricated."

"You may be right," the investigator said. "As soon as we get back to Houston, I'm going to try to talk to Pilgrim. I've been making inquiries about the pension scam, so he may be on the defensive. Maybe I can get him to crack."

"Good luck on that," Stella said. "If my uncle bumped off Randall to keep him from talking, Pilgrim would be a fool to go up against him. Have you located the doctor yet?"

"I'm working on it," she said. "So far I've determined that the same doctor was involved in at least five instances, but I'm not sure that's unusual. He probably had some kind of contract with the city."

"Is he still around?" Stella asked. "Can you get in touch with him?"

"I don't want to do that yet," Brenda said, following Stella into the parking lot. "Once I go through all the claims, we'll decide how to proceed."

Seeing her car, Stella glanced at her watch. It was almost six and she was supposed to be at Sam's house for dinner at seven. "I have to go," she said. "I should be home by nine or ten at the latest. If you think of anything else, give me a call at the house."

"Wait," Brenda said, having saved the best for last. "Did the clicking noises sound like the ones you heard that night?"

"Yes," Stella said. "They sounded exactly like the sounds I heard." A question mark appeared on her face. "How did you do that, by the way? I've been trying to match those sounds for years."

Brenda reached into the pocket of her black slacks and pulled out a silver Zippo lighter, the sun bouncing off the shiny metal. She flicked it several times, moving her hand around so the lid tapped against the bottom section of the lighter, making a metallic sound.

"That's it," Stella said excitedly. "I always thought it was a lighter, but I never thought of one like that. I always compared it to the Bic lighters everyone uses today, and they don't sound the same."

"Well, I guess one mystery's been solved," Brenda said, smiling. "Now do you know what the metal pieces are and why they're so important?"

"Hot damn," Stella said. "You're a genius, Brenda. It was a Zippo lighter, wasn't it? That's how the arsonist set the fire."

"Here's what I think happened," she said, leaning back against Stella's car. "The killer came in through the basement. Randall said the window leading to the basement was standing open. That's how he got back inside the house, remember? The killer might have been hiding down there when Randall came in, and he simply kept silent. He was probably using the lighter for light so he could see, not wanting to turn the light on and risk getting caught. That's why you heard the clicking noise so many times. He was walking around down there, flicking the lighter, probably looking for something flammable."

"He didn't have to look far," Stella told her. "We had a gas furnace with an open flame. If he flicked that lighter anywhere near the furnace, it would have blown sky high."

"See," Brenda said, "they thought the fire originated in your bedroom, but the furnace was probably right under your bed. When the floors collapsed after you managed to get out of the house, there was no way to tell if the fire started in your room or the basement. If the killer had flicked the lighter near the furnace, he would have been killed as well. He must have ignited something dry in the basement, and it flared up later after he'd left."

"You think the killer's initials or name were on the lighter?" she asked. "You know, the writing?"

"Yep," Brenda said, placing the Zippo back in her pocket. "But I don't think the inscription says Clementine Cataloni. There's a *C* visible on one of the metal chunks, but there's also a *U* and several *N*'s on the others."

"Are you certain?"

"Fairly certain," she said. "We have to see the missing piece, though, before we can figure out what it says."

"Maybe you're just not reading the letters right. They were melted, so—"

"I've got the crime lab working on it now," Brenda said. "Keep your fingers crossed that they find the missing piece in Houston, and that your uncle didn't have someone swipe it from the evidence room. Without it, we may never figure out what the damn thing says." She paused, thinking. "Just for the record, did your uncle smoke?"

"Absolutely," Stella answered. "I remember because my mother wouldn't let him smoke in the house. She always made him go out on the front porch. Wait," she said, another thought coming to mind, "maybe the lighter was a souvenir from the Knights of Columbus. That might be where the letter *U* comes in."

Brenda nodded. "You might be right, Stella."

A feeling of satisfaction spread throughout Stella's body. "Revenge," she said. "I can almost taste it, Brenda, and boy is it sweet."

The two women embraced, and Brenda headed back to the building. Stella reached up and touched the scar on her face, tracing the uneven abrasion with her fingers. For the first time she didn't feel a jolt of revulsion. Brushing the hair on the right side of her face back behind her ear, she tilted her head up and closed her eyes, letting the sun's warm rays wash over her entire face.

Even though the sun was setting, the temperature was still in the eighties and the humidity was oppressive. Janet Hernandez was used to it, though. The house she shared with her husband didn't have air-conditioning. Sitting on the steps of the Fannin Street complex, she slapped at a mosquito that had landed on her arm, cursing her husband under her breath. Just then a dark blue Camaro pulled up at the curb. The driver honked, and she raced down the steps.

"You're late," she said, opening the passenger door and climbing inside with her husband. Tossing her backpack in the seat behind her, she snapped, "I'd rather take the bus than wait for you all night. If you're going to be late, Ray, all you have to do is call."

Ray Hernandez was a good-natured man, with wavy dark hair, olive skin, and a perpetual smile. "What's got you so bent out of shape?" he asked, laughing at her intensity. "Ah," he said a few moments later, "must be the wicked witch again. What did Holly do today?"

"Nothing," Janet said, gazing out the window. They rode in silence for several miles. When they

282

came to a stoplight, Ray reached over and tickled her in the ribs, causing her to giggle. "Stop that," she said, knocking his hand away. "You don't understand, Ray. I went to the building inspector's office today on my lunch hour. They gave me the runaround, claiming it could take months to find the information I need. That is, if they still have it. I don't know what to do now. I don't want to go back to Holly empty-handed."

Ray cranked the powerful engine on the Camaro and took off. "Tell me again what you're looking for."

"Well," she said, "like I told you yesterday, Stella's father was a building inspector. Holly wants to find out what he was working on at the time of his death. Maybe he knew something or saw something that he shouldn't have, and someone decided to kill him because of it."

"Oh, I see," Ray said, his inherent curiosity taking hold. After working for the *Houston Chronicle* for eight years in a variety of low-level jobs, he had recently landed a position as a reporter. He was so taken with his new role in life that he had started consuming gallons of coffee and running on nervous energy, emulating the ragged reporters he had always admired. "You should go through the archives at the paper," he told her. "If this Cataloni guy stumbled across something big enough to get him killed, it was probably newsworthy enough to make the paper. If you want, we can go to the office and check it out right now."

"I don't know what to look for," Janet replied.

"That's why I thought it best to start with the building inspector's office."

"Look for some kind of calamity," Ray told her, steering the Camaro up the ramp for the freeway. "A building that burned due to faulty wiring, a roof that collapsed. Something along those lines."

Janet leaned over and kissed him on the cheek. "I love you," she said. "You're the best."

Once they arrived at the offices of the *Chronicle*, Ray led Janet into a small, cramped room lined with file cabinets and computer terminals. Four cluttered desks were positioned along the walls next to several microfiche machines covered in a fine coat of dust. "Almost all the files have been transferred to computer now," he said, flipping the switch on one of the terminals. Sitting down, he tapped a few keys and pulled up a date-retrieval screen. "Just put in the dates you're interested in," he said, "and wait for the computer to respond." He stood, indicating that Janet should take his seat. "There's a huge data base, so don't panic if your information doesn't pop up right away. I'll go check my voice mail, make a few calls. If you want, I can come back in an hour."

Janet watched her husband disappear through the doorway. She was tired, and her stomach was growling. All she'd had was an apple for lunch, and it was already past seven. Her husband seemed to be able to survive on thin air since he had been made a reporter, but Janet was different. When she didn't eat, she became light- headed and irritable.

Deciding to check articles at least a month before the fire, she inserted the dates and waited for the computer to respond. Page by page, she scanned the text, her eyes burning as she focused on the small print on the computer screen. By the time her husband stuck his head in the door an hour later, she was ready to give up and go home. "One more page," she told him, hitting the return key. "I have to do this, Ray," she added. "If I don't, Holly will refuse to give me a letter of recommendation."

"She can't do that," he said, his pleasant expression changing to one of annoyance. "It's one thing for Holly to ask you to do her work for her, but she can't refuse to give you a recommendation. You've always done a good job for her."

"You don't know Holly," Janet said, leaning back in her chair and stretching her arms over her head. Returning to the text on the computer screen, she said, "Look at this, Ray." The header read DISASTER AT DAY SCHOOL. The article went on to describe how the floor had collapsed at the Happy Day Kindergarten. "This occurred two days before the fire that killed Stella's parents." Two children had died and many others had sustained serious injuries. "My God," Janet said, after reading through the article, "those poor kids. A sinkhole opened up under the foundation. That's why they think the floor collapsed."

Janet reacted to the sorrow of the situation, whereas Ray responded as a reporter. Sinkholes didn't just spring out of nowhere. Most of them developed for a reason. Natural gas pipelines, landfills, underground wells. Adrenaline coursed through Ray's wiry body. One of his biggest stories since he had been made a reporter had involved a crude-oil pipeline that had burst underneath a local cemetery. What a lawsuit that had been. Coffins had floated to the surface. In some cases, the bodies themselves had surfaced, covered in an oily black scum. Relatives of the dead had been awarded huge sums from the oil company. Could something similar have happened at Happy Day?

He quickly nudged Janet out of the chair, replacing her in front of the computer. "Now we have to check all the subsequent articles and determine if there is any mention of Stella's father or an investigation into what caused the cave-in." His fingers flew over the computer keys. "I think you found something, babe."

"What do you mean?" Janet asked, peering over his shoulder. "Wasn't this just an accident?"

"Not necessarily," Ray said. "I'm not saying someone purposely caused the floor to cave in, but I'll bet you anything it involved some kind of negligence. Ask yourself this question," he said, turning to look her in the eye. "Would you have wanted to own the land Happy Day was sitting on?"

Janet shook her head.

"Besides," he continued, "Stella Cataloni is the biggest news in Houston right now. If we can prove her innocence and find the real killer, trust me, you won't need Holly and her stupid letter. You'll end up a household name, and I'll get the story of a lifetime."

Janet reached over and tousled her husband's

286

hair. "I think I'm going to like this," she said, a broad smile on her face.

After she called Sam to tell him she was running late, Stella took a quick shower and then dressed in a pair of jeans and a Polo shirt. Sam had told her he was cooking outside on the grill. Even though the temperature would drop a few degrees in the evening, Stella knew it would still be warm, and she wanted to dress comfortably.

When she arrived at Sam's house in North Dallas, she knocked on the door and waited. The house was brick and had a colonial-style overhang over the front porch. Built on one level, from the outside it looked enormous, but Stella knew looks were deceptive. Lovely magnolia trees dotted the front yard, and Sam had planted zinnias and pansies along the winding walkway. The mailbox had a little duck on it, not the type of ornament Stella had expected to find in a house occupied only by males.

The boy came to the door in his swim trunks. He was a good-looking kid, with curly black hair like his father's. Stella decided he must be tall for his age, since he was only an inch or so shorter than she was. "You must be Adam," she said, smiling at him.

"Yeah," he said, displaying a mouth full of metal braces as he grinned. "Dad's in the backyard. I just got out of the pool. I have to get changed or he's going to get mad at me. I'm all wet, see." He stopped and swiped at his runny nose. Then he darted off inside the house, leaving Stella standing at the door.

For a few moments she just stood there, uncertain whether she should wait for the boy to come back or go inside. Finally she stepped through the doorway, spotting Sam in the backyard through the sliding glass door in the den. Wearing a short-sleeve shirt and an apron over his jeans, he was scraping the barbecue grill with a wire brush. She looked around at the furnishings, finding them surprisingly warm and inviting. The sofas were covered in a floral print, video games were scattered on the floor, and one whole wall was covered with framed snapshots.

Stella walked over and looked at the pictures. Most of the shots were of Adam and Sam, but she saw one photo with a woman that looked older than the other photos. It had to be Sam's wife, she thought. The woman was lovely. Her hair was a shimmering shade of blond, her eyes a soft blue, and she was cradling a tiny infant in her arms. She looked delicate. Stella wondered if she was already ill when the photo was taken. She was thin and even though she was smiling, her eyes were troubled.

"Stella," Sam said, stepping in through the sliding glass door with a plate containing three steaks in his hands, "how long have you been here? Where's Adam? I'm about to put the steaks on the grill. I hope you like them well done. That seems to be the only way they ever turn out."

"He's getting dressed," she said. "I was just looking at the pictures. Is this your wife?"

"Yes," he said. Placing the plate on an end table, he stepped up behind her and wrapped his

288

arms around her waist, bending down and kissing the top of her head.

Stella pried his hands off. "I don't think we should do this in front of Adam, particularly since he thinks I'm a criminal."

Sam put his arms back in the same position, holding Stella even tighter than before. "I don't believe in that," he told her. "You know, hiding things from my kid. He already knows I care about you. He sees dead bodies on TV all the time. I don't think he's going to be traumatized by seeing two adults embrace."

"Oh," she said, not knowing what else to say. She tensed when she heard the boy's voice behind them. How long had he been standing there?

"Want to see my room?" Adam said. He had changed from his bathing suit to a pair of neon orange shorts and an Astros T-shirt.

"Sure," Stella said, pulling away from Sam. She followed Adam down the hall, glancing in the rooms as they passed. "Is this the maid's room?"

"Lois isn't really a maid," Adam said. "Dad won't let her clean up after us. She's been with us a long time. She used to be kind of a baby-sitter, but I guess now she's more of a friend." He puffed out his chest. "I'm too big for a baby-sitter."

"Where is she?" Stella asked.

"Today's her day off. She comes back tomorrow." He stopped in front of a room, and motioned for Stella to step inside. Against one wall was an oak desk with a computer and what appeared to be a laser printer.

"So you like computers, huh?" Stella said, taking a seat on his twin bed. "Wish you could teach me to use one. I mean, I know a little, but they still make me want to pull my hair out."

"They're easy," he said. "If you want, you can come over one day and I'll show you some things. I've had a computer for as long as I can remember."

"Well," she said, laughing lightly, "you come from another generation, Adam. In my day we just had pencils and paper."

She turned her head to the wall, shocked when she saw what was tacked up on his bulletin board. All the articles on the Pelham case were there, one of them with Stella's picture in it. "I-I can't believe you have these," she stammered. "Did your father put them up here?"

"No," Adam said, "I did. I want to be a lawyer, see, but I don't want to do stupid divorces like Dad does. Who'd want to do that? All those people screaming and yelling at each other all day. No," he said, "I want to be a criminal attorney like you, maybe even a D.A. I want to put bad guys away like that Pelham guy."

Stella was flabbergasted. "You followed the Pelham case?"

"I follow all the big cases," he said. "I even have a complete law library on CD-Rom. Want to see it? My dad bought it for me last year as soon as it came out. He has one at the office too. That way, he doesn't have to have all those books and waste all that space."

"Sounds great," Stella said, standing up to

watch over his shoulder as he sat down in front of the computer and booted it up.

"The steaks are almost done," Sam said from the doorway.

"This is amazing," Stella said. "I had no idea you could get all this on a computer. This is a smart kid you've got here, Sam."

"Tell me about it," he said, beaming with pride. "Adam can run circles around me. I guarantee he'll pass the bar on the first try. I don't know about you, but it took me three times."

Dinner consisted of grilled steaks, baked potatoes, and freshly sliced tomatoes. It was simple but delicious. By the time they finished eating, Stella felt as if she had known Sam's son for years. He was inquisitive, bright, and talkative. Before she knew it, she was telling them about her experience in the virtual reality lab.

"That's so cool," Adam said. "I never thought of them using it that way, you know, to help someone remember. I thought it was mostly just for games and things. Now you're going to find the real killer, aren't you?"

"I sure hope so, Adam," Stella said, smiling at him across the table. She glanced over at Sam and felt a touch of envy. He might have lost his wife, but he had a wonderful son and had made a good life for the two of them. Feeling her eyes mist over, she excused herself and rushed to the bathroom.

Sam followed, and she heard his voice through the door. "What's wrong, Stella? Are you sick? I know my cooking is bad, but surely it's not that bad."

"I'm fine," Stella said, opening the door.

"No, you're not fine." He entered the bathroom with her and closed the door behind them so Adam couldn't hear. "What upset you?" He could see she was about to break down and cry.

"If I hadn't had a miscarriage, I might have a son like Adam," she said, leaning back against the sink. "It's just so hard to imagine. My whole life would have been different."

"You're a young woman, Stel," he told her. "You can still have children if you want to." He paused, then asked a question that had been on his mind. "Why didn't you have a child with Brad? You were certainly married long enough."

"He didn't want children," Stella said, resentment sparking in her voice. "Besides, we had my brother. Mario was like our son. I can't really hold it against him, Sam. All the operations I had cost a fortune, and money was tight then."

Sam looked over at her and smiled. "I wouldn't mind having a few more kids some day. Come on, let's go back outside. We're having ice cream for dessert." Taking her hand, he led her to the yard, dispatching Adam to the kitchen to serve the Ben & Jerry's.

Stella and Sam curled up on the grass on an old blanket. She leaned back and snuggled her head against his neck. "Adam seems so mature for his age. I felt like I was talking to an adult, not a child. Do you know he has clippings of me in his room?"

"Yeah," Sam said. "He's been a fan of yours for a long time. Even before I told him I was handling your divorce, he made me take him down to the courtroom to watch you."

"Which case?" Stella asked, flattered.

"Rodriguez."

Stella was surprised. "That was a rape case, Sam. You'd really let him watch something like that at his age?"

"Why not?" Sam said. "Like I said earlier, he sees a lot worse on television."

Adam came out and they dug into their desserts. The sun had set and the night was clear. Dozens of stars lit up the sky. The temperature was still in the high seventies, but it was no longer uncomfortable. "Look," Adam said, pointing upward. "There's the Big Dipper."

"You need to go to bed, kid," Sam said. "You know, let us grown-ups have some time alone."

"So you can neck, I bet," he said, laughing and punching his father in the arm. "Are you going to come back tomorrow night?" he asked Stella. "If you bring your swimsuit, we can go for a night swim. It's really fun when the lights are all off."

"That's enough," Sam said, shooing him away. "What are you trying to do? Steal my date? Get your own girl, guy. This one is mine."

After Adam reluctantly headed off to his room, Sam pulled Stella into his arms and kissed her passionately. "Tomorrow the housekeeper will be back. We'll go to your place."

"Good idea," Stella said, kissing his forehead, his cheeks, his chin. "I was afraid you were going to tell me it was all right for Adam to watch."

"I'm progressive," Sam laughed, "but not that progressive."

Stella stood and brushed herself off. "I should head for home." They held hands as they walked through the house. "It was a great evening," she said at the door. "I feel almost normal again, as if all this other stuff is nothing more than a dream. Thanks, Sam. I mean it. Not just for tonight, but for everything."

He pulled Stella's head over and whispered in her ear, "Save your gratitude for tomorrow, okay?"

Stella laughed, waving at him over her shoulder as she headed down the steps to her car.

As soon as Stella arrived at the office the next morning, her secretary told her Holly Oppenheimer was on the line.

"We found the missing evidence," Holly said. "Someone misfiled it in the evidence room."

"Good," Stella said. "Can we test it right away?"

"Be my guest, but I won't allow you to take evidence out of Houston. Name a lab here and I'll get Winters to take it over and wait while they perform the tests. There's such a thing as chain of evidence, Stella, in case you've forgotten."

"I'll have to call you back," Stella said. "We'll have to locate a lab in Houston."

"Either you take it and test it," Holly said, "or I'm going to send it to our lab this afternoon. Don't expect me to just sit on it while you figure out what to do. We have time constraints here, you know. I'm being more than cooperative."

Holly's voice was so shrill and her tone so demeaning that Stella had to bite down on the inside of her mouth to keep from saying something she would later regret. "You know what really chaps me, Holly?" she said, unable to remain silent. "Remember all the court appearances I made for you when you were going through your problems with Growman? You know how many hours I was working back then? I hadn't been on the job that long, and some of the things you asked me to do were beyond my capabilities. I could have been fired, and you never even thanked me."

"Don't be silly, Stella," Holly said, "that was years ago. I was appreciative. Maybe I didn't say it, but—"

As Holly's voice trailed off, Stella sensed an opportunity. "Tell me about Mario's case," she said. "Are you still planning to file it as a felony? He's never going to cooperate with you, Holly. I don't know how you could ever think that he would. He's my brother. Besides, he doesn't know anything incriminating. You're wasting your time."

"You're reaching," Holly barked. "If you want to know about your brother's case, ask your damn brother. You know I can't release confidential information."

"You could if you wanted to," Stella shot back. "Don't tell me you haven't done it before, because I know you have. You leaked information to me about Randall's statement that day in your office. Have you forgotten?"

"Up yours," Holly said. "You may pull this

shit on Growman and all your other little pals, but you're not pulling it on me." She stopped and sucked in air. "I wouldn't worry about Mario. I'd say your brother was the least of your problems. Victor Pilgrim positively identified you from a photo lineup about thirty minutes ago. The game is over, Stella."

Stella continued holding the phone to her ear, even though Holly had disconnected. She listened to the incessant drone of the dial tone, unable to separate it from the rushing sound inside her head. Finally she opened her fingers and let the receiver fall, placing her head down on the desk.

Stella could see it all unfolding. Victor Pilgrim, former police officer, slowly turning his head on the witness stand, his eyes cold and accusing. Then she saw his finger go out, the trump card every prosecutor dreamed of possessing, as he positively identified the person who had killed Tom Randall.

Lifting her head, she fingered the paperwork on her desk. She couldn't concentrate on her work, not while her future was leaning toward a jail cell. They had charged her with three separate counts of homicide, along with an additional count of arson. If she rolled the dice, she could spend the remainder of her life in prison.

Perspiration appeared on her forehead. Her chest felt constricted, and acid bubbled back into her throat. How many times had she negotiated plea agreements, looked into the tired eyes of defendants as their attorneys explained the risks inherent in a jury trial. How many of these poor souls had been innocent, the system squeezing them until they gave in? Stella had never given it a second thought. Was she really any different than Holly? Hadn't it always been the conviction that mattered, foreshadowing any concern she might have over the defendant's guilt or innocence?

Even though she found the thought repugnant, Stella knew the time was coming when she would have to contact Fitzgerald and take a long, hard look at her options. What would they offer her? Voluntary manslaughter? Only one charge of murder instead of three? She cringed, picking up her purse and walking out of her office.

chapter

FOURTEEN

Stella and Brenda Anderson arrived in Houston on the four o'clock shuttle, bedraggled and somber. The investigator insisted on being present when Carl Winters transported the evidence to a Houston lab. Stella had only one agenda to pursue in Houston: Victor Pilgrim.

The two women made their way through the Hobby Airport to the rental car counter, where they arranged for a late-model sedan. By the time they picked up their car and drove to the police station, it was after six and Winters had already left for the day.

"Can't you call him at home and ask him to come back down?" Brenda asked the officer in the evidence room. "This is really important. We flew here from Dallas to take care of this, and we'd like to handle it this evening."

The officer looked up Winters's home number and called him. A few moments later, he stuck his head out the window and said the detective wasn't home. "I can't let you take it," he said. "You'll have to wait until tomorrow."

"Great," Brenda said, frustrated. "We should have taken an earlier flight, Stella. I was afraid this was going to happen."

Realizing that the man they were speaking to was the same officer from the day they'd examined the evidence, Stella impulsively stepped up to the window. "A friend of mine used to be an officer here," she said, smiling flirtatiously.

"Really?" the man said. "What's his name?"

"I probably shouldn't tell you his name," Stella said, glancing behind her nervously. "He retired not long ago on disability. I'm curious, though. There's not a thing wrong with him. How did he manage to get disability? He said Captain Cataloni arranged it for him. What do you think? Is he telling the truth?"

"I know who you are," the man said. "Where do you get off saying things like that about the captain? He's your fucking uncle, isn't he?"

Brenda was appalled. She yanked Stella away, and then promptly lit into her as they headed back down the corridor. "What are you doing, Stella? Are you trying to get yourself killed? You might as well paint a target on your back."

"I don't care anymore," Stella snapped. "If Uncle Clem comes after me, that's fine with me. I'm not going to take this lying down, Brenda."

"You're staying with me tonight at the hotel," Brenda said, still annoyed. "I can't let you out of my sight now."

"But I want to talk to Mario," Stella protested. "I've got to get him into a treatment program. If he does what I say, I might be able to convince the court to place him on probation."

They exited the police station and headed for their car in the parking lot. "Call him on the phone," Brenda said, climbing into the driver's seat of their rented Ford.

Stella was circling to the other side when she spotted Clementine Cataloni walking to his car a few feet away. She stopped and froze in place. "Look who's here," she said, tapping on the window to get Anderson's attention.

"Get in the car," Brenda yelled from inside. Once Stella did what she said, she added, "Did he see us?"

"I'm certain he did," Stella answered, her bravado of a few moments ago gone. "He looked right at me. See, he's looking over here now."

"Shit," Brenda said, throwing the gearshift into reverse, making a quick left and then squealing out of the parking lot. "We have to get to Pilgrim right now."

"Do you have his address?"

"Look in that folder," Brenda said, checking her rearview mirror. "I don't think Clem's following us. If he is, he knows what he's do- ing. I can't see a thing."

Stella found the page and read out an address in Galveston Bay. "Okay," Brenda said, "do you know how to get there?"

"Sure," Stella said. "Galveston Bay is near Clear Lake, over by the space center. It's a long drive. Maybe we should call first and make certain he's home."

Brenda jerked her head to the side, surprised that Stella would suggest they announce themselves. But Stella was full of surprises today, and Brenda found it disturbing. "Did you really mean to say that, Stella?"

"No," Stella said, flushing, "I guess not."

Janet Hernandez met her husband for dinner at the Steak and Ale restaurant on Inwood Road, having caught a ride from another secretary at the courthouse. Ray had been held over at the paper, and Janet was too antsy to wait for him to pick her up. Once they were seated and had placed their food orders, he said, "What's going on? You look like the cat who swallowed the canary. You're not mad at me because I had to work late again, are you?"

Janet shook her head. "I went back to the building inspector's office today on my lunch hour," she told him. "I asked if they had a file on the Happy Day disaster and they did, Ray. Tony Cataloni inspected the structure when the kindergarten was first built, and he was the person assigned to look into the cave-in."

"No shit," Ray said, smiling. "What else did you find out?"

"Mr. Cataloni hadn't finished preparing his

report and compiling his findings when he died," Janet continued, "but he did leave a handwritten note in the file that he suspected the foundation was not properly reinforced. The note was dated the day of the fire. He said he was planning to collect a sample of the foundation the following day and have it tested for rebar. But of course, he died, so nothing ever came of it."

"Didn't they assign another building inspector?"

"No," Janet said, pausing as the waitress delivered their drinks. "The people who took over the investigation were claims examiners with the various insurance companies that were involved. The school was built on a landfill, Ray. That's what caused the sinkhole to develop, and of course, the parents of the injured children filed an enormous class-action lawsuit against the development company who sold the school the land. The people at the building inspector's office probably never saw Cataloni's notes. Either that, or someone bribed them to look the other way."

"What exactly is rebar?" Ray asked. "Isn't it some type of steel rods?"

"Yes," Janet said. "Except in a few isolated instances, the building code calls for it. The problem is compliance is hard to enforce because you can't tell if the people have used it or not. Once the foundation is poured, it just looks like concrete and there's no way to tell if it's been reinforced with rebar."

"Now I get the picture," Ray said, his eyes sparkling with interest. "The sinkhole wouldn't have been a problem if the foundation had been reinforced. Isn't that what you're saying? If that's the case, why didn't the victims sue the builders instead of the company that owned the land?"

"They must not have known the foundation wasn't reinforced," she said. "The guy at the building office told me that there are landfills all over the city. Erecting a structure on top of a landfill isn't the optimum situation, but they generally only see some minor settling damage. Most of the time, nothing happens at all. Foundations rarely collapse the way Happy Day's did, causing a major cave-in."

The waitress arrived with their food. Ray had ordered a thick sirloin steak and a baked potato. Janet's meal was a grilled breast of chicken salad. Her husband picked up his knife and fork to begin eating, but his wife gave him a disapproving look, then handed her plate back to the waitress. "Can you keep our food warm in the kitchen, please?" she asked. "We're in the midst of an important conversation."

"No problem," the woman said. "Don't blame me if your steak is overcooked, though."

Ray frowned, watching as the woman picked up his plate. "I can talk and eat at the same time," he said. "Don't you think you're getting a little carried away with this detective stuff?"

"Two children died, Ray," she said. "And don't forget, twenty-three kids were seriously injured. I think you can hear me out, don't you?"

Ray rested his head in one hand. "What was the outcome of the lawsuit?"

"The company that sold the kindergarten the land was held liable," Janet told him. "The court ruled against them because they failed to disclose that there was a landfill underneath the property when they sold it to Happy Day. The settlements were huge, Ray. We're talking millions of dollars here. Isn't that enough to make someone desperate?"

"Who?" he said. "I'm a little lost, Janet."

"That's because you haven't been paying attention," she snapped, her voice loud enough that several diners at adjoining tables turned around. "The people who laid the foundation were responsible for what happened, Ray, not the development company."

"Okay," he said. "Who laid the foundation?"

The fire vanished from Janet's eyes. "I don't know," she said. "I haven't gotten that far yet. I found out the name of the company who built the structure, but a lot of the work was done by subcontractors, and their names aren't listed in the file. Littlefield Construction went out of business not long after the fire, so it's going to be difficult to track down the principals."

"You're doing good, babe," Ray said, flagging down the waitress to bring them their food. "Let's eat, okay? Then I'll give you some suggestions on how to proceed."

Galveston was a Mecca for tourists, particularly during the summer months. An enormous traffic jam blocked Highway 145, which led to Galveston Bay, and teenagers and young adults were hanging out of car windows, while their stereos blasted out rock music. "You should come here during spring break," Stella said to Brenda. "It's a zoo."

Finally the traffic opened up, and they passed a lovely recreational area with a marina, restaurants, and antique and specialty shops. The sun was setting and the sky was awash with brilliant colors. Dozens of sailboats were tacking toward the harbor, their sails billowing in the ocean breeze. "This is one thing they don't have in Dallas," Stella said, enjoying the view out of her window. "Water. Sometimes I miss it. You know, my father always wanted to have a boat. His own father was a fisherman in Italy. He used to drive us down here on Sundays after mass just to watch the yachts come into the harbor."

"We have to find Shoreline Drive," Brenda told her. "Does the map have the smaller streets, or just the major thoroughfares?"

"Turn right," Stella said, leaning forward and peering out the window. "I'm almost certain Shoreline Drive cuts in to the right. It's one of the streets that overlooks the harbor."

Approximately twenty minutes later, they pulled up in front of a modest beach house, squeezing the Fairlane into the only parking spot left on the street. Even though the house was little more than a cottage, they both realized Victor Pilgrim had paid a tidy sum for it. Any property near the water was expensive, and Pilgrim had the Gulf of Mexico right in his backyard. Kids were zipping by on skateboards, or walking with surfboards balanced on their heads. People were carrying sacks of food and supplies to their boats in the nearby marina. Several cars roared by, clearly exceeding the speed limit, occupied by what appeared to be intoxicated teenagers. "Looks like fun," Brenda quipped. "How many people do you think they kill here a year? A dozen, two dozen? Most of these kids aren't old enough to buy beer."

"It's a good place if you want a tan," Stella said. "Other than that, it sucks."

"I don't really need a tan," Brenda said. She reached for the door handle, then added, "You have to wait in the car. Pilgrim will recognize you."

Brenda walked up and rang the bell. After waiting some time, a woman opened the door. She was plain-looking, with grayish hair, wearing a blue shirtwaist dress. "Is Victor Pilgrim home?" Brenda said, flipping her shield and then quickly shoving it back in her purse. "I'm with the D.A.'s office, ma'am. I need to ask him a few questions."

"Wait here," the woman said, disappearing into the house. When she returned, she had a puzzled look on her face. "He was here just a minute ago, but now I can't find him. Maybe he went for a walk on the beach. Would you like to come in and wait? I'm certain he'll be back soon. He never walks for very long because of his leg."

Brenda was intrigued by the woman's face. Something about her eyes struck Brenda as strange. She never focused on the investigator's face, but seemed to be looking right past her. On impulse she waved her hand in front of her. The woman didn't blink. Then Brenda looked down and saw the cane in her hand. "If you don't mind, we'll come back later. Oh, and what's wrong with your husband's leg?"

"It still hurts him," she said. "He was hit when he worked for the police department. He was writing a ticket on the freeway and a drunk driver slammed into the car behind him."

"Which department was that?"

"I'm sorry," she said, "I didn't catch your name."

"Brenda Anderson," she said, sticking out her hand to shake, then feeling foolish when the woman just stood there, her arms straight at her sides.

"I have to go," she said, closing the door in the investigator's face.

When she got back inside the car, Brenda turned to Stella. "Victor Pilgrim's wife is blind."

"Where's Pilgrim?"

"I may have blown it," Brenda continued. "I think I said the wrong thing."

"What did you say?"

"I asked which department her husband was with when he was injured."

"What's so bad about that?"

"Think about it," she said. "Pilgrim's getting a pension from Houston. Don't you think he should have incurred the leg injury while he was with the Houston P.D., not while he was still employed in San Antonio?"

"I don't understand," Stella said. "If this is a scam, he wouldn't be disabled at all."

"Not necessarily," Brenda told her. "It's usually very difficult for a cop to get disability retirement. As long as you can stand upright, most departments want you on the job. You know, the government thinks a warm body is better than nothing, particularly when they know the alternative is dishing out a pension every month."

"Are they really that callous?" Stella asked, appalled at what she was hearing.

"You bet," Brenda said. "But at the same time, the officers brought a lot of this down on themselves. They take a few tumbles and then cry wolf, claiming their injuries are worse than they really are. Sometimes they lose their nerve, you know. Something spooks them. A near miss. A particularly nasty scene. A supervisor that's all over their ass. Where do you go when you've been a cop for ten years? Go to work for the sanitation department? So they want out, and disability is a way to get what they want and still get paid for it."

"But Pilgrim sounds legitimately disabled," Stella said. "If so, why would he need my uncle's help?"

Brenda paused, thinking she saw Victor Pilgrim returning home. But the man had no limp, and she resumed her explanation. "It all fits together," she continued. "Let's say some of these men were legitimately injured, but they just couldn't get their superiors to classify them as disabled. Like I just told you, the doctors see so many phony claims that the criteria have become very stringent and many legitimate cases are probably turned down. These guys meet your uncle, and he makes the necessary arrangements. To guys like this, your uncle must be a saint."

"I see what you mean," Stella said.

"Not only that," she said. "If Pilgrim's wife is blind, he'd have an even greater reason to want disability retirement. Cops work long shifts, and the poor woman would be alone all the time."

For a long time, they just sat there, both of them immersed in their thoughts. Finally Stella said, "Are we just going to sit here? He might not come back for hours."

"No," Brenda said, engaging the engine, "let's get something to eat. Then we'll come back and see what Mr. Pilgrim has to say."

Over dinner, the two women tried to keep their conversation light. The day had been stressful and they both were ready to set talk of the case aside. "Have you ever thought of getting married?" Stella asked.

"I was married for about three years," Brenda said, dabbing at her mouth with a napkin. "It was the worst three years of my life."

"What happened?"

"You know," she said, popping a french fry in her mouth, "not a lot of black guys want to be married to a cop. If you want to know the truth, it's hard to find someone who hasn't been arrested at one time or the other."

"I think you're exaggerating," Stella said. "There's all kinds of black professionals out there. Doctors, engineers, lawyers. How can you say that?"

"Because it's true," Brenda answered. "Do you have any idea how many black men are in prison? Just look at the statistics. And the educated professionals you just mentioned, well, a lot of them marry white women."

"Then marry a white guy," Stella said. "Why would that be so bad?"

Brenda laughed. A few moments later, she fell serious again. "Men in general don't like women with authority, Stella, and black men are the worst. It's an ego thing with them. If anyone carries a gun, they think it should be them."

"Was your husband in law enforcement?"

"I don't date cops anymore," Brenda said, toying with the salt shaker. "And to answer your question, yes, he was. I got promoted to sergeant while he remained in patrol. Didn't sit too well, evidently. He moved out the following week, but not before he tried a little attitude adjustment. He broke four of my ribs. In return, I gave him a black eye and a ruptured spleen." She forced a wry grin. "That's one good thing about being a cop. When some guy tries to beat the shit out of you, you at least have the skills to retaliate."

"Well, in my situation," Stella said, "Brad didn't beat me, but he resented my career horribly." That reminded her of her financial problems. "I'm waiting to hear from Sam tonight. He's trying to negotiate our financial agreement so I can get a loan and hire an attorney."

"I thought he was meeting with your husband the other day," Brenda said, pushing her plate away. "Isn't that what you told me?"

"Sam set up a time for them to meet, but when he got to Brad's office, he wasn't there. What a prick, huh? I'm sure he stood him up on purpose.

He's pissed because I refused to sign over everything we owned the day he came to the jail."

Brenda insisted on picking up the check even though Stella protested. "I'll charge it back to the city," she lied, determined not to let Stella find out that she was working without pay. "You need to watch your nickels right now, Stella."

"Thanks," she said. "If the city ever finds out about this, I'll be in hock the rest of my life."

"Being in hock is better than being in prison," Brenda told her.

They drove back to Victor Pilgrim's house, and Brenda went to the door again. After ringing the bell repeatedly and knocking, she finally gave up and returned to the car. "They're in there. I can even hear the television set, but they won't come to the door. I guess Pilgrim doesn't want anyone to ask him any questions about his pension."

"Are you going to try again?" Stella asked, grasping her arm. "We have to crack him, Brenda. It's the only way I'm ever going to clear myself. Can't you come back another day?"

"Probably not," Brenda said. "If your uncle has warned him to keep quiet, he'll never talk to me. But there are dozens of ways to discredit a witness. You, of all people, should know that. Don't lose faith, Stella. It may take some time, but we'll get the goods on Pilgrim."

"Damn," Stella said. The strain of the day finally struck home and she leaned her head back against the headrest. They rode the remainder of the way in silence.

★ ★ ★

It was after ten o'clock by the time they arrived at the Holiday Inn. The air-conditioning in the Fairlane had gone out as soon as they had left Galveston, and Stella was hot and sticky. "I get the first go at the shower," she said, getting out and grabbing her suitcase from the backseat.

"No problem," Brenda said, waiting until Stella stepped aside and then reaching into the backseat for her computer case. The only other luggage she had brought was a small cosmetic case. Now she wished she had brought a change of clothing, as her blouse was damp with perspiration, and she didn't have anything fresh to wear the following day. Catching sight of the hotel's swimming pool, she yearned to submerge herself in the cool water. "If I'd brought a bathing suit, I'd jump in the pool. Think I could get away with skinny dipping?"

"Hey," Stella answered, "as far as I'm concerned, you can do anything you want. I won't tell a soul."

"I'm kidding, Stella," Brenda said, chuckling at her. "You're an intelligent person, but for some reason, you never know when I'm teasing you."

"That's because you're always so serious," Stella said, bumping shoulders with her as they walked across the courtyard to the main entrance. "I don't think I ever heard you laugh before we started working together on my case. Why are you so quiet at the office?"

"It's hard to explain," Brenda told her. "I guess I want people to see me as a professional, to know that I take my work seriously."

"Well, you've got that—"

Brenda suddenly stopped and stared across the parking lot. Stella followed her line of sight, wondering why she stopped. "Get down," Brenda screamed, pushing hard on the top of Stella's head.

"Why?" Stella said, fighting to keep her head up so she could see why Brenda was so excited. "What's going on?"

The investigator leaped in front of Stella just as a blast of gunfire rang out. Six shots came in rapid succession. In no time, the air reeked of cordite. Stella heard Brenda let out a scream and then felt her body fall on top of her, pinning her to the asphalt. "Help," Stella shouted, "someone's shooting at us. Are you all right, Brenda?"

"Run, Stella," the investigator said, struggling as she tried to work her gun out of her shoulder holster. When it was finally in her grip, she rolled off Stella onto her stomach. "I'll cover you," she said, panting. "Go to the lobby and call for help. Tell them it's a sniper. He's on the south side of the courtyard. It looks like the fifth room from the left."

"Oh, God, no," Stella exclaimed, seeing a pool of blood spreading under the investigator's waist, "you've been shot, Brenda. I can't leave you here. You're bleeding. We've got to get you to a hospital."

"Get out of my line of fire," Brenda shouted, bringing her service revolver up and bracing it in both hands.

Stella couldn't move. Brenda's hands were covered in blood, and the pool beneath her was rapidly expanding. "You're going to bleed to

312

death," Stella cried. "Please, Brenda, let me get you to the hospital. We'll go in the car. You're bleeding too badly to wait for an ambulance."

"Get the fuck out of here before you get us both killed," Brenda said, swiping at her mouth with the back of her hand and leaving a bloody streak. "Now, Stella! Do what I say. Take off! He's probably reloading right this minute."

Stella took off, running in the direction of the lobby, expecting a bullet to tear into her flesh any second. But when she glanced toward the area where the shots had come from, all she saw was an open window, the curtains flapping back and forth in the breeze.

"Call an ambulance and the cops," she said, pounding the counter to get the clerk's attention. "Hurry, a police officer has been shot. Keep everyone inside. Don't let anyone go outside or they could get hurt. He's shooting from across the courtyard . . . from one of the rooms."

As soon as Stella saw the clerk pick up the phone, she rushed back outside. With no concern for her own safety, she ran across the courtyard and dropped to her knees next to Brenda Anderson. The woman had tumbled over onto her back and a gaping, bloody hole was visible in her abdomen. Her eyes were closed, her skin ashen, and a trickle of blood oozed out of the corner of her mouth. Stella shook her shoulder. "Brenda, can you hear me? God, talk to me. Please, don't die," she pleaded, tears coursing down her face.

With trembling fingers Stella felt for the pulse in Brenda's neck, relieved when she felt the faint beat of her heart beneath her hand. Then she bent down and placed her cheek next to her mouth, relieved to feel the woman's breath brush across her skin.

Glancing toward the lobby, she saw people lined up in front of the glass, watching and waiting. Yanking off her blouse, she rolled it into a ball and pressed it against the open wound to stop the bleeding. "You're going to be okay, Brenda," she told her, leaning down close to her ear. "It's not bad," she lied. The blouse was quickly soaked with blood. She knew her friend might be only moments away from death. "You're going to be just fine. Just hold on. Keep fighting. You're strong. You can do it."

From a distance Stella heard the squeal of sirens. "Please, God, don't let her die," she whispered under her breath.

A minute later a black-and-white police unit roared up and parked, an ambulance pulling up right behind it. By the time the first two officers had exited their units, four more police cars had pulled into the circular driveway. The cars formed a shield around Brenda and Stella.

"What happened?" an officer said, bending down next to Stella. Behind them, paramedics were unloading medical supplies and a gurney from the back of the ambulance. Police officers were scattering across the courtyard, several of them with shotguns in their hands.

"We were just walking to the lobby," Stella said, "when someone started shooting at us. They were over there across the courtyard, in one of the rooms. They must have been shooting out the window."

"Is she a cop?" the officer asked as the paramedics appeared and started working over Anderson. "The dispatcher said this was an officer assist."

The paramedics motioned for the officer and Stella to move away to give them some space. Men were running in the direction of the open window with their guns drawn, while another team of men entered the hotel to access the room from inside. "Just in case he's still around," the officer said, "why don't we talk in the lobby?"

Once they were inside, the officer told all the people gathered around the door to go back to their rooms. Stella wouldn't leave the area by the glass doors because she wanted to see what was happening with Brenda. It dawned on her that she was wearing only her bra and slacks now, and she was grateful when the officer got a blanket and tossed it over her shoulders. "The sniper must have fled," she said. "If he was still around, he would have shot me when I came back outside."

"Did you see him?"

Stella shook her head, pulling the blanket tightly around her, then stopping to wipe her bloody hands on her slacks. "He was too far away. I don't know what Brenda saw, though. She must have seen him, because she pulled me down. Thank goodness, you got here when you did. Another minute, and I'm certain she would have bled to death."

"When you call in an officer assist," the man

315

told her, "we run like hell." His eyes scanned the parking lot. "Almost every unit within fifty miles responded. Even the S.O. sent deputies. Is this woman really an officer?"

"D.A.'s investigator," Stella told him. "And she's the best there is."

"Have any idea who did this?"

"Yes, I do," she said, immediately clamming up. They were lifting Brenda into the ambulance now and Stella opened the door to go outside. "I'm going with her."

"I don't think that's a good idea," the officer said, grabbing an edge of the blanket. "We need to get your statement, find out what happened out here. If you know who the sniper is, you better tell us right now."

"No," Stella snapped, jerking away from him. "If you want to know who did this, call Jack Fitzgerald at the D.A.'s office and have him meet me at the hospital. I won't talk to anyone but him."

While the officer stood there with a baffled look on his face, Stella rushed over to the ambulance and climbed in the back with the paramedics. "How is she?"

"Touch and go," the female paramedic said, busy adjusting the IV over Anderson's head. Then she looked over at Stella. "Who are you? You can't come in here like this."

"I'm a D.A.," Stella said, taking on an authoritative demeanor. "This woman works for me and I'm not going to leave her. She's my responsibility."

"Well," the woman said, "she's lost a lot of

blood. She's in shock right now and her pulse is extremely weak."

Stella's voice quavered as she asked, "Will she make it?"

"Your guess is as good as mine," the woman said, shrugging. The rear doors slammed shut, and the paramedic seemed to measure Stella for a second before she explained, "It depends on where the bullet went once it entered her abdomen. If it lodged in her lungs, her heart, her kidneys, it could have done an enormous amount of damage. We're not going to know much until we get her to the hospital and take some X-rays."

As the ambulance raced down the highway, Stella edged over next to Brenda and picked up her hand. "She's going to be okay," she said, yelling over the shrill of the siren. "I'm not going to let you go, Brenda," she shouted at the unconscious woman. "Do you hear me? You're going to be just fine."

chapter

FIFTEEN

The clock in the waiting room at Methodist Hospital read 3:08. Stella was exhausted and sick with worry. A member of the hospital staff had given her a green surgical shirt to wear, but she was still dressed in the same bloodstained slacks.

Seated on a small, orange vinyl sofa, she was sipping a cup of lukewarm coffee.

Brenda Anderson's parents were seated in two chairs across from her. As soon as they were notified, they had caught the first flight to Houston. By the time they arrived, however, their daughter was already in surgery.

The X-rays had indicated the bullet was lodged dangerously close to Brenda's aorta, and no one could say for certain if she would survive the operation. All they could do now was wait and pray.

Before Anderson's parents had arrived, Stella had spent the better part of an hour on the phone. She called both Growman and Sam. Then she reached Mario, wanting him to know that they were all in imminent danger. Sam wanted to fly to Houston immediately, but Stella told him there was nothing he could do. In Growman's case, however, Stella agreed that it was wise that he come as soon as possible. Anderson was a county employee, and people would want to know what she was doing in Houston.

Milton Anderson was a tall, distinguished-looking man, with a spattering of gray in his neatly trimmed hair. Stella decided Brenda took her height and regal bearing from him, but her eyes and mouth resembled her mother's. Dressed in a full skirt and a colorful print blouse, Eleanor Anderson was reserved and dignified. She wasn't crying or wringing her hands. She sat quietly without speaking, a lightweight cotton sweater tossed over her shoulders. In her hands she held a pocket-sized Bible.

"She should be out of surgery by now," her father said, standing and pacing. "They said three o'clock, didn't they? It's after three."

"Should I go check?" Stella asked.

"No, no," he said, his voice resonant. "They'll come in when they know something. Let them do their job. No use bothering them."

"Brenda is a wonderful person," Stella said, looking down at her hands. "This wouldn't have happened if she hadn't been trying to save my life. I'm certain they were after me. She shoved me aside, took the bullet for me. I've never known anyone that brave."

"She was just doing her job," her father said. Walking over, he softly patted Stella on the back. "She wouldn't want you to feel bad. Our Brenda isn't like that."

Stella heard a commotion outside in the hall and leaped to her feet. She and Milton Anderson rushed out to the corridor to see what was going on. Jack Fitzgerald was standing in the hall yelling, a thick black cigar clamped between his teeth. "It's not lit, okay," he said. "Can't you cut me some slack, Lois? You've been riding my ass for twenty years now."

"Fine," an older nurse with a no-nonsense look said. "I'll just hold it for you, then." She reached over and snatched the cigar out of his mouth.

"Damn you, woman," he barked. "Give that back to me. That cigar cost me three bucks and change."

"Six times I've caught you smoking this filthy thing in my hospital," she said, waving the cigar in his face. "No more, you hear me? I don't care if you're the president, Jack. You're not smoking on my floor."

When the nurse had marched off, cigar in hand, Fitzgerald spotted Stella and walked over. "This is Milton Anderson," she said. "He's Brenda Anderson's father, the woman who was shot tonight."

"Jack Fitzgerald," he said, pumping Anderson's hand. "Pleased to meet you. Sorry about your daughter. Nasty affair, huh?"

Milton Anderson just stared at him. Then he returned to the waiting room to check on his wife.

Once they were alone, Fitzgerald said, "What's going on, Cataloni? Patrol said you refused to talk to anyone but me. I'm here, so let's get on with it. You didn't get a fellow out of bed for nothing, I hope."

"I don't want to talk here," Stella said. "Come with me. There's another waiting room down the hall."

An hour had passed. At the thirty-minute mark, Stella had excused herself and checked to see if Brenda was out of surgery yet. She met the surgeon in the hall, just as he had finished speaking to Brenda's parents. Things had gone well, he said, but the injury was serious, and Anderson's condition would be listed as critical for the next twenty-four hours. If her condition was stable by then, he advised, the chances were good that she would make a full recovery. Feeling a measure of relief, Stella returned to Jack Fitzgerald to conclude their conversation.

"This is some story," Fitzgerald said, leaning

back in his chair and stretching his legs out. "The strange part about it is someone else was concerned about this pension thing. I think it was a few years back, though, and I don't recall the specifics. If I'm not mistaken, it was the city controller who brought it up."

"Don't you see?" Stella said. "My uncle saw us at the police department when we went to transfer the evidence to the lab. He knew I was back in town. That alone might have been enough to force his hand."

"Then you went to see this Pilgrim fellow," he said, rubbing the side of his face. "Pilgrim must have been the icing on the cake."

"Exactly," Stella said. "When I talked to the officers here at the hospital, they told me they think the sniper used a high-powered assault rifle with a scope. I know my uncle has a gun like that because I saw it in his gun cabinet just the other day. I'm not certain if it was an assault rifle, but I know the gun I saw had a scope and a long barrel."

"That's not enough to issue an arrest warrant, though," Fitzgerald said.

"Why not?" Stella asked. "You arrested me with practically no evidence. I don't see why you can't arrest my uncle. Brenda has been making all kinds of inquiries regarding the pension scam. It's not like we're asking you to go into this empty-handed. Once I get all her notes correlated, we should have the beginnings of a pretty solid case."

Fitzgerald pushed himself to his feet, reaching in his pocket for a fresh cigar. He started to put it in his mouth and then thought better of it, rolling it in his fingers instead. "Let me get my people on this. We want to see what the crime lab comes up with. Maybe they picked up some decent evidence from the hotel room."

"Doubtful," Stella said, scowling. "My uncle was a police captain. If he did this, you won't find a thing." Seeing Fitzgerald was about to walk out the door, she called out to him. "Wait," she said. "You have to do something for me. I need those metal pieces. I want you to release them to me."

"I can't do that," Fitzgerald said, sticking the cigar in his mouth, plastic wrapper and all. "You know I can't release evidence in a homicide."

"You have to," Stella pleaded. "I don't know who's involved in this, who we can trust. Those pieces of metal are the most valuable evidence we have right now. You turn them over to Carl Winters or someone else at the P.D. and they may disappear. How do we know how many people are mixed up in this? For all I know, Holly Oppenheimer is involved as well."

"That's preposterous," the older D.A. said. "This pension scam, if there is such a thing, only involves police officers. Why would you think my people would be involved?"

"Winters isn't one of your people, remember?" Stella said. "He's a cop, Jack, and he's been out to railroad me for years. If Winters is involved, then Oppenheimer can't be trusted either. She and Winters are tight. Holly is a jealous, vindictive woman. She'll do anything to convict me."

"Hmmmm," he said, pondering her request. "You're asking me to do something that could

322

compromise our case. Not only that, it's highly irregular."

Stella leaped to her feet. "What case?" she shouted. "The case against me? There is no case. Don't you realize that now? If I'm the bad guy, why is someone trying to kill me?" She thrust her chin out in defiance. "A good woman was shot tonight, Fitzgerald. Add up the deaths. My parents, Randall, and now, Brenda Anderson almost lost her life. How long is it going to be before you wise up?"

"Don't take that tone with me," he said, narrowing his eyes. "You're still facing murder charges, young lady, no matter what happened tonight. This here shooting may have no connection to the crimes you've been charged with. Just because a man is running a pension scam doesn't mean he's a murderer. For all I know, you're simply trying to pull a fast one on us, take advantage of this situation."

Blood rushed to Stella's face. "I resent that," she snapped. "I'm trying to put together your damn case, Fitzgerald. Not only did you put me on trial for something I didn't do, your idiot prosecutors created a fucking nightmare. If you hadn't gone after me, Randall would be alive and Anderson wouldn't have been shot tonight. When I turn up with a bullet in my head—"

Fitzgerald held up a hand. "Calm down, okay," he said. "Let's say I do agree to give you this evidence and see what you can make of it, where exactly would you want me to send it?"

Stella knew the name of the lab, but it had momentarily disappeared from her memory, so she made up a name of a lab and jotted down Mario's address beneath it. "Anderson was certain those metal chips came from a Zippo lighter. If we can make out the inscription, you might have enough evidence to bring charges against my uncle."

Fitzgerald still looked unconvinced. "And the information on the pension scam," he said, scratching the side of his face. "Where is it?"

"Anderson probably stored it in her computer," Stella told him. "Why don't we make a deal? I'll give you what we have on Clem Cataloni. In exchange, you send me the metal chips. As soon as I get the results, I'll send a copy of the report directly to your office, along with the evidence."

"I didn't say I'd do it," he drawled. "I have to look into this and give it some serious thought. You know, I have people of my own I can trust."

"You owe me, Fitzgerald," she said, fixing him with an icy gaze. "Do you know what I've been through? I could have been killed out there tonight. At least give me a chance to protect myself and prove who's behind all this." Stella could see her plea for compassion was falling on deaf ears, so she switched tactics. "I could sue for unlawful detainment, false arrest, loss of wages, and libel. My career is seriously tarnished, and I was flying high before this went down. This was the most trumped-up case I've ever seen, Jack." She pointed a finger at him. "I'm a D.A., for Christ's sake. Let me try to put this together before you and your people end up looking like a bunch of idiots."

Fitzgerald drew himself to full height. "I'll let you know," he said, shuffling toward the door.

"Whatever you do," Stella cautioned, "you better do it fast. If you don't, more lives will be lost."

Stella stopped to check on Anderson's parents, and then took a taxi to the hotel, her eyes smarting in the early morning sun. She was relieved to find the car was still in the hotel parking lot and that the police had not towed it off as evidence. Because the shooting had occurred outside, she assumed they didn't think anything could be accomplished by examining it. She needed to find Anderson's computer, but after checking inside the car, she remembered that the investigator had been carrying it at the time of the shooting. The police had more than likely taken the computer in with the rest of the evidence. Now Stella would have to go through miles of red tape to get it back.

She picked up her key at the desk and headed upstairs to her room, thinking that tomorrow she would have to switch hotels. It was doubtful that the shooter would come back tonight, though, she decided, unlocking the door to her room. She didn't believe he would be stupid enough to try to ambush her again in the same hotel.

She had ripped off her clothes and entered the shower when she heard the phone ringing in the other room. Grabbing a towel, she rushed to answer it.

"Is this Stella Cataloni?" a man's voice said.

"Yes," she said. "Who is this?"

"Victor Pilgrim," he said. "I need to talk to you."

Stella had not slept all night. By the time she arrived at Jack Fitzgerald's office at nine o'clock, her eyes were bloodshot and her skin had an unhealthy pallor. Growman was waiting in the outer office, having just arrived from Dallas. "I called your hotel from the airport," he said, eyeing the man standing next to her. "They said you left instructions that I should come straight here. What's going on, Stella?"

"This," Stella said, tilting her head to the side, "is Victor Pilgrim, the state's primary witness."

"I see," Growman said. "Want to fill me in?"

"There's no use telling the story twice," she said. "Is Fitzgerald here yet? I called him at home and told him we were coming."

Growman walked over to the secretary's desk, waiting as she buzzed the district attorney over the intercom. Once Fitzgerald's secretary had announced them, they entered his musky office and took seats in the heavy oak chairs around his desk. "Mr. Pilgrim has something to say," Stella said. "Go on, Vic. Tell them what you told me."

Victor Pilgrim was a plain-looking man, with light brown hair and a thin mustache. He was dressed in a pink polo shirt and cotton slacks. At one time he was probably robust and fit, but at present he was stooped-shouldered and whatever muscles he had once possessed had turned to flab. "Where do I start?" he said, a pathetic look on his face.

"Start from the beginning," Stella said. "Tell them exactly what you told me."

He hesitated a moment, then sighed. "I was injured on duty," he said slowly, "when I was a deputy with the San Antonio Sheriff's Department a number of years back. In the beginning I didn't have any beefs. My medical care was adequate and everyone at the department was supportive. But once my sick leave was used up, the brass demanded that I come back to work. They said I could have a desk job until I could go back to patrol." He cleared his throat. "I knew I could never go back to patrol. It isn't just my leg, see, it's my wife."

"She's legally blind," Stella said. "Victor said she was raped. During the attack the rapist hit her over the head with a baseball bat. The blows to the head caused both her retinas to detach."

"Everything just happened at once," Pilgrim continued. "First, my accident and then my wife was attacked. I didn't want to put her in a nursing home. I love my wife. How could I leave her alone all day by herself?"

"Please go on," Fitzgerald said, firing up a cigar and puffing clouds of smoke out into the room. "If you were legitimately disabled, why didn't the San Antonio department give you a pension?"

"Don't think I didn't fight for it," Pilgrim said. "I got an attorney and everything, but we still lost. These people, I don't know," he said, his voice trailing off. "Seems as if they do everything in their power to make it tough on guys like me. They said I was malingering, you know, making it up. The county physician swore there was no physical reason for me to limp. Maybe he was right and I just didn't want to leave my wife. A person's mind is a strange thing."

"How did you meet Cataloni?" Growman asked.

"Well, while I was out on leave after the accident," Pilgrim told him, "I got involved in the Knights of Columbus. It was just something to do, a way to keep myself occupied. We had a big affair in Houston and that's where I met Clem." He stopped, as if searching for words. "I don't know exactly how it went down. I mentioned something about my problems, and Clem said he could help. All I had to do was transfer to Houston, he told me. He promised he'd get me hired without a physical. I just had to hide the limp." Pilgrim shrugged. "He even suggested that I learn to walk in a certain way so it seemed as if the limp was nothing more than a distinctive walk. Kind of like a swagger, he said. That's the exact words he used too." He paused and looked Fitzgerald in the eye. "Just swagger, he told me, and they'll never know the difference."

"Tell them what happened after you got to Houston," Stella interjected.

"Well, nothing much happened," he said. "I went to work in patrol. It was hard, but I took a lot of pills and tried my best not to limp or get in a foot pursuit. My wife stayed in San Antonio with her sister. After about six months Cataloni gave me these papers, certifying me as permanently disabled. They were signed by the city doctor, but I never even met the guy."

"How were you supposedly injured?" Growman asked.

"One night he staged an accident, see, making it appear as if I had hurt my leg on duty. He set it up to look like a hit and run, but I never went to the hospital. He supplied me with papers that said I went to the hospital. I even had bills from the hospital, but I guess they were all just phonies he had made up at some printing company. Regardless, the city accepted them and I finally got my pension."

"Aren't you forgetting something?" Stella said, leaning forward. When Pilgrim gave her a blank look, she said, "What about the money, Vic?"

"Oh," he said, "Cataloni made me pay him twenty grand for the documentation papers. I didn't have that much saved, so he agreed to let me pay him in installments. I think I still owe him about five grand." His face flushed. "That's why I agreed to do it, see. He said he'd wipe my debt clean if I did it, and with my wife's problems, money is hard to come by right now."

"Do what?" Growman said. "Spell it out, Pilgrim."

"Say I saw a woman in a white rental car leaving the scene of the Randall homicide."

Although Stella had already heard his story, she found it hard to suppress her outrage. Fidgeting in her seat, she said, "It was more than that, wasn't it, Vic? You positively identified me from a photo lineup."

"Clem coerced me into doing it," he said defensively. "He said they needed a positive ID, and just saying I saw a woman in a white car wasn't good enough."

"Your statements were all lies?" Fitzgerald said, biting down hard on his cigar. "I want to make sure I'm hearing this right. Everything you told the police was fabricated, fed to you by Clem Cataloni? You never saw this woman at the scene of the crime?"

"Yeah," Pilgrim said, scratching at an angry rash on his forearm. "But I didn't know Clem was the one who shot and killed the guy. I would never get involved in something like that—a murder, for God's sake. This is what he told me, see. He told me his niece had murdered his brother and sister-in-law and got away with it. He said she killed this Randall guy as well, but they'd never be able to prove it if I didn't help them. I thought I was doing a public service, you know, getting some dangerous criminal off the street."

"Did you really believe that?" Growman asked.

"Yeah," Pilgrim said, completely earnest. "I swear I did. If I had thought the woman was innocent, I'd never have agreed to do it. I was a cop, see, a damn good cop. I may not be a cop anymore, but I still have values." He started scratching at his arm again. "I'm not a bad person, really," he said, glancing down at the rash and seeing that he had drawn blood. "I never wanted to hurt anyone." He grimaced. "Now I'm fucked, aren't I?"

"What made you come forward today?" Fitzgerald asked.

"Because he shot that lady," he shouted, the first time he had raised his voice. "She was one of us, in law enforcement, you know. How could I remain silent and let him get away with that? This Anderson woman didn't kill anyone. She was just trying to do her job."

"When you say he," Growman said, thinking they should be recording Pilgrim's statements, "are you referring to Cataloni? These are serious allegations. You have to be specific."

"Of course it was Cataloni," Pilgrim said, glowering. "Who else have I been talking about?"

"How can you be sure he was the one who shot her?"

"Easy," Pilgrim said. "He tried to get me to do it for him and I refused."

The room fell silent. Fitzgerald looked over at Stella and then at Growman, shocked at what he had heard. Pilgrim started clawing at his arm again. Stella pulled a tissue out of her purse and handed it to Pilgrim to blot the blood. "When Brenda Anderson and I came to your house," she said, "why didn't you come clean then? If you had, this poor woman wouldn't be in a hospital right now fighting for her life."

"I was afraid," Pilgrim said, his eyes widening. "Captain Cataloni isn't the only one involved in this pension deal. No one wanted this thing to come to light."

"Aren't you afraid now?" Stella asked. "If you give us the names of these individuals you just mentioned, we can have warrants issued for their arrest."

"Not on your life," he answered, letting Stella

331

know that she was reaching the end of the line. He had stepped forward and admitted his involvement, but he would not roll over on his fellow officers. At least not until he had been offered the right incentive. "Are you guys going to offer me immunity?"

"Now wait just a minute," Fitzgerald said. He had been nodding off, the lack of sleep from the night before taking its toll. When he heard the word *immunity*, he sprang back to life. "I'm a little confused here. Who did Cataloni want you to shoot? Brenda Anderson?"

"No," Pilgrim said, pointing at Stella. "She's the one he wanted dead. Didn't you hear what I said a few minutes ago? He thought she killed his brother."

"What about Randall? Did Cataloni kill Randall?"

"I don't know," Pilgrim said. "He could have, I guess, but he tried to make me think his niece had done it." He paused, looking around the room, as if he wasn't certain where to direct his next question. "What are you guys going to offer me? I can't go to jail because of my wife. Are you going to grant me immunity in exchange for my testimony?"

Growman started to speak, then deferred to Fitzgerald. He would have no say as to what happened to Victor Pilgrim as the crimes had occurred outside of his jurisdiction.

Fitzgerald's beady eyes flashed, and a glimpse of the feisty young prosecutor he had once been reappeared. "In this city, Mr. Pilgrim," he said forcefully, "you do the crime, you do the time.

332

If you're looking for a free ride, you've come to the wrong town."

By two o'clock that afternoon, Fitzgerald had secured an arrest warrant for Stella's uncle for multiple counts of fraud, along with one count of attempted murder in the shooting of Brenda Anderson.

"I can't believe it," Stella told Growman. "Are they moving too fast? Do they have enough to make the charges stick? I pushed them, but I don't want them to do anything to compromise the case."

"They have Pilgrim," he said. "Right now that's all they need. Once they arrest your uncle, they'll search his house. Then they'll run ballistics tests on the guns in his gun cabinet. If they find the weapons used to shoot Brenda and Randall, your uncle's down for the count."

As soon as Stella finished speaking to Growman, she left the D.A.'s office and rushed to the hospital to see Brenda Anderson. The investigator had still not regained consciousness.

"What does the doctor say?" she asked, finding Anderson's parents in the waiting room outside the intensive care unit.

"She's in a coma," Milton Anderson said. "The longer she stays out, the greater the chance the coma could be permanent."

Stella put her hand over her mouth, trying to keep from crying. She glanced through the glass windows to Brenda's room and saw all the tubes and equipment. Once she regained her composure, she asked the nurse if she could go in to see her.

"Are you family?" she asked.

"Yes," Stella said, overlooking the fact that her skin was a different color.

"I guess it's all right then," the nurse said, bending her head back down to her chart.

Stella walked into the room. She was shocked when she saw Brenda's face. She looked so different, so helpless and frail. Leaning close to the bed, she spoke into her ear. "You have to wake up, Brenda. Everyone's here for you. Your mother and father are here. I'm here. We all love you and want you to get well."

For a long time Stella just stood there, not knowing what to say or do. It was such a tragic situation. Stella felt her heart wrenching as she pressed Brenda's limp hand. "We're going to get him, Brenda. I only wish you could be there," she said. "We're going to arrest my uncle this evening at five o'clock. Pilgrim confessed to everything. Because of you, I'm going to be cleared."

Stella felt a tiny flicker in the palm of her hand. Brenda's eyes were still shut, but Stella was certain she could hear her. "You're a hero," she continued. "Don't you want to bask in the glory? I bet you'll get a commendation and everything. In fact, I'll make certain of it."

Brenda's fingers twitched again inside her palm. Bringing the woman's hand to her chest, Stella held it there a few moments and then placed it back under the covers, before rushing out to tell the Andersons the good news.

The units were assembled at the base of the hill leading up to Clem Cataloni's house. Stella was waiting inside a squad car while Sergeant Phil McDonald finished instructing his men. It was five twenty-five and the sun was still high in the sky, but the searing heat of the past week had finally lifted and a gentle breeze brushed across Stella's face. Dressed in their riot gear, the black-garbed police officers appeared out of place under the pale blue sky. "Looks like an invasion," she said when McDonald walked over to speak to her.

"I hear you want to go in with us," the sergeant said, speaking to her through the window. McDonald had wheat-colored hair, a rugged face, and the coldest blue eyes Stella had ever seen. At forty-nine, he was six feet three and built like a linebacker, his body as fit as a man of thirty.

"We cleared it with Fitzgerald," Stella said. "Didn't he tell you?"

"Yeah, he told me," McDonald said, the muscles in his body tensing. "I'd like to have a few minutes alone with him, though," he added. "That is, if you don't mind."

The sergeant's animosity hit Stella right between the eyes. Was McDonald one of her uncle's co- conspirators? She pulled her head back from the window, a jolt of fear darting up her spine. For a long time, McDonald continued to glare at her, then he finally turned and headed up the winding driveway.

The young officer Stella was riding with started the car, taking up a position behind the sergeant. One by one, the other men followed suit, lining up their squad cars and inching along as the sergeant led the procession on foot. Throughout her tenure as a prosecutor, Stella had gone out on dozens of big busts. There was always an excited buzz in the air, and the officers would joke and posture. Glancing out the back window of the police car at the string of cars and the somber-faced men inside, she knew there would be no jokes and laughter tonight.

Once the sergeant had reached the front of the house, several officers exited their units and joined him on the front porch. McDonald stepped forward, and rang the bell. After three or four minutes, Sarah Cataloni appeared, and a few moments later, the men pushed their way through the doorway. "Let's go," Stella said, reaching for the door handle.

The young officer threw his arms across Stella's chest, pinning her in the seat. "Stay put," he shouted. "Sergeant McDonald wants to talk to Captain Cataloni first. He gave me specific orders. I'm not supposed to let you go inside until he gives me a signal."

Stella was furious. Fitzgerald had made a mistake sending the Houston P.D. out to arrest one of their own. Were they going to allow her uncle to slip out the back door? Clem had ample funds. He could flee the country. "Get your hands off me," Stella snarled. "You have no right to do this to me. Fitzgerald said—"

"I'm sorry," the officer said. "I can't let you go."

Stella tried to pry his arm off, but the man was too strong. She began to panic, certain something sinister was unfolding, and determined to stop it. With one hand on the door, she sank her teeth into the officer's arm. The second he yelped and jerked away, Stella leaped out the passenger door and sprinted toward the front of the house.

The front door was standing open. The living room was empty, but Stella could hear men's voices coming from the back of the house. She headed down the hall and came to the door to her uncle's study. Clem Cataloni was seated behind his desk, listening as the sergeant read off the charges from the arrest warrant.

Stella pushed her way inside the room, shoving several officers out of her way.

When her uncle saw her, the strained look on his face turned to rage. "You," he said, pointing an accusing finger at her. "You just couldn't leave me alone, could you? You killed my brother and now you're trying to destroy me."

"You destroyed yourself," Stella said, her lip curling. "I hope you like small places, because you'll probably never see the outside of a prison cell again." She sucked in a breath. "My father was on to you, wasn't he?" she shouted. "He knew all about your little pension scam. That's why you had to get rid of him." Whipping her hair back from her face, she said, "That's why I look like this. I'll look like this until I die, thanks to you. But at least I survived, huh? Mom and Dad weren't that lucky."

"You're a lying whore," Cataloni snarled. "You disgust me."

"Pilgrim confessed," Stella spat. "The jig is up. You can call me names all you want. It won't get you out of this mess."

"That's enough," McDonald growled, stepping in front of Stella. His uniform was damp with perspiration, and a look of hatred shot from his eyes. Stella recoiled, fearful the man was going to strike her. "You had your say," he spat. "Now leave us alone, and let us do our jobs."

Stella moved backward one step at a time, never taking her eyes off the sergeant. McDonald shook his head, made a little smacking noise with his mouth, and then turned back to Clem Cataloni. "I'm sorry, Captain, but we've got to take you in now," he said. "There's no use making it any worse than it is, sir."

A group of officers approached her uncle, and in the small room, Stella was suddenly surrounded by a sea of blue suits. Someone yelled, "Watch out. He has a gun."

A single shot rang out, and everyone panicked. Stella found herself crushed on the floor under several officers. Feet pounded all around her. Voices were screaming and barking orders. Someone crushed Stella's hand beneath his heel. "Fuck," she said, shaking her fingers once the man moved away. Pushing herself up on her hands and knees, she began crawling across the room. She touched something sticky and wet on the floor.

"He's gone," a deep voice said. "Get these men out of here. We need some air. Peters, get an ambulance and medical examiner en route."

Stella managed to get to her feet. Her hands were covered with blood and a gray mushy substance that resembled oatmeal. When she saw the top of her uncle's head, she realized the gray matter on her hands was brain tissue. Clementine Cataloni was still seated behind his desk, but the top of his head was completely gone. Loose flaps of skin obscured his face. One hand was resting on the desk, the skin splattered with blood. The other hand was dangling over the side of the armrest, the gun resting beneath it on the floor.

"Swallowed his gun," Sergeant McDonald said, looking over at Stella and then back to what was left of her uncle. "Are you satisfied now?" he said, his chest heaving. Exploding, the sergeant reached out and grabbed Stella's blouse near the collar, lifting her off her feet. "I guess the thought of jail wasn't that appealing, huh?" he said. "He was my son's godfather. You want to come to my house and tell my son that his godfather blew his frigging head off?"

An officer came up behind the sergeant and touched his arm. "Let her go, Sarge," he said. "You don't want to do this."

"Get the fuck away," McDonald shouted, unable to calm down. "All Clem was trying to do was help our guys cut through the red tape and get what they deserved. Because of this fucking bitch, he's dead."

Stella's blouse was so tight around her neck that she felt as if she was strangling. Gasping for air, she kicked out and managed to connect with the sergeant's knee, causing him to release her. She fell to the floor, landing on her seat in a puddle of blood.

Stella felt her stomach turning over and over like a beach ball. Wiping her hands back and forth on her pants, she had to struggle to keep from vomiting. "He didn't have to kill himself," she muttered under her breath. "It wasn't my fault. Please, believe me, I—"

The other officers were watching and listening. One man's eyes were glistening with tears, and he pulled out a handkerchief and blew his nose. A long silence ensued. The only sound in the room was the ping, ping, ping of her uncle's blood as it dripped off the corner of the desk and splashed onto the wood flooring.

Stella saw another officer unholster his gun, and she quickly scrambled to her feet, knowing a threat when she saw one. "My aunt," she said. "Where's my aunt?"

"In the bedroom," the man with the handkerchief said, tilting his head toward the back of the house.

"Does she know?" Stella asked.

"She knows," he said.

Stella found Sarah Cataloni face down on the bed, her shoulders shaking as she sobbed. Walking over, Stella softly touched the back of her neck. "I'm so sorry, Aunt Sarah," she said. "Is there anything I can do? Anyone I can call for you? You shouldn't be alone right now."

"Get out of my house," the woman cried, lifting her head off the pillow. "I refused to believe

Clem when he told me you were responsible for your parents' deaths, but I know now he was right. What's wrong with you? Why are you such a twisted, ugly person? Your parents were good people. They tried to give you a nice home."

"I loved my parents," Stella said. "And whether you believe it or not, I had nothing whatsoever to do with their deaths. Uncle Clem killed them. He killed them to cover up his illegal activities."

"That's a lie," she said, sniffling. "Clem's a great man. Everyone worships him. He's never broken the law in his life."

"You have to believe what you have to believe," Stella said, realizing that it had been a mistake to try to comfort her after they had been estranged for so long. "If you ever want to know the truth, though," she added, handing her a card, "all you have to do is call."

After leaving her uncle's house, Stella went to the hotel to shower and change clothes, and then headed to Methodist Hospital to check on Brenda Anderson. Her condition had improved somewhat, and Stella was pleased. She was semicomatose, but was now able to communicate by squeezing people's hands. Her parents had worked out a system where she would tighten the muscles in her right hand for an affirmative response, and do the same with her left hand for a negative.

"She looks better today," Stella said. "Her color has improved. She's isn't as pale."

"Go on," her mother urged, giving Stella a

little push to get her to move closer to Brenda's bed. "Try to talk to her. She can hear you, but she can't speak. But she will," she added, "it's just going to take her some time." She bent down in her daughter's face. "You have a visitor, sugar. Don't you want to talk to her? Come on, wake up for your momma. Be a good girl, Brenda. I know you can do it if you try."

"Brenda," Stella said, "my uncle committed suicide. It's over. As soon as you're better, we're going to celebrate." Lifting the woman's hand, she added, "Do you understand? It's finally over. I can go back to my life. You're the one who made it possible."

Brenda's lips moved, but no sound came out. A few seconds later, she opened her eyes.

"Praise the Lord," Eleanor Anderson said, rushing back to her daughter's bedside, her husband right behind her. "Thank you, Jesus," she continued, looking up at the ceiling. "My baby is back."

Brenda looked up at Stella's face. "What did I do?" she said weakly. "I heard you talking."

"Not much," Stella said, feeling her heart soar, "you just saved my life." She leaned down and kissed Brenda's cheek. "My uncle shot you, Brenda," she told her. "He meant to shoot me, but you stepped in front of me. He's dead. He blew his head off."

Brenda's mother cared only about her daughter's recovery. "How do you feel?" her mother said, stroking Brenda's forehead. "I knew you'd come back to us. I knew God wouldn't let a wonderful person like you die."

"How're you doing, pumpkin?" her father said in his soft voice, stroking her arm. "Can I get you anything? Something to eat, a drink maybe."

Brenda grimaced, moving her hand over her stomach. "I'll get the nurse," Stella said. "She's in pain."

"Don't go," Brenda said. "What did you find out about the Zippo lighter?"

Stella laughed. "Always the investigator, huh?"

"Damn right," she said, managing a small smile.

"I don't think it really matters anymore."

"Okay," Brenda said. "Then get me a shot or something. I hurt like a bitch." She touched the bandages on her stomach, but this time her grimace was not from pain. "I'll never be able to wear a bikini again. All those damn situps were for nothing."

Not wanting to spend the night alone, Stella showed up on Mario's doorstep. "What are you doing here?" he said, moving back as she stepped through the doorway.

"Can I stay with you?" Stella asked. "Uncle Clem killed himself tonight. I was there."

Mario was speechless.

"I always suspected it was Dad who set the fire," she told him, once they had taken seats in the living room and Stella had filled him in on all the facts. Mario had insisted Stella drink a glass of wine to relax her, and she gulped it down in a few swallows.

"You never told me that," Mario said. Seeing

Stella's wineglass was empty, he reached over and filled it up again.

"The look on his face that night, and the way he was holding the ax over his head," she said. "I was certain he was trying to kill me. You have no idea how relieved I am to know my fears weren't true."

The two lapsed into silence. "Do you remember the time Clem pulled a shotgun on me?" Mario said. "Danny was still living with them at the time, and he was always getting into fights. One night, the police brought him home in a squad car, and Uncle Clem went ballistic. That's when I had to get out of there. I thought Clem got carried away with me that night because of all the problems they were having with Danny. I never suspected he had anything to do with the fire. In retrospect, I guess holding a shotgun on your nephew is pretty radical."

Her uncle and aunt had been childless, and Stella had forgotten about the foster child they had taken in not long before the fire. Although she had only seen the boy on one occasion when they went to her uncle's house for Sunday dinner, she remembered Danny as a big, strapping sixteen-year-old, a troubled young man who never smiled. "They should have never taken in a foster child that old," Stella said. "I'm surprised Clem ever agreed to do it. He should have known it would never work out. Aunt Sarah must have pushed him into it. When a child is that old, their personality has already been formed." Stella drained the last of her wine, then set her glass on the end table. "What ever happened to Danny?"

"Who knows?" Mario shrugged. "He's probably in jail somewhere." Something came to mind and he added, "A box came today. I don't know what it is, but the return address is from the Houston D.A.'s office. It was addressed to some lab, so I just assumed it was for you. Do you want me to get it? It can't be anything significant. It's about the size of a ring box."

"No," Stella said, her voice weary and strained. "I know what it is, but I'm not in the mood to deal with it tonight. Just hold on to it for me."

Stella went into the kitchen to use Mario's phone. She filled Sam in on what had transpired. "It was awful, Sam. I've never been so frightened in my life."

"When are you coming home?"

"I don't know," Stella said. "I'll probably have to spend all day tomorrow at the police station giving them my statement. They're going to want to document everything, and I need to find out where Brenda put all the paperwork she collected on the pension scam."

"Why don't I come down on Friday?" Sam said. "That will give you all day tomorrow and the next day to conclude your business with the police and the court. I think I'll bring Adam along, if that's all right. We'll all stay in a hotel, make it like a mini-vacation."

Stella rubbed her eyes. "I'm so tired right now," she told him, "I might need more than a mini-vacation, Sam." His mention of her business with the court finally struck home. "I want to pay you back," she said. "As soon as they officially drop the charges, they have to refund the bail money."

"Don't worry about that, Stella," Sam said. "I'm not coming to get my money back. I want to see you, spend the weekend with you and Adam. I thought we'd go to a ball game at the Astrodome. Adam has been begging me for years to take him to an Astros game."

"Sure," Stella said. "Did you ever talk to Brad, by the way?"

"Not in person," he said. "Didn't I tell you he stood me up?"

"Yes," Stella said, "but weren't you supposed to see him yesterday?"

"According to his secretary," he said, "he was called away on urgent business. My guess is he took his girlfriend to Vegas or something. But look, Stella, he called me and I made a pretty good pitch over the phone. I told him you were going to get off, that you had evidence that would prove your innocence." Sam paused. "Will they drop the charges now on the fire?"

"I'm almost certain they will," she said. "Even though I won't need the money for an attorney, Sam, I'm really anxious for the divorce to be final. How did he sound when you talked to him? Was he agreeable to the terms I suggested?"

"I worked him hard," he answered. "I think he's weakening. Probably by next week we should be able to strike a deal with him." He paused and his voice dropped to a low murmur. "I want you to be free too, Stella."

"I miss you terribly," she said.

"Not as much as I miss you," he answered.

"I haven't been sleeping, Stella. I've been too worried about you."

"You don't have to worry anymore, Sam," Stella reassured him. "Seeing my uncle blow his head off wasn't a pretty sight, but I'm relieved that it's finally over."

"Until Friday then," Sam said.

"I'll be waiting," Stella told him, slowly replacing the phone in the cradle.

chapter

SIXTEEN

Holly strode past Janet Hernandez without speaking, slammed the door behind her, and promptly exploded. Picking up all the files and papers from her desk, she began hurling them across the room. "Fuck," she yelled, tossing the last file at the door and watching as the papers tumbled out onto the carpeting.

Hearing all the commotion in Holly's office, Janet cracked the door and looked in. "Are you okay?" she said. "It sounded like you were throwing things."

"No," Holly shouted, hurling another file at the wall, "I'm not okay. I did all this work for nothing. I look like an idiot now, and Stella Cataloni is the toast of the town." She picked up the morning paper and tossed it at the woman. "Her picture's on the front page of the fucking *Chron-*

icle. Not only did she solve the Randall homicide, they're talking like she saved the city from bankruptcy and swept the police department clean of corruption. Shit," she sneered, "Stella might as well run for mayor. She'd probably win by a landslide."

"I've already seen it," the woman said meekly. "Ray works at the *Chronicle*, remember?" She started to leave and then added, "You asked me to check the newspaper articles around the time of the fire. I found something, Holly. Two days before the fire, the foundation in the Happy Day Kindergarten caved in and twenty-three children were seriously injured. Two children were killed. Evidently the school was built on top of a landfill and a sinkhole developed, causing the foundation to collapse."

"What's interesting about that?" Holly said. "What could a kindergarten have to do with a homicide case?"

"Because you also asked me to check with the building inspector's office," Janet said. "You wanted to find out what Stella's father was working on when he died."

"So," Holly said, flicking the tips of her fingernails, "what was he working on? This Happy Day thing, I gather. A floor caving in doesn't sound sinister enough to cause someone to commit murder. It was an accident, right? There was no intent involved. The development company probably wasn't aware there had ever been a landfill on the property."

Janet advanced to Holly's desk and took a chair facing her. "The developers who sold the kindergarten were sued by the school, and ended up paying for all the damages. Then all the parents of the injured children sued."

At last Holly was paying attention. "Go on," she said. "I'm listening."

"Here's the interesting part," Janet said, flipping through the papers in her lap. "Landfills are everywhere, Holly. For all we know, the building we're in right now might be sitting on top of an old landfill. As long as the foundation is sturdy, there shouldn't be a problem." She removed an eight-by-ten photo from the file and handed it to her. "Look at this, and maybe you'll understand the enormity of what occurred at the Happy Day school."

Holly stared at the picture. The words Happy Day were written across the top margin in magic marker. An enormous hole was visible in the center of a room. Chairs were toppled toward the hole, the concrete cracked in huge jagged chunks. But it was the images of the children that shook Holly and made her want to cry. This could be her own daughter. Tiny bodies were laid out on stretchers, blood and debris were all over their faces, their eyes stark with terror. The children's drawings on the walls, the scattered toys, the brightly painted furniture looked almost obscene next to the destruction.

"Awful," Holly said, placing the photo down on her desk. "Can you imagine how horrifying it must have been for the children to be sucked into a hole like that? These kids were probably traumatized for life. No wonder there were lawsuits. The person responsible for this should be taken out and shot."

"When I was little," Janet said, "I used to have nightmares about the devil pulling me under the ground. I guess these kids lived it for real, huh?"

"Yeah," Holly said, then she snapped out of it. "Hey, what do I care, huh? My career's in the drink. Maybe I should just resign and go to work for the Legal Aid Society or something. I'll never be anything but a peon around this place."

"That's not true, Holly," Janet said. "Don't you see? Maybe the pension scam and Stella's uncle had nothing to do with the fire that killed her parents. According to Randall, her father was arguing with someone on the front lawn. It could have been over the Happy Day cave-in."

"Everyone is convinced Clem Cataloni killed Randall," Holly said. "Why would he kill Randall if he wasn't guilty of setting the fire?"

"Maybe he didn't kill Randall," Janet said.

"Then who did?"

"The person or persons who poured the Happy Day foundation."

Holly suddenly saw a way out of her career morass. She leaned back in her chair and studied the ceiling. "Let me see if I understand you right," she said. "If the foundation wasn't reinforced, then the liability would fall on the people who poured the foundation rather than the development company who sold them the land?"

"Right," Janet said. "They were probably cutting corners, see, trying to save on materials. They do things like this all the time in the building trade. They quote a high sum and then scrimp, using inferior materials or skipping certain aspects of the job that they think no one will notice. They can pocket a lot of money this way, and in most cases no one's the wiser."

"Okay," Holly said, leaning forward and placing her palms on the desk, "who poured the foundation?"

Janet cleared her throat. "I don't know yet," she said. "The Sterling Corporation handled the land transaction. I managed to find out that a company named Littlefield Construction contracted to build the school. Littlefield subcontracted a lot of the work to other people, though, and this is where I hit a brick wall. They went out of business shortly after the fire, Holly. After sixteen years I don't know if we'll ever be able to get our hands on the records to find out who poured the foundation."

"Of course you can," Holly said. "Get the court file on the lawsuit. It should list all the subcontractors they used."

"You're right," Janet said. "Even if they don't have the file in the regular stacks at the courthouse, they should have it in archives."

"They've got to have it somewhere," she shrugged. "Get right on it. I might be able to turn this whole thing around, don't you see?" She grinned broadly. "Then Stella will be the one with egg on her face instead of me."

She picked up the phone to make a call, dismissing Janet with a flick of her hand. "You won't believe what I came up with, Frank," she told Minor. "I've been working night and day on it, and let me tell you, we're going to blow everyone out of the ballpark if I'm right." As Janet rose from her chair, Holly looked right through her as if she were a ghost. "Sometimes I amaze myself. This might be the most brilliant work I've ever done."

Janet stood there with her mouth open. She had been the one to put it together, and now Holly was going to take all the credit. She stormed out of the room. She would have been happy with just a few words of appreciation, but she knew they would not be forthcoming. Holly was a consummate consumer. It wasn't goods and services she gobbled up, however, it was human beings. She took whatever talents a person possessed and used them as her own.

Seething, Janet called Ray at the *Chronicle*. "I can't take it anymore," she told him. "I'm so angry right now that I'm shaking. Holly didn't appreciate anything I did. You should hear her, Ray. She's in there bragging to Frank Minor, telling him she did all the work herself."

"Whatever you want to do," he said. "If you want to start to law school in September, that's fine with me. Turn in your resignation, baby, and get the hell out of there. I've got some money set aside. We'll get by."

"Fine," Janet said. "But I'm going to do more than just quit, Ray." Before he had a chance to ask her what she meant, Janet disconnected.

Sitting down at her word processor, she typed out her resignation, signed it, and braced it against her computer. Then she placed all four phone lines on hold, and picked up the paperwork she had worked so hard to prepare. Grabbing her purse off the desk, she walked straight out of the building.

The day was as long and hectic as Stella had anticipated. She spent the better part of the morning sequestered in an interview room at the Houston P.D., going over her statement. After lunch, the police agreed to release Brenda Anderson's laptop computer, and Stella drove to Mario's apartment to try and find the information Brenda had stored regarding the pension scam. "Damn," she said, "I just can't figure this out. Do you know anything about computers, Mario?"

"A little," he said, pulling up a chair next to her at the kitchen table. "What seems to be the problem?"

"I don't know where to start," Stella sighed, staring at a blank screen. "No matter what Pilgrim told us, we have to substantiate it. Brenda has all the names of the officers involved, plus all the stuff from the other police agencies. I agreed to deliver this information to Fitzgerald right away. Aunt Sarah has already hired an attorney."

"The first thing you have to do is pull up the menu," Mario said, leaning across Stella and striking a few keys. Once the menu flashed on the screen, he hit the list files button and a long list appeared. "Now all you have to do is figure out which file it's in," he told her. "Does anything on this list ring a bell?"

"No," Stella said, peering at all the words and symbols as Mario clicked through the pages.

"Then you'll have to look in every file."

"That could take days," she said. "As soon as I get Fitzgerald this information, they're going to drop the charges against me. I need to find this stuff today, Mario. Sam is coming to Houston tomorrow and I want to be able to get his money refunded. A hundred grand can earn a lot of interest. It's not right that he's deprived of his savings because of me."

"Move over," Mario said, standing to take Stella's seat. "I'll try to find it."

"Are you sure?" Stella said. "You don't mind?"

"Not at all," he said, smiling. They exchanged places, and he was about to hit a key when he looked over and said, "I'm clean, you know. I haven't used in over a week."

"A week isn't a very long time," she said softly. "You need to get in a treatment program. You know you can't do it by yourself. Besides, if you're in a program when you go to court, they'll be more receptive to granting you probation."

"I've already checked a few programs out," he told her. "But I don't need to go in a hospital. I just need a support group. Narcotics Anonymous is a good program. What do you think? I went to one of their meetings a few days ago, and it was pretty good."

"Well, if you like it," Stella said, "that's half the battle right there. I've heard good things about N.A. What about your court case?"

"It's scheduled for next week," he said. "Should I hire an attorney?"

"Absolutely," she said. "Do you have the money?"

Mario frowned. "I'm a little short on cash right now."

"Figures," she said. "You've been snorting everything you earn, right?"

"More or less," he said, then took a deep breath. "Since we're on the subject of my disgusting behavior, I might as well let it all hang. I got involved with Holly, Stella. I didn't mean to get mixed up with her. It just happened."

"What are you saying?" Stella said, a fluttering sensation in the pit of her stomach. "You mean you cut a deal with her?"

"No," he said. "I slept with her."

"You what?" she shouted.

"You heard me," he said, shifting uncomfortably in his seat. "It's over now. I just feel bad that I didn't tell you. To be perfectly honest, I was with Holly the night before Randall was shot. That's why I was so nervous when you started quizzing me. I knew you'd go through the roof."

She sprang to her feet and began pacing. "How did this come about?"

"After they decided to file charges against you," he said, "Holly called me up and told me she would be handling my drug case. I was thrilled, you know. I thought I had an edge going. She asked me to stop by her house later that night and discuss it. You may think I was a fool, Stella, but when I slept with her, I really thought it would benefit both of us. I thought she was on our side, and the closer I got to her, the easier it would be for you to get off. It was only later that I realized the truth, that she wanted me to testify against you." He ran his fingers through his hair. "I refused, Stella. I told her I'd rather go to prison than do anything to hurt you."

"Great," Stella said, stopping to face him squarely. "Are there any other secrets you want to tell me about? I mean, maybe you robbed a few banks along the way."

"That's it," Mario said, standing and walking over to her. "I'm sorry, Stella." He reached out to embrace her, but his sister moved away. "Don't do this to me, Stel," he said. "Don't freeze me out. I'm only human. For years I've carried around all this guilt over the fire. It made me feel like two cents knowing that you were burned and I walked away without a scratch."

"And that's why you were using cocaine?" she said. "There's no other reason? So it's all my fault."

"No," he said, "you're right. I'm just making up excuses."

They stood there for some time before Stella weakened and pulled him into her arms. "I love you," she said. "Promise me you'll never put that shit in your body again."

"I won't," he said, hugging her tight. When he pulled away he was smiling. "If you want me to find those files, I better get busy."

Three o'clock rolled around and Mario still hadn't retrieved the information Stella needed. "I've got an idea," Stella said. Picking up the phone, she dialed Sam's home number. "Is this Adam?" she said when a young voice answered.

"Yeah," the boy said. "Who's this?"

"Stella Cataloni," she said. "How's it going, Adam?"

"My dad's not home yet," he told her. "Want me to have him call you when he gets here? We're coming to see you tomorrow night, you know. I've never been to an Astros' game, and they're one of my favorite teams."

"I didn't call to talk to your father," Stella told him. "I thought maybe you could help me, Adam. I've got a problem finding something in a friend's computer."

"Really?" he said. "What kind of computer is it?"

"Hold on, I'm going to let you talk to my brother," Stella said, handing the phone over.

They talked for a while and Adam gave Mario a few suggestions, but they still couldn't retrieve the information. Finally Adam asked if the computer had a modem. When Mario said he thought it did, Adam told him how to hook it up to the phone line. "I bet what you're looking for is in her E-mail," he said. "If she sent out a lot of inquiries, the people probably answered her back that way."

Adam walked Mario through the procedure to get into Anderson's electronic mailbox. "Wow," Mario said, shocked at the number of messages. "There's fifty- three messages," he said. "This must be the right place."

"Look at the dates," the boy said. "Some of them could be from a long time ago. Sometimes people forget to delete the messages once they've read them."

"Most of them are from yesterday or the day before," he said. "Now what do I do?"

"Read them, I guess," Adam said. "Hey, you're on your own now. I've got to get my homework done before my dad gets home. What grade are you in, anyway?"

Mario laughed. "School's over for me, sport."

"You mean you dropped out?" Adam said. "See, that wouldn't have happened if you'd learned how to use a computer. It's not too late, though. You can always go back. Besides," he added in a conspiratorial whisper, "there's all these neat bulletin boards where you can meet girls. You can flirt with them all you want and they don't even know how old you are."

"Gee, thanks," Mario said, hanging up the phone. "Some kid you turned me on to," he told Stella, chuckling. "Real smart ass."

"Smart ass doesn't apply if you're really smart." Stella took a seat next to Mario and they began to read through the messages. They hadn't scrolled through the first screen when she thought of a way to speed up the process. "Can't we just print all this stuff and divide it up?"

"Good idea," Mario said. "It'll only take a few minutes to hook up the printer. For that, I don't even need the whiz kid."

Once they printed out the messages, Mario gave Stella half of them and took the other half for himself. Over the next hour, they compiled a list of more than a hundred men who had received disability pensions as a result of their uncle's scam. They came from departments all over the state. "Why did he have to stay within the state?"

Mario asked, looking over the dates. "The man was so greedy, why didn't he recruit on a national basis?"

"Simple," Stella explained. "Police officers have to be trained and certified in the state where they work. Since many of them were legitimately disabled, they would have never made it through another police academy."

"I see," he said. "Just think—over a hundred salaries. Do you realize how much money we're talking about?"

"A lot," Stella said. "And don't forget, this could be just the tip of the iceberg. Anderson only went over the records of officers who had transferred in from other departments. There's no telling how many men who were already with the Houston P.D. went for Uncle Clem's scheme."

"Let's say the average monthly pension is a grand a month, or twelve thousand a year per man," Mario said, jotting some numbers down on a piece of paper. "The city would be out a hundred twenty grand a year. Then you have to determine how many years these guys have been on the take. One guy has been receiving a pension for over eighteen years. That's"—he did the math in his head—"over two hundred thousand dollars."

"And don't forget all the medical benefits," Stella pointed out. "When you retire on full disability from an on-duty injury, you receive the same insurance and benefits that a regular officer receives."

Mario gave a low whistle. "No wonder the city

is in financial trouble," he said. "They should give you a medal, sis."

"I'll settle for the money I owe Sam," Stella said. The phone rang and she picked it up at the counter.

A feminine voice said, "I'm sorry, but I may have the wrong number. I'm trying to locate Stella Cataloni. The jail gave me this number. Stella listed it for her next of kin when she was booked."

"Who's calling?" Stella asked, fearful it might be a reporter. The press had been waiting out front when she'd left the police station. As soon as Stella had seen them, she'd turned around and slipped out the back instead.

"My name's Janet Hernandez," the woman said. "Do you remember meeting me? Until today, I was Holly Oppenheimer's secretary."

"Certainly, I remember you," Stella said, thumping Mario on the back to get his attention. "You said 'until today,' Janet. You no longer work for Holly?"

Janet didn't want to take the time to explain. "Listen," she said, "I have something for you. Can you meet me at the corner of Oak and Clover in about thirty minutes? There's a Mobil station on the north side of the street. I'll be waiting in a blue Camaro."

"I can't get away right now," Stella said. "If you need a letter of reference—"

Janet interrupted. "It's not that," she said. "I think I've got a lead on the person who killed your parents."

chapter

SEVENTEEN

When Holly came out of her office at the end of the day, she saw the note Janet Hernandez had left. Snatching it off her desk, she crumpled it up in her fist. "Bitch," she said, heading to Frank Minor's office to advise him that her secretary had jumped ship. No wonder she had got so much work done, she thought. The phones had all been on hold.

Halfway down the corridor, she remembered the information Janet had given her and went back to the office to retrieve it. Now that she was gone, she'd have to find someone else to continue the research. She started flinging open drawers in Janet's desk and digging through all her files, but she didn't find it.

Returning to her own office, she found Janet's home number and called her. "I don't give a shit that you quit," she told her, "but the least you could have done was leave me the damn paperwork on the Cataloni case. Where is it?"

"What paperwork?" Janet said. "I don't know what you're talking about, Holly."

"If you don't tell me what you did with that paperwork, I'll make certain you never get another job in this town."

Janet knew Holly meant it, but she no longer

cared. She'd been about to walk out the door to meet Stella when Holly had called. "I think I put it in the trash," she lied. "If you look, Holly, I'm sure you'll find it."

"Great," Holly said, hanging up and rushing to the other room to check the trash can. It was completely empty. She ran next door to the adjoining office and yelled at the secretary, "Did they just come to pick up the trash?"

"A long time ago," the woman told her. "They always pick it up around lunchtime."

"Where do they take it?"

"To the incinerator, I guess," she said, shrugging. "I'm not really sure."

Holly reviewed her options. "Where do the janitors stay?" she asked.

"In the basement somewhere," the woman answered.

Holly had already boasted to Minor that she was on to something big. She had to get the paperwork back before it went up in smoke. Kicking off her heels, she sprinted down the hall in her stocking feet.

Friday morning Stella got up and showered, trying to be quiet so she didn't wake Mario. Once she was dressed, she went to make a pot of coffee. The living room floor was strewn with cardboard boxes, file folders, and bound transcripts, and she had to step around them to get to the kitchen. The materials were from the Happy Day lawsuit, courtesy of Janet Hernandez.

Mario, Janet, and Stella had worked until three in the morning, sifting through the mounds of paperwork in an attempt to find the name of the subcontractor who had poured the foundation. But there was simply too much paperwork, and Stella knew it would take more than a night's work to sort through it.

The realization that someone other than her uncle might be behind her parents' deaths had left Stella reeling in confusion and disbelief. Had she brought another senseless tragedy to the Cataloni family? She had tossed and turned in her bed, unable to sleep, asking herself why her uncle had committed suicide. If Janet's speculations were true, it didn't make sense. Once the ballistics tests were in, she told herself, things would be more conclusive. If they came back with a positive match on her uncle's gun, then she would know he was the person who had shot Brenda Anderson.

Stella poured water into the coffeepot, inserted the prepackaged filter, then stood at the kitchen window staring off into space. Too many conflicting thoughts were racing through her head, and she decided to wake Mario after all. Walking into his room, she gently shook his shoulder.

"God, Stella," he mumbled, "what time is it?"

"Six," she said. "I'm going out to visit Mom and Dad's grave. I thought you might want to go with me. I have to be in court at nine. After the hearing, we'll go back to work on the transcripts from the lawsuit."

Mario dropped his head back to the pillow and groaned. "I don't want to go to the cemetery," he said. "I feel like I just went to bed, Stella. Can't we go another time?"

"No," Stella said. "I'm going back to Dallas this weekend. If you don't want to go, forget it. I just thought I'd ask." She turned to leave the room when Mario called out to her.

"I'll go," he said. "Just give me a few minutes to put my clothes on."

On the drive over, the morning air was fresh and crisp. A fragrant breeze from the Gulf of Mexico drifted in through the open window. "If Janet is right," Stella said, "and Clem didn't set the fire, why did he kill himself? Do you think he did it just to avoid going to jail over the pension scam?"

"Yeah," Mario said. "You know how tough it must be for a cop in prison." He shivered, imagining the kind of abuse his uncle would have suffered. "Shit, I'd probably blow my head off too if I was a cop facing a prison sentence. Then again, Stella," he added, "nothing may come of this stuff from the lawsuit. Just because Dad had something to do with the Happy Day kindergarten disaster doesn't mean someone killed him over it."

The cemetery was located on a hill overlooking the Houston Ship Channel, and the air was heavy with the scent of the sea. Stella reached in the backseat and pulled out a bouquet of flowers she had purchased at a grocery store on the way to the cemetery. "Have you ever been out here?" she asked.

"No," Mario said. "I've never seen a reason to come out here. Mom and Dad are dead and gone. It doesn't make sense to stand around and stare at a grave. What does that accomplish?"

Stella got out of the car and Mario reluctantly followed her. They trudged across the grass, both of them searching for the markers bearing their parents' names. "It's a matter of respect," she said. Once they located the graves, she bent down and placed the flowers between the two stones.

A gust of wind came up, whipping Stella's hair back from her face. Mario stared at her scar. "I never even knew them," he said, pulling his eyes away.

"You've just forgotten," Stella whispered.

While Stella stood there without speaking, a strange feeling descended on Mario. Things he hadn't thought of in years came to mind. "Dad called me sport, didn't he?"

"Yes," Stella said.

"He used to take me down to that park on the corner and play catch every Saturday," he continued. "I don't know why he called me sport, though. I was a terrible athlete. Mom was always pumping me full of carbohydrates. I was so fat I couldn't run for shit." He turned and glanced behind him at the ship channel. "Didn't he take us to watch boats or something?"

"In Galveston Bay," Stella answered. "We used to go on Sundays after mass."

"He built a boat in the garage one time," Mario said, chuckling at the memory. "I remember because we took it down to the lake to try it out, and it sank in about ten minutes."

"That's why I insisted on this cemetery," Stella

told him. "I wanted Dad to be near the water. He always loved it."

For five or ten minutes, they both stood perfectly still, each lost in thought. Mario moved closer and squeezed Stella's hand. She leaned against him. "I'm glad you came."

"I guess I knew them better than I thought," Mario sighed. "I should have come a long time ago, Stella. For some reason, being here brings back a lot of memories."

"It's all right," Stella said, linking arms with him as they headed back to the car. "You'll come now."

As they got closer to the street, Stella saw a dark brown Chrysler parked at the curb behind her rental car. "Was that car here before?"

"I don't remember," he said. "Why?"

Stella turned and looked behind her at the cemetery. "We're the only people here, Mario, and I'm certain that car wasn't here when we arrived. It looks like an unmarked police car."

"Over there," Mario shouted, yanking on Stella's arm. "Quick, get behind the tree."

Stella threw herself on the ground instead, placing her hands over her head. "Get down, Mario," she shouted, certain someone was about to open fire. When her brother had dropped to the ground beside her, she panted, "What did you see?"

"Shsssh," he said. "Look through the branches of that tree, Stella. Do you see it? It looks like the barrel of a shotgun."

"Oh, God," she said in terror. "We have to get out of here. We can't just wait for them to kill us." She scrambled to her feet, in full panic, but Mario pulled her back down.

"If you run for it, Stella," he said, his eyes glued on the object in the trees, "they'll pick you off in a second. Just stay calm. Maybe it's a piece of wood or something, and I was mistaken."

Stella clenched her eyes shut and prayed. A few moments later, she heard leaves crunching, followed by the sound of a man's voice. "Well, look what we've got here," the voice said, kicking out and connecting with Mario's rib cage. Mario started to retaliate when the man swung a shotgun from his side and placed the muzzle against Mario's cheek. "Two birds in the bush instead of one," he said. "This must be my lucky day."

Stella's eyes flew open. Sergeant Phil McDonald was standing over her, his blue eyes burning with hate. He laughed, dropping the shotgun back to his side. "You fucking bastard," she snarled. "What are you doing? Following me?"

Phil McDonald walked off, turning to yell back over his shoulder. "Better be careful out here, Stella," he said. "You don't want to end up in one of these graves."

Dressed in a pale blue suit with pink trim, Stella made her way to Judge Maddox's courtroom, her heels tapping on the linoleum as she walked down the corridor. Once she had dropped Mario at his apartment and dashed inside to change her clothes, she had driven to Fitzgerald's office to tell him what had occurred at the cemetery. He had been sympathetic, but he had not been reassuring. His best advice was for Stella to leave Houston immediately. He could reprimand Sergeant McDonald, he'd told her, but he could not control the entire police department.

Stella's steps slowed, then faltered as she saw Brad waiting outside the door to the courtroom. "What are you doing here?"

"I was worried about you," he said. "I read about what happened in the paper. It was terrible. How's that woman, the one who was shot?"

"She's getting better," Stella said. Glancing at her watch, she saw it was almost nine. "Are you going to stay for the hearing?" she asked. She couldn't help feeling pleased that he had come.

"Might as well," Brad answered. "I thought I'd take you out to lunch when you're finished. Are you available?"

Her suspicions flared. "To discuss the financial agreement?"

"Not exactly," he said. "I thought we'd talk, you know. Spend some time together."

Stella didn't know what to think. His face was haggard and pale, and he looked older than his fifty-four years. Was he ill? Had something happened with his girlfriend? Or did he have something else up his sleeve? Maybe he was trying to soften her up so she would go easy on him when they finally got around to settling their affairs. "Let's see how it goes in court," she said, opening the door and stepping through.

Stella parted company with her husband and took her seat at the counsel table. Judge Maddox called the case, then looked at Holly. "I was informed that the People are prepared to dismiss in this matter. Is that correct?"

"No, Your Honor," Holly said, glancing over at Stella and seeing the look of surprise register on her face. "New information has recently surfaced regarding this crime. Whereas the people are prepared to admit that Ms. Cataloni may not have been responsible for the deaths of her parents, we are not willing to terminate these proceedings until she returns the evidence that's currently in her possession."

"What evidence are you referring to?" Judge Maddox asked.

"The pieces of metal found in the house," Holly answered. "This evidence should never have been released directly to Ms. Cataloni, Your Honor. We agreed that the defense could conduct their own examinations, but the evidence was to be under our control at all times. I'm not even certain where it is right now."

"Ms. Cataloni," the judge said, tossing the ball to Stella.

"Your Honor," Stella said, "the evidence in question is presently in my brother's apartment. Because of what occurred, I never had it sent to a lab. All I need is an hour or so to drive to my brother's apartment to retrieve it."

"If so," Judge Maddox said, "and it's agreeable to the prosecution, we could trail to the end of today's calendar and resolve this issue then."

"I'm sorry, Your Honor," Holly said, a smile flickering on her lips. "I have a sentencing hearing this afternoon and I anticipate it's going to run late. We'll have to continue until Monday morning or later in the week."

Stella tensed. If she stayed in Houston, she might not survive until Monday. After the incident in the cemetery, she knew her uncle's friends would stop at nothing to get back at her. "It's not even ten o'clock," she said. "With the court's permission, I can call and see if my brother can bring the metal chips to me right now. That way we can take care of this before the noon break."

"That's not going to work," Judge Maddox said, studying her calendar. "I have another matter set for ten that will run all the way to lunch. Ms. Oppenheimer, would you consider dismissing and taking Ms. Cataloni's word that she will return the evidence?"

"No, Your Honor," Holly said. "We must have this evidence. As I just stated, we have new activity on this case and may find ourselves prosecuting another individual in the future. We refuse to dismiss until we have the evidence back in our possession." She paused, thinking. "In addition, we need time to examine this evidence and verify that it's in the same condition as when it was delivered. My suggestion is to have Ms. Cataloni get the evidence to us today. Then we'll have a chance to conclude this matter next week."

"Monday it is, then," Judge Maddox said, jotting down the date and time in the file. "This matter is continued until ten o'clock Monday."

Stella was furious. Grabbing her briefcase, she gave Holly a scathing glance before heading down the aisle.

"Stella, wait," Holly said, catching up to her. "I need to talk to you."

"I have nothing to say to you."

They hit the double doors at the same time. "You're making a mistake," Holly said. "Didn't you hear what I just said in there? Your uncle might not have been the one who set the fire. My secretary left me in a bind, or I would have been able to follow through on this by now."

"Oh, really?" Stella said, arching an eyebrow. "You're a little behind, Holly. Fitzgerald told me the ballistics tests on my uncle's gun came back this morning. The tests were positive. My uncle shot Brenda Anderson. His cronies at the police department probably don't believe it, but we have the evidence to prove it."

Holly massaged her temples. "But this is something different, Stella."

"You couldn't even trust me to return those stupid pieces of metal?" Stella shouted, "If you had, I could get out of this frigging town. Because of you, I'm stuck here until next week." She saw Brad emerge from the courtroom, and before he had a chance to speak, she snapped, "I can't go to lunch. I have too much to do."

"Stupid pieces of metal?" Holly exclaimed. "For all I know, those pieces of metal could be the key to this entire case. If you were in my shoes, you'd have done the same thing."

"Sure, right," Stella said. "And I'd fuck your brother too."

Holly's face turned ashen. She recovered quickly, though, and the same confident look appeared on her face. "What's the big deal,

Stella? We're both single. I didn't seduce him, anyway. He seduced me. You can't have me disbarred for sleeping with your brother. Except for the cocaine, he's a nice guy. To tell you the truth, I kind of like him."

"You tried to manipulate him," Stella spat at her. "It was bad enough you agreed to prosecute me, but going after my brother was disgusting."

When she arrived at Mario's apartment to pick up the metal chips, Stella found the door locked. After searching in her purse for the spare key he had given her and not finding it, she started beating the door with her fists. "Shit, damn, hell," she yelled. Where was Mario? If she didn't get the evidence back today, they might not be able to examine it and the case would be held over again.

A horrid thought passed through her mind. Was Mario inside unconscious or dead? She checked the door, but couldn't detect any signs of forced entry. Peering in through the windows, she saw no evidence of a struggle inside. The boxes and paperwork appeared to be in the same spots as before. Calm down, she told herself. You're getting paranoid. After she had called Mario from Fitzgerald's office and told him the news about the ballistics tests, he had probably gone out for breakfast.

Returning to her car, Stella searched through the glove box, then looked on the floor to see if the key had fallen out of her purse. She thought of trying to get in through one of the windows, but Mario had an alarm and having the police respond was clearly not in her best interest. Finally she gave up, leaving a note on Mario's door that she had gone to the hospital to see Brenda Anderson and asking him to get in touch with her the second he came home.

Brenda was asleep when Stella entered her room. She had been moved from intensive care, though, and was now in the surgical wing of the hospital. "How is she?" Stella asked Brenda's mother.

"The pain has been horrible," the woman said, "but the doctors say she's doing as good as can be expected."

Brenda opened her eyes. "Stella," she said weakly, "what's going on with the case?"

"They're going to dismiss," she told her, "but Holly's being her customary bitchy self."

"What'd she do now?" Brenda said.

Stella pulled up a chair by her bed, and caught her up to date on everything that had occurred since the shooting. "They're certain now that my uncle shot you. Ballistics completed their tests yesterday. The bullet they removed from your stomach came from my uncle's AR-15 assault rifle, the same one I saw in the gun case that day."

"What about the Randall homicide?" Brenda said. "Did the police trace ownership of the gun they found at the scene back to your uncle? Were his fingerprints found on it?"

Stella shook her head. "As far as I know, the fingerprints found on the gun were never identified. Ballistics confirmed it was the weapon used to shoot Randall, though. My uncle was smart,

Brenda. He knew holding on to the murder weapon would be a mistake. Uncle Clem probably took that gun off some crook years ago. That's why he wasn't concerned about leaving it at the scene."

"He didn't dispose of the assault weapon he used to shoot me," Brenda told her. "Most criminals follow a certain pattern of behavior, Stella. Your uncle had a mammoth ego. He thought his contacts in law enforcement would protect him. Besides, he was a gun collector." She paused and let her mother give her a sip of water. Her voice had become hoarse from talking. "What about this Happy Day thing?"

"I don't think anything is going to come of it," Stella answered. "Even if we find out the name of the contractor who poured the foundation, we might not be able to find him."

"Maybe Holly shot Randall?"

"What are you saying?" Stella said, her stomach in knots. "What motive would Holly have to shoot Randall? Are you saying my uncle shot you, but Holly shot Randall? Were they crime partners or something? Is this another of your Mafia scenarios?"

Brenda moaned in pain. Her mother rushed over and placed a fresh pillow behind her head, trying to make her more comfortable. "I'm not professing to know exactly how all this all went down," Brenda said. "We're only speculating. I've got plenty of time to think right now, you know, so forgive me. If I'm not making sense, just tell me to shut up. All these drugs, well—"

"Go on," Stella said.

"Holly is insanely jealous of you, Stella. She knew prosecuting you would give her great notoriety, the kind of fame you achieved with the Pelham case. After Randall made statements implicating you, and you pitched a fit at their office that day, perhaps she decided that killing Randall was the answer to all her problems."

"This is ridiculous," Stella said, scowling.

"Just listen," Brenda continued, rolling over onto her side. "First, you told me yourself that Holly was involved with Growman, that they had an affair a few years back. I was there when she accused you of sleeping with him. So, she's jealous and bitter. She's also overly ambitious, Stella. Combine those two and you've got yourself a fairly lethal mix. She kills Randall, knowing all the suspicion will fall on you. Then she can destroy you, her competitor and nemesis, and embarrass the hell out of Growman for endorsing you. At the same time, she has an opportunity to enhance her status in the legal community by trying a sensational case. That gives her not just one motive, but several."

"I don't buy it," Stella said.

"Well," Brenda continued, "I thought it was a long shot, but I like to be thorough. So, I checked on Holly's whereabouts at the time Randall was killed. I just forgot to mention it to you the other day."

Stella's eyes expanded, but she didn't speak.

"Holly disappeared from the courthouse a few minutes after nine," Brenda explained. "She didn't return until after lunch. She could have rented a car similar to the one you rented from

Hertz, shot Randall, and then returned it before driving her own car back to the courthouse. She knew how to get in touch with Randall. All she had to do was call and ask him to meet her somewhere to discuss the case."

The phone rang and Anderson's mother answered it. "It's your brother," she said, handing the phone to Stella.

"My apartment's been burglarized," Mario said, sounding scared. "The police are here now."

"No," Stella said. "I was just there."

"You should see it," he said. "The burglar tore the place apart. The strange part is there's nothing of value missing. My stereo's still here, my television, my cameras."

"What about the files from the lawsuit?"

"Everything looks like it's here," Mario said. "Of course, there's no way to know if anything's missing. The police think the intruder was looking for drugs. They know I was arrested for possession, so—"

"Shit, the metal pieces," Stella said, her eyes enormous. "God, Mario, did they take the box?"

"What box?"

"The box that came for me earlier in the week."

"Hold on," he said, "I'll have to check."

"Mario's apartment was ransacked," Stella told Brenda while she was waiting for her brother to return to the phone. "Someone else must be after those metal chips. It certainly can't be my uncle. He's on a slab in the morgue."

Mario came back on the line, out of breath.

"The box is here," he said. "I have it in my hands. I put it on top of the refrigerator. It must have fallen behind it. I had to move the damn refrigerator to get to it."

"Stay right there," Stella said, "I'm on my way. Don't let that box out of your sight, Mario. Something's going on. Watch what you say to the police. Some of Uncle Clem's police buddies could be behind this. Whatever you do, don't let them get their hands on those metal chips."

Mario's apartment was ripped asunder. Furniture was overturned, the upholstery on the sofa had been slit, and the stuffing had spilled out onto the carpeting. Papers from the cardboard file boxes were scattered everywhere. Stella's heels punctured some of the papers as she made her way to the back of the house to find Mario. All the drawers in his bedroom were hanging open and his clothes littered the floor. "How did they get in?" Stella asked, stepping over the rubble.

"Broke out the front window," Mario said. "Didn't you see it when you came in?"

"Where's the box?" she said.

Mario went to the kitchen and returned, handing her a small package wrapped in brown paper. "You really think they broke in here for this?" he said.

"I don't know," she said, a bewildered look on her face. Taking the box, she placed it in her purse. "I'm going to deliver this to Holly right now before something else happens. What time is it?"

"Almost three," Mario said.

"Sam's arriving on the four o'clock shuttle. If he calls looking for me, tell him to call me at the Holiday Inn. I should be there by six at the latest."

"I'll go with you," Mario said. "I'm frightened for you, Stella. I thought all this stuff was over. What's going on?"

"Stay here and clean up your apartment," Stella told him, kicking a stack of clothing out of her way. "And you'd better call and have the glass replaced in the window, or the person could come back later tonight while you're sleeping."

chapter

EIGHTEEN

Instead of surrendering the metal chips to Holly as she had planned, Stella took them with her to the Holiday Inn.

The moment she entered her room, she ripped open the box and dumped the pieces of metal out on the bed. Now that they were all present and accounted for, she might be able to make sense of them. Picking up each chip and holding it under the light, she was able to see a few letters, but she had no idea what they said. Grabbing a pen and paper, she jotted down the letters she had seen, and then carried all the chips to the small desk. After thirty minutes of staring at them, she gave up. Some of the letters were so faint and distorted that she couldn't make them out. She needed a magnifying glass. Tomorrow, she decided, she'd go out and buy one.

Seeing her message light illuminated, Stella picked up the phone and called the front desk. Sam had left a message telling her to check out of her hotel and meet him at his room at the Ritz-Carlton. She glanced at her watch, realized she was already late, and then jumped in the shower. She'd wanted everything to be perfect. By now, she had expected her legal problems would be resolved. She slapped the tile in frustration. How could this be a victory celebration when she was more confused and frightened than ever? Cops were stalking her with shotguns. Someone had ransacked her brother's apartment, and murder charges were still hanging over her head.

"This will not spoil the weekend," she said several times before turning the water off and getting out.

Stopping at the mirror before she left the room, Stella rearranged her hair and dabbed at a speck of lipstick on her teeth. Dressed in an all-white pantsuit, she liked the look of the outfit against her dark hair, but the jacket gaped in front and she was concerned that her bra might show. Racing to the gift shop in the lobby, she purchased a lacy body suit and ducked into the ladies' room to put it on under her clothes.

Stella knocked on Sam's hotel door at eight o'clock. The moment he appeared, he pulled her into his arms. "God, I've missed you," he said. "The past few days have seemed like a lifetime."

She looked past him into the room. "Where's Adam?"

"Visiting with his aunt," Sam explained. "Madeline lives here in Houston. She's bringing Adam back around midnight."

Sam had not rented a mere room. When Stella walked in and looked around, she was overwhelmed. Fresh flowers stood in the crystal bowl in the entryway, filling the air with their fragrance. The living room area was elegantly furnished, with two blue velvet sofas positioned around a mahogany coffee table. The room had a built-in bar, and an antique writing desk sat on an angle in one corner. Lovely framed prints covered the walls, and the ceiling was finished with intricate crown molding. "Is this the honeymoon suite?" she asked.

Sam laughed. "No, but we could pretend if you want."

Stella then saw the table, set up with fine china and crystal. "This is most beautiful room I've ever seen," she told him. "Are we eating here?"

"Any time you're ready," Sam said, bowing at the waist. Dressed in a casual pair of slacks and a short-sleeve shirt, he looked handsome and sexy.

Stella caught a glimpse of Sam's dark chest hair protruding from the front of his shirt. She felt like ripping his clothes off and dragging him straight to the bedroom. Instead, she flopped down on one of the blue velvet sofas and kicked her shoes off. "I love this hotel, Sam. The Holiday Inn was beginning to feel like the jail."

"No, you don't," Sam said, extending his hand and pulling her back to her feet. "I have another surprise for you." Leading her to the bathroom, he pointed to a Jacuzzi tub filled with water. "Your bath awaits you, madam."

"Oh," Stella said, "I've already showered, Sam."

"A Jacuzzi is not for the purpose of getting clean," he said, unbuttoning the front of her jacket. "Didn't anyone ever tell you that?"

"I guess not," Stella laughed.

Sam pushed her jacket down on her shoulders, then sighed. "I'll leave you alone," he said. "I have to call room service, anyway, and get them to bring up our dinner now that you're here."

Stella's face fell. "I don't have your money, Sam," she said. "I'm almost certain they're going to drop the charges, but Holly refused to do anything until Monday."

"It doesn't matter, Stella," he said, bracing himself against the door frame. "Let's not talk about money tonight, okay? Let's just enjoy ourselves."

"I saw Brad today," she blurted out. "He came to the hearing. He might have broken up with his girlfriend. The way he was acting, I thought he might be trying to patch things up between us."

"Is that what you want, Stella?" Sam said. "If so—"

"Of course not," she said. Feeling somewhat bold, she removed her arms from the jacket and showed Sam her lacy bodysuit. "What do you think? Pretty sexy, huh?"

"I love it," he said, staring at her nipples

381

through the lace. "If you don't hurry, though, your bathwater is going to get cold."

Sam left the room and Stella removed the rest of her clothing, folding it neatly and placing it on top of the commode. Once she lowered herself into the hot water, she sighed in pleasure.

As Sam had left the bathroom door cracked, Stella yelled at him once she heard him get off the phone, "How much does a room like this cost?"

Sam stuck his head in the door. "Why do you always steal my lines?"

"What do you mean?"

"I'm Jewish," he said. "Let me worry about the cost of things, okay? I got a deal. I have a friend who owns a travel agency."

"Shrewd guy," she said. "Are you coming in?"

"I didn't think you'd want me to," he said.

"See how much you know?" she said, laughing. "Get your butt in here, Sam."

"Wait," he said, excitement flashing in his eyes, "I have a bottle of champagne on ice."

Darting into the other room, he returned with the bottle of champagne, and placed it on the edge of the tub. Stella watched as he unbuttoned his shirt, her eyes riveted on his sinewy chest and the way the hair ran down his stomach and disappeared inside his pants. Feeling her breath catch in her throat, she sank lower in the tub until the water tickled her nose.

The moment was immensely titillating. Her body in the warm, fragrant water, nude and vulnerable, Sam only a few feet away, virile and handsome. With the mirrors fogged up and steam rising from the hot water, the room had an intimate, surreal atmosphere that served to enhance her excitement.

She looked away, but out of the corner of her eye, she could see Sam's slacks sliding down his thighs. Catching a brief look at his green-and-blue-striped jockey shorts, she sucked in a breath and held it. The next thing you knew, the shorts were gone as well, and Stella's breath escaped in a gasp.

As he stepped into the tub, she watched his legs, mesmerized by the way the water swirled around them in gentle ripples. Every sound and light seemed to be magnified, as if she had consumed some type of mind- altering drug. Peering up at his genitals as he lowered himself into the tub, she realized that the drug was Sam himself. From what should be an unflattering perspective, she saw only perfection and masculine beauty.

Once he was in the tub, Sam leaned back, extending his long legs until they brushed against the sides of Stella's hips under the water. He reached for the champagne bottle and brought it to his lips, then handed it to Stella.

Maintaining eye contact, Stella tipped the bottle to her mouth, but she was so distracted that she failed to seal her lips. Icy liquid streamed down her chin and dribbled onto her neck and chest, causing her to shiver.

Just then they heard a knock on the door in the other room. "That must be our dinner," Sam said. "Are you hungry?"

Stella shook her head.

"They'll go away," he said, finding the button for the jets. Water instantly bubbled around them. "Feels good, doesn't it?"

Stella took another drink of the champagne and then passed the bottle back to him. When he reached out for it, their fingertips touched and his legs moved against the sides of her body again. Stella stretched her legs out next to his and leaned her head back against the opposite edge of the tub. A jet was positioned right at the base of her spine. Closing her eyes, she tried to push everything out of her mind except the wonderful, pulsating sensation.

Suddenly Sam closed his legs, trapping Stella in the center of them. She bolted upright, escaping the pressure of his legs by pushing herself to her knees. Before she knew it, however, Sam had pulled her on top of him and was probing the inside of her mouth with his tongue, his fingers laced tightly in her damp hair.

"I want you," he whispered. "It's a good thing they didn't send you to prison. If they had, I would have had to figure out a way to bust you out."

Stella kept her eyes closed as Sam picked up the bar of soap and rubbed it over her breasts, her stomach, her buttocks. Then she heard the soap splash in the water beside her and felt Sam's slick fingers between her legs. Arching backward, she moaned as his tongue flitted across her nipples. With the pulsating jets massaging her, it was as if she were having sex with not one but a dozen lovers, their hands all stroking and kneading her flesh at the same time.

At that moment Stella wanted Sam more than she had ever wanted anything in her life. With one hand she reached down into the water and found his erection. Closing her fingers on it, she guided him effortlessly inside her body, opening her eyes so she could look at his face. His eyes were closed now, his nostrils flared with passion. He was so beautiful, she thought. She drank in the strands of thick, wet hair on his forehead, his moist skin, his gradually sloping nose, his strong chin. She'd never noticed how long his eyelashes were, but now she could see them fluttering against his cheeks, and with the tip of her finger, she reached out to touch them, caress his eyelids, trace his lips like a person examining a priceless sculpture.

Sam reached out and pulled her back down to his body. "I love you," he said. "I thought I'd never feel this way again." He wrapped his arms around her and held her tightly, refusing to release her when she tried to continue their love-making.

Stella buried her head in the crook of his neck. Their feelings for each other overshadowed their sexual desires, taking the moment to another level of intensity and meaning. For a long time they were both silent, curled in each other's arms in the now tepid water.

For the first time Stella knew that what she felt was genuine. Unlike her teenage fling with Tom Randall, this was not girlhood infatuation or youthful exploration. Unlike her marriage to Brad, her feelings didn't spring from gratitude or respect for a man who had helped her after a devastating tragedy.

"I do love you," she said.

Sam smiled, trapping her nose with his fingers. "Don't worry," he said, "I've already figured that out."

By nine o'clock, Stella and Sam had moved their lovemaking to the bedroom, continuing what they had begun in the Jacuzzi. Stella had never been so free and uninhabited, never felt such overwhelming pleasure. Pushing Sam over onto his back, she started at his feet and crawled up his body inch by inch, ultimately straddling him. She rode him with her head tossed back, her mouth open and panting. Her hair tickled her upper shoulders and neck, and she felt completely at ease with her body, giving no thought whatsoever to her unsightly scars.

Women were peculiar creatures, she thought. A man could be the greatest lover in the world and still not be able to satisfy his partner. To let go, a woman had to feel trust and total acceptance. It was similar to falling off a cliff and knowing that someone was there to catch you. In that moment of release, a woman moved outside herself, gave herself completely and freely. Stella knew she could make love to dozens of men, but the one she allowed to satisfy her would be the one who owned her.

"Oh, God," Stella cried, her muscles stiffening as she reached a powerful orgasm, so intense that she collapsed limp and wasted onto Sam's sweaty chest. It was as if she had somehow reached inside and pulled out all the pain, all the sorrow, all the bitterness. She felt empty and filled at the same time.

What she felt, she decided, was normal. For the first time since the fire, Stella didn't see herself as deformed or ugly. She felt whole, beautiful, complete.

Once Stella had rolled over onto her back, Sam spread her legs, lifting them and draping them over his shoulders. When he began to move inside her, she felt the full force of his desire. Some time later, his face twisted in a grimace as he exploded inside her.

Finally it was over. Without speaking, they remained in each other's arms, the room dark and still, nothing but the shadows surrounding them.

chapter

NINETEEN

"Wake up," Stella whispered. "It's after eleven, and Adam will be here soon. I have to go."

"Why don't you stay?" Sam said, nuzzling his face in her hair.

"I have some things to do," she told him, flipping on the bedside light. "Besides, I don't want Adam to know we're sleeping together."

Sam sat up in the bed, watching as Stella

crossed the floor to the bathroom. "What do you have to do this time of night?"

Stella was putting on her clothes when Sam appeared in the bathroom doorway. "I want to go back to Mario's and finish going through the paperwork from the Happy Day cave-in," she told him. "I have to get to the bottom of this before I go back to Dallas."

"You're overdoing it, Stel," he cautioned, grabbing a towel and wrapping it around his lower body. "Let the police handle it now. If something's going on, why put yourself in the eye of the hurricane? Haven't you had enough problems?"

"The police, huh?" she smirked, not having told him about the incident in the cemetery. "The police have been my problem all along."

Sam was concerned. Stella had a sense of urgency about her, as if she were rushing to catch a last-minute flight. "Maybe I should drive you?" he said. "If we hurry, I should be able to get back before midnight. Besides, my sister-in-law won't just drop Adam off at the curb. If I'm a few minutes late, they'll wait in the lobby."

"Don't be ridiculous," Stella said, sitting down on the toilet seat as she pulled on her panty hose. "Adam will be here any minute," she said, standing and pulling on her slacks. "I'll be fine, Sam. I'm going straight to Mario's apartment."

Once Stella stepped into her shoes, Sam walked her to the door. "The game starts at one o'clock. Wait," he said, disappearing into the bedroom. When he returned, he handed Stella a small brown envelope. "I bought an extra ticket for your brother. I thought he might want to go to the game with us. Should I pick you both up at his apartment?"

"Mario's apartment is near the Astrodome," Stella said, placing the tickets in her purse. "I'll meet you in front of the stadium around noon, near the ticket booth. I'm not sure if Mario will come, Sam, but it was nice of you to think of him." She leaned over and kissed him. "When I get back to Dallas, everything will be great."

"You sure?" he said, yawning.

"Tonight was wonderful," Stella said, giving him another peck on the cheek before she darted out the door.

Stella jogged to her car in the parking lot, her mind racing like a jet engine. While Sam had been sleeping, she had remained awake in the dark room, events long buried in her subconscious suddenly appearing in her mind. She recalled awakening in the middle of the night only a few days before the fire, worrying how she could ever tell her parents she was pregnant. Seeing her rental car and climbing inside, she closed her eyes and tried to bring forth the same memory, hoping that now she was alone, she could remember the incident in greater detail. For several minutes, her mind lacked focus, but she slowed her breathing and it all came clear.

The narrow, dark hall stretched out in front of her. Stella's bare feet were soundless on the cold wood floor as she made her way to the kitchen. A cup of hot milk might help her to fall asleep. When she saw the light burning at the end of the corridor, she wondered if she had been the last one in the kitchen. Money was tight, and her father had a fit when they left the lights on.

"Are you okay, Dad?" she said, seeing her father passed out at the kitchen table, a half-empty bottle of bourbon in front of him.

"Oh," he mumbled, raising his head, "is it morning?"

"No," Stella said. "It's only three o'clock. Haven't you been to bed yet?" Her father reached for the bottle to refill his empty glass, but Stella seized it and held it in the air. "Please, Dad, don't drink any more of this stuff. Why are you doing this? I've never seen you drink anything but beer."

"You don't understand," her father said, his eyes bloodshot and his speech slurred. He reached for her arm and pulled her closer, his voice a tense whisper. "People may say things, baby. You must not believe them."

"What do you mean?" Stella asked. The way he was talking frightened her. Her father had always been a tower of strength. She had never seen him this way.

Bracing himself with his hands, her father struggled to his feet, then threw his arms around his daughter. His breath reeked of bourbon, and Stella recoiled. It wasn't just his breath, though. The smell seemed to be seeping from his pores. A second later, she felt her father trembling and realized that he was sobbing. "I tried to be a good father," he cried. "I only wanted the best for my family. I would never do anything to hurt anyone. Never in my life would I harm a child."

"It's okay, Dad," Stella said, her own eyes

misting over. She led him to the foot of the stairs, allowing him to lean on her to maintain his balance. "Get some sleep," she told him. "You've had too much to drink. You'll feel better in the morning."

Stella was so entrenched in her memories that she missed the on-ramp to the freeway. Gunning the Ford's engine, she made a fast U-turn and sped off in the opposite direction, leaving a streak of rubber on the asphalt. She had to find the name of the contractor who had poured the Happy Day foundation. If necessary, she would stay up all night, go through every scrap of paper relating to the lawsuit.

When she had returned to the kitchen for her cup of milk, she had found the newspaper next to her father's half- empty bottle of bourbon. The entire front page had been dedicated to the Happy Day disaster. She remembered the pictures of injured children, the gaping hole in the center of the room, the scattered and crushed toys. But it was the words her father had spoken that night that made the fine hairs on Stella's arms stand straight up. Like everything else that had occurred right before the fire, the incident in the kitchen had simply vanished from her memory.

Hearing a strange bleeping sound, Stella glanced in her rearview mirror. When she saw the police car behind her, she realized the officer had given her a quick blast from his siren to get her to stop. "Shit," she said, taking her foot off the gas pedal. She prayed the officer was with the highway patrol, and not with the Houston police. Recognizing the markings on the car, though, she knew she had not been so lucky. She let the car come to a rolling stop, and then sucked in a deep breath.

"Don't panic," she muttered, watching as the officer exited his police unit and approached her car. Her fingers locked on the steering column.

"Can I see your driver's license and registration, please?" the officer said, training his flashlight on Stella's face.

"Certainly," she said, blinking in the bright light. All she could see was the top of the officer's head as the flashlight was positioned in front of his face. Reaching inside her purse, she pulled out what she thought was her driver's license and passed it to him through the window. "It's a rental car," she said, reaching for the glove box and then dropping her hands back to her lap. Never reach for the glove box with a cop, she reminded herself. He might think she was reaching for a gun. "I'll have to find the registration, Officer. I'm not sure where it is."

"This isn't your driver's license," the officer said, handing Stella back the tickets Sam had given her. "Going to an Astros game, huh?" The beam of light struck Stella's face again. "How many drinks have you had this evening?"

"Oh," Stella said, finally retrieving her license from the bottom of her purse. "I guess I should carry a wallet, Officer." How many glasses of champagne had she consumed? Was it enough to classify her as legally intoxicated?

"Can you answer the question, ma'am?" the

officer said, his voice loud and stern. "How many drinks have you had?"

"One glass of champagne," Stella lied.

"I'm sorry, but I'm going to have to give you a field sobriety test," the officer said. "I stopped you because you made an illegal U-turn, but I also observed you driving erratically. You were weaving across the yellow line back there."

The officer walked back to his unit, either to run a check for outstanding warrants or to call a back-up unit now that he thought he might make an arrest. Stella prayed the officer was a rookie, hired after her uncle had already retired. She watched out her rearview mirror, afraid she was going to end up in jail. Several hours had passed since she had consumed the champagne. Even though she didn't feel intoxicated, she was terribly nervous. Could she walk a straight line? She closed her eyes and tried to touch her nose, her fingertips connecting with her eyelid instead. "Damn," she said, slapping the steering wheel. How could she get herself arrested for drunk driving? And now, of all times, when she was finally on the verge of uncovering the truth.

When the officer passed through the light, Stella finally got a good look at his face. "It can't be," she said, craning her neck around to get a better look. The officer was standing next to his car, his portable radio in his hand, shining the flashlight on Stella's driver's license. He jerked his head up, looking straight at her.

Danny!

Stella was thunderstruck. It couldn't be Danny. Her uncle's foster son was a Houston police officer! Stella began to shake. Perspiration poured out of her pores, instantly soaking her jacket. Black spots danced in front of her eyes, and she thought she might faint. She'd had no idea that Danny was still in Houston, let alone on the police force.

Just then the headlights went black.

What was he doing? Stella looked out the window, thankful for the streetlights. Checking the rearview mirror again, she saw a dark shadow in the front seat of the police unit. Was he calling Sergeant McDonald, telling him to organize a lynch squad? She strained her eyes trying to see inside the police car, wondering if another officer might be in the car as well.

Minutes ticked off in slow motion. How much time elapsed, Stella didn't know, but it seemed like an eternity. She hummed to herself, tapping her fingernails on the steering column. It's going to be okay. Stay cool. She took several deep breaths, telling herself she could be mistaken and the officer was not who she thought he was. She tried to think of Sam and the wonderful evening they had shared. A sense of foreboding fell over her, however, and she found herself staring in the rearview mirror, too frightened to turn away.

When she heard a voice outside her window, she jumped in her seat. "You have to move your car," the officer said. "There's too much traffic on this street to conduct a field sobriety test."

"Where do you want me to go?" Stella kept her eyes focused straight in front of her. If it was Danny, he had to know who she was. He had her damn license. She hadn't seen Danny in sixteen years, not since he was a teenager. She snuck in several quick side glances, but all she could see was a shadowy face that looked exactly like the boy she remembered. She couldn't go on without knowing. She opened her mouth to confront him when he began speaking.

"Drive your car down there and park," he said, pointing off in the distance. "I'll follow you."

Stella recognized the voice inflections. It was Danny all right. The boy had been in numerous foster homes before moving in with her aunt and uncle, but he had spent four years with a couple from Russia which had left him with a slight Russian accent. Danny had been in constant trouble with the law, racking up juvenile offenses right and left, the majority of them involving acts of violence. How had he become a police officer? Her uncle, of course, she quickly reasoned. If Clem had managed to get hundreds of officers approved for disability, getting his foster son a job would have been easy.

Stella looked toward the area Danny had indicated. It was pitch black, not a streetlight in sight. Her fear intensified. Why didn't he say something? Why didn't he scream at her, vent his rage over her uncle's death? Why was he playing games with her, pretending he didn't know who she was? When she turned back to the window, she saw Danny was already walking back to the police car.

Stella cranked the ignition, and slowly pulled away from the curb, watching in her rearview mirror as the police car took up a position behind her. The location he had asked her to drive to appeared deserted and poorly lit. His story about the traffic didn't make sense. Not one car had passed the whole time Stella had been waiting. Alarms sounded in her mind. Releasing the steering wheel, she wiped her sweaty palms on her slacks. She had to make a decision fast. If she hesitated, it would be too late. They were about to reach the ramp leading to the freeway.

Stomping on the gas pedal, Stella floored the Ford and took off, squealing up the freeway ramp in a cloud of exhaust smoke. She heard the sirens engage on the police car, but she refused to look behind her. Instead, she watched the speedometer climb: seventy, eighty, ninety. "Come on," Stella yelled, rocking back and forth in the seat as if she thought it would make the car go faster.

Traveling now on the two-lane divided highway, Stella was darting in and out of traffic, desperately trying to control the speeding car and avoid a collision. Seeing a dirt pass-through to the opposite side of the freeway, she decided it was her only chance. As she made the turn, her car fishtailed and spun out of control. She steered into the skid, managing to correct it. Instead of continuing straight, though, Stella turned right and crossed diagonally to the shoulder on the opposite side, barely missing a speeding car that she had failed to see earlier.

The police car was entering the dirt pass-through, but several cars were approaching, and Danny had to wait until they zipped past to enter the lanes of traffic.

Stella panicked, seeing a second police car two car lengths behind Danny's unit. The Fairlane wasn't fast enough. She knew she could never outrun two police cars with high-performance engines. Slamming on the brakes, she left the engine running, grabbed her purse, and leaped out of the car before it came to a complete stop. Tossing the strap to her purse over her head, she ran toward the embankment. Inside her purse were the metal chips. No matter what happened, she couldn't lose them.

The embankment was a gradual slope, but it was thick with shrubs, weeds, and discarded rubbish. Stella tripped and fell into a patch of prickly branches. She managed to get back on her feet, but her jacket was torn and her arms were scraped and stinging. On the road above, she heard the sirens stop, and fell back to the ground, crawling the rest of the way on her hands and knees.

A beam of light zigzagged through the brush, illuminating discarded aluminum cans, broken bottles, and various paper products people had tossed out the windows of their cars. Stella looked for a place to hide, but the bushes were too low to conceal her. She heard twigs snapping, as Danny started climbing down the embankment. "Over here," he called out to the other officer.

Stella was crouched low to the ground, hiding in a patch of knee-high weeds. Now there were two beams of light crisscrossing the embankment, and one passed right by her head. She looked to the bottom of the slope, seeing a narrow access road, and only a few feet away, a blinking neon sign for what looked like a diner. If she could get to the restaurant, she would be safe. Danny and the other cop wouldn't harm her in front of witnesses. No one would be that stupid.

The beams of light moved a few feet to her right, and Stella knew it was time to make her move. She scurried down the embankment, slapping the branches away with her hands. Reaching the road, she kicked off her one remaining shoe, and sprinted toward the diner. It was farther away than she thought, and Stella's chest felt as if it were about to burst. When she finally reached the door, she yanked it open and stumbled inside.

"Where's the bathroom?" she shouted, her eyes searching the room, then darting back to the windows. Danny's face was pressed against the glass as he peered inside, the second officer standing behind him.

A blond waitress passed Stella carrying a tray laden with plates of scrambled eggs and bacon. "Oh, honey," she said, seeing the scratches and dirt on Stella's face, her ripped and filthy clothes, the wild look in her eyes. "Were you raped? Do you want me to call the police?"

"Too late," Stella mumbled, her hand pressed over her mouth. Through the window, she saw Danny speaking to the other officer, then saw the officer walk off. When she saw Danny enter the restaurant, Stella vomited right at the waitress's feet, the contents of her stomach spewing out through her fingers.

Stella was seated in the passenger seat of the police car. "Are you feeling better?" Danny asked, glancing over at her.

"Does this mean I'm under arrest?" Stella

asked, her voice weak and shaky. "I thought prisoners had to ride in the back."

"I'm not going to arrest you," he said. "I was concerned, though, when I first stopped you. You probably don't realize it, Stella, but you were weaving all over the place."

"Why didn't you say something?" she asked, her arms wrapped around her chest. "You know, acknowledge that you knew me."

"Oh," Danny replied, pulling the police unit behind Stella's rental car and killing the engine, "when you have to arrest someone, it's better if you don't make it personal. I learned that in the police academy. I've only been a member of the force for two years." He sighed. "I try to do everything by the book, particularly now after what happened with Clem."

A tense silence ensued. Stella felt uncomfortable sitting in the dark car with him. She reached for the door handle, when Danny began speaking. "Clem wasn't a good man," he said. "He was cruel, Stella. He treated Sarah like dirt, always barking orders at her, never showing her any respect."

"And you?" she said.

The muscles in his body became rigid, but he didn't speak.

"That bad, huh?" Stella whispered.

"Whatever Clem got, he deserved," Danny said, turning to face her. "There are people at the department who don't feel that way, though. There's been talk, Stella. It's one of the reasons I sent the officer who responded for backup away once I found you in the restaurant. If another one of our guys tries to stop you in the next couple of days, you might be better off doing what you did tonight."

"Try to outrun them?" Stella asked.

"Yeah," Danny said. "Either that, or buy yourself a gun."

Stella opened the door and stepped out, leaning back in through the window. "Thanks," she said. "If I can ever do anything to help you, you know where to find me."

Standing in the kitchen with Mario, Stella was nibbling on a piece of toast as sunlight streamed in through the open window. Her brother was wearing jeans, but had not yet put on his shirt, and Stella was still swaddled in her terry-cloth robe. "Why didn't you wake me last night?" he said.

"I was so scared, Mario," Stella answered, her upper lip trembling. "Other than the night of the fire, I don't think I've ever been that afraid. I was certain they were going to drag me off in handcuffs, take me somewhere, and kill me. If it hadn't been Danny who stopped me—"

Mario scowled. "The police can't do this, Stella. The way Danny described it, they're planning to ambush you or something. We should call the federal authorities and ask them to investigate the entire Houston Police Department."

"Sounds like a plan," she said, dropping what was left of her toast in the trash can. "How bad is my face?" she asked, touching it with her fingers. "Can I cover it up with makeup?"

Mario walked over and tilted her head up.

"There's only a few scratches." He pushed up the sleeve of her robe. "The ones on your arms are the worst, Stella, but they should be fine in a few days. You're lucky you didn't crash the car."

"I don't want Sam to know what happened," she said. "I've put him through enough as it is. Once the baseball game is over, he's flying back to Dallas with Adam. He won't leave if he finds out what happened last night."

"What are you going to do about the stuff in the living room?" Mario asked. "I mean, this is a small place, Stel. I can barely walk with all those boxes."

"I'll work on it after Sam leaves," she said, sighing. "Are you going to come with us to the game? Sam bought you a ticket."

Mario stood, angry and agitated. "You're going to a fucking baseball game? You can't be serious, Stella. You're just going to skip off as if last night never happened, after everything Danny told you? Have you lost your mind?"

Stella glowered at him, refusing to answer.

"Look at you," Mario continued, pacing back and forth in front of her. "You haven't slept. Your face is all marked up. You're a nervous wreck." He stopped and grabbed her by the shoulders. "Give it up, Stella. Don't you know when to quit? Your life is in danger. Now is the time to walk away."

Stella knocked his hands away. "I can't walk away," she snapped. "I'm too close."

He shook his head. "You always been stubborn, but—"

Stella pushed her way past him, stopping at the doorway. "Everything's coming back," she told him. "Dad was involved in the Happy Day cave-in, and not just as a building inspector. I remember seeing the newspaper article on the kitchen table only a few days before the fire." She paused, taking a long breath. "Janet Hernandez was right, Mario. The answers are in those boxes. All we have to do is find them."

Mario was silent, thinking. "I'll go through the remaining paperwork while you're gone."

"Thanks," Stella said.

"Oh, Brenda Anderson's mother called last night," Mario added. "They're taking her back into surgery this morning."

"No," Stella said, her jaw dropping. "Why?"

"She's allergic to the material the surgeons used to stitch her up, so her mother said they have to go back in and replace it. Mrs. Anderson insists she's going to be fine, though, and asked me to tell you not to worry." Mario removed a piece of paper from a bowl on the kitchen counter where he kept coupons and receipts. "Brenda told her mother to deliver this message. I have no idea what it means. Here," he said, handing the paper to Stella, "maybe you can figure it out."

Stella saw only one word on the paper: *Partners*. "Is this all she told you?"

"Strange, huh?" Mario said. "Brenda had already been sedated when her mother called last night, so we couldn't clarify what she meant." He looked at the wall clock. "The surgery was scheduled for ten o'clock. If you stick around,

Stella, Brenda should be awake in an hour or so and we can talk to her."

Stella was confused. "It must relate to the cave-in. Brenda has to be referring to the subcontractors who poured the foundation."

"Not necessarily," he answered. "Maybe she's talking about the pension scam. Didn't you suspect that Uncle Clem had partners? His partners were probably police officers. I think what happened to you last night and what we went through in the cemetery more or less confirms that, don't you?"

Stella thought of Carl Winters. Had the detective been her uncle's partner? Had he been the one to do her uncle's dirty work, like setting the fire at her house? She felt like tracking Winters down and beating the truth out of him. Mario was right. She was reaching the breaking point. "I have to go," she said. "Today means too much to Sam."

"Go, then," Mario said. "I'll call Janet and see if she'll come over and give me a hand looking through the files. Who knows? Maybe we'll find something."

Stella hadn't been to a baseball game since she was a child, and the Astrodome was far from an ordinary baseball field. Adam was a walking almanac. "Did you know Evil Knievel jumped thirteen cars here in 1971?" he said. They were standing in line at the concession stand. "They call this place the Eighth Wonder of the World."

"I don't think they call it that anymore, big guy," Sam said, ruffling his hair. "They called it that because it was the only enclosed playing field. Now there's a number of them."

Adam reached up and knocked his father's hand away. "Don't do that to my hair," he said, "it makes me look like a baby. See," he continued, "when they first built it, they tried to use real grass, but it died because there wasn't enough sunlight. Guess what they did then?"

"They invented AstroTurf," Stella said.

"No," he said, "that was later. First, they sprayed the dead grass with paint. Isn't that funny? Didn't they know when they built it that the grass wouldn't grow? Bunch of knuckleheads, huh?"

Stella laughed and leaned into Sam. Being with Sam and his son gave her a sense of well-being. "There's something about a baseball game, isn't there? Look at all these people. Everyone seems so happy, so up. Why can't they be this way all the time?"

"Maybe it's the hot dogs," Sam said, stepping up to order their food.

Once he had paid, Sam dispensed their hot dogs and sodas. Reaching for a wad of napkins, he shoved them in his pocket, then took a handful of plastic packets filled with mustard and ketchup. "Follow me, gang," he said, leading them toward the entrance to their seating section.

Stella was juggling her hot dog and soda in her hands when she felt someone bump into her, and her soda splashed all over the floor. In the same instant, she realized her purse had disappeared from her shoulder. Looking up, she saw a man darting in and out through the crush of people ahead. "My purse," she shouted back to Sam, tossing her hot dog aside. "Call security. I have to get it back."

Shoving people out of her way, Stella dashed after the thief. The metal pieces were in her bag, and Holly would never drop the charges if she didn't get them back. Every few feet she jumped in the air, trying to see over people's heads. The purse snatcher had been wearing an Astros cap and a dark- colored T-shirt. Sam was calling to her but she didn't stop. If she did, the man would get lost in the crowd and they'd never find him.

Stella bent over to catch her breath when a group of people parted and she caught sight of a purse swinging through the air. She couldn't see the man, but she was certain it was her purse. Just as she was about to catch up to him, Adam darted past her and tackled the man around the ankles. They both tumbled to the ground, the boy trying to wrench the purse out of the man's hands.

Although she was still a good distance away, Stella saw the contents of her purse spill out onto the floor. The man was on his back now, and Adam was straddling him, pummeling at his face with his fists. Right by the man's feet was the small brown box containing the metal chips. The man kicked out, and the box went sailing across the floor, disappearing under the feet of a group of onlookers who were huddled together watching the drama unfold.

"Get away, Adam," Stella screamed. "Let him have the purse." She saw a dark object on the floor next to her hairbrush. "Oh no!" She stopped running and stood perfectly still. Before leaving Mario's, she had placed the revolver Brenda had given her in her purse, and it was now only a few feet from the purse snatcher's hands.

"The gun," she yelled. She ran a few more feet and then threw herself on the floor on her stomach, stretching her arms in front of her to reach the revolver. The man growled and tossed Adam off his chest. Stella's fingers were touching the gun, but Adam slammed into her side, and the gun went skittering away. She pushed herself to her feet, but by the time she did, the gun had disappeared.

Stella heard Sam's voice again, and called out to him, "Find the gun, Sam." More onlookers had assembled in the corridor, forming a wall between Stella and Sam, who was trying to fight his way through the crowd.

Stella jerked her head back to Adam, and gasped. "Br- Brad," she stammered. Her husband had his forearm pressed against Adam's throat and was scooting backward across the floor, his face partially obscured by the baseball cap.

"Get back or I'll shoot the boy," he shouted, holding the gun to Adam's head.

Stella's feet felt as if they were nailed to the floor. Was she hallucinating? The man turned his head, and she saw his profile. "Good lord, Brad," she cried, "why are you doing this?"

"Get back," Brad shouted again. His face was drenched with sweat, and mucus dripped from his nose. "I'll shoot, Stella. I have nothing to lose now."

The onlookers scattered, running into each other as pandemonium broke out. Sodas, hot dogs, and napkins littered the floor. Several people slipped and fell, then scrambled back to their feet. "He's got a gun!" someone cried.

Sam ran past Stella to get to his son. She managed to catch his arm. "It's Brad . . . my God, Sam, it's Brad!"

Sam stared at the man with his son, his chest heaving from exertion. "Did he mistake Adam for the purse snatcher?"

"No," Stella said, shaking her head. "Don't go near him. Something is terribly wrong." Seeing the small brown box containing the metal chips on the floor where a group of onlookers had been, Stella raced over and retrieved it. "He wanted my purse," she told Sam, showing him the box in her hand. "The metal chips were inside."

Sam was horrified. "Let the boy go," he called out, his voice shaking. "Please, he's only a kid. Give him the box, Stella. If that's what he wants, give it to him."

Hearing the disturbance, two men in security uniforms rushed over. When they saw what was going on, one of them said, "Call the police. Tell them we've got a hostage situation." The officer glanced toward the ramps leading into the enclosed stadium. People were still walking in and out, heading to the snack bar and toilets. "And get some men stationed at the gates," he barked to the other security officer. "Have them make an announcement inside the arena. We can't let these people walk out here like this. We have to contain this situation."

Stella's fear and confusion turned to rage. She tossed the box at Brad, snarling like a mad woman, "Take it, you fucking prick." She lowered her voice, realizing it was a mistake to provoke him. "Did you think you could frame me with the chips, Brad? I don't need your stupid money. Let the boy go, and I won't ask you for another cent."

Releasing his hold on Adam long enough to grab the box, Brad shoved it into the waistband of his pants, then placed his arm back on Adam's throat. "You got what you wanted," Sam yelled. "Now be a man and let my son go."

Adam's face was pasty and pale. Several times he tried to wrench away from Brad, but Sam called out to him. "Don't move, Adam. Just be still. He's going to let you go. He doesn't want to go to jail." All the onlookers had been dispersed now, and Sam's voice echoed in the empty space.

Inside the stadium, the announcer came on the loudspeaker and advised the spectators to stay in their seats and not exit the stadium until the police resolved the situation outside. The announcer tried to assure them they weren't in danger, that it was only a minor police matter, but people were already scrambling from their seats and rushing up the stairs toward the exits before the announcer had even finished speaking. The players stood still on the playing field, wondering what was going on. Several of the coaches and other officials huddled together, trying to make a decision as to what to do. One coach checked in with the control booth via his headset. "Are we playing ball today or not? What's going on?"

"They have a man with a gun," the announcer reported. "If you don't want people to get trampled to death, I'd suggest you play ball. If you stop the game, the crowd will assume the worst and panic."

The game resumed.

Hundreds of people had already rushed the exit doors, however, and were beating on them with their fists. The security force had locked the doors from the outside, and now had men stationed in front of each exit. But the doors were straining as the people's hysteria intensified.

Stella and Sam were standing in the same position, several security guards beside them. Brad started scooting backward again, dragging Adam with him. Sam, Stella and the security guards advanced, and then stopped, fearful Brad would panic. "Please, Brad," Stella pleaded, "let him go. Whatever problems we have can be resolved. I'll do anything you ask of me. I swear. You can even keep the house. What you're doing now is insane."

"If he keeps moving," the security guard whispered to Sam, "he's going to make it to the stairwell. We're going to go out this entrance and then come in behind him. You don't want him to get down the stairs."

"No," Sam said. "Don't do anything. Wait for the police. They're trained to handle situations like this. Besides, if you try to get inside the stadium, the people are going to rush the doors and stampede. My son will be trampled."

The security guard shrugged. "The exit leading to the parking lot is right at the bottom of those stairs. If this guy gets the boy outside—"

Sam looked at Stella and then back to the security guard. He turned around in a small circle, running his fingers through his hair, anguished over what they should do. When he looked back at Brad, he had scooted another foot or so toward the stairwell. "Do it," he said, keeping his voice low. "Just block his way, though. Don't confront him. Don't do anything unless Emerson tries to take my son outside of the arena."

"You know this guy?" the guard said.

"Yes," Sam said, glaring at Stella. "It's a divorce situation."

Adam's feet were spread out in front of him, and his face had turned a bright shade of red. As Stella watched, a dark stain appeared in front of his pants. He had lost control of his bladder. Tears streamed down her face. He was so afraid, and there was nothing they could do to help him. "Oh, God," she said, tugging on Sam's shirt, "we have to do something. We can't just stand here. Adam is so scared, Sam. Look at him."

"It's your fucking husband," Sam snapped, a tortured look in his eyes. "Why don't you tell us what he's capable of, huh? Will the bastard kill my son if we jump him?"

Stella started to reply when Brenda's message appeared in her mind. "Brad was my father's business partner at one time," she said. "Brenda tried to warn me this morning."

"I thought your father was a building inspector," Sam answered, swiping at his mouth with the back of his hand. "You're not making sense, Stella."

"He opened his own construction company some time before the fire," Stella said, her speech rapid-fire. "Brad was one of the principals. The company went bust after only a few months." It was all coming together now. "Don't you see, Sam? My father's company must have poured the foundation at Happy Day." She recalled the night she had seen her father, the Happy Day headlines in the newspaper. People may say things, he had said. Had the fire been her father's way of committing suicide, his guilt over the Happy Day disaster more than he could handle? She shook her head as if to clear it. Too many things were happening at once.

Sam had a blank look in his eyes. All he cared about was his son. Stella stood by his side in silence. Although only a few minutes went by, it seemed like hours before they saw five or six uniformed police officers running toward them. Several plainclothes officers were right behind them. Stella's jaw dropped when she realized one of the men was Carl Winters.

Winters pulled Stella aside, while the other officers conferred with Sam, trying to get a handle on what was going on.

"What happened?" Winters said. He had been running, and his gray Stetson was sitting at an odd angle on his head.

"It's my husband," Stella said, tossing her arms in the air. "He took my purse, and the boy tackled him. We thought he was a purse snatcher." Her suspicions regarding Winters flared, and she eyed him warily. "I thought you only worked homicides, Carl. Why are you here?"

"I'm one of the department's hostage negotiators," he advised. "What does your husband intend to gain by this?"

"I'm not one hundred percent certain," Stella said, narrowing her eyes as she turned back to Brad. "But I have a fairly good idea. I had the metal chips from the fire in my purse. My guess is they came from a lighter, and that lighter has my husband's name on it. Why else would he want them?"

"I see," Winters said, although he looked more befuddled than before. He asked one of the men for the bullhorn. The Houston P.D. had secured the exits now, and no one other than the parties involved and the police were present in the corridor.

"Okay, Emerson," Winters said into the bullhorn, "this is Detective Winters with the Houston P.D. Throw the gun out in front of you and let the boy go. There's no way you'll ever get out of the ballpark. We have officers stationed at every exit. You have nowhere to go."

Stella stood beside Winters. A captain as well as a lieutenant had arrived. "Has he made any demands?" the captain said, a tall, slender man in his late thirties, his light brown hair cut close to his head. "You know, does he want money, transportation?"

"Not that I know of," Winters answered, dropping the bullhorn to his side.

The captain turned to Stella, and she shook her head. Brad looked as frightened as Adam, and she doubted if he had given any thought to what he would do next. Yanking the bullhorn out of Winters's hands, she tried to reason with him. "Listen to me, Brad," she said, "I know you were involved in the cave-in at Happy Day. There's nothing to hide anymore. If you let Adam go, the police won't try to apprehend you. They've given me their word."

"They're lying," Brad barked. "As soon as I let the boy go, they'll open fire."

"You're wrong, Brad," Stella continued. "No one wants any bloodshed." When she turned around, she saw her husband's fears in the flesh. Twelve officers from the tactical squad had lined up behind her, each holding a high-powered rifle with a scope. "You can't use sharpshooters," she told the captain. "If you try to shoot my husband, you may shoot Adam instead."

"Look," the captain said, "you don't know how good these men are. They can pick a fly off the wall from a block away. This is a volatile situation here. This creep is going to panic any second and kill the kid."

Adam suddenly went skidding across the floor on his seat, propelled by a mighty shove from Brad.

Brad's hindquarters rose in the air in a running stance. The police officers took off after him, but he had disappeared down the stairwell. A gunshot rang out, and the police officers halted. A second shot rang out, and then was quickly followed by a third.

The gunshots must have been heard inside the stadium, as the doors to the arena burst open and the police officers were pushed aside by the crowd of people who forced their way through. The captain started barking orders on the portable radio, and his officers formed a chain, blocking the area near the concession stand. This time, the officers had their nightsticks out and were not hesitating to use them to keep the crowd at bay.

Sam scooped up Adam in his arms and took off running toward the concession area. Stella raced to the stairwell. Brad was face down on the floor at the foot of the stairs, his hands cuffed behind his back, several police officers hovering over him. Once Stella had descended, the men gave her a strange look and then stepped aside.

"Roll him over," she said. "If you don't know already, this disgusting piece of shit is my husband."

Once the officer had done what Stella said and rolled his prisoner onto his back, Brad Emerson looked up into his wife's eyes. The baseball cap was no longer in place, and his silver hair sparkled in the overhead lights. "I wouldn't have hurt the boy," he mumbled.

"Right," Stella said, exploding and kicking him in the ribs. Brad winced in pain, but he didn't cry out. One of the officers stepped forward and seized Stella by the arm, but she kicked out again, her foot striking the edge of Brad's jaw this time. "You're the most contemptible human being who ever lived," she said. "I hope you rot in hell."

chapter

TWENTY

Holly had been about to walk out the door to go to a cocktail party when Jack Fitzgerald called her at home and told her to report to his office. Why would the district attorney want to speak to her at six o'clock on a Saturday evening? On the drive over, she decided it could only be one thing. A sensational case had come in, and Fitzgerald wanted her to try it.

Strolling into his office with a confident look on her face, Holly did a double take. Janet Hernandez was seated in a chair facing Fitzgerald's desk. Holly knew this spelled trouble, but she slowly lowered herself to her seat, giving nothing away. "What's going on, Jack?"

"I'll tell you what's going on," the older D.A. barked, a cigar locked between his teeth. "I've got a damn nut case posing as a prosecutor, that's what."

Holly placed a hand over her chest. "What the—"

"Shut up and listen," Fitzgerald said, grimacing. "You see this woman over here. She's a secretary, right?"

"She was *my* secretary," Holly said, kicking her leg back and forth. Wearing a short black dress trimmed in sequins, dark hose, and high heels, she looked out of place in Fitzgerald's cluttered office. "She walked off the job last week."

"She's not a law clerk," Fitzgerald said, "and she's not an attorney. Do we agree on these points?"

"Of course," Holly said, glaring at Janet. "What has she been telling you? To be perfectly honest, Jack, I don't think Janet is emotionally stable. She's been acting peculiar for several months now."

"I have not," Janet shot back. "You're the one who has been throwing things and acting like a lunatic."

Fitzgerald held up a hand. "Miss Oppenheimer, did you or did you not assign specific and vital research to Miss Hernandez? Research your supervisor instructed you to handle yourself."

"Absolutely not," Holly lied, tossing her head. "Why would I ask her to do my research? She can't even spell." She leaned forward, her voice almost a whisper. "This poor woman is a basket case. I don't know if she's going through a divorce or what's wrong with her, Jack, but she's got major problems."

"Let me ask you something," Fitzgerald said, rolling his cigar in his fingers. "Whatever happened to the search for truth? Isn't that what your job is all about, Oppenheimer? If you had done what the county pays you to do, an innocent woman would not have been charged with murder, a respected investigator would not have been shot, and this agency would have been spared considerable embarrassment." Holly opened her mouth to defend herself, but Fitzgerald silenced her with a look. "As if this weren't enough, additional charges of impropriety have been brought to my attention. Mario Cataloni claims you seduced him in an attempt to get him to testify against his sister. Prosecutors don't sleep with criminal defendants, Miss Oppenheimer, at least not in my agency."

"He's lying," Holly shouted. "Mario Cataloni is only trying to worm his way out of drug charges. He's a damn cocaine addict, Jack."

"Here's what I want you to do," Fitzgerald said forcefully. "I want you to remove all your personal effects from your office, then walk out the door of this building. Do you understand? As of this second, you are relieved of your duties. If you have any questions, you can contact personnel next week."

Holly stood, then fell back to her chair. "You can't be serious!"

Fitzgerald stuck his cigar in his mouth, then pointed his finger at the door. "I'll give you three minutes to vacate my office, Oppenheimer. If you don't, I'll have security come and cart you away."

Stella stood next to Carl Winters in the dark room, peering through the one-way glass at Brad Emerson. The clock behind her read nine-fifty. Sam and Adam were waiting for her at the Ritz-Carlton. As soon as Stella concluded her business at the police department, they would return to Dallas on the next available shuttle.

"You shouldn't be here," Winters said. "But

I guess I owe you something after all the hell I put you through."

Stella wasn't listening. She couldn't take her eyes off Brad. He wasn't her husband, she told herself. The man she was looking at was a stranger. "He'll never waive his rights," she said. "You're wasting your time, Carl."

"You never know," Winters said, a sly look on his face. "Things may work out better than you think. Your brother came through, you know. He found the documentation in the Happy Day files. Emerson Construction poured the foundation."

"Brenda Anderson figured it out before Mario," Stella said, her eyes trained on the glass. "I told her my father had been in business with Brad for a short period of time. I guess she finally put two and two together."

"How is she?"

"I called the hospital earlier. Her mother says she's doing very well." Stella turned to face him. "Never in all the years we were together did I have a reason to believe my husband was involved in the fire."

"Too bad Mario didn't uncover the truth before he told Brad you were at an Astros game, huh?" Winters said, smacking his lips. "It would have saved us all a lot of trouble."

"Yeah," Stella said pensively. "What about the metal chips? Could the lab make anything out of them?"

"Nah," Winters said, glancing through the glass at Brad. "Isn't life a bitch? This guy was panicked over those scraps of metal, and they were so melted, no one would have ever figured it out."

Detective Winters stepped into the interview room, placing his tape recorder in the center of the small round table. He read Brad his Miranda rights off a small card, then asked him if he was willing to speak without an attorney. "I'll talk," Brad said, fidgeting in his seat. "I'd like a cigarette, though. You've had me cooped up in this room for hours."

As Brad had already been booked into the county jail earlier in the day, he was dressed in a jail-issued white jumpsuit. Winters had asked that the handcuffs be removed during the interview, but Brad's legs were shackled at the ankles.

"Not supposed to smoke in a city building," Winters said, shrugging. He studied his subject, sensing a coldness that he knew he had to penetrate. His eyes drifted to the one-way glass. He wanted Emerson to confess, for Stella's sake more than anything. "Were you ever in the military, Emerson?"

"No," Brad said.

"Ever been arrested before today?" Winters asked.

"Never," he answered.

Quietly slipping out of the room, Winters returned with a pack of Winston cigarettes and a book of matches, pilfered from one of the homicide detectives' desks. "Sometimes rules are made to be broken," he told Brad, smiling as he handed him the cigarettes.

"I haven't had a cigarette in ten years," Brad

419

said, lighting the cigarette and then exhaling a stream of smoke.

The detective sprawled out in one of the chairs, tipping his Stetson back on his head. "Let's start at the beginning. I understand you and Stella's father were business partners. Is that correct?"

"Yeah," Brad said, flicking his ashes on the floor. "All the partners put in ten G's, but we used my name and called the company Emerson Construction. I'd been a subcontractor for a number of years, so we decided to trade off my reputation. It worked out better that way. Tony being a building inspector and all, we decided using his name was too risky."

"Was that the name on the lighter?" Winters asked. "The writing says Emerson Construction?"

"Yeah," Brad said, a question mark on his face. "Don't you guys already know that? You have the metal chips, right?"

"When you refer to the partners," Winters continued, ignoring Brad's questions, "who exactly are you referring to?"

For a long time Brad didn't respond, and Winters didn't press him. He'd take it slow and easy. If they had to stay here all night, so be it. His eyes roamed to the windows again. Stella deserved to know the truth, and he wanted to be the one to bring it to her.

"There were three of us," Brad said at last, his body hunched over at the waist. "Clem, myself, and Tony Cataloni. Clem was a silent partner. All he did was put up the money. He didn't participate in the day-to-day business of running the company."

Winters removed his cowboy hat and ran his hand over his head. His eyes were as small and dark as the buttons on his jacket. "You're trying to tell me that Captain Cataloni was your business partner, that he was involved in this Happy Day mess?"

"That's what I said," Brad answered. Dropping his cigarette on the linoleum floor, he extinguished it with the heel of his shoe, the chains jangling around his ankles. "Your little captain wasn't such a big hero after all. If it hadn't been for Clem, the Happy Day foundation wouldn't have collapsed."

"Oh, really?" Winters said, thinking Brad Emerson was handing him a pack of lies. Cataloni was dead, and a dead man was the perfect patsy. "You want to explain that statement?"

Brad said, "Clem worshiped money, and he was as shrewd as they come when it came to business. You guys uncovered the pension scam, so I guess you know about his business sense."

"Were you involved in this pension thing?" Winters asked, keeping his voice low and steady.

"Nah," Brad said. "I knew Clem had a sweet little deal going, but I didn't share in the profits. No one profited from Clem's schemes but Clem. He taught me everything I know about the building trade, though. Stella's father didn't know anything. Tony was the Last Boy Scout."

"Let's go back to Clem," Winters said, straightening up in his seat. "How did you meet him?"

421

"Stella's father introduced us. We were looking for investors and he thought his brother would be interested."

"You said Clem was responsible for the cave-in," Winters said. "If he wasn't involved in the daily operations of the company, how could that be true?"

"When we got the Happy Day contract," Brad continued, "Clem suggested that I shave some of the costs by not using rebar to reinforce the foundation. What's the big deal? he said. Everyone cuts corners. If you don't cut corners, you'll be out of business in sixty days. The school was a big contract for us, but we'd won it by submitting a ridiculously low bid. If we hadn't done some cost containment, we would have lost money on the job."

"Is the rebar the only thing you scrimped on?"

"Hardly," Brad said, reaching for another cigarette. "If you mean on this particular job, yeah, but on other jobs, we cut corners everywhere we could. We used cheap materials, failed to reinforce beams, used plywood instead of sheetrock. Hey, it was a competitive business. People want the world, but they don't want to pay diddly squat. We were trying to establish a name for ourselves, get some money in the company's coffers, then we would have produced some quality work."

"Did Stella's father know about this?"

"No," Brad said, flicking his ashes. "Last Boy Scout, remember? He was our inside man. If we did a really shoddy job, we made sure Tony went out to inspect it. Most of the stuff is hard to

422

detect once the building goes up, but he let a lot of small stuff pass. You know, he didn't mind looking the other way on things that couldn't hurt anyone."

"The cave-in wasn't a small thing," Winters said. "How did he react?"

"Tony only found out about the rebar problem after the damn floor caved in." Brad pointed a finger at him. "We didn't cause this by ourselves," he said. "I'm not about to take full responsibility for those kids getting killed. The property was on a landfill, and the development company never advised us of that fact. If they had, we would have reinforced the foundation."

"Tell me about the night of the fire," Winters said, quickly checking the tape recorder to make certain he was recording.

"After the cave-in," Brad said, "Tony panicked. I mean, we were all going nuts, but Tony posed a more serious problem. He wanted us to turn ourselves in once he found out we hadn't used rebar in the foundation." Brad paused and wiped the sweat off his face with his hand. "He took a sample of the foundation home with him, then told me he was going to turn it over to the authorities the following day. He said he couldn't live with something like that on his conscience. I told him we'd all be sued and never work again, but he refused to listen. I even offered him money, a shitload of money if you want to know the truth."

"So," Winters said, "you were the man arguing with Stella's father on the lawn that night?"

"Yes," Brad answered, another cigarette

hitting the floor. This one he didn't stomp out, though. He just let it simmer. "When Tony wouldn't go along with the program, I decided to see if I could get the sample of the foundation back, thinking it would buy us more time. Clem insisted his brother would come around, but I knew better. The brothers weren't even speaking to each other by this time. If Tony said he was going to the authorities, I knew it was a done deal."

"Did you find this sample?" Winters asked, trailing his fingers across the table.

"I went in through the basement window," he said. "I was afraid if I turned the lights on, someone might see them under the door, so I used my cigarette lighter to see what I was doing. I found the concrete block and left. I guess I dropped the lighter somewhere in the basement, or it fell out of my pocket when I crawled back out through the window."

"What about the fire?" Winters said, arching an eyebrow.

"I didn't purposely set it," Brad said defensively. "I must have ignited some dry papers or connected with something flammable when I was walking around in the dark. I didn't smell smoke or anything, but of course, we both know the house went up in flames." He stroked the side of his face. "When I saw how seriously Stella was burned, my heart wrenched in two. She was such a pretty girl before the accident. Seeing her all scarred up like that was the saddest day of my life."

"Your heart must not have wrenched too

long," Winters said. "You married the damn woman."

Brad laughed, but it wasn't genuine, more of a nervous response. "It was a pretty strange situation, I admit," he said, leaning back in his chair. "But I had to do something for them, you know. I felt responsible, so I decided this was the thing to do." When Winters didn't seem impressed, he added, "I raised Stella's brother, treated him like my own son. I also paid for her hospital bills and all the reconstructive surgery she had done. I mean, I'm not a monster or anything. I did my best to make amends."

"Bully for you," Winters said, having almost had his fill of Brad Emerson. He glanced at his watch. It was past ten, and the Dallas police should have called him by now. He had waited all day to question Brad, hoping to have more ammunition. "Did you shoot Tom Randall?"

"I'm not your shooter, pal," Brad said, his palms on the table. "Clem was the marksman. He took Randall out himself."

Winters repositioned himself in the seat. "Because Randall saw you on the lawn that night?"

"Sort of," Brad said, a smile flickering on his lips. "See, after the tragedy, I denied ever being at the house. Clem would have killed me in a second if he'd known I had anything to do with the fire. So, I tracked down Randall and gave him five G's to say Stella was responsible, then get his ass out of town. I knew no one would ever prosecute her. Hell, she was just a kid, and her face was ruined. I had to place the blame on someone or Clem would have eventually found out the truth." He let out a whistle. "Hell, you knew Clem. You know he was a tough son-of-a-bitch. I bet he enjoyed popping Randall."

"Why would Cataloni kill Randall?" Winters asked. "Randall was willing to testify against Stella. Didn't he believe Stella killed his brother? Isn't that what you told me?"

Brad looked as if his lies were strangling him. His face was red, and his eyes bulged in their sockets. "I'm not saying anything else until I talk to my attorney."

"Let me tell you how it went down," Winters said, his voice booming out over the small room. "You shot Tom Randall because he saw you on the lawn that night. When Stella told you he was back in town, you knew you had to take him out. You couldn't take a chance that the truth would come out, that you bribed him to incriminate your own wife. What you feared the most, though, was Clem Cataloni. If he found out that you were responsible for his brother's death, you knew he would kill you." Winters tapped the top of the tape recorder, then smirked. "You told us that yourself, Emerson. Hell, I think you might be right. You better wait for your attorney."

"I wasn't afraid of Clem," Brad said, trying to retract his earlier statements.

"You and Clem might have been buddies sixteen years ago," Winters countered, "but once you married Stella, you went to the top of his shit list. Without additional evidence, though, Clem knew the courts would never convict her."

426

"You can't prove any of this," Brad said, his voice shaking.

"Well," Winters said, "you might be right, Emerson, but we're certainly going to try."

When Stella saw Winters get up and leave, she assumed the interview was over. Brad was staring at the one-way glass, though, as if he knew she was there. A hard ball of rage formed in her stomach, and she wanted to rip the flesh right off his body. She pounded the glass with her fists instead, stopping only when she saw Winters step back in the room.

The detective had a piece of paper in his hands, and was waving it in front of Brad's face. "While we were having our little talk," the detective said, his voice coming out over the speakers in the observation booth, "the Dallas P.D. was searching your house. We found the receipt for the gun you used to shoot Randall, and the airlines just verified that you booked a flight from Dallas to Houston the morning of the murder. Another bonus came through . . . we've matched your fingerprints to the ones we lifted from the murder weapon. Because your prints weren't on file, it took us a while to put this together." He paused and cackled. "You're a little sloppy, Emerson. You're about as good at murder as you were at pouring foundations. Dropping the murder weapon at the scene of the crime is stupid, but only an idiot would fail to wipe off his fingerprints."

Brad's eyes blazed, but he didn't speak.

"You've got balls, though," Winters

continued, his voice laced with venom now. "I've got to hand it to you. To cause a woman's parents to die, scar her for life, then end up married to her takes one hell of an asshole." He stood, slamming his chair back to the table. "I've been a cop a long time," he told him. "I've dealt with murderers, rapists, men so mean and callous they couldn't be classified as human beings. But I'll tell you the God's honest truth," he said, looking the other man squarely in the eye. "In my entire career, I've never met a bastard as sick as you."

Stella's palms were pressed against the glass. Dropping her hands to her sides, she stood perfectly still, taking a final look at the man who had been her husband.

She watched as Winters left the interview room, taking his tape recorder with him. A few moments later, a uniformed officer entered and led Brad away.

Her skin pricked as she sensed another presence beside her. Craning her neck around, she searched the shadows thinking Winters had come in without her knowledge. In her emotional state, Stella knew she was probably imagining things, but it was as if her father were in the room with her. She closed her eyes, bringing forth his face, the sound of his voice, the distinctive smell of his aftershave. Was he telling her to go on with her life? Did he know what Brad had done to her? She wanted to shake her fist in fury, cry out at the top of her lungs. She couldn't walk away. She'd waited too long to extract her vengeance, rid herself of the hate. She took a deep breath, then slowly let it out. She would leave the evil

428

here, she decided, with Brad, the man who had created it.

Stella walked to the door and stopped, looking back into the darkness. "It's okay, Dad," she whispered. "You don't have to worry about me anymore."

IF YOU HAVE ENJOYED READING THIS
LARGE PRINT BOOK AND YOU
WOULD LIKE MORE INFORMATION
ON HOW TO ORDER A WHEELER
LARGE PRINT BOOK, PLEASE WRITE
TO:

WHEELER PUBLISHING, INC.
P.O. BOX 531
ACCORD, MA 02018-0531